Praise for *New York Times* bestselling author Diana Palmer

"Palmer proves that love and passion can be found even in the most dangerous situations."
—*Publishers Weekly* on *Untamed*

"You just can't do better than a Diana Palmer story to make your heart lighter and smile brighter."
—*Fresh Fiction* on *Wyoming Rugged*

"Diana Palmer is a mesmerizing storyteller who captures the essence of what a romance should be."
—*Affaire de Coeur*

"The popular Palmer has penned another winning novel, a perfect blend of romance and suspense."
—*Booklist* on *Lawman*

"Diana Palmer's characters leap off the page. She captures their emotions and scars beautifully and makes them come alive for readers."
—*RT Book Reviews* on *Lawless*

T0205111

Dear Reader,

I can't believe that it has been over thirty years since my first Long, Tall Texans book, *Calhoun*, debuted! The series was suggested by my former editor Tara Gavin, who asked if I might like to set stories in a fictional town of my own design. Would I! And the rest is history.

As the years went by, I found more and more sexy ranchers and cowboys to add to the collection. My readers (especially Amy!) found time to gift me with a notebook listing every single one of them, along with their wives and kids and connections to other families in my own Texas town of Jacobsville. Eventually the town got a little too big for me, so I added another smaller town called Comanche Wells and began to fill it up, too.

You can't imagine how much pleasure this series has given me. I continue to add to the population of Jacobs County, Texas, and I have no plans to stop. Ever.

I hope all of you enjoy reading the Long, Tall Texans as much as I enjoy writing them. Thank you all for your kindness and loyalty and friendship. I am your biggest fan!

Love,

Diana Palmer

A LONE STAR HERO

NEW YORK TIMES BESTSELLING AUTHOR
DIANA PALMER

Two Heartfelt Stories
Donavan
and
Jordan (Previously published as *Cattleman's Pride*)

SPECIAL RELEASE

 **Harlequin®**
SPECIAL RELEASE

Recycling programs for this product may not exist in your area.

ISBN-13: 978-1-335-48498-7

A Lone Star Hero

Copyright © 2024 by Harlequin Enterprises ULC

Donavan
First published in 1991.
This edition published in 2024 with revised text.
Copyright © 1991 by Diana Palmer
Copyright © 2024 by Diana Palmer, revised text edition

Jordan
First published as Cattleman's Pride in 2004.
This edition published in 2024 with revised text.
Copyright © 2004 by Diana Palmer
Copyright © 2024 by Diana Palmer, revised text edition

For questions and comments about the quality of this book, please contact us at CustomerService@Harlequin.com.

TM and ® are trademarks of Harlequin Enterprises ULC.

 Harlequin Enterprises ULC
22 Adelaide St. West, 41st Floor
Toronto, Ontario M5H 4E3, Canada
www.Harlequin.com

Printed in U.S.A.

CONTENTS

A prolific author of more than one hundred books, **Diana Palmer** got her start as a newspaper reporter. A *New York Times* bestselling author and voted one of the top ten romance writers in America, she has a gift for telling the most sensual tales with charm and humor. Diana lives with her family in Cornelia, Georgia. Visit her website at dianapalmer.com.

Books by Diana Palmer

Long, Tall Texans

Fearless
Heartless
Dangerous
Merciless
Courageous
Protector
Invincible
Untamed
Defender
Undaunted

The Wyoming Men

Wyoming Tough
Wyoming Fierce
Wyoming Bold
Wyoming Strong
Wyoming Rugged
Wyoming Brave

Visit the Author Profile page
at Harlequin.com for more titles.

DONAVAN

For a special reader—Peggy

CHAPTER ONE

FAY FELT AS if every eye in the bar was on her when she walked in. It had been purely an impulse, and she was already regretting it. A lone female walking into a bar on the wrong side of town in south Texas late at night was asking for trouble. Women's lib hadn't been heard of this far out, and several pairs of male eyes were telling her so.

She could only imagine how she looked in her tight designer jeans, her feet encased in silk hose and high heels, a soft yellow knit sweater showing the faint swell of her high breasts. Her long dark hair was around her shoulders in soft swirls, and her green eyes darted nervously from one side of the small, smoke-filled room to the other. There was a jukebox playing so loud that she had to yell to tell the bartender she wanted a beer. That was a joke, too, because in all her twenty years, she'd never had a beer. White wine, yes. Even a piña colada down in Jamaica. But never a beer.

Defiance was becoming expensive, she thought, watching a burly man separate himself from his companions with a mumbled remark that made them laugh.

He perched himself beside her at the bar, his narrow eyes giving her an appraisal that made her want to run. "Hello, pretty thing," he said, grinning through his beard. "Wanta dance?"

She cupped her hands around the beer mug to stop them from shaking. "No, thank you," she said in her soft, cultured voice, keeping her eyes down. "I'm... waiting for someone."

That was almost true. She'd been waiting for someone all her life, but he hadn't shown up yet. She needed him now. She was living with a mercenary, social-climbing relative who was doing his best to sell her to a rich friend with eyes that made her skin crawl. All her money was tied up in trust, and she was stuck with her mother's brother. Rescue was certainly uppermost in her mind, but this rowdy cowboy wasn't her idea of a white knight.

"You and me could have a good time, honey," her admirer continued, unabashed. He smoothed her sweater-clad arm and she withdrew as if his fingers were snakes. "Now, don't start backing away, sweet thing! I know how to treat a lady."

No one noticed the dark face in the corner suddenly lift, or saw the dangerous glitter in silver eyes that dominated it. No one noticed the look he gave the girl, or the colder one that he gave her companion before he got gracefully to his feet and moved toward the bar.

He wore jeans, too. Not like Fay's, because his were working jeans. They were faded and stained from work, and his boots were a howling thumbed nose at city cowboys' elegant footwear. His hat was blacker than his thick, unruly hair, a little crumpled here and there. He was tall. Very tall. Lean and muscular and quite well-known locally. His temper, in fact, was as legendary as the big fists now curled with deceptive laxness at his sides as he walked.

"You'd like me if you just got to know me—" The

pudgy cowboy broke off when the newcomer came into his line of vision. He became almost comically still, his head slightly cocked. "Why, hello, Donavan," he began uneasily. "I didn't know she was with *you*."

"Now you do," he replied in a deep, gravelly voice that sent chills down Fay's spine.

She turned her head and looked into diamond-glinted eyes, and lost her heart forever. She couldn't seem to breathe.

"It's about time you showed up," he told Fay. He took her arm, eased her down from the bar stool with a grip that was firm and exciting. He handed her beer mug to her, and with a last cutting glare at the other man, he escorted her back to his table.

"Thank you," she stammered when she was sitting beside him. He'd left a cigarette smoking in the dented metal ashtray, and a half-touched glass of whiskey. He didn't take off his hat when he sat down. She'd noticed that Western men seemed to have little use for the courtesies she'd taken for granted back home.

He picked up his cigarette and took a long draw from it. His nails were flat and clean, despite traces of grease that clung to his long-fingered, dark hands. They were beautiful masculine hands, with no jewelry adorning them. Working hands, she thought idly.

"Who are you?" he asked suddenly.

"I'm Fay," she told him. She forced a smile. "And you…?"

"Most people just call me Donavan."

She took a sip of beer and grimaced. It tasted terrible. She stared at it with an expression that brought a faint smile to the man's hard, thin mouth.

"You don't drink beer, and you don't belong in a bar.

What are you doing on this side of town, debutante?"
he drawled.

"I'm running away from home," she said with a
laugh. "Escaping my jailers. Having a night on the town.
Rebelling. Take your pick."

"Are you old enough to do that?" he asked pointedly.

"If you mean, am I old enough to order a beer in a
bar, yes. I'm two months shy of twenty-one."

"You don't look it."

She studied his hard, suntanned face and his unruly
hair. With a little trimming up and proper dressing,
he might be rather devastating. "Are you from around
here?" she asked.

"All my life," he agreed.

"Do you…work?"

"Child, in this part of Texas, everybody works." He
scowled. "Most everybody," he amended, letting his
eyes linger pointedly on her diamond tennis bracelet.
"Wearing that into a country bar is asking for trouble.
Pull your sleeve down."

She did, obeying him instantly when she was known
for ignoring anything that sounded like a command at
home. She flushed at her instant deference. Maybe she
was drunk already. Sure, she mused, on two sips of beer.

"What do you do when you aren't giving orders?"
she taunted.

He searched her green eyes. "I'm a ranch foreman,"
he said. "I give orders for a living."

"Oh. You're a cowboy."

"That's one name for it."

She smiled again. "I've never met a real cowboy before."

"You aren't from here."

She shook her head. "Georgia. My parents were killed in a plane crash, so I was sent out here to live with my uncle." She whistled softly. "You can't imagine what it's like."

"Get out," he said simply. "People live in prisons out of choice. You can always walk away from a situation you don't care for."

"Want to bet? I'm rich," she said curtly. "Filthy rich. But it's all tied up in a trust that I can't touch until I'm twenty-one, and my uncle is hoping to marry me off to a business associate in time to get his hands on some of it."

"Are you for real?" he asked. He picked up the whiskey glass and took a sip, putting the glass down with a sharp movement of his hand. "Tell him to go to hell and do what you please. At your age I was working for myself, not for any relatives."

"You're a man," she pointed out.

"What difference does that make?" he asked. "Haven't you ever heard of women's lib?"

She smiled. At least one person in the bar had heard of women's lib. "I'm not that kind of woman. I'm wimpy."

"Listen, lady, no wimpy girl walks into a place like this in the middle of the night and orders a beer."

She laughed, her green eyes brilliant. "Yes, she does, when she's driven to it. Besides, it was safe, wasn't it? You were here."

He lifted his chin and a different light came into the pale, silvery eyes. "And you think I'm safe," he murmured. "Or, more precisely, that you're safe with me?"

Her heart began to thud against her ribs. That was a very adult look in his eyes, and she noticed the corresponding drop of his voice into a silky, soft purr. Her lips parted as she let out the breath she was holding.

"I hope I am," she said after a minute. "Because I've done a stupid thing and even though I might deserve a hard time, I'm hoping you won't give me one."

He smiled, and this time it was without mockery. "Good girl. You're learning."

"Is it a lesson?" she asked.

He drained the whiskey glass. "Life is all lessons. The ones you don't learn right off the bat, you have to repeat. Get up. I'll drive you home."

"Must you?" she asked, sighing. "It's the first adventure I've ever had, and it may be the last."

He cocked his hat over one eye and looked down at her. "In that case, I'll do my best to make it memorable," he murmured dryly. He held out a lean, strong hand and pulled her up when she took it. "Are you game?"

She was feeling her way with him, but oddly, she trusted him. She smiled. "I'm game."

He nodded. He took her arm and guided her out the door. She noticed a few looks that came their way, but no one tried to distract him.

"People seem to know you in there," she remarked when they were outside in the cool night air.

"They know me," he returned. "I've treed that bar a time or two."

"Treed it?"

He glanced down at her. "Broken it up in a brawl. Men get into trouble, young lady, and women aren't always handy to get them out of it."

"I'm not really handy," she said hesitantly.

He chuckled. "Honey, what you are is written all over you in green ink. I don't mind a little adventure, but that's all you'll get from me." His silvery eyes narrowed. "If you stay around here long enough, you'll learn that I don't like rich women, and you'll learn why. But for tonight, I'm in a generous mood."

"I don't understand," she said.

He laughed without humor. "I don't suppose you do." He eyed her intently. "You aren't safe to be let out."

"That's what everybody keeps saying." She smiled with what she hoped was sophistication. "But how will I learn anything about life if I'm kept in a glass bowl?"

His eyes narrowed. "Maybe you've got a head start already." He tugged her along to a raunchy gray pickup truck with dents all over it. "I hope you weren't expecting a Rolls-Royce, debutante. I could hardly haul cattle in one."

She felt terrible. She actually winced as she looked up at him, and he felt a twinge of guilt at the dry remark that was meant to be funny.

"Oh, I don't care what you drive," she said honestly. "You could be riding a horse, and it wouldn't matter. I don't judge people by what they have."

His pale eyes slid over her face lightly. "I think I knew that already," he said quietly. "I'm sorry. I meant it as a joke. Here. Don't cut yourself on that spring. It popped out and I haven't had time to fix it."

"Okay." She bounced into the cab and he closed the door. It smelled of the whole outdoors, and when he got in, it smelled of leather and smoke. He glanced at her and smiled.

He started the truck and glanced at her. "Did you drive here?" he asked.

"Yes."

He paused to look around the parking lot, pursing

his lips with faint amusement when he saw the regal blue Mercedes-Benz sitting among the dented pickup trucks and dusty four-wheel-drive vehicles.

"That's right, you don't need to ask what I drove here in," she muttered self-consciously. "And yes, it's mine."

He chuckled. "Bristling already, and we've only just met," he murmured as he pulled out into the road. "What do you do when you aren't trying to pick up strange men in bars?"

She glared at him. "I study piano, paint a little and generally try to stay sane through endless dinner parties and morning coffees."

He whistled through his teeth. "Some life."

She turned in the seat, liking the strength of his profile. "What do you do?"

"Chase cattle, mostly. Figure percentages, decide which cattle to cull, hire and fire cowboys, go to conferences, make financial decisions." He glanced at her. "Occasionally I sit on the board of directors of two corporations."

She frowned slightly. "I thought you said you were a foreman."

"There's a little more to it than that," he said comfortably. "You don't need to know the rest. Where do you want to go?"

She had to readjust her thinking from the abrupt statement. She glanced out the dark window at the flat south Texas landscape. "Well… I don't know. I just don't want to go home."

"They're having a fiesta down in San Moreno," he said with an amused glance. "Ever been to one?"

"No!" Her eyes brightened. "Could we?"

"I don't see why not. There isn't much to do except dance, though, and drink beer. Do you dance?"

"Oh, yes. Do you?"

He chuckled. "I can when forced into it. But you may have trouble with the beer part."

"I learned to like caviar," she said. "Maybe I can learn to like beer."

He didn't comment. He turned on the radio and country-western music filled the cab. She leaned her head back on the seat and smiled as she closed her eyes. Incredible, she thought, how much she trusted this man when she'd only just met him. She felt as though she'd known him for years.

The feeling continued when they got to the small, dusty town of San Moreno. A band of mariachis was playing loud, lively Mexican music while people danced in the roped-off main square. Vendors sold everything from beer to tequila and chimichangas and tacos. The music was loud, the beer was hot, but nobody seemed to mind. Most of the people were Mexican-American, although Fay noticed a few cowboys among the cele-brants.

"What are we celebrating?" Fay asked breathlessly as Donavan swung her around and around to the quick beat of the music.

"Who cares?" He chuckled.

She shook her head. In all her life, she couldn't re-member being so happy or feeling so carefree. If she died tomorrow, it would be worth it, because she had to-night to remember. So she drank warm beer that tasted better with each sip, and she danced in Donavan's lean, strong arms, and rested against his muscular chest and breathed in the scent of him until she was more drunk on the man than the liquor.

Finally the frantic pace died down and there was a slow two-step. She melted into Donavan, sliding her arms around him with the kind of familiarity that usually came from weeks of togetherness. She seemed to fit against him, like a soft glove. He smelled of tobacco and beer and the whole outdoors, and the feel of his body so close to hers was delightfully exciting. His arms enfolded her, both of them wrapped close around her, and for a few minutes there was nobody else in the world. She heard the music as if through a fog of pure pleasure, her body reacting to the closeness of his in a way it had never reacted before. She felt a tension that was disturbing, and a kind of throbbing ache in her lower body that she'd never experienced. Being close to him was becoming intolerable. She caught her breath and pulled away a little, raising eyes full of curious apprehension to his.

He searched her face quietly, aware of her fear and equally aware of the cause of it. He smiled gently. "It's all right," he said quietly.

She frowned. "I… I don't quite understand what's wrong with me," she whispered. "Maybe the beer…"

"There's no need to pretend. Not with me." He framed her face in his lean hands and bent, pressing a tender kiss against her forehead. "We'd better go."

"Must we?" she sighed.

He nodded. "It's late." He caught her hand in his and tugged her along to the truck. He was feeling something of the same reckless excitement she was, except that he was older and more adept at controlling it. He knew that she'd wanted him while they were dancing, but things were getting ahead of him. He didn't need a rich society girl in his life. God knew, one had been the ruin of his family. People around Jacobsville, Texas, still remembered how his father had gone pell-mell after a local debutante without any scruples about how he forced her to marry him, right on the heels of his wife's funeral, too. Donavan had turned bitter trying to live down the family scandal. Miss High Society here would find it out eventually. Better not to start something he couldn't finish, even if she did cause an inconvenient ache in his body. No doubt she'd had half a dozen men, but she might be addictive—and he couldn't risk finding out she was.

She was pleasantly relaxed when they got back to the deserted bar where she'd left her Mercedes. The spell had worn off a little, and her head had cleared. But with that return to reality came the unpleasantness of having to go home and face the music. She hadn't told anyone where she was going, and they were going to be angry. Really angry.

"Thank you," she said simply, turning to Donavan after she unlocked her car. "It was a magical night."

"For me, too." He opened the door for her. "Stay out of my part of town, debutante," he said gently. "You don't belong here."

Her green eyes searched his gray ones. "I hate my life," she said.

"Change it," he replied. "You can if you want to."

"I'm not used to fighting."

"Get used to it. Life doesn't give, it takes. Anything worth having is worth fighting for."

"So they say." She toyed with her car keys. "But in my world, the fighting gets dirty."

"It does in mine, too. That never stopped me. Don't let it stop you."

She lowered her eyes to the hard chest that had pillowed her head while they danced. "I won't forget you."

"Don't get any ideas," he murmured dryly, flicking a long strand of hair away from her face. "I'm not looking for complications or ties. Not ever. Your world and mine wouldn't mix. Don't go looking for trouble."

"You just told me to," she pointed out, lifting her face to his.

"Not in my direction," he emphasized. He smiled at her. The action made him look younger, less formidable. "Go home."

She sighed. "I guess I should. You wouldn't like to kiss me good-night, I guess?" she added with lifted eyebrows.

"I would," he replied. "Which is why I'm not going to. Get in the car."

"Men," she muttered. She glared at him, but she got into the car and closed the door.

"Drive carefully," he said. "And wear your seat belt."

She fastened it, but not because of his order—she usually wore a seat belt. She spared him one long, last look before she started the car and pulled away. When she drove onto the main highway, he was already driving off in the other direction, and without looking back. She felt a sense of loss that shocked her, as if she'd given up part of herself. Maybe she had. She couldn't remember ever feeling so close to another human being.

Her father and mother had never been really close to her. They'd had their own independent lives, and they almost never included her in any of their activities. She'd grown up with housekeepers and governesses for companionship, and with no brothers or sisters for company. From lonely child to lonely woman, she'd gone through the motions of living. But she'd never felt that anyone would really mind if she died.

That hadn't changed when she'd come out to Jacobsville, Texas, to live with her mother's brother, Uncle Henry Rollins. He wasn't well-to-do, but he wanted to be. He wasn't above using his control over Fay's estate to provide the means to entertain. Fay hadn't protested, but she'd just realized tonight how lax she'd been in looking out for her own interests. Uncle Henry had invited his business partner to supper and hadn't told Fay until the last minute. She was tired of having Sean thrown at her, and she'd rebelled, running out the door to her car.

It had been almost comical, bowlegged Uncle Henry rushing after her, huffing and puffing as he tried to match his bulk to her slender swiftness and lost. She hadn't known where she was going, but she'd wound up at the bar. Fate had sent her there, perhaps, to a man who made her see what a docile child she'd become, when she was an independent woman. Well, things were going to change. Starting now.

Donavan had fascinated her. She tingled, just remembering how he hadn't even had to lift a hand in the bar to make the man who'd been worrying her back down. He was the stuff of which romantic fantasies were made. But he didn't like rich women.

It would be nice, she thought, if Donavan had fallen madly in love with her and started searching for her. That would be improbable, though, since he didn't have a clue as to her real identity. She didn't know his, either, come to think of it; all she knew was what he did for a living. But he could have been stretching the truth a little. He hadn't sounded quite forceful when he'd said he was a foreman.

Well, it didn't really matter, she thought sadly. She'd never see him again. But it had been a memorable meeting altogether, and she knew she'd never forget him. Not ever.

CHAPTER TWO

THE FEEDLOT OFFICE was quiet, and Fay York was grateful for the respite. It had been a hectic two weeks since she started this, her first job. She was still faintly amazed at her own courage and grit, because she'd never thought she'd be able to actually do it. She'd surprised her uncle Henry as much as herself when she'd announced her plans to get a job and become independent until her inheritance came through.

It had been because of Donavan that she'd done it. Her evening with him had changed her life. He'd made it possible for her to believe in herself. He'd given her a kind of self-confidence that she hadn't thought possible.

But it hadn't been easy, and she'd been scared to death the morning she'd walked into the office of the gigantic Ballenger feedlot to ask for a job.

Barry Holman, the local attorney who was to handle her inheritance, had suggested that she see Justin Ballenger about work, because his secretary was out having a baby and Calhoun Ballenger's wife, Abby, had been reluctantly filling in.

She could still remember her shock when she'd gone to Mr. Holman to ask for a living allowance until her inheritance came through, something that would give her a little independence from her overbearing uncle.

That was when the blow fell. "I'm sorry," Holman

said. "But there's no provision for any living allowance. According to the terms of the will, you can't inherit until you're twenty-one. Until that time, the executor of your parents' estate has total control of your money."

She gasped. "You mean I don't have any money unless Uncle Henry gives it to me?"

"I'm afraid so," he said. "I realize it probably seems terribly unfair to you, Fay, but your parents must have thought they were doing the right thing."

"I can't believe it," she said, feeling sick. She wrapped her arms around her body. "What will I do?"

"What you originally planned. Go ahead and get a job. You'll only need it for a couple of weeks, until you get your inheritance."

The statement helped her fight out of her misery. Involuntarily, she smiled, liking the blond attorney. He was in his early thirties, very good-looking and successful. He was married, because on his desk was a photograph of a young woman with long, brown hair holding a baby.

"Thank you," she said.

"Oh, it's my pleasure. Don't worry, you won't even have to look far for a job. I just happen to know of an opening. Know anything about cattle?"

She hesitated. "Not really."

"Do you mind working around them?"

"Not if I don't have to brand them," she murmured dryly.

He laughed. "It won't come to that. The Ballenger brothers are looking for a temporary secretary. Their full-time one was pregnant and just had a complicated delivery. She'll be out about two months and they're looking for someone to fill in. Calhoun Ballenger's wife has been trying to handle it, but you'd be a godsend right now. Can you type?"

"Oh, yes," she said. "I can handle a computer, too. I took several college courses before my parents died and I had to come out here to comply with the terms of their will."

"Good!"

"But surely they've found someone…"

"There aren't that many people available for part-time work," he said. "Mostly high-school students, and they don't like the environment that goes with the job."

She grinned. "I won't care, as long as I make enough to pay my rent."

"You will. Here." He scribbled an address. "Go and see Justin or Calhoun. Tell them I sent you. Trust me," he added, rising to shake hands with her. "You'll like them."

"I hope so. I sure don't like my uncle much at the moment."

He nodded. "I can understand that. But Henry isn't a bad man, you know. And there could be more to this than meets the eye," he added reluctantly.

That statement gave her cold chills. The way Uncle Henry had been throwing her headlong at a rich bachelor friend of his made her uneasy. "I suppose so." She hesitated. "Do you know just how my uncle's been managing my affairs in the past two months?"

"Not yet," Barry Holman replied. "I've asked for an accounting, but he's refused to turn over any documents to me until the day you turn twenty-one."

"That doesn't sound promising," she said nervously. "I understood my father to say he had at least two million dollars tied up in trust for me. Surely Uncle

Henry couldn't have gone through that in a few weeks, could he?"

"I hardly think so," he assured her. "Don't worry. Everything will be all right. Go and see the Ballengers. Good luck."

"I think I'll need it, but thanks for your help," she said as she left the office.

THE BALLENGER FEEDLOT was a mammoth operation. During the short time she'd been in Jacobsville, Fay had never gotten a good look at it. Now, up close, the sheer enormity of it was staggering. So was the relative cleanliness of the operation and the attention to sanitation.

It was Justin Ballenger who interviewed her. He was tall and rangy, not at all handsome, but kind and courteous.

"You understand that this would only be a temporary job?" he emphasized, leaning forward. "Our secretary, Nita, is only going to be out long enough to recuperate from her C-section and have a few weeks with their new baby."

"Yes, Mr. Holman told me about that," Fay said. "I don't mind. I only need something temporary until I get used to being on my own. I was living with my uncle but the situation was pretty uncomfortable." Without meaning to, she went on to explain what had happened, finding in Justin a sympathetic listener.

Justin's dark eyes narrowed. "Your uncle is a mercenary man. I think you did the right thing. Make sure Barry keeps a close watch on your holdings."

"He's doing that." She gnawed her lower lip worriedly. "You won't mention it to anyone...?"

"It's nobody's business but yours," he agreed. "As far as we know, you're strictly a working girl who had a minor disagreement with her kin. Fair enough?"

"Yes, sir," she said, smiling. "I'm not really much more than a working girl, since everything is tied up in trust. But only for a few more weeks." She smiled. "Money doesn't really mean that much to me. Honestly I'd rather marry someone who loved me than someone who just wanted an easy life."

"You're a wise girl," he replied quietly. "Shelby and I both felt like that. We're not poor, but it wouldn't matter if we were. We have each other, and our boys. We're very lucky."

She smiled, because she'd heard about Shelby Ballenger and the circumstances that had finally led to her marriage to Justin. It was a real love story. "Maybe I'll get lucky like that one day," she said, thinking about Donavan.

"Well, if you want the job under those conditions, it's yours," he said after a minute. "Welcome aboard. Come on and I'll introduce you to my brother."

He preceded her down the hall, where a tall blond man was poring over figures on sheets of paper scattered all over his desk.

"This is Fay York," he said, introducing her. "Fay, my brother, Calhoun."

"Nice to meet you," she said sincerely, and shook hands. "I hope I can help you keep things in order while Nita's away."

"Abby will get down and kiss your shoes," Calhoun assured her. "She's been trying to keep one of our boys in school and the other two in day care and take care of the house while she worked in Nita's place this week.

She's already threatened to open all the gates if we didn't do something to help her."

"I'm glad I needed a job, then," she said.

"So are we."

Abby came barreling in with an armload of files, her black hair askew around her face, her blue-gray eyes wide and curious when they met Fay's green ones.

"Please be my replacement," she said with such fervor that Fay laughed helplessly. "Do you take bribes? I can get you real chocolate truffles and mocha ice cream…"

"No need. I've already accepted the job while Nita is out with her baby," Fay assured the other woman.

"Oh, thank *God*!" she sighed, dropping the files on her husband's desk. She grinned at Calhoun. "Thank you, too, darling. I'll make you a big beef stew for dinner, with homemade rolls."

"Don't just stand there, go home!" he burst out. He grinned sheepishly at Fay. "She makes the best rolls in town. I've been eating hot dogs for so many days that I bark, because it's all I can cook! This has been hard on my stomach."

"And on my stamina." Abby laughed. "The boys have missed me. Well, I'll show you what to do, Fay, then I'll rush right home and start dough rising."

Fay followed her back to the desk out front and listened carefully and made notes while Abby briefed her on the routine and showed her how to fill in the forms. She went over the basics of feedlot operation as well, so that Fay would understand what she was doing.

"You make it sound very easy, but it isn't, is it?"

"No," Abby agreed. "Especially when you deal with

some of our clients. J. D. Langley alone is enough to make a saint throw in the towel."

"Is he a rancher?"

"He's a…" Abby cleared her throat. "Yes, he's a rancher. But most of the cattle he deals in are other people's. He's general manager of the Mesa Blanco ranch combine."

"I don't know much about ranching, but I've heard of them."

"Most everybody has. J.D.'s good at his job, don't get me wrong, but he's a perfectionist when it comes to diet and handling of cattle. He saw one of the men use a cattle prod on some of his stock once and he jumped the man, right over a rail. We can't afford to turn down his business, but he makes things difficult. You'll find that out for yourself. Nobody crosses J.D. around Jacobsville."

"Is he rich?"

"No. He has plenty of power because of the job he does for Mesa Blanco, but it's his temperament that makes people jump when he speaks. J.D. would be arrogant in rags. He's just that kind of man."

Abby's description brought to mind another man, a rangy cowboy who'd given her the most magical evening of her life. She smiled sadly, thinking that she'd probably never see him again. Walking into that bar had been an act of desperation and bravado. She'd never have the nerve to do it twice. It would look as if she were chasing him, and he'd said at the time that there was no future in it. She'd driven by the bar two or three times, but she couldn't manage enough courage to go in again.

"Is Mr. Langley married?" Fay asked.

"There's no woman brave enough, anywhere," Abby

said shortly. "His father's marriage soured him on women. He's been something of a playboy in past years, but he's settled somewhat since he's been managing the Mesa Blanco companies. There's a new president of the company who's a hard-line conservative, so J.D.'s toned down his playboy image. There's talk of the president giving that job to a man who's married and settled and has kids. The only child in J.D.'s life, ever, is a nephew in Houston, his sister's child. His sister died." She shook her head. "I can't really imagine J.D. with a child. He isn't the fatherly type."

"Is he really that bad?"

Abby nodded. "He was always difficult. But his father's remarriage, and then his death, left scars. These days, he's a dangerous man to be around, even for other men. Calhoun leaves the office when he's due to check on his stock. Justin seems to like him, but Calhoun almost came to blows with him once."

"Is he here very often?" Fay asked with obvious reluctance.

"Every other week, like clockwork."

"Then I'm very glad I won't be around long," she said with feeling.

Abby laughed. "Not to worry. He'll barely notice you. It's Calhoun and Justin who get the range language."

"I feel better already," she said.

HER FIRST DAY was tiring, but by the end of it she knew how many records had to be compiled each day on the individual lots of cattle. She learned volumes about weight gain ratios, feed supplements, veterinary services, daily chores and form filing. If it sounded simple just to feed cattle, it wasn't. There were hundreds of details to be attended to, and printouts of daily averages to be compiled for clients.

As the days went by and she fell into the routine of the job, Fay couldn't help but wonder if Donavan ever came here. He was foreman for a ranch, he'd told her. If that ranch had feeder cattle, this was probably where they'd be brought. But from what she'd learned, it was subordinates who dealt with the logistics of the transporting of feeder cattle, not the bosses.

She wanted badly to see him, to tell him how big an impact he'd had on her life with his pep talk that night she'd gone to the bar. Her horizons had enlarged, and she was independent for the first time in her life. She'd gone from frightened girl to confident woman in a very short time, and she wanted to thank him. She'd almost asked Abby a dozen times if she knew anyone named Donavan, but Abby would hardly travel in those circles. The Ballengers were high society now, even if they weren't social types. They wouldn't hang out in country bars with men who treed them.

Her uncle had tried to get her to come back to his house when word got out that she was working for a living, but she'd stood firm. No, she told Uncle Henry firmly. She wasn't going to be at his mercy until she inherited. And, she added, Mr. Holman was going to expect an accounting in the near future. Her uncle had looked very uncomfortable when she'd said that and she'd called Barry Holman the next morning to ask about her uncle's authority to act on her behalf.

His reply was that her uncle's power of attorney was a very limited one, and it was doubtful that he could do much damage in the short time he had left. Fay wondered about that. Her uncle was shrewd and underhanded. Heaven knew what wheeling and dealing he might have done already without her knowledge.

Pressure of work caught her attention and held it until the early afternoon. She took long enough to eat lunch at a nearby seafood place and came back just in time to catch the tail end of a heated argument coming from Calhoun's office.

"You're being unreasonable, J.D., and you know it!" Calhoun's deep voice carried down the hall.

"Unreasonable, hell," an equally deep voice drawled. "You and I may never see eye to eye on production methods, but while you're feeding out my cattle, you'll do it my way."

"For God's sake, you'd have me out there feeding the damned things with a fork!"

"Not at all. I only want them treated humanely."

"They *are* treated humanely!"

"I wouldn't call an electric cattle prod that. And stressed animals aren't healthy animals."

"Have you ever thought about joining an animal rights lobby?" came the exasperated reply.

"I belong to two, thanks."

The door opened and Fay couldn't drag her eyes away from it. That curt voice was so familiar…

Sure enough, the tall, lithe man who came out of the office in front of Calhoun was equally familiar. Fay couldn't help the radiance of her face, the softness of her eyes as they adored his lean, dark face under the wide brim of his hat.

Donavan. She could have danced on her desk.

But when he turned and saw her, he frowned. His silvery eyes narrowed, glittered. He paused by her desk, his head cocked slightly to one side, a lit cigar dangling from his fingers.

"What are you doing here?" he asked her bluntly.

"I'm filling in for Nita," she began.

"Don't tell me you have to work for a living now, debutante?" he asked in a mocking tone.

She hesitated. He sounded as if he disliked her. But she knew he'd enjoyed the fiesta as much as she had. His behavior puzzled her, intimidated her.

"Well, yes," she stammered. "I do." And she did. For the time being.

"What a hell of a comedown," he murmured with patent disbelief. "Still driving the Mercedes?"

"You know each other?" Calhoun asked narrowly.

Donavan lifted the cigar to his mouth and blew out thick smoke. "Vaguely." He glanced at Calhoun until the other man sighed angrily and went back to his office with a muttered goodbye.

"You've been driving by the bar fairly regularly," he remarked curtly, and she blushed because she couldn't deny it. She'd been looking for him, hoping to have a chance to tell him how he'd helped her turn her life around. But he seemed to be putting a totally different connotation on her actions. "Is that where you found out I did business with the Ballengers?" He didn't even give her time to deny it. "Well, no go, honey. I told you that night, no bored debutante is going to try to make a minor amusement out of me. So if you came here hoping for another shot at me, you might as well quit right now and go home to your caviar and champagne. You're not hard on the eyes, but I'm off the market, is that clear?"

She stared at him in quiet confusion. "Mr. Holman told me about the job," she said with what dignity she had left. "I don't have a dime until my twenty-first birth-day, and I'm living on my own so I have to pay rent. This was the only job available." She dropped her gaze to her computer. "I drove by the bar a time or two, yes. I wanted to tell you that you'd changed my life, that I was learning to stand on my own feet. I wanted to thank you."

His jaw tautened and he looked more dangerous than ever. "I don't want thanks, teenage adulation, hero wor-ship or misplaced lust. But you're welcome, if it mat-ters."

He sounded cynical and mocking. Fay felt chastised. She'd only been grateful, but he made her feel stupid. Maybe she was. She'd spun a few midnight dreams about him. Except for some very innocent dates with boys, she'd never had much attention from the oppo-site sex. His protective attitude that night in the bar, his quiet handling of what could have become a bad inci-dent, had made her feel feminine and hungry for more of his company. He was telling her that she'd made too much of it, that she was offering him affection that he didn't want or need. It was probably a kindness, but it hurt all the same.

She forced a smile. "You needn't worry. I wasn't planning to follow you around with a wedding band on a hook or anything. I just wanted to thank you for what you did."

"You've done that. So?"

"I…have a lot of work to get through. I'm only tem-porary," she added quickly. "Just until Nita comes back. When I get my legacy, I'll be on the first plane back to Georgia. Honest."

His dark eyebrows plunged above the straight bridge

of his nose. "I don't remember asking for any explanations."

"Excuse me, then." She turned her attention back to her keyboard; her hands were cold and numb. She forced them to work. She didn't look up, either. He'd made her feel like what came out of a sausage grinder.

He didn't reply. He didn't linger, either. His measured footsteps went out the door immediately, leaving the pungent scent of cigar smoke in their wake.

Calhoun came back out five minutes later, checking his watch. "I have to be out of the office for an hour or so. Tell Justin when he comes back, will you?"

"Yes, sir," she said, smiling.

He hesitated, his narrowed eyes registering the hurt on her face that she couldn't hide. "Listen, Fay, don't let him upset you," he added quietly. "He doesn't really mean things as personally as they sound, but he rubs everybody the wrong way except Justin."

"He saved me from a bad situation," she began. "I only wanted to thank him, but he seemed to think I had designs on him or something. My goodness, he thought I came to work here because he did business with you!"

He laughed. "Can't blame him. Several have, and no, I'm not kidding. The more he snarls, the harder some women chase him. He's a catch, too. He makes good money with Mesa Blanco, and his own ranch is nothing to laugh at."

"Mesa... Blanco?" she stammered, as puzzle pieces began to make a pattern in her mind.

"Sure. Didn't he introduce himself before?" He smiled ruefully. "I guess not. Well, that was J. D. Langley."

CHAPTER THREE

FAY GOT THROUGH the rest of the day without showing too much of her heartache. She'd had hopes that Donavan might have felt something for her, but he'd dashed those very efficiently. He couldn't have made it more obvious that he wanted no part of her or her monied background. He wouldn't believe that she had to work. Well, of course, she didn't, really. But he might have given her the benefit of the doubt.

It hadn't been a terrible shock to learn that he was J. D. Langley. He did live down to his publicity. Later, she'd found out that Donavan was his middle name and what he was called locally, except by people who did business with him. She certainly understood why the Ballengers hated to see him coming.

She was sorry about his hostility, because the first time she'd ever seen him, there had been a tenderness between them that she'd never experienced. It must have all been on one side, though, she decided miserably.

Well, she told herself as she lay trying to sleep that night, she'd do better to stop brooding and concentrate on her own problems. She had enough, without adding the formidable Mr. Langley to them.

But fate was conspiring against her. The next day, she tried a new cafeteria in Jacobsville and came face-to-face with J. D. Langley as she sat down with her tray.

He gave her a glare that would have stopped traffic. He'd obviously just finished his meal. He was draining his coffee cup. Fay turned her chair so that she wasn't looking directly at him and, with unsteady hands, took her food off the tray.

"I told you yesterday," Donavan said at her shoulder, "that I don't like being chased. Didn't you listen?"

The whip of his voice cut. Not only that, it was loud enough to attract attention from other diners in the crowded room.

Fay's face went red as she glanced at him apprehensively, her green eyes huge as they met the fierce silvery glitter of his.

"I didn't know you were going to be here…" she began uneasily.

"No?" he challenged, his smile an insult in itself. "You didn't recognize my car sitting in the parking lot? Give it up, debutante. I don't like bored little rich girls, so stop following me around. Got that?"

He turned and left the cafeteria. Fay was too humiliated by the unwanted attention to enjoy much of her meal. She left quickly and went back to work.

Following him around, indeed, she muttered to herself while she fed data into her computer. She didn't know what kind of car he drove. The only vehicle she'd seen him in was a battered gray pickup truck, had he forgotten? Perhaps he thought she'd seen his car when he'd come to the feedlot, but she hadn't. The more she saw of him the less she liked him, and she'd hardly been hounding him. She certainly wouldn't again, he could bank on that!

Abby came in the next afternoon with an invitation. "Calhoun and I have to go to a charity ball tonight. I know it's spur-of-the-moment, but would you like to come?"

"Will my uncle be there, do you think?" Fay asked.

"I hardly think so." Abby grinned. "Come on. You've been moping around here for two days, it will be good for you. You can ride with us, and there's a very nice man I want to introduce you to when we get there. He's unattached, personable and rich enough not to mind that you are."

"Uh, Mr. Langley…?"

"I heard what happened in Cole's Café." Abby grimaced. "J.D. doesn't go to charity balls, so you aren't likely to run into him there."

"Thank God. He was so kind to me the night I met him, but he's been terrible to me ever since. I only wanted to thank him. He thinks I have designs on him." She shuddered. "As if I'd ever chased a man in my life…!"

"You're not J.D.'s kind of woman, Fay," the older woman said gently. "Your wealth alone would keep him at bay, without the difference in your ages. J.D.'s in his early thirties, and he doesn't like younger women."

"I don't think he likes *any* women," Fay replied with a sigh. "Especially me. But I wasn't chasing him, honestly!"

"Don't let it worry you."

"You're sure he won't be there tonight?"

"Absolutely positive," Abby assured her.

PROPHETIC WORDS. Abby and Calhoun picked Fay up at her apartment house, and drove her to the elegant Whitman estate where the charity ball was already in progress. Fay was wearing a long, white silk dress with one shoulder bare and her hair in a very elegant braided bun atop her head. She looked young and fragile…and very rich.

They went through the receiving line and Fay moved ahead of Calhoun and Abby to the refreshment table while they spoke to an acquaintance. She bumped into someone and turned to apologize.

"Again?" J. D. Langley asked with a vicious scowl. "My God, do you have radar?"

Fay didn't say a word. She turned and went back toward Abby and Calhoun, her heart pounding in her chest.

Abby spotted J.D. and grimaced. "I didn't know," she told a shattered Fay. "I swear I didn't. Here, you stick close to us. He won't bother you. Come on, I'll introduce you to Bart and that will solve all your problems. I'm sorry, Fay."

"It wasn't your fault. It's fate, I guess," she said dryly, although her eyes were troubled.

"Arrogant beast," Abby muttered, sparing the tall, elegant man in the dinner jacket a speaking glance. "If he were a little less conceited, you wouldn't have this problem." She drew Fay forward. "Here he is. Bart!"

A thin, lazy-looking man with wavy blond hair and mischievous blue eyes turned as his name was called. He greeted Abby warmly and glanced at Fay with open curiosity and delight.

"Well, well, Greek goddesses are back in style again, I see. Do favor me with a waltz before you set off for Mount Olympus, fair damsel."

"This is our newest employee, Fay York," she introduced them. "Fay, this is Bartlett Markham. He's president of the local cattlemen's association."

"Nice to meet you," she said, extending a hand. "Do you know cattle?"

"I grew up on a ranch. I work for a firm of accountants now, but my family still has a pretty formidable Santa Gertrudis purebred operation."

"I don't know much, but I'm learning every day," Fay laughed.

"I'll leave her with you, Bart," Abby said. "Do keep her away from J.D., will you? He seems to think she's stalking him."

"Do tell?" His eyebrows levered up and he grinned. "Why not stalk me instead? I'm a much better catch than J.D., and you won't need preventive shots if you go out with me, either."

Insinuating that she would with J.D., she thought. Rabies probably, she mused venomously, in case he bit her. She smiled at Bart, feeling happier already.

"Consider yourself on the endangered species list, then," she said.

He laughed. "Gladly." He glanced toward the band. "Would you like to dance?"

"Charmed." She gave him her hand and let him lead her to the dance floor, where a live band was playing a bluesy two-step. She knew exactly where J. D. Langley was, as if she really did have radar, so she was careful not to look in that direction.

He noticed. It was impossible not to, when she was dancing with one of his bitterest enemies. He stood quietly against a wall, his silver eyes steady and unblinking as he registered the fluid grace with which she followed her partner's steps. He didn't like the way Markham was holding her, or the way she was responding.

Not that he wanted her, he assured himself. She was nothing but another troublesome woman. A debutante, at that, and over ten years his junior. He had no use for her at all, and he'd made sure she knew it. Their one evening together had sent him tearing away in the opposite direction. She appealed to him terribly. He couldn't afford an involvement with a society girl. He knew he was better off alone, so keeping this tempting little morsel away from him became imperative. If he had to savage her to do it, it was still the best thing for both of them. She was much too soft and delicate for a man like himself. He'd break her spirit and her heart, because he had nothing to give. And his father's reputation in the community made it impossible for him to be seen in public with her in any congenial way. He'd accused her of stalking him, but gossip would have it the other way around. Another money-crazy Langley, critics would scoff, out to snare himself a rich wife. He groaned at just the thought.

He didn't like seeing her with Markham, but there was nothing he could do about it. He shouldn't have come tonight.

He turned away to the refreshment table and poured himself a glass of Scotch.

"You aren't really after Donavan, are you?" Bart asked humorously.

"He flatters himself," she said haughtily.

"That's what I thought. Like father, like son," he said unpleasantly.

"I don't understand."

He made a graceful turn, carrying her with him as the music's tempo increased. "After Donavan's mother died, Rand Langley got into a financial tangle and was about to lose his ranch. My aunt was very young then, plain and shy, but she was filthy rich and single, so Rand set his cap for her. He kept after her until he seduced her, so that she had to marry him or disgrace her family. She was crazy about him. Worshiped the ground he walked on. Then, inevitably, she found out why he really married her and she couldn't live with it. She killed herself."

Fay grimaced. "I'm sorry."

"So were all of us," he added coldly, glaring at J. D. Langley's back. "Rand didn't even come to the funeral. He was too busy spending her money. He died a few years later, and believe me, none of us grieved for him."

"That wasn't Donavan's fault," she felt bound to point out.

"Blood will tell," came the unbelieving reply. "You're well-to-do."

"Yes, but he can't stand me," she replied.

"I don't believe that. I can't imagine J.D. passing up a rich woman."

"How many has he dated over the years?" she asked with faint irritation.

"I don't keep up with his love life," he said tersely, and all his prejudices showed quite clearly. Fay could see that he wouldn't believe a kind word about J. D. Langley if he had proof.

"The two of you don't get along, I gather."

"We disagree on just about everything. Especially on his ridiculous theories about cattle raising," he added sarcastically. "No. We don't get along."

She was quiet after that. Now she understood the situation. It couldn't have been made clearer.

She danced with several eligible bachelors and several married men before the evening ended. It surprised her that J. D. Langley was still present. He remained on the fringes of the dance floor, talking to other men.

He asked no one to dance. Fay was sadly certain that he wouldn't ask her.

But in that, she was surprised. The band was playing a soft love song and she watched Bart glance in her direction. But before he could get across the room, Donavan suddenly swung her into his arms and onto the dance floor.

Her heart skipped wildly as she felt the firm clasp of his hand on her waist, his fingers steely as they linked her own.

"This is not a good idea," she said firmly. "I'll think you're encouraging me."

"Not likely. By now Bart's filled you in, hasn't he?" he replied with a mocking smile.

She averted her eyes to the white ruffled shirt he wore under his dinner jacket. On another man it might look effeminate. On Donavan, it looked masculine and very sexy, emphasizing his dark good looks. "I got an earful, thanks," she replied.

He shook her gently. "Stiff as a board," he mused, looking down at her. "Are you afraid to let your guard down? There's very little I could do to you on a dance floor in front of half of Jacobsville."

"You've made your opinion of me crystal clear, Mr. Langley," she said without looking up. "I haven't been stalking you, as you put it, but you're free to think what you like. Do try to remember that I didn't ask you to dance."

"That was the whole purpose of the exercise," he said carelessly. "To make sure you didn't set your cap for me."

"Then why are you dancing with me?"

His lean arm whipped her close on a turn, but he

didn't let her go afterward. His dark face was all too close, so that she could smell his tangy aftershave, and his silver eyes bit into hers at point-blank range. "Don't you know?" he asked at her lips.

Her heart tripped as she felt his breath. "Oh, I see," she said suddenly. "You're trying to irritate Bart."

He lifted his head and one eyebrow quirked. "Is that it?"

"What else?" she asked with a nervous laugh, averting her eyes to a fuming Bart nearby. "Listen, I'm not going to be used for any vendettas, by you or your hissing kin."

His fingers curled into hers and drew them to his broad chest. It rose and fell heavily, and he stared over her dark head without seeing anything. "I don't have any vendettas," he said quietly. "But I won't be accused of following in my father's footsteps."

She could feel the pain in those terse words, but she didn't remark on it. Her eyes closed and she drank in the delicious masculine scent of him. "I won't be rich for another week or two," she murmured. "Until the legal work goes through, I'm just a temporary secretary."

He laughed in spite of himself. "I see. For two weeks you're on my level. No Mercedes. No mansion. No padded checkbook."

"Something like that." She sighed and snuggled closer. "How about a wild, passionate affair? We could throw the coats on the closet floor and you could have your way with me under somebody's silver fox stole."

He burst out laughing. His steely arm drew her close as he made a sudden turn, and her body throbbed with the sensations it caused in her untried body.

"Hasn't anyone told you yet that I belong to two animal rights groups?"

"So you're one of those people who protest lab animal experiments that save little children's lives and throw paint on people who wear fur coats?" she asked, her temper rising.

"Not me. I'm no fanatic. I just think animals have the right to humane treatment, even in medical facilities." His arm tightened. "As for throwing paint on fur coats, a few lawsuits should stem that habit. The idea is to stop further slaughter of wild animals. A fur coat is already a dead animal."

She shivered. "You make it sound morbid."

One silver eye narrowed. "Do you wear fur?"

She chuckled. "I can't. Fur makes me break out in hives."

He began to smile. "A rich girl with no furs. What a tragedy."

"I have plenty of velvet coats, thanks very much. I think they're much more elegant than fur and they don't shed." She moved closer, shocked when his hand caught her hip and contracted painfully. "Ouch!" she protested.

He moved her back an inch. "Don't push your luck," he said, his voice low and faintly threatening, like his glittery eyes. "You're pretty sexy in that little number you're wearing, and I'm easily aroused. Want me to prove it?"

"No, thanks," she said quickly. "I'll take your word for it."

He laughed as he spun her around in a neat turn. "For a sophisticated debutante, sometimes you're a contradiction. Is that a blush?"

"It's hot in here."

"Ah. The conventional excuse." He leaned close and brushed his cheek against hers. "Too bad you're rich."

"Is it? Why?" she asked in a tone that sounded, unfortunately, all too breathless.

He nibbled gently on her earlobe. "Because I'm dynamite in bed."

"Do tell?" She hid her face against him. "Are you?" she whispered shakily.

His lean hand slid up her back and into the coiled hair at her nape. He caressed it gently while he held her, the music washing over them in a sultry silence.

"So I've been told." His chin rubbed softly against her temple, his breath coming roughly. "But why take someone else's word for it?"

She forced a laugh. "Isn't this a little sudden? I mean, just a day ago you were giving me hell for eating lunch in the same restaurant with you."

"I'm sure Bart told you the problem. Rich, you're right off my Christmas list. Poor, you're an endangered species." His hand contracted, coaxing her face up to his glittery eyes.

"Should I cut and run?" she asked, her voice husky.

"Do you really want to?" he whispered.

As he spoke, he moved closer, and his powerful thighs brushed hers. Even through all the layers of fabric, she felt the imprint of them, the strength. His hand slid down her back to her waist and pulled, very gently, so that she was pressed right up to him, welded from breast to thigh. He watched her eyes and something masculine and arrogant kindled in his gaze as he felt the faint shiver of her soft body.

"Do you like Chinese food?" he asked.

She nodded.

"I like to drive up to Houston for it. There's a good restaurant just inside the city limits. How about it?"

Her heart jumped. "Are you asking me out?"

"Sounds like it," he mused. "Don't expect steak and lobster. I make a good salary, but it doesn't run to champagne."

She colored furiously. "Please, don't," she said quickly. "I'm not like that."

He touched her face gently. "Yes, I know. It makes it harder. Do you think I enjoyed hurting you?" he asked harshly, and for an instant something showed in his eyes that startled her. He looked away. "There's no future for us, little one."

She felt him hesitating. Any second, he was going to take back that supper invitation.

"Just Chinese food," she prompted, one slender hand poking him gently in the ribs.

He started, and she grinned at him. "And no moonlight seduction on the way home," she added. "As you said, it isn't wise to start things we can't finish."

"I could finish that," he murmured dryly.

She cleared her throat. "Well, I don't take chances. I'll risk my stomach with you, but not my heart."

He cocked an eyebrow. "Does that mean that making love with me might enslave you?" he teased.

"Exactly. Besides, I never sleep with a man on the first date."

There was the faintest movement of his eyelashes. He averted his gaze to a point beyond her head. He couldn't admit that it bothered him, thinking of her with other men. She was a debutante and filthy rich, surely there had been a steady stream of suitors. She might have more experience even than he did. He'd never thought about a woman's past before. It had never occurred to him to wonder how experienced his lover of the evening actually was. But with Fay, he wondered.

"What's wrong?" she asked curiously.

He glanced down at her. She looked very innocent until she smiled, and then her eyes crinkled and there was a sophistication in them that made him feel cool. "Nothing."

"That's usually the woman's line, isn't it?"

"Equal rights," he reminded her. "Friday night. I'll pick you up at six."

"I don't live with Uncle Henry anymore," she began.

"I know where you live," he replied. "We'll eat Chinese food and you can show me what you know. It should be quite an experience…"

LONG AFTER THE dance was over and she was back in her apartment, she worried over that last statement. She felt as if she were about to get in well over her head.

She wanted Donavan more than she'd ever wanted anything in her life. A date with him was the gold at the end of the rainbow. But she'd pretended to be something she wasn't, and she didn't know what she was going to do if he took her up on it.

ABBY NOTICED FAY'S preoccupation the next day when she stopped by to see Calhoun.

"You're positively morose!" Abby exclaimed. "What's wrong?"

"Donavan asked me out."

Her eyebrows went up. "J.D. asked you out? But he hates rich women."

"Yes, I know. I told him I was going to be poor for two

more weeks, so I guess he thought it was safe enough until my inheritance comes through."

"I see." Abby didn't say anything, but she began to look worried herself. "Fay, I never thought to mention it, because J.D. was giving you such a hard time, but he's something of a womanizer…"

"I figured that out for myself," she murmured with a smile. "It shows."

"He's a gentleman, in his way. Just don't give him too much rope. He'll hang you with it."

"I know that, too. I'll be careful."

Abby hesitated. "If it helps, I know how you feel. I was crazy about Calhoun, but he liked a different kind of woman altogether. We had a very rocky path to the altar."

"He's crazy about you, though. Anyone can see that."

Abby smiled contentedly. "Of course he is. But it wasn't always that way."

"Donavan already said that he doesn't want commitment. I'm not going to get my hopes up. But an evening out with him… Well, it's going to be like brushing heaven, you know?"

"I do, indeed." Abby smiled, remembering her first date with Calhoun. She glanced back at Fay, her eyes wistful. She only hoped their newest employee wasn't going to be badly hurt. Everyone locally knew that J. D. Langley wasn't a marrying man. But Abby would have bet her prize bull that Fay was as innocent as Abby herself had once been. If she was, she had a lot of heartache in store. When J.D. found out, and he would, he'd drop Fay like a hot rock. Innocents were not his style.

FAY WENT THROUGH the motions of working like a zombie for the next week, with a dull and tedious weekend in between that did little for her nerves. Donavan didn't come by the feedlot at all, and when she left the office the next Friday afternoon, she still hadn't heard from him. For all she knew, he might have forgotten all about her.

The phone was ringing even as she got in the door, and she grabbed up the receiver as if it were a life preserver.

"Hello?" she said breathlessly.

"I'll be by in an hour. You hadn't forgotten?" Donavan drawled.

"How could I?" she asked, adding mischievously, "I love Chinese food."

He chuckled. "That puts me in my place, I guess. See you."

He hung up and Fay ran to dress. The only thing in her closet that would suit a fairly casual evening out was a pale green silk suit and she hated wearing it. It screamed big money, something sure to set Donavan's teeth on edge. But other than designer jeans and a silk blouse, or evening gowns, it was all she had. The cotton pantsuit she'd worn to work today was just too wrinkled and stained to wear out tonight. It wouldn't have been suitable anyway.

She teamed the silk suit with a nice cotton blouse and sat down to wait, after renewing her makeup. She only hoped that he wasn't going to take one look at her and run. If he didn't throw her over entirely, she was going to have to invest in some medium-priced clothing!

CHAPTER FOUR

JUST AS FAY had feared, Donavan's first glimpse of her silk suit brought a scowl to his face.

"It's old," she said inadequately, and looked miserable. She locked her fingers together and stared at him with sadness all over her face.

He shoved his hands into the pockets of his gray slacks. He was wearing a white cotton shirt and a blue blazer with them, a black Stetson cocked over one eye and matching boots on his feet. He looked nice, but hardly elegant or wealthy. Her silk suit seemed to point out all the differences between the lifestyle she was used to, and his own.

"You look very nice," he said quietly.

"And very expensive," she added on a curt laugh. "I'm sorry."

"Why?"

"I didn't want you to think I wore this on purpose," she said, faltering.

He lifted an eyebrow and smiled mockingly. "I'm taking you out for a Chinese dinner. A proposal of marriage doesn't come with the egg roll."

She blushed furiously. "I know that."

"Then why bother about appearances?" He shrugged. "A date is one thing. A serious relationship is something else." His silver eyes narrowed. "Let's settle that at the outset. I have nothing serious or permanent in mind. Even if we wind up as the hottest couple in town between the sheets, there still won't be anything offered in the way of commitment."

"I knew that already," she said, steeling herself not to react to the provocative statement.

"Good." He glanced around the apartment, frowning slightly. "This is pretty spartan, isn't it?" he asked, suddenly realizing how frugally she seemed to be living.

"It's all I could afford on my salary," she told him. She wrapped her arms across her breasts and smiled. "I don't mind it. It's just a place to sleep."

"Henry doesn't help you financially?" he persisted.

"He can't," she explained. "He's got his own financial woes. I'll be fine when he turns over my affairs to Mr. Holman and I can get to my trust."

Donavan didn't say a word, but suddenly he was beginning to see things she apparently didn't. If Henry was having money problems, surely his control of Fay's estate would give him the means of solving them, even if he had to pay her back later. The fact that he was suffering a reversal didn't bode well for Fay, but she seemed oblivious. Perhaps like most rich women she didn't know or care much about handling money.

He was aware that he'd been silent a long time. He took his hands out of his pockets and caught her slender fingers in his. They were cold, like ice. "We'd better go," he said, drawing her along with him.

Fay had never realized how exciting it could be to hold hands with a man. He linked her fingers into his as they walked, and she felt the sensuous contraction all the way to her toes. It was like walking on a cloud, she thought. She could almost float.

Donavan was feeling something similar and fighting it tooth and nail. He hadn't really wanted this date at all, but something stronger than his will had forced him into it. Fay was a delicious little morsel, full of contradictions. He'd always liked puzzles. She was one he really wanted to solve, even if his inclination was to get her into the nearest bed with all possible haste.

She had to be experienced. He'd never denied that. He wondered if pampered rich boys were as anemic in bed as they seemed when he saw them at board meetings. His contempt for the upper classes was, he knew, a result of his father's ruthless greed.

He could still barely believe the whole episode, his father running pell-mell after a woman half his age when his wife of twenty years was just barely in her grave. It had disgusted and shocked him, and led to a confrontation of stellar proportions. He hadn't spoken to his father afterward, and his presence at his father's funeral two years later was only a nod to convention. It wasn't until much later that he'd learned why Rand Langley had been so ruthless. It had been to save the family ranch, which had been Langley land for three generations. Not that it excused what he'd done, but it did at least explain it. Rand had wanted Donavan to inherit the ranch. Marrying money had been the only way he could keep it.

"You're very quiet," Fay remarked on the way to Houston. "Are you sorry you asked me out?"

He glanced at her. "No. I was remembering."

"Yes?"

He was smoking one of the small cigars he favored, his gray eyes thoughtful as they lingered on the long road ahead. "My father disgraced himself to marry money, to keep the ranch for me and my children, if I ever have any. Ironic, that I've never married and never want to, because of him."

She folded her hands primly in her lap. It flattered her that he was willing to tell her something so personal.

"If you don't have children, what will happen to your ranch?" she asked.

"I've got a ten-year-old nephew," he said. "My sister's boy. His father's been dead for years. My sister remarried three years ago, and she died last year. Her husband got custody. But he's just remarried, and last month he stuck Jeffrey in a military school. The boy's in trouble constantly, and he hates his stepfather." He took a long draw from the cigar, scowling. "That's why I was sitting in that bar the night you walked in. I was trying to decide what to do. Jeff wants to come out here and live with me."

"Can't he?"

He shook his head. "No chance. His stepfather and I don't get along. He'd more than likely refuse just to get at me. His new wife is pregnant and he doesn't seem to care about Jeff at all."

"That's sad," she said. "Does he miss his mother?"

"He never talks about her."

"Probably because he cares too much," she said. "I miss my parents," she added unexpectedly. "They died in a plane crash. Even if I never saw much of them, they were still my parents."

"What do you mean, you never saw much of them?"

She laughed softly. "They liked traveling. I was in school, and they didn't want to interrupt my education. I stayed at home with an elderly great-aunt. She liked me very much, but it was kind of lonely. Especially during holidays." She stared out the window, aware of his curious stare. "If I ever have kids, I'll be where they are," she said suddenly. "And they won't ever have to spend Christmas without me."

"I suppose," he began slowly, "there are some things money won't buy."

"An endless list," she agreed. "Beginning and ending with love."

He chuckled softly, to lighten the atmosphere. He glanced sideways at her. "Money can buy love, you know," he murmured.

"Well, not really," she disagreed. "It can buy the illusion of it, but I wouldn't call a timed session in bed 'love.'"

He burst out laughing. "No," he said after a minute. "I don't suppose it is. They say that type of experience is less than satisfying. I wouldn't know. I couldn't find any pleasure in a body I had to pay for."

"I can understand that."

There was a pleasant tension in the silence that dropped between them. Minutes later, Donavan pulled up in front of a Chinese restaurant and cut off the engine.

"This is it," he said. He helped her out of the car and escorted her inside.

It was a very nice restaurant, with Chinese music playing softly in the background and excellent service.

Donavan watched her covertly as he sampled the jasmine tea the waitress had served. "Tell me about your job. How does it feel to work for a living?"

Her eyes brightened and she smiled. "I like it very much," she confessed. "I've never been responsible for my own life before. I've always had people telling me

what to do and how to do it. The night I met you at
the bar really opened my eyes. You made me see what
my life was like, showed me that I could change it if I
wanted to. I wasn't kidding when I said you turned my
world around."

"I thought the job was a means to an end," he confessed, smiling at his own folly. "I've been chased before,
and by well-to-do women who saw me as a challenge."

"You're not bad looking," she said demurely, averting
her eyes. "And you're very much a man. But I meant it
when I said I wasn't chasing you. I have too much pride
to behave that way."

Probably she did. He liked her honesty. He liked
the way she looked and dressed, too. She wasn't beautiful, but she was elegant and well-mannered, and she
had a big heart. He found himself wondering how Jeff
would react to her.

They ate in a pleasant silence and talked about politics and the weather, everything except themselves.
All too soon it was time to start back for Jacobsville.

"How are you and your uncle getting along?" Donavan asked on the way back.

"We speak and not much more. Uncle Henry's worried about something," she added. "He gets more nervous by the day."

He'd never thought of her uncle as a nervous man.
Perhaps it had something to do with Fay's inheritance.

"Suppose you inherit only a few dollars and an apology?" he asked suddenly.

She laughed. "That isn't likely."

"But if it was?"

She thought about it seriously. "It would be hard,"
she confessed. "I'm not used to asking the price of any-

thing, or denying myself a whim purchase. But like anything else, I expect I could get used to it. I don't mind hard work."

He nodded. That would make her life easier.

He turned off onto a farm road just at the outskirts of Jacobsville.

"Where are we going?" she asked, glancing around at unfamiliar terrain.

"I'm going to show you my ranch," he said simply. His eyes lanced over her and he smiled wickedly. "Then I'm going to shove you into the henhouse and have my way with you."

"Do you have a henhouse?" she asked excitedly.

"Yes. And a flock of chickens to go with it. I like fresh eggs."

He didn't add that he often had to budget in between cattle sales, even on the good salary he made.

"I guess you have your own beef, too?" she asked.

"Not for slaughter," he replied. "I like animals too much to raise one to kill. Mesa Blanco has slaughter cattle, but I don't spend any more time around them than I have to."

The picture she was getting of him didn't have a lot to do with the image he projected. An animal lover with a core of steel was unusual.

"Do you have dogs and cats?"

He smiled slowly. "And puppies and kittens," he said. "I give them away when the population gets out of control, and most of mine are neutered. It's criminal to turn an unneutered animal loose on the streets." He slowed as the road curved toward a simple white frame house. "Ever had a dog or cat of your own?"

"No," she said sadly. "My parents weren't animal

lovers. My mother would have fainted at the thought of cat hair on her Louis Quinze furniture."

"I'd rather have the cat than the furniture," he remarked.

She smiled. "So would I."

His heart lifted. She wasn't at all what he'd expected. He pulled up in front of the ranch house and cut off the engine.

There were flowers everywhere, from shrubs to trees to beds of them right and left around the porch. She could see them by the fierce light of the almost-full moon. "How beautiful!" she exclaimed.

"Thank you."

"You planted them?"

"Nobody else. I like flowers," he said defensively as he got out and helped her out of the car.

"I didn't say a word," she assured him. "I like flowers, too."

He unlocked the front door while she glanced covetously along the long front porch at the old-fashioned swing and rocking chair. Somewhere nearby cattle made pleasant mooing noises.

"Do you keep a lot of cattle here?" she asked.

"I have purebred Santa Gertrudis," he told her. "Stud cattle, not beef cattle."

"Why doesn't that surprise me?" she teased.

He laughed, standing aside to let her enter the house.

The living room was done in Early American, and it looked both neat and lived-in. For a bachelor, he was a good housekeeper. She said so.

"Thanks, but I can't take all the credit. My foreman's wife looks after things when I can't."

She was insanely jealous of the foreman's wife, all at once.

He saw her expression and smiled. "She's fifty and happily married."

She blushed, moving farther into the room.

"Look out," he warned.

Before the words went silent, her foot was attacked by a tiny ball of fur with teeth.

"Good heavens!" she exclaimed, laughing. "A miniature tiger!" she kidded.

"I'm training her to be an attack cat. I call her Bee."

"Bee?"

He grinned. "Short for Beelzebub. You can't imagine what she did to the curtains a day or so ago."

She reached down and picked up the tiny thing. It looked up at her with a calico face and the softest, most loving blue-green eyes she'd ever seen, with black fur outlining them.

"Why, she's beautiful!" she exclaimed.

"I think so."

The kitten's eyes half closed as it began to purr and knead her jacket with its tiny paws.

"She'll pick that silk," he said, reaching for the kitten.

She looked at him curiously. "That doesn't matter," she said, surprised by his comment.

His silver eyes registered his own surprise as they looked deeply into hers. "That suit must have cost a small fortune," he persisted. He extricated the kitten, despite her protests, and carried it into the bedroom, closing the door behind him.

"Want some coffee?" he asked.

"That would be nice."

"It will only take a minute or so." He tossed his hat onto the hat rack and went into the kitchen.

Fay wandered around the living room, stopping at a photograph on the mantel. It was of a young boy, a studio pose. He looked a lot like Donavan, except that his eyes were dark, and he had a more rounded face. He looked sad.

"That's Jeff," he told her from the doorway. He leaned against it, waiting for the coffee to brew. His long legs were crossed, like his arms, and he looked very masculine and sexy with his jacket off and the top buttons of his shirt unfastened over a thicket of jet black hair.

"He favors you," she remarked. "Did your sister look like you?"

"Quite a lot," he said. "But her eyes were darker than mine. Jeff has his father's eyes."

"What does he like?" she asked. "I mean, is he a sports fan?"

"He doesn't care much for football. He likes martial arts, and he's good at them. He's a blue belt in tae kwon do—a Korean martial art that concentrates on kicking styles."

"Isn't that a demonstration sport in the summer Olympics?"

He smiled, surprised. "Yes, it is. Jeff hopes to be able to participate in the 1996 summer games in Atlanta."

"A group of Atlantans worked very hard to get the games to come there," she recalled. "One of my friends worked in the archives at Georgia Tech—a lot of the people on campus were active in that committee."

"You don't have many friends here, do you?" he asked.

"Abby Ballenger is a friend," she corrected. "And I get along well with the girls at the office."

"I meant friends in your own social class."

She put the picture of Jeff back on the mantel. "I never had friends in my own social class. I don't like their idea of fun."

"Don't you?"

He moved closer. His hands slid around her waist from behind and tugged her against him. His cheek nuzzled hers roughly. "What was their idea of fun?"

"Sleeping around," she said huskily. "That's…suicidal these days. All it takes is the wrong partner and you can die."

"I know." His lips slid down her long, elegant neck. His tongue tip found the artery at her throat and pressed there, feeling it accelerate wildly at his touch. His fingers slid to her slender hips and dug in, welding her to his hard thighs.

"Donavan?" she whispered unsteadily.

His hands flattened on her stomach, making odd little motions that sent tremors down her long legs and a rush of warmth into her bloodstream.

She didn't act very experienced. The camouflage was only good at long range, he thought as he drank in the gardenia scent of her skin. He should have been disappointed, because he'd wanted her badly tonight. But something inside him was elated at his growing suspicion that she was innocent. He had to find out if it was true.

"Turn your mouth up for me, Fay," he whispered at her chin. "I want to taste it under my own."

The words sent thrills down to her toes and curled them. Blind, deaf, she raised her face and turned it, feeling the sudden warm pressure of his mouth on her parted lips.

It wasn't at all what he'd expected. The contact was explosive. He'd been in complete control until he touched her. Now, suddenly he was fighting to keep his head at all. He turned her in his arms and caught his breath as he felt her body melt hungrily into his.

It shouldn't have happened like this. He could barely think. His hands bit into the backs of her thighs and lifted her, pulled at her, needing the close contact as he'd never needed anything. His legs began to tremble as his body went taut and capable, and his hands became ruthless.

Fay moaned. Never at any time in her life had she felt such a sudden, vicious fever of longing. She could always pull back, until now. With a tiny gasp, she lifted her arms around his neck and gave in completely. She felt him against her stomach, knew that he was already painfully aroused. She couldn't manage enough willpower to deny him, whatever the cost, whatever the risk. He was giving her a kind of pleasure she'd never dreamed of experiencing.

He invaded the silk jacket and the blouse she wore under it. He unbuttoned them and drew the fabric aside seconds before his mouth went down against the bare curve of her breast above her lacy bra. She'd never been touched like that. She clung to him, shivering as his lips became ruthless, his face rubbing the bra strap aside so he could nuzzle down far enough to find the hard, warm nipple.

She cried out. It was beyond bearing, sensation upon hot sensation, anguished joy. Her fingers tangled in his thick, dark hair and pulled at it as he suckled her in a silence throbbing with need.

"You taste of gardenias," he breathed urgently. "Soft and sweet... Fay...!"

His hands were as urgent as his voice. He unfastened her bra and slid it, along with her half-unbuttoned jacket and blouse, right down to her waist. His glazed eyes lingered for one long minute on the uncovered pink and mauve beauty of her naked breasts with their crowns hard and tip-tilted. Then his mouth and his hands were touching them, and she was glorying in his own pleasure, in the sweet delight of his ardor.

"So beautiful," he whispered as he drew his face over her soft breasts. "Fay, you make my body throb. Feel it. Feel me..."

One hand went to gather her hips close to his, to emphasize what he was saying. She moaned and searched blindly for his mouth, inviting a kiss as deep and ardent as the hand enjoying her soft breasts in the stillness of the room.

"Little one," he said huskily, "do you know what's going to happen between us now? Do you want me?"

"Yes!" she whispered achingly, hanging at his lips.

His body shivered with its blatant need. It had never been so urgent before, with any woman. He bit at her mouth. "Do you have anything to use? Are you on the pill?"

She hesitated. "No."

No. The word echoed through his swaying mind. No, she wasn't protected. He could have her, but he could also make her pregnant. Pregnant! He said something explicit and embarrassing, then he put his hands on her upper arms and thrust her away from him. He went blindly toward the kitchen and slammed the door behind him.

Fay sat down on the sofa, fastening hooks and buttons with hands so unsteady that she missed half the buttons and had to start over. It was a long time before she was back in order again, and only a few seconds after that, Donavan came in with a tray of coffee.

She couldn't look at him. She knew her face looked like rice paper. She was still trembling visibly, too, her mouth red and swollen, her breathing erratic and irregular.

He put a cup of black coffee in front of her without saying anything.

She didn't raise her eyes when she felt the sofa depress near her. She reached for the cup, barely able to hold it for the unsteadiness of her icy fingers.

A big, warm hand came to support hers, and when she looked up, his eyes weren't angry at all. They were faintly curious and almost affectionate.

"Thank you," she stammered as she sipped the hot, black liquid.

He smiled. A real smile, not the mocking ones she was used to. "You're welcome."

"I'm so sorry…!" she began nervously.

He put a long finger over her soft lips. "No. I am. I shouldn't have let it go so far."

"You were angry," she said hesitantly, her eyes glancing with sheer embarrassment off his before they fell to her cup.

"I was hotter than I've been in years and I had to stop," he said simply, and without anger. "It doesn't put a man in a sparkling mood, let me tell you."

"Oh."

He leaned back and sipped his own coffee, his eyes

quiet and faintly acquisitive. "Why are you still a virgin?" he asked suddenly.

The coffee cup made a nosedive, and she only just caught it in time. Her gaze hit his with staggering impact. "What did you say?"

"You heard me," he accused softly. "You can't even put on an act, can you? The second I touch you intimately, you're mine."

She flushed and looked away. "Rub it in," she invited.

"Oh, I intend to," he said with malicious glee. "I'm not sure I've ever made love to a virgin in my life. It was fascinating. You just go right in headfirst, don't you? There's not even a sense of self-preservation in you."

She glared at him. "Having fun?"

"Sure." He rested his arm over the back of the sofa and his gaze was slow and thorough as it fell to her breasts and watched their soft rise and fall. "Pretty little creature," he mused. "All pink and dusk."

"You stop that, J. D. Langley," she muttered hotly. "It isn't decent to even talk about it."

One eyebrow went up. "This is the nineties," he reminded her.

"Wonderful," she told him. "Life is liberal. No more rules and codes of behavior. No wonder the world's a mess."

He leaned back, chuckling. "As it happens, I agree with you. Rules aren't a bad thing, when they prevent the kind of insanity that's gripping the world today. But periodically, people have to find that out for themselves. Ever heard of the Roaring Twenties?" he added.

"Gin flowed like water, women smoked, sexually

transmitted diseases ran rampant because everybody was promiscuous…"

"You're getting the idea. But it's nothing new. People had cycles when rules were suspended even back in the Roman Empire. There were orgies and every evil known to man thrived. Then society woke up and the cycle started all over again. The only certain thing in life, Miss York, is change."

"I suppose so. But it's discouraging."

"Maybe you haven't heard, but the majority of people in this country feel exactly the same way you do," he said. "America is still a very moral place, little one. But it's what's different that makes news, not what's traditional."

"I see." She smiled. "That's encouraging."

"You come from wealth. Odd that you don't have an exaggerated sense of morality to go with it."

"You mean, because I was rich, I should be greedy and pleasure-loving and indifferent to my fellow man?" she teased. "Actually, that's a stereotype."

"I get the picture." He stared at her silently, his eyes growing dark with memory. "I wanted you like hell. But in a way, I'm glad you aren't on the pill."

She eyed him curiously. "You didn't sound glad."

"Wanting hurts a man when he can't satisfy it," he explained matter-of-factly. "But you weren't on the pill and I didn't have anything with me to protect you from pregnancy. That's one risk I'll never take."

She smiled at him. "I feel the same way."

His eyes warmed. "We'd better not create any accidental people," he said softly. "That's why I stopped. That," he added, "and the fact that I'm too old-fashioned to dishonor a chaste woman. Go ahead. Laugh," he invited. "But it's how I feel."

"Oh, Donavan, you and I are throwbacks to another time," she said heavily. "There's no place for us on earth."

"Why, sure there is, honey," he disagreed. "I'll carry you to church with me one Sunday and prove to you that we're not alone in the way we think. Listen, it's the radicals who are the minority." He leaned closer. "But the radicals are the ones who make news."

She laughed. "I guess so. I'd like to go to church with you," she said shyly. "I haven't been in a long time. Our housekeeper used to let me go to services with her, but when she quit I had no way to get there. It was before I was old enough to drive."

"Poor little rich girl," he said, but he smiled and the words sounded affectionate.

She smiled back. Everything had changed, suddenly. She looked at him and knew without question that she could love him if she was ever given the chance.

He reached out and tapped her cheek. "Let's go. And from now on, stay out of lonely ranch houses with amorous bachelors. Got that?"

"You were the one who dragged me here," she exclaimed.

"That's right, blame it all on me," he agreed after he'd put the coffee things away and then escorted her out the door. "It's always the man who leads the sweet, innocent girl into a life of sin."

She frowned. "Isn't it the woman who's supposed to lead the innocent man into it?"

He raised both eyebrows as he locked the door. "There aren't any innocent men."

"A likely story. What about priests and monks?"

He sighed. "Well, other than them," he conceded.

"I like your house," she said.

He opened the car door and put her inside. "I like it, too." He got in and started the engine, pausing to glance her way. "We may be heading for a fall, but I'm game if you are."

"Game?" she asked blankly.

He slid a lean hand under her nape and brought her face under his, very gently. He bent to kiss her, with tenderness and respect. "In the old days," he whispered, "they called it courting."

She felt a wave of heat rush over her. Wide-eyed, she stared helplessly up at him.

He nodded, his face solemn. "That's right, I said I didn't believe in marriage. But there's always the one woman who can make a man change his mind." His eyes dropped to her mouth. "I want Jeff. If I'm married I have a good chance of getting him. But you and I could give each other a lot, too. If you're willing, we'll start spending time together and see where it leads."

"I'm rich," she began hesitantly.

"Don't worry. I won't hold it against you," he whispered, smiling as he kissed her again. What he didn't mention was that he had his own suspicions about her future. He didn't think she was going to inherit anything at all, and that would put her right in his league. She'd be lost and alone, except for him, when the boom fell. She was sweet and biddable and he wanted her. Jeff needed a stable environment. It wouldn't hurt his chances with the new president of Mesa Blanco to be a settled family man, either, but that was only a minor consideration. Jeff came first. He'd worry about the complications later. Right now, he was going to get in over his head for once without looking too closely at his motives.

CHAPTER FIVE

IT WAS ALL Fay could do to work the next day. She was so lighthearted that she wondered how she managed to keep both feet on the floor.

Her dreams of being with Donavan honestly hadn't included marriage because he'd said that he didn't believe in it. In fact, he'd given her hell for chasing him. How ironic that she'd landed in his orbit at all.

Probably, she had to admit, he needed a wife so that he could gain custody of his nephew, and to help him get ahead in his job. He didn't want a rich wife.

But why, then, was he paying her any attention at all? She'd been honest with him. She'd told him that in a couple of weeks she stood to inherit a fortune. Hadn't he believed her?

Work piled up and she realized that she was paying more attention to her own thoughts than she was to her job, so she settled down to the job-related problems.

"How's everything going?" Abby asked when she came by to meet Calhoun for lunch.

"Great!"

Abby lifted a curious eyebrow. "Really?"

She glanced around her and leaned forward. "Donavan's taking me out."

"J.D.?"

"Don't look so horrified," Fay laughed. "He's serious. He was the perfect gentleman last night and he actually talked about a commitment."

"J.D.?"

Fay nodded. "J.D. Did you know he had a nephew and there's a custody suit in the offing?"

"Yes," Abby said, sobering at once. "The poor little boy's had a hard time. I don't like J.D. a lot, but I'll give him credit for caring about Jeff. He really does." She frowned. "Is that why he's talking seriously?"

"Probably," Fay said, then she smiled. "I don't have any illusions that he's suddenly discovered undying love for me. But he might learn to love me one day. Love takes time."

"Yes," Abby said, remembering. "But you're still rich."

"He said it wouldn't matter."

Abby didn't say another word, until she was alone with Calhoun. "I'm afraid Fay's heading for a bad fall," she told him when they were sharing a quick lunch. "J.D. doesn't seem to mind about her inheritance, but you know how he is about rich women."

"I think he's got some suspicions that her uncle Henry isn't telling her everything. I have some of my own," he added. "I wonder if Fay has anything left to inherit."

"I had the same feeling. Poor Fay. J.D. doesn't love her, I know he doesn't. He's too much of a womanizer to feel anything deep for a woman."

Calhoun lifted an eyebrow and pursed his lips. "He may be a reforming womanizer." He covered her hand with his and clasped it affectionately. "We all meet our Waterloo eventually. God, I'm glad I met mine with you!"

"Oh, so am I, my darling," she said softly. She leaned forward and kissed him tenderly, despite the amused looks from other diners. "You and the boys are my whole life."

"We've had a good beginning," he agreed. "And the best is still yet to come. We're very lucky."

"Very. I hope Fay fares as well," she added before she concentrated on her food instead of her sexy husband.

FAY DIDN'T SEE Donavan again for a few days. He'd phoned just to say that he was going out of town on business and that he'd call her when he got back. He hadn't sounded anything like an impatient lover, although he had sounded impatient, as if he hadn't wanted to call her in the first place. She'd been morose ever since, wondering if he'd had second thoughts. Her joy deflated almost at once.

From the day Donavan left, her life went downhill. Two days later she had to go to see Barry Holman about her inheritance. A nervous Uncle Henry was in the office when she got there, and Mr. Holman didn't look very happy.

"Sit down, Fay," Barry said quietly, standing until she was seated.

"It's bad news, isn't it?" she asked, looking from one of them to the other with quick, uneasy eyes.

"I'm afraid so," Barry began, and went on to tell her the bad news. She was penniless.

"I'm sorry, honey," Uncle Henry said heavily. "I did my best, honest to God I did. I pushed you at Sean because I hoped the two of you might hit it off. Sean's rich." His shoulders moved helplessly. "I thought if you married him, you wouldn't have to give up so much."

"Why didn't you tell me?" she asked miserably.

"I didn't know how," he replied. "Your father was a speculator, but for once, he picked the wrong thing to speculate on. I didn't know until a few weeks ago myself, when I tried to liquidate the stock. It fell almost overnight. There's nothing left. Just nothing." He spread his hands. "Fay, you can always come back and live with me…"

"I have a job," she said thinly, remembering almost at once that it was only a temporary job and would soon end. She felt like crying.

"You still have the Mercedes," Barry said surprisingly. "Your father had the foresight to take out insurance that would pay it off if he died. That's yours, and it has a high resale value. I could handle that for you, if you like. Then you'd have a little ready capital and enough over to buy a smaller car."

"I'd appreciate that," she said dully. "I'll get the papers together and bring them by in the morning, if that's all right."

"That will be fine. There are just a few more details, and I'll need your signature in several places…"

Fay hardly heard anything else that was said. She felt numb. In shock. Just a week ago, she'd been in Donavan's arms with a whole future to look forward to and an inheritance to fall back on. Now she had nothing at all. Even Donavan had seemed to have second thoughts, because he'd certainly dropped her flat.

What if he'd only wanted her for the money in the first place? she thought with hysteria. Or to help him provide a settled home so that he could get custody of his nephew?

The more she worried it in her mind, the worse it

got. Donavan hadn't wanted her when she was rich, he'd made sure she knew it. Then all at once, about the time he decided to fight for custody of his nephew, he became suddenly interested in her.

It all fit. The only thing that didn't was his abrupt lack of interest. Had he decided he didn't need her after all? Well, she wouldn't do him much good now, she thought wildly. She was just another member of the working class, and what was she going to do when her job folded?

She went through the motions of her job for the rest of the day, white-faced and terrified. Calhoun noticed, but when he asked what was wrong, she only smiled and pretended it was a headache.

That didn't fool him. He knew too much about women. He picked up the phone and called Barry Holman.

"I know it's all confidential and you can't tell me anything," Calhoun said. "But you can pause in significant places. I only want to help. Fay didn't get a damned thing did she?"

There was a long pause.

"That's what I thought," Calhoun said quietly. "Poor kid."

"She really needs that job," Barry replied. "Knowing it's only temporary is probably eating her up. She's never had to depend on herself before."

"No problem there," Calhoun returned, smiling. "Fay's got a job here as long as she can type. We'll find a niche for her. Damn Henry!"

"Not his fault," Barry said. "A bad investment gone sour, that's all. The old story, but a tragic one for Fay.

All she's got left is the Mercedes. And you didn't hear this from me," he added firmly.

"Of course not! I'll just sort of mention that she's working out too well to let go and we want to keep her on."

Barry chuckled. "She'll appreciate that."

"We appreciate her. For a debutante, she's a hell of a hard worker." His eyes narrowed. "See you," he said, and hung up. He had another call to make.

He dialed J. D. Langley's number.

"Hello?" came the abrupt reply.

"I thought you were out of town," Calhoun said curtly.

"I was. I just got in fifteen minutes ago. I was having a cup of coffee. What's wrong?" he asked. "Something about the cattle?"

"Something about Fay York," Calhoun said.

There was a deathly hush. "Has anything happened to her?" he asked, feeling as if the ground had been cut out from under him. "Is she all right?"

Calhoun felt relieved. That was genuine concern in the other man's voice. Of course, and he hated himself for thinking of it, it could be that J.D. was counting on Fay's money to help him get his nephew. If he was, he was going to do Fay a big favor.

"I'm going to tell you something I'm not supposed to know," he said. "You aren't supposed to know it, either, so don't let on."

"What?"

"Fay didn't get a penny. Her father lost everything. All she inherits is the Mercedes."

J.D. didn't say anything, and Calhoun felt sorry for

Fay. Until the sound of soft laughter came over the line and eased his mind.

"So she's busted," Donavan said warmly. "I had a feeling it would work out like that. I'm sorry for her, but I'm damned glad in a way. I wouldn't want people to think another Langley was taking the easy way out with a rich wife."

"You're really serious about her?" Calhoun asked, surprised.

"Why is that so hard to believe? You must have noticed that she's got a heart as big as all outdoors," he replied. Then he spoiled it all by adding, "She's just the kind of foster mother Jeff needs."

"You aren't going to marry her over a custody suit?"

"Whatever it is, is none of your business, Ballenger," J.D. said with icy politeness. "If Fay wants to marry me, that's her affair."

"And if she loves you, what then?"

"She isn't old enough to love anyone yet," Donavan said carelessly. "She's infatuated with me, and she needs a little security. I can give her enough to make her happy."

Calhoun called him a name he wouldn't have wanted Abby to hear. "You're lower than I gave you credit for," he added coldly.

"And it's still none of your damned business. I'll be in to check on the Mesa Blanco stock in the morning." He hung up, leaving Calhoun furious.

AFTER HANGING UP on Calhoun, Donavan sipped his coffee without really tasting it. He was fond of Fay, and physically she appealed to him as no other woman had.

She was innocent, and that alone excited him. He could make her happy.

But the thing was to get Jeff, to rescue the boy who was his sister's only child from the hell he was living in. It had taken all his powers of persuasion and a lot of tongue-biting to get his venomous brother-in-law to let Jeff come up here just for the spring holidays. Possession was nine-tenths of the law. He had Jeff and he was going to keep him. He'd already talked to the lawyer he shared with Mesa Blanco about filing for custody, so the wheels were turning.

"Are you sure you won't mind having me around, Uncle Don?" Jeff asked from his sprawled position in the armchair. With his crewcut and husky physique, he looked the very picture of a boy who was all boy.

"No, sport, I won't," Donavan said. "We get along pretty good most of the time."

Jeff smiled. "Sure we do. Can we go riding tomorrow?"

"Maybe. First we have to go to the feedlot and check up on the feeder cattle. There's someone I want you to meet."

"Fay, right?" he asked, smiling again at his uncle's surprise. "She was all you talked about on the plane," he added.

Donavan lit a cigar and didn't look at the boy. He hadn't realized that he'd been so transparent. He'd missed Fay, but he didn't like admitting it even to himself. He'd been footloose all his life. Even if he married Fay for Jeff's sake, he didn't intend giving up his freedom.

"Aren't you going to call her?" Jeff asked.

"No," Donavan said, frowning. He did want to, but he wasn't going to give in to his impulse. Better to start the way he meant to go on, and acting like a boy with a crush wasn't going to keep him in control of his life.

"It's nice here," Jeff said after a minute. "I hate military school. You can't do anything without permission."

"Don't expect to be able to run wild here," his uncle cautioned.

"No, I don't. But you like me, at least. My stepfather hates my guts," he added coldly. "Especially now that he's married *her* and they're expecting their own child. He didn't even love my mother, did you know?"

Donavan's face hardened. "I knew," he said. He didn't elaborate on it, but he knew very well that his brother-in-law's blatant affairs had all but killed his sister. She'd loved the man, but his womanizing had depressed her to the point of madness. A simple case of pneumonia had taken her out of this world, out of her torment, leaving a heartbroken brother and son behind to mourn her. Donavan had hated Jeff's stepfather ever since. Better his sister had stayed in mourning for her first husband than pitch headlong into a second marriage that was doomed from the start.

"What did she see in him?" Jeff asked miserably. "He drinks like a fish and he's always off somewhere. I think he's running around on his new wife already."

It wouldn't surprise Donavan. After all, he thought viciously, he was running around with his current wife while he was still married to Donavan's sister.

"Let's forget he exists for a few days," he told Jeff. "How about a game of chess?"

"Super!"

WHILE DONAVAN AND JEFF were playing chess, Fay was trying to come to grips with her new situation.

She'd always secretly wondered how she would cope if she ever lost everything. Now was her big chance, she thought with black humor, to find out. If she could conquer her fear of having her livelihood depend on her own efforts, she could manage. Thank goodness Donavan had made her take a good look at herself and start learning independence. If she'd still been living with Uncle Henry now, she really would have been terrified.

She understood now why her uncle had been so eager to push her at his business associate, Sean. It had been out of a misplaced protective instinct. He'd hoped she'd marry Sean and be secure when she found out there was nothing left of her parents' estate.

Even though she was grateful for his concern, she wished he'd told her sooner. She put her face in her hands. Well, she could always write to Great-Aunt Tessie and beg for help if things got too bad. She and the old lady had always kept in touch. In fact, there was no one else who loved Tessie just because of her sweet self and not her money. Fay always remembered the elderly woman's birthday. She wondered if anyone else ever had. Certainly not her parents.

She wiped the tears away and wondered when Donavan was coming back. He might not want her now. She had to face the fact that without her wealth, despite what he'd said about not wanting a wealthy woman, he might walk away without looking back. Time would tell. For now, she had enough to keep her busy. She got up from her chair and went to find the paperwork on the Mercedes. At least it would bring a tidy sum, and give her a badly needed nest egg.

The next morning after she'd dropped the papers off at Barry Holman's office, she was working away when the office door opened and Donavan Langley came in with a dark-haired boy at his side.

So he was back. And that had to be Jeff. Her heart ran wild, but she pinned a polite smile to her face as he approached her desk.

"Good morning," she said politely.

"This is Jeff," he replied without answering her. "Jeff, this is Fay York."

"Nice to meet you," Jeff said. He was watching her with open curiosity. "You're pretty."

She flushed. "Thank you."

Jeff grinned. "My uncle likes you."

"That's enough," Donavan drawled. "Go out and look at the cattle. But don't get in the way, and stay out of the pens."

"Yes, sir!"

He was off at a dead run, barely missing one of the amused cowboys. "Keep an eye on him, will you, Ted?" Donavan called.

"Sure thing, Mr. Langley," the cowboy replied, and turned on his heel to follow Jeff.

"He's impulsive and high tempered," Donavan told her. "I have to watch him like a hawk so that he doesn't hurt himself." He searched her eyes with no particular expression on his lean face, but his silver eyes were glittery with contained excitement. She stirred him up. He'd missed her more than he wanted to admit. But she wasn't receptive today. That smile was as artificial as the ficus plant in the pot beside her desk.

"Did you have a nice trip?" she asked for something to break the silence.

He nodded. "Jeff and I got in last night."

And he hadn't called. Well, now she knew where she stood. The fixed smile didn't waver, even if she had gone a shade paler. "He's a nice looking young man."

"He favors his mother. How about lunch? You can go with us to the hamburger joint."

She wanted to, but it was better to break this off now even if it killed her. Things could only get worse, and her life was in utter turmoil.

"I can't today, but thanks anyway."

He started. "Why can't you?"

"I have to see Mr. Holman about selling the Mercedes," she said with stiff pride. "You'll find out sooner or later, so I might as well tell you. I don't have any money. My parents left me without a dime." She lifted her chin and stared at him fearlessly. "All I have is the Mercedes and it's going on the market so that I'll have a nest egg for emergencies."

He didn't like the way she said that. She made it sound as if his only interest in her was what she had. Didn't she know it was her wealth that had stood between them in the first place?

He scowled. "The money didn't matter."

"Didn't it?" she asked bravely.

His gray eyes narrowed. "So you did believe Bart after all. You think I'm as money-crazy as my father." His expression went hard with contained rage. He'd thought she knew him better than that. It hurt to realize that she was just like several other people in Jacobsville who tarred him with the same brush they'd used on his father. "All right, honey. If that's the kind of man you think I am, then take your damned Mercedes and go to hell with it," he said cuttingly. He turned and went after Jeff.

Fay couldn't believe she'd said such a thing to him. Not that it would make any difference, she kept assuring herself. He didn't want her in the first place, so all she'd done was save herself a little more heartache.

Donavan didn't come back through the office on his way out. He took Jeff with him the back route, stormy and unapproachable, smoking his cigar like a furnace all the way to the car.

"What's eating you?" Jeff asked curiously.

"Nothing. What do you want for lunch?"

"A cheeseburger. I thought you said Fay was coming with us? Didn't she want to?"

"She was busy," he said curtly. "Get in."

Jeff shrugged. He wondered if he was ever going to understand adults.

Calhoun paused by Fay's desk, noticing her worn expression and trembling hands.

"J.D.'s been by, I gather," he said dryly.

She lifted her miserable eyes to his. "You might say that. He had Jeff with him."

"And left you here?"

She sat up straighter. "I told him I didn't have any money. He left."

He whistled. "Not a wise move, Fay," Calhoun said gently. "Donavan's touchy about money. You knew that his father—?"

"Yes, I knew," she cut him off gently. "It's for the best," she said. "He didn't really care about me. If he wanted me at all it was because he had a better chance of keeping Jeff if I was around. I'm not stupid. I know he doesn't love me."

Calhoun wanted to deny that, to reassure her, but it was patently obvious that she was right, J. D. Langley wasn't the hearts-and-roses type, but he sure didn't act like a man in love.

"It's early days yet," he told her, wanting to say something positive. "Give him time. J.D.'s been a loner ever since I've known him. He's a lot like Justin. Maybe that's why they get along so well. I have to admit, he and I have never been particularly friendly, but that doesn't have anything to do with you."

"I guess I should apologize," she began.

"Oh, not yet," he said, smiling. "Let him sweat for a while. It will do him good to be on the receiving end for once."

"You mean, he's usually the one who does the jilting," she said, sighing as she remembered how experienced he was. "I guess he's done his share of breaking hearts."

"Be careful of yours," Calhoun said seriously. "There's something I want to mention to you. I told you that this job was temporary, just until Nita came back." He hesitated, noticing her depressed look as she nodded. "Well, I want to offer it to you permanently. I need a secretary of my own, and Nita works a lot better with Justin than she does with me. What do you say? We've been thinking of adding a secretary, but until you came along, we weren't sure exactly what we wanted. You suit me and we seem to work pretty well together. Besides," he added on a chuckle, "Abby might divorce me if I let you go. She thinks a lot of you."

"I think a lot of her." Fay brightened magically. "You really mean it?"

"I mean it. If you want the job permanently, it's yours."

"And Nita won't mind working just for Justin?"

"I've already asked her. She almost kissed my feet. It seems that she's only been putting on a brave face about handling the workload for both of us. Getting some relief has given her a new lease on life. She said she was actually thinking of staying home with the baby just to get away from the work."

"Then I'd love the job, thank you," she said brightly. "You have no idea how much I enjoy working here. Besides," she confessed, not realizing that he already knew her situation, "I'm afraid I'm going to have to work for the rest of my life. My parents didn't leave me anything. I'm flat broke."

"In that case, we'll be helping each other out," he said. "So welcome aboard."

"Thanks, Calhoun," she said, and meant it. "Thanks very much."

"My pleasure."

She turned her attention back to her computer with an improved outlook. At least she had a job, even if she didn't have J. D. Langley. But that might still be for the best. She'd only have been letting herself in for a lot of heartache. It was better not to even begin something that was blighted from the start. And it wasn't as if he loved her. She had to keep remembering that.

THE MAN DRIVING back toward home was trying to keep it in mind himself, while he fumed inwardly at Fay's attitude. He wasn't mercenary, but she thought he was. Like father, like son. He groaned inwardly. Would he never be free of the stigma?

Jeff hadn't said a word, and Donavan couldn't bring himself to tell the boy why Fay wouldn't come to lunch with them. She thought he'd only been keeping company with her because of her money, when he'd already told her he didn't like rich women.

But in all honesty, he had to admit that he'd given her no real reason to think she was of value to him as a person. He'd talked much more about getting custody of Jeff than of wanting her for herself. He'd made love to her lightly, but even that could have convinced her that it was desire mingled with the need for a woman to aid his case to keep Jeff.

He frowned. He hadn't given her any chance at all. To compound it, he'd told her that he'd been back in town for almost a whole day and hadn't even bothered to phone her. He groaned inwardly. He'd made so many mistakes.

Worst of all, he hadn't considered her feelings. She'd just been told that she'd lost everything. All she had to her name was a Mercedes-Benz that she was going to have to sell. It was more than an inheritance she'd lost—it was her whole way of life. She had to be terrified at being responsible for herself. She was only twenty-one, and so alone, because she and her uncle weren't close. She'd needed comfort and help, and he'd told her to go to hell.

"You look terrible, Uncle Don," Jeff broke the tense silence. "Are you sure you're okay?"

"Not yet. But I will be," he said, and abruptly turned around in his own front yard and headed right back toward town. It was quitting time, so Fay would most likely be at home. He didn't know what he was going to say to her. He'd think of something.

CHAPTER SIX

FAY HAD THOUGHT about staying late at the office, just to keep her mind busy, but in the end she decided she would be equally well-off at home. She said good-night to her coworkers and drove the short distance back to her apartment house.

The Mercedes felt uncomfortable now that she was a working girl. It was just as well that Mr. Holman was going to help her sell it. There would be no more luxury cars, no more shopping sprees that didn't include looking at price tags. There would be no more designer clothes. No bottomless bank account to fall back on. She could have cried. She would make it. She knew she would. But getting used to her circumstances was going to take a little time.

She got out of the car and was walking onto the front porch when she heard the roar of a vehicle and saw Donavan driving up next to the Mercedes with Jeff beside him.

Not another fight, she prayed silently, her wan face resigned and miserable even if her eyes did light up helplessly at the very sight of him when he got out and approached her.

He stopped just in front of her, his own expression somber. She looked bad. The camouflage she'd hidden her fears behind had vanished now, because she was tired and her guard was down. He reached out and touched her mouth, dry and devoid of lipstick.

"I'm sorry," he said without preamble. "I didn't think about how you must feel until I was back home."

The unexpected compassion, on top of the emotional turmoil she'd been through, cracked inside her. Tears poured down her cheeks.

"I'm sorry, too," she managed brokenly. "Oh, Donavan, I didn't mean it…!"

His breath caught at her vulnerability, and he was glad he'd made the decision to come back. Without a word, he bent and lifted her in his hard arms and started back toward his car, kissing the tears away as he went, whispering comforting things that she didn't quite hear.

Jeff saw them coming and, with a grin, moved into the backseat. Donavan winked at him before he slid Fay into the passenger seat and trussed her up in her seat belt.

"Stay put," he told her. "We're kidnapping you."

"What will my landlord think?" she asked with a watery smile.

"That you're being kidnapped, of course. We'll take her home and hold her prisoner until she cooks supper for us," he told Jeff, who was smiling from ear to ear. "If she's a good cook, I'll marry her right away."

Fay was trying not to choke. "But you told me to go to…!" she began.

"Not in front of the boy," he said with a mock glower. "He isn't supposed to know words like that."

"What century is *he* living in?" Jeff asked, rolling his eyes. "Gimme a break, man!"

"Too much TV," Donavan said. "We'll have to take a plug out of the set."

Fay's head was whirling. "But, Donavan, I can't cook. That is, I can," she faltered, wiping at her eyes. "But only omelets and bacon."

"No problem," he said as he started the car. "I like breakfast. Don't you, Jeff?"

"Sure!"

She gave up. In the scant minutes it took them to get to the ranch, she'd dried her tears and managed to gather her composure. She still didn't understand what had prompted Donavan to come after her, despite the way she'd insulted him, but she wasn't going to question a kindly fate.

Jeff was in a flaming rush to get to the living room for one of his favorite TV programs, leaving Donavan to escort a worn Fay into the kitchen.

"Mind Bee," he murmured, stepping around the kitten as she rushed toward them.

"I'll take care of her, Uncle Don," Jeff interrupted. He scooped up the kitten, popped back into the living room and closed the door behind him. The blare of the television could be heard even through it.

"The noise takes a little getting used to," Donavan said slowly. He studied Fay, whose hair was straggly as it came loose from its neat chignon. "Why do you wear it like that, anyway?" he asked gently, moving far too close to her. His lean hands deftly separated hairpins from upswept strands, loosening the dark cloud of her hair around her shoulders. "That's better," he whispered. "Now you look like my Fay again."

A tiny sob broke from her lips at the tenderness. Somehow she'd never associated it with him until now.

"I said such terrible things to you," she whispered back, her eyes eloquent.

"I said such terrible things back," he murmured, smiling. "We had a lovers' quarrel. Nothing to lose sleep over. Everything's all right now."

"We aren't lovers," she protested.

His eyes searched hers. "We're going to be, though."

She flushed. "I'm not like that."

He bent and drew his lips with aching tenderness over her own, gently parting them. His hands went to her hips and brought them firmly into the cradle of his, so that she could feel every vibrant muscle and tendon of him close, close against her softness.

"Come on, baby," he breathed into her open mouth. "Don't make me fight for it…"

She lost the will to protest the second she felt his tongue going past her lips, into the darkness beyond. A white-hot flash of sensation rippled her body in his arms, stiffened her. She caught her breath and then released it in a long, shuddering sigh that he could feel and taste.

"Yes," he said huskily. "That's it. That's it!"

He lifted her by the waist, turning her deftly to the wall. He pinned her there with his body, his long legs pushing between her thighs as he penetrated her mouth with quick, hard thrusts that simulated a kind of joining she'd never experienced.

When he finally lifted his head, she couldn't see anything except his swollen mouth. Her body was throbbing, like the tiny breaths that pulsed out of her, like her heart in her throat.

He leaned closer and bit her lower lip, not hard enough to hurt, but quite hard enough to make her aware of the violence of his passion.

She couldn't move. He had her pelvis completely

under his, her legs supported by his, her breasts pinned beneath the heavy pressure of his chest. Behind her, the wall was cold and hard, not warm and alive like the man who had her helpless.

"I think you'd better marry me, Fay," he said huskily. "I don't know how much longer I can protect you."

"Protect me from what?" she asked, dazed by passion.

"Do you really need to ask?" he murmured against her bruised mouth.

"Marriage is a big step," she said weakly.

"Sure it is. But you and I are getting more explosive by the day. I want you like hell, honey, but not in the back seat of my car or some out-of-the-way motel when time permits. You're a virgin. That puts you right off-limits."

"I'm poor," she said. "No, don't look like that," she pleaded, touching his thick eyebrows where they clashed to smooth away the scowl. "I mean, I'd be a burden on you. I'll work, but I can't make much…"

"How do you think other couples manage?" he asked. "For God's sake, I don't care if you're poor! So am I, in a lot of ways. You're much more desirable to me without money than you were with it, and I think you know why."

"Yes. I shouldn't have said what I did. I was so afraid that you wouldn't want me anymore."

He lifted an eyebrow. "Does it feel like I don't want you?" he asked pleasantly.

He hadn't moved, but what he felt was rather blatant and she blushed.

He laughed softly as he let her slide down against him until her feet touched the floor. He loomed over her as he searched her flushed face with indulgent amusement.

"You're priceless," he murmured. "Will you faint on our wedding night, or hide in the bathroom? I'll wager you've never seen a naked man, much less an aroused one."

"I guess I'll get used to it," she replied gamely.

He chuckled. "I guess you'll have to. Yes or no?"

She took a deep breath. "Yes, then," she said, refusing to worry about his motives or even her own. She wanted him and he wanted her. She'd worry about the rest of the problems later.

He didn't speak for so long that she was frankly worried that he was regretting the proposal. Then he lifted her hands to his mouth and kissed them with breathless tenderness, and the look in his silver eyes made her feel humble. Whatever he felt right now, it wasn't reluctance. Her heart lifted and flew.

Jeff was called in minutes later and told the news. He literally jumped for joy.

"When?" he asked them.

Fay hesitated. Donavan didn't. "Next week," he said, his eyes daring Fay to challenge him.

"Then," Jeff said, as if he was reluctant to put it into words, "can I stay for the wedding?"

Donavan studied him in a silence that became more tense by the second. "As far as I'm concerned, you can stay until you're of legal age."

"That goes for me, too," Fay said without prompting.

Jeff looked embarrassed. He colored and averted his eyes. Like his uncle, very little showed in his face unless he wanted it to. But his uneasiness was a dead giveaway.

"I'd like that," Jeff said. "But wouldn't I be in the way?"

"No," Donavan said tersely. "We won't have time for

a honeymoon right away, and you'll need to be registered in school here, even though it's almost the end of the school year."

Jeff's eyes widened. "You mean I won't have to go back to military school?"

"Not unless you want to," Donavan told him. "I've already started custody proceedings for you."

"Gosh, Uncle Don," Jeff said enthusiastically. "I don't even know what to say!"

"Say okay and go back and watch television with Bee," Donavan mused, glancing warmly at Fay. "I haven't finished kissing Fay yet."

"Oh. That mushy stuff," Jeff said with a sly grin.

"That mushy stuff," Donavan agreed, smiling at Fay's wild-rose blush. "You'll understand in a few years."

"Don't bet on it," the boy murmured. He reached down to retrieve Bee, who was tangling his shoelaces. "I'd like to stay here," he said without looking at them. "I'd like it a lot. But my stepdad won't ever agree."

"Let me worry about that," Donavan told him. "We'll call you when supper's ready."

"Okay. I won't hold my breath or anything, though," he added dryly, and closed the door behind him.

Fay stared up at Donavan and felt as if every dream she'd ever had was about to come true. She had nothing. But if she had Donavan, she had the world.

She said so. He looked briefly uncomfortable. She didn't know that he was unsure of his own reasons for wanting to marry her. He wanted to keep Jeff. He felt a furious physical longing to make love to Fay. But beyond that, he was afraid to speculate. He'd done without love all his life. He wasn't sure he knew what it was.

"I haven't embarrassed you?" she asked worriedly.

He moved forward and drew her slowly into his arms. "No," he said. His eyes searched hers. "It's going to be hard for you getting used to my lifestyle. I like my own way. I budget like a madman. There's no provision for pretty dresses and expensive cosmetics and a trip to the hairdresser once a week..."

Daringly, she put her fingers against his hard mouth. "I won't miss those things." She traced his lean cheek and his firm mouth and chin, loving the way he tolerated her exploration. "Oh, glory," she said on an unsteady breath. "I'll get to sleep with you every night."

He stiffened at the way she said it, as if being in his arms would lift her right up to heaven. He brought her closer and bent to kiss her with slow, expert thoroughness.

She reached up to hold him back, giving in with exquisite delight pulsing through her body, loving him as she'd never dreamed she could love someone.

He lifted his head feverish seconds later and clasped her shoulders firmly while he looked down at her. "I hope I'm going to be man enough to satisfy you in bed," he said on a husky laugh. "You are one wild little creature, Fay."

She flushed. "I hope that's a compliment."

"It's a compliment, all right," he replied, fighting for enough breath to talk. She confounded him. For an innocent, which he was almost certain she was, there was no reticence in her when he started kissing her. She made his knees weak. In bed, she was going to be the end of his rainbow.

She studied him with soft, worried green eyes. "I haven't ever slept with anyone," she began nervously.

He smiled gently. "I know that. But you've got promise, honey. A lot of it." He leaned close and brushed his lips over her nose. "I'm glad it's going to be with me, Fay," he whispered huskily. "Your first time, I mean."

Her heart ran wild. "So am I."

His lips probed gently at her mouth, teasing it open. "Do you know what to expect?" he breathed.

"I...think so."

His eyes opened at point-blank range, silver fires that burned while she felt his coffee-scented breath on her lips. "I've never been gentle," he whispered. "But I will be. With you."

"Donavan," she breathed, her eyes closing as she pulled him down to her.

He didn't know if he was going to survive the soft heat of her body, the clinging temptation of her mouth. He groaned under his breath as the kiss went on and on, burning into his very soul.

"I can't bear it," he groaned at her lips. "Fay...!"

The tormented sound gave her the willpower to pull gently out of his arms and move away. Her knees felt weak, but he looked as if he was having a hard time standing up straight.

"It's like being thirsty, isn't it?" she asked breathlessly. "You can't quite get enough to drink."

"Yes." He turned away from her and lit a cigar with hands that were just faintly unsteady.

She stared at his long back lovingly, at the body that would one day worship hers. He was going to be her man, her very own. Losing her fortune seemed such a tiny sacrifice to make to have Donavan for the rest of her life.

She smiled to herself. "If you'll show me where the eggs are, I'll make you and Jeff an omelet," she offered. "I'm sorry I can't cook anything else just yet, but I'll learn."

"I know that. Don't worry about it," he added with a fairly calm smile. "I can cook."

"You can teach me," she mused.

"To cook," he agreed. His eyes fell to the visible tautness of her breasts. "And other things."

She smiled with barely contained excitement as she followed him to the refrigerator.

SUPPER WAS A gleeful affair, with Jeff laughing and joking with his uncle and Fay as if he'd never had a solemn, sad day in his life. He rode back with them when Donavan eventually drove Fay home and sat in the car while they walked to the door of Fay's apartment house.

"I can't believe the change in Jeff," he remarked as they paused on the darkened porch. "He's not the same boy who came out here with dead eyes and even deader dreams."

"Does his stepfather care about him?"

"Not so anyone would notice," he replied. "He was always jealous of the way my sister got along with Jeff, always resentful of him. He made Jeff's life hell from the very beginning. Since my sister died, it's been much worse."

"Will he fight you over custody, do you think?"

"Oh, I'm convinced of it," Donavan said lightly. "That's all right. I don't mind a good fight."

"That's what I've heard," she murmured dryly.

He chuckled. "I grew up swinging. Had to. My father made sure of that." His eyes darkened and the smile faded. "You'll have that to live down, too, if you marry me. Some people won't know that you've lost your inheritance. There will be talk."

"I don't mind," she murmured. "While they're talking about me, they'll be leaving someone else alone."

"You don't get depressed much, do you?" he asked quizzically.

"I used to, before you came along." She toyed with a button of his shirt, loving the feel of him close to her, the warm strength of his hands on her shoulders. She looked up, her eyes shadowed in the darkness of the porch. "I'm much too happy now to be depressed."

He frowned. "Fay... I've been alone a long time. Jeff's taking some getting used to. A wife...well, I may make things difficult for you at first."

"Just as long as you don't have women running through the house in towels or anything," she said with an impish smile.

He chuckled. "No chance of that. I've kept to myself in recent years." He bent and brushed her mouth lightly with his, refusing to let the kiss ignite this time. "Good night, little one. Jeff and I will pick you up for lunch tomorrow."

"Cheeseburgers, right?"

"Right," he murmured. "I wish we were already married, Fay, and that we were completely alone. I'd carry you up those steps and take an hour stripping the clothes off you."

"Hush!" She giggled. "I don't wear *that* many!"

"You don't understand, do you?" he whispered. "You will."

"That first time we went out, you wouldn't even kiss me," she recalled suddenly.

"I didn't dare. I wanted it too much." He smoothed

back her hair. "I figured you'd be addictive, Fay. I was right, wasn't I?"

"I'm glad I am," she said fervently.

"So am I. Good night, sweet."

He turned and left her, and he didn't look back, not even when he'd started the car and drove away. Jeff waved, and she waved back. But Donavan hadn't even glanced in the rearview mirror.

It made her nervous, realizing that he didn't seem to look back. Was it an omen? Was she doing the right thing to marry a man whose only feeling for her was desire?

She worried it all night, but by morning, the only thing she was certain of was that she couldn't live without Donavan. She went into the office resolute, determined to make the best of the situation.

"Is it true?" Abby asked the minute she came in the door later that morning, looking and sounding breathless.

Fay didn't have to ask any questions. She laughed. "If you mean, am I going to marry J. D. Langley, yes."

"Fay, you're crazy," Abby said gently. She sat down beside the younger woman. "Listen, he wants custody of Jeff, that's all. I'll absolve him of wanting your money, but if you think he's marrying you for love…"

Fay shook her head. "No, I'm not that crazy," she assured her friend. "But I care too much to refuse," she added quietly. "He may learn to love me one day. I have to hope that he will."

"It's not fair," Abby argued worriedly.

"It's fair to Jeff," Fay reminded her. "He stands to lose so much if he has to go back to live with his stepfather. He's a great boy, Abby. A boy with promise."

"Yes, I know. I've met him." She sat down on the edge of Fay's desk with a long sigh. "I hope you know what you're doing. I can't see J.D. passionately in love. Calhoun said he was actually cussing you when he left here yesterday."

"He was," she replied dryly. "And I was giving as good as I got. But we made up later."

Abby raised an eyebrow at the blush. "So I see."

"I can't say no, regardless of his reasons for wanting to marry me," Fay said urgently. "Abby, I love him."

The older woman didn't have an argument left. She looked at Fay and saw herself several years before, desperately in love with Calhoun and living on dreams. She knew that she'd have done anything Calhoun had asked, right down to living with him.

She smiled indulgently. "I know how that feels," she said finally. "But I hope you're doing the right thing."

"Oh, so do I!" Fay said with heartfelt emotion.

When Donavan came to pick her up for lunch, the office was empty. Calhoun and Abby had their midday meal together most of the time, and the office girls took an early lunch so that they could be back during the regular lunch hour.

"Where's Jeff?" she asked, surprised that the boy wasn't with him.

"Gone to the movies," Donavan told her, smiling. "He thinks engaged people need some time alone. That being the case," he murmured, tugging her up by one hand, "suppose we buy the ingredients for a picnic lunch and find a secluded spot down by the river where we can make love to each other after we eat?"

She blushed, smiling at him with her whole heart. "Okay."

He chuckled as he pulled her along with him, standing aside to let the first of the office crew back in the building before he escorted her out to his car.

"We're raising eyebrows," he murmured. "Do they know we're engaged?"

"Everybody seems to," she replied.

"Small town gossip. Well, it doesn't matter, does it?"

She shook her head. "Not at all."

They stopped by a grocery store in a nearby shopping center and bought lunch at the take-out deli, adding soft drinks and ice for a small cooler. It wasn't a fancy or expensive lunch, but Fay felt as if it were sheer elegance.

"You look like one of those posed pictures of a debutante at a garden party," he remarked, his eyes on the way her gauzy white-and-green patterned dress outlined her body as she lay across from him on a spot of grass.

"I feel that way, too," she mused, tossing her long hair as she arched her back and sighed. Her eyes closed. "It's so peaceful here."

"If that's a complaint..."

The sound of movement brought her eyes open just in time to find Donavan levering his jean-clad body over hers. He was smiling, but there was a kind of heat in the smile that made her body begin to throb.

His elbows caught his weight as he eased down on top of her, his long legs cradling hers in a silence tense with promise. His eyes dropped to her mouth.

"This is as good a time as any for you to start getting used to me," he whispered. His hips shifted slowly, first to one side, then to the other. The faint movement aroused him and he tensed as the familiar heat shot through him like fire.

Fay watched his face contort slightly even as she felt

the changing contours of his body. Her lips parted on a held breath.

"A hundred years or so ago, when I was young and hot-blooded, that was a frequent and worrying occurrence. These days," he mused, watching her flushed face, "it's more of a delightful surprise. I like the way my body reacts to you."

"It doesn't…react to other women like this?" she asked, torn between embarrassment and curiosity.

He shook his head. "Only to you, apparently. I must be getting old. Either that, or a diet of virginal shock is rejuvenating me."

"It isn't shock. Well, not exactly," she faltered.

"No?" He bent and gently parted her lips. One long, powerful leg began to ease its way between hers, parting them and spreading her skirt on the cool ground. He felt her gasp and lifted his head. "We don't have a lot of time for courtship," he breathed. "We need to get used to each other physically before we marry. It will make it easier."

"I've never done this," she said nervously.

"Not even this far?" he asked, surprised.

She shook her head. "My parents were very strict. So were the relatives I used to stay with. They all said it was a sin to let a man do what he liked to a woman's body."

"Perhaps in some respects it is," he replied quietly. "But you and I are going to be married. One day, I'm going to put my seed deep in your body and you're going to have my baby. That won't be a sin of any kind."

The words, so carelessly spoken, had a very uncareless reaction on Fay. Her eyes went wide and watchful, and her face went scarlet.

He felt her sudden tension, saw it in her face. "That

excites you, does it?" he whispered huskily. His eyes fell
to her breasts, and he watched the nipples go hard with
quiet pride before he caught her shocked eyes again.
"You have pretty breasts."

The blush exploded and he chuckled. "I shouldn't
tease you, Fay. Not about something so profound. But
it's irresistible. As irresistible as...this."

And as he spoke, he bent suddenly and put his open
mouth over the hard tip of her breast.

CHAPTER SEVEN

FAY THOUGHT THAT if she died and flew into the sun she couldn't have felt any greater explosion of heat. The feel of Donavan's hot mouth on her body, even through the cloth, was incredible.

She arched against him and made a sound, half gasp, half groan, while her nails bit into his hard shoulders.

His teeth nipped her delicately, before his tongue began to swirl around the hard tip and make it unbearably sensitive to the moist heat of his mouth.

"Please," she whispered huskily. "Please, please, please…!"

He barely heard her through his own need. His fingers were quick and rough on her bodice, painful seconds passing before he managed to disarrange the hated fabric that kept her soft skin from his mouth. He found her with his lips and his hands simultaneously, and she clung to him, no thought of protest in her whirling mind as she fed on the feverish tasting of his mouth, the hot sensuality of his hands on her body.

"Don…avan!" she sobbed.

He lifted his head abruptly and looked at her.

"My God, you're beautiful, Fay," he said unsteadily. "The most beautiful creature unclothed that I've ever seen in my life!"

"I want you," she said weakly.

"I want you, too."

"Here."

He shook his head, fighting for sanity. He had to drag his eyes away from her body to meet her own. "No. Not now. We aren't married, little one."

"It...doesn't matter!" she wept, her body racked with need.

"Yes, it does." Gently he disengaged her hands and put her clothing to rights. When she was dressed again, he rolled onto his back and pulled her down into his arms. He held her while she cried, his voice soothing, his hands gentling her while the storm passed.

"I'm a lucky man, Fay," he said when she was quiet again. "A very lucky man."

"I think I'm the lucky one," she said breathlessly, clinging.

He bent and kissed her, his silver eyes looking straight into hers while his lean hands framed her flushed face gently. "We're taking a big step together," he said then, and looked solemn. "I hope for both our sakes, and Jeff's, that it's the right one."

"It will be," she assured him. Somehow, she knew it. But it didn't escape her notice that he looked unconvinced.

THE NEXT WEEK went by in a pleasant haze. Fay spent every free moment with Donavan and Jeff, taking just time enough to go shopping with Abby for her wedding gown. She chose an oyster-hued suit, which was sensible, because it would go with everything she had left in her wardrobe. She splurged on a hat, too, and a veil to drape over it. She worried about the amount of money she'd spent, because it was no longer possible to buy without looking at price tags. But Donavan only smiled when she mentioned that, and told her that getting married certainly warranted a little splurging.

The ceremony was held at the local church where Donavan was a member, and half the population of Jacobsville turned out for the occasion. Most everyone knew by now that Fay had lost everything, and even Donavan's cousin Bart was civil to him.

Jeff stayed with the Ballengers while Donavan drove himself and his new bride all the way to San Antonio for their two-day honeymoon. They had supper on the Paseo del Rio, where lighted barges went past with mariachi bands and music filled the flower-scented air.

"There can't be any place on earth more beautiful than this," she commented when she finished the last bite of her apple pie à la mode and looked at her new husband with quiet possession.

He cocked an eyebrow, very handsome in the pale gray suit he'd worn to be married in. He hadn't changed. Neither had she. She was still wearing her off-white suit, because they hadn't wanted to take the time to change earlier.

"Aren't you disappointed that I couldn't offer you a week in Nice or St. Tropez?"

She smiled and shook her head. "I'm very happy. I hope I can make you that way, too."

His returning smile became slowly wicked. "Suppose I take you back to our room now? I want to see how many times I can make you blush before I show you what physical love is."

Her heart beat faster. "All right," she whispered with barely contained excitement, and was unable to meet his eyes as he paid the bill and led her out into the sweetly scented night.

"Are you afraid of it, Fay?" he asked in the elevator, where they were briefly alone.

"A little, I think," she confessed with a nervous laugh. She looked up at him. "I don't want to disappoint you. I know you aren't innocent..."

He smiled gently. "I've never been married, though," he reminded her. "Or had a virgin to initiate." The smile faded. "I'll try not to hurt you too much."

"Oh, I'm not worried about...that," she faltered.

"Aren't you?" he mused knowingly as the elevator stopped.

They entered the room and he locked the door behind them, but when her cold hand went toward the light switch, he caught it.

"It will be easier for you in the dark," he whispered as he brought her gently close. "I don't want you to see me just yet."

"Do you have warts?" She laughed, trying to make a joke of it.

"No. You'll understand a lot better in the morning. For now," he said, swinging her up in his arms as he started toward the bed, "let's enjoy each other."

She'd never dreamed that she could lie quietly while a man took her clothes off, but she did. Donavan made what could have been an ordeal into a breathless anticipation, kissing her between buttons and catches, stroking her body gently to relax her while he slowly and deftly removed every stitch she had on. Then he pulled her against him, and she felt the faint abrasion of his suit while he began to kiss her.

"You...you're still dressed," she whispered.

He bit at her mouth with lazy delight. "I noticed. Open your mouth a little more. That's it." He kissed her very slowly and his hand smoothed down over her taut breasts, making her gasp, before it left a warm trail down her flat belly to the soft inside of her thighs. "Don't faint," he whispered as he touched her intimately for the first time and felt her tense. "Relax, Fay," he breathed at her lips as he trespassed beyond even her wildest and most erotic dreams. She cried out and he made a rough sound, deep in his throat. "My God, this isn't going to be the best night of your life. Listen, sweetheart, do you want to wait until you can see a doctor?" he asked, lifting his head. "I don't want to frighten you, but this barrier isn't going to be easily dispensed with. You know, don't you, that I'm going to have to break it before I can take you?"

"Yes." She swallowed. "Will it hurt you, too, if you do?"

"More than likely." He rolled onto his back and pulled her close, his body pulsating with its denied need while he fought his inclination to say to hell with it and go ahead. He needed her, but he didn't want to hurt her, to make intimacy something that would frighten and scar her.

"I didn't know," she said hesitantly. "I've never had any female problems, and I didn't think I needed a pre-nuptial checkup..."

He smoothed her long hair gently. "I'm not fussing, am I?" he murmured.

"I'll bet you feel like it," she said miserably. She laughed and then began to cry. "I've ruined everything!"

"Don't be absurd." His arms tightened and he rolled over against her, his mouth warm and soft and slow as his hand moved down her body again. Instead of probing, this time it touched, lightly, sensually. She gasped and instinctively caught his hand, but it was already too late. The pleasure caught her by surprise and for minutes that seemed never to end, she was oblivious to everything except her husband.

A long time later, he got up, leaving her wide-eyed and more than a little shaken on the bed. He turned the lights on and looked at his handiwork, from the drowsy, sated green eyes to the pink luxury of her sprawled body. She was too fulfilled to even protest the intimacy now, and his expression was just faintly smug.

"No need to ask if you liked it," he murmured unforgivably and began to take off his clothes.

She watched him with visible pleasure. He had a stunning body, very powerful and darkly tanned, except for a pale band where she imagined his swimming trunks normally rested. He was lightly feathered all over with dark, curling hair, except for his chest and flat stomach, where it was thickest. He turned toward her and she caught her breath, unable to take her eyes off him. Even like this, he was any woman's dream. Especially like this.

He knelt over her, his eyes glittering with unsatisfied desire. "Now it's my turn," he whispered, easing down beside her. "I want what I gave you."

"Anything," she choked. "Teach me…!"

His mouth covered hers, and lessons followed that banished her shyness, her fear, her inhibitions. When he cried out a second time and was still, she lay against him with drowsy pleasure and closed her eyes in satisfied sleep.

They went back home the next morning. Donavan

murmured dryly that he wasn't spending another night playing at sex when they could have the real thing after she saw the doctor. She did, first thing Monday morning, although the minor surgery was a little embarrassing. The doctor was pleased at Donavan's care, because, he added, it would have been an unpleasant experience for both of them if her new husband had been impatient. He sent her home with a smile and she dreamed for the three days it took for the discomfort to pass.

It was going to be the most exciting night of Donavan's life, Fay promised herself as she got everything ready. She'd already asked Abby to keep Jeff for that one evening, without telling her why, and Jeff had agreed with a murmured dry remark about newlyweds needing some privacy. Nobody knew that the marriage hadn't been consummated. But tonight it was going to be.

Fay had a bottle of champagne chilling. She'd cooked a special meal and made a crepe dessert, things she'd had Abby show her how to do. Everything looked delicious. Even Fay, who was wearing one of the only sexy dresses she possessed, a little strappy black satin number that showed off her full breasts and her long, elegant legs in the nicest possible way. She'd left her hair loose around her shoulders, the way Donavan liked it, and sprayed herself with perfume. He'd been exquisitely patient and caring for the past few nights, contenting himself with a few gentle kisses and the feel of her in his arms and nothing more. Tonight, she was going to make him glad he'd been so considerate.

She heard his car pull up in the driveway, very impatiently, and heard the vicious slam of his door. Something must have upset him at work, she thought as she quickly lit the candles on the table. Well, she had the cure for that.

She turned as he threw open the front door and came in. That was when she realized that what had upset him wasn't the job. He was staring at her with undisguised fury, his whole look accusing and violent.

"You didn't tell me you had a great-aunt who could buy and sell Miami Beach."

She blinked and had to think hard. "You mean Great-Aunt Tessie," she faltered. "Well, yes, but..."

His face hardened. His lean hand almost crushed the hat he'd just swept from his damp hair. "Your uncle Henry had a call a few minutes ago. He wanted me to break the news to you." He took a steadying breath. "Your great-aunt died last night. You inherit everything she owned, and that includes millions of dollars."

He was white in the face. Now she knew why. She sat down heavily. "Tessie is dead? But I had a letter from her just last week. She was fine..."

"You didn't tell me," he ground out. "Why?"

She lifted her eyes. "I never thought of it. Honestly," she said dully. Tears stung her eyelids. She'd been very fond of Tessie. "I loved her. Her money never made any difference to me. I expected she'd leave it to charity. She knew I didn't need it."

"Didn't, as in past tense." He nodded. "But now you're not a woman of property. Or are you?"

"I can always refuse it," she began.

"Don't bother. I assume you'll want to fly down there," he said shortly. "Your uncle will go with you. He said he'd make the travel arrangements and let you know later." He tugged at his tie, glaring at her.

"It's not my fault," she said huskily, tears pouring down her cheeks.

"Don't you think I know that?" he replied, his eyes cold and dark. "But it changes everything. I won't stay married to you. Not now."

"What about Jeff?" she gasped. "The custody suit?"

"I don't know…"

He was uncharacteristically hesitant. She went closer to him. "We don't have to tell anyone," she said. "I'll swear Uncle Henry to secrecy. We can stay married long enough for you to get Jeff away from his stepfather. Then we can get a…a divorce."

"Divorce?" he asked with a curt laugh. "An annulment." She flushed. "Had you forgotten, baby?" he asked mockingly. "We played at sex, but we never had it. Now it's just as well that we didn't. No harm done. You can find yourself some society boy in your own circle and get married again."

"And you?"

He shrugged indifferently and turned away before she could see his face. "I'll have Jeff."

"You don't want me?"

"What I want or don't want doesn't enter into it anymore," he said coolly, careful not to let her see his face. "The last thing I can afford is to have Jacobsville start gossiping about another Langley marrying for money, especially when I've got Jeff's future to think about."

"Oh, I see."

She did, painfully. Donavan would never want her with millions. He was a proud man. Much too proud to withstand the snide remarks and gossip. Even if he was less proud, there was Jeff. The boy shouldn't have to suffer for things he'd never done.

"I'll...just phone Uncle Henry," she said, but Donavan didn't answer her. He went out and closed the door.

THE NEXT MORNING, he drove her and her uncle to the airport and put them on a plane. The Ballengers had been very understanding about her absence from work for a couple of days, and Abby was glad to fill in for her under the circumstances. They all put down Fay's apathy to her fondness for her great-aunt, so it was just as well they didn't see her with Donavan. His fierce scowl might have changed their minds.

"Thanks for driving us here," Henry said uncomfortably. "Fay, I'll wait for you on the concourse."

"Yes." She watched him go with dull eyes before she lifted her own to Donavan.

"You haven't slept, have you?" he asked formally. And he had to ask, because he'd moved out of her bedroom the night before without a word.

She shook her head. "I was fond of Great-Aunt Tessie. We were good friends."

"I wasn't very sympathetic last night," he said stiffly. "I'm sorry..."

Her chin lifted proudly. "I haven't asked for anything from you, have I, Donavan?" she asked with expression. "And I won't. I'll stay with you until the custody hearing. Then, as you suggested, we can get an annulment."

"What will you do?" he asked.

She only laughed. She felt a million years old. "What do you care?" she asked without looking at him. She picked up the case he'd been carrying for her. "I haven't told the Ballengers about what I'll inherit, and I hope you won't," she said over her shoulder. "Until I talk to her lawyers, nothing is really certain."

"Don't make some stupid decision about that money out of misplaced loyalty to me," he said coldly, forcing himself to smile as if he didn't give a damn about her. Letting her give up millions to live a modest lifestyle with him, out of nothing but desire, would be criminal. "I only married you to get Jeff. Maybe I wanted you, too," he added when she looked at him. "But bodies come cheap, honey. I've never gone hungry."

Her face went, if possible, a shade paler. "It's nice to know that I'll be leaving you heart-whole and unencumbered. Goodbye, Donavan."

"Not goodbye," he said carelessly. "So long."

She shook her head. "No, I meant it. I'll come back. I'll stay, for Jeff. But in every other way, it's goodbye." Her eyes fell away from his and she tried not to feel the bitter wound of rejection that made her insides hurt. Every step was one less she'd have to repeat. She thought about that as she counted them. She didn't look back, either. She was learning, as he apparently already had, not to ever look back.

THE TRIP TO Miami was long and tiresome. She and Uncle Henry spent two days dealing with Great-Aunt Tessie's possessions, saving keepsakes and arranging for disposal of everything else. The very last stop was the lawyer's office, where Fay sat beside her uncle with dead eyes, hardly aware of her surroundings.

"I know the will seems cut-and-dried," the attorney said apologetically, glancing at Fay and grimacing, "but I'm afraid it was altered just recently without my knowledge. Tessie's maid found the new will in her bedside table, witnessed and properly signed."

Henry's eyebrows raised. "Did she leave the whole shooting match to her cats?" he asked with a chuckle.

"Oh, it's a little better than that," the attorney returned, reading over the document. "She left it to open a chain of hostels that would house the families of children with incurable cancer. It seems her housekeeper's sister had a child with leukemia and was having to drive a hundred miles a day back and forth because she couldn't afford to stay in a hotel… Mrs. Langley, are you all right?"

Fay was aghast. Delighted. Unbearably pleased. She looked at the attorney. "You mean, I don't have to take the money?"

Her wording shocked him, when very little ever had. "You don't want it!"

"Oh, no," she agreed. "I'm quite happy as I am."

"Well, I'm not," Henry muttered. "She could have left me a few sticks of furniture or something."

"But she did," the attorney recovered himself enough to add. "There's a provision for the contents of her apartment to be sold at public auction and the proceeds split between the two of you. I should say it will amount to very nearly a quarter of a million dollars. There is, too, her jewelry, which she wanted to go to Mrs. Langley— provided none of it is sold. Heirlooms, you know."

Fay smiled. "Some of the pieces date back three hundred years to European royal houses. I'd never sell it. It should go to descendants." She realized that she wouldn't have any now, and her face fell.

"At least we got something," Henry told her once they were outside. "I don't feel so bad that your inheritance didn't come through, now."

"There was nothing you could have done," Fay assured him. "I don't have any hard feelings."

He stared at her curiously. "You didn't want Tessie's money?"

She shook her head as they walked back to the rented car. "Not at all. Donavan would never have married me in the first place if I'd been rich."

"Yes. He does have a sore spot about his father." He glanced at her. "Well, this slight in Tessie's will should make your marriage a little more stable. I can imagine what J. D. Langley would have thought if you'd inherited all that money."

"Yes. Can't you, though?" Although she was thinking that if he'd loved her, money wouldn't have mattered at all. He'd tossed her out on her ear because he thought she was inheriting Tessie's money. He didn't want her rich. Well, that was all right with her. A relationship based on money—no matter if it was too much or too little—wasn't the right kind. She'd go on with her job at the feedlot and tell him that her inheritance was going to be tied up for a time. Beyond that, he didn't really need to know anything else. He'd thrown her out. She had to consider that maybe he'd done her a favor. She was falling more in love with him by the day. But aside from his need to keep Jeff and his desire for her, there was nothing on his side worth fighting for. As he'd already said, he could have all the women he needed. What would he want with Fay?

She did feel somewhat responsible for Jeff, though, since she'd agreed to the marriage in the first place partly to help rescue him from his stepfather. She liked the boy. For his sake, she wasn't going to walk out on J. D. Langley. She'd stick with them until the court case was settled one way or the other. Then she'd make whatever decisions had to be made.

It was ironic, though, that she'd gone to her marriage bed a virgin and left it still a virgin, even if she had learned quite a lot about pleasure in the process. She wondered if she could get into *The Guinness Book of Records*?

She packed her things and got ready to head back to Jacobsville. She didn't seem fated to be rich anymore, and she was rather glad about it. It was one thing to be born into money, quite another to learn to make it in the world without a big bankroll to fall back on.

If Donavan had loved her, she'd have had everything. She remembered so many good times with him, so much sweetness and pleasure. He'd genuinely seemed to like her at times, and his desire for her had been quite unmistakable. But desire wasn't love.

She couldn't settle for a man who looked at her as an infrequent dessert that he could live without. She wanted to be loved as well as wanted, to be cherished just for herself. Donavan had put conditions on their relationship that she couldn't meet. Be poor and I'll want you, he'd as good as said. If he'd loved her, whether she was rich or poor wouldn't have mattered. And all the gossip in the world wouldn't have made any difference.

Donavan had never loved, so he couldn't know that. But Fay did. She had to go back to him now and pretend that she didn't love him, that they were simply two people living together for the sake of a child. They weren't even legally married, because the marriage hadn't been consummated. She laughed bitterly. Jeff's stepfather could have had plenty of fun with that charge in court, but nobody knew except Donavan and herself, thank God.

She closed the case she'd been packing and went to phone the bellhop station. She had to go home and face Donavan, and the future.

CHAPTER EIGHT

WHEN FAY AND her uncle arrived at the airport, it was a shock to find Donavan waiting for them.

She shot a curious glance at her uncle, but he looked as surprised as she did.

"We could have gotten a cab," she began, her very calm voice belying the turmoil that the sight of Donavan engendered in her.

"It was no hardship to pick you up," he said easily. He was smoking a cigar, wearing working clothes that were clean if not new. His Stetson was cocked over one eye so that it wasn't possible to see the expression on his lean face. Just as well, too, he thought, because he wasn't ready for Fay to find out how glad he was to see her. The days had been endless since she left, and his conscience was hurting him. He'd been unkind to her at a time when she'd needed compassion and a shoulder to cry on.

"This is decent of you, Donavan," Henry said as he shouldered cases and followed Donavan out to the car. "I hate cabs."

Fay didn't comment. She clutched her purse and her overnight bag tightly, not returning Donavan's quiet, close scrutiny. She didn't care what he did or said anymore, she told herself. He'd hurt her for the very last time.

He dropped Henry off and not a word was spoken until he escorted Fay into the house.

"Jeff's in school," he told her when she noticed the sudden hush in the house. Only Bee, the kitten, was in evidence when Donavan came back from depositing her bags in her room. He picked her up with a faint smile and deposited her in a chair.

"You enrolled Jeff in school here, then?" she asked.

"Yes." He stopped just in front of her, his silver eyes probing as he looked down at her in the off-white suit she'd been married in. It brought back painful memories.

"How are you?" he asked.

"Still kicking," she replied dryly. "I'm not bleeding, Donavan, so you don't need to worry over me. I won't be a problem. Now, if you'll excuse me, I'll unpack and change. Then I'll see about starting something for supper."

"You don't have to…" he began irritably.

"I don't mind." She turned away, cutting him off before he could sway her resolve. "You've said it all already," she added without turning. "Let's just leave it alone. Have you heard from your lawyer about the custody hearing?"

"Yes," he said after a minute. "It's scheduled for next week."

She didn't know what else to say, so she nodded and left him there. It was some small consolation that he seemed as ill at ease as she felt. Their marriage was over before it had even had a chance to begin. She wished they could start again. But she doubted that Donavan believed in second chances any more than she did herself.

It was a silent meal. Jeff looked from one of them to the other with curiosity and faint uneasiness.

"I'm sorry about your great-aunt, Fay," Jeff said when they were eating the pudding she'd made for dessert. "I guess you're still sad."

"Yes," she agreed without argument. "Great-Aunt Tessie was special. She was a renegade in a day and age when it wasn't popular."

"Was she really rich?"

Fay hated the question, but she couldn't very well take out her wounds on the boy. "Yes, Jeff, she was. Very rich. But money isn't the most important thing in the world. It won't buy good health or happiness."

"Yeah, but it sure would buy a lot of Nintendo games!" he enthused.

She laughed despite herself. But Donavan was silent all through the meal, and afterward.

While Fay was washing dishes, he came into the room. His hands were dangling from the thumbs in his jeans pockets, his silver eyes watchful in a face like a carving in a stone cliff.

"I heard you call Abby Ballenger just before supper. Why? Did you tell her you were resigning?" he asked slowly.

"I'm not resigning. You do realize that paperwork and so forth takes time?" she added, playing for time. "I don't automatically inherit. Neither does Uncle Henry."

"You wouldn't have known that by the way he was talking on the way to his house," he reminded her with a calculating smile. "He's already got his money spent. Or he will have, by the time he actually gets it."

She didn't speak. He made her nervous. It was impossible to be in the same room with him and not re-

member how it had been between them that one night of
their honeymoon. Even without the ultimate intimacy,
she'd had a taste of Donavan that still could make her
head spin. She loved him with all her heart. It wouldn't
have mattered if he'd owned several multinational corporations or only a rope and an old horse. She loved him
so much that his circumstances would never have made
any difference. But he didn't feel the same about her,
and she didn't need him to put it into words. She had
money—or so he thought—and he didn't, so he didn't
want her. Nothing would alter his opinion one iota, and
she knew that, too.

"I should have stayed there with you, shouldn't I?"
he asked unexpectedly. "You look worn to a nub, Fay.
All that grief and your uncle to deal with at once. I suppose all the details were left up to you."

It was a question, she supposed. "Yes," she replied.
"Uncle Henry was able to make the funeral arrangements, though, with the attorney's help. I sorted out the
things in the apartment—" She stopped, blinking to stay
the tears. She washed the same plate again, slowly. "It
was so empty without her."

He hesitated. "So was this house, without you in it,"
he said gruffly.

She swallowed. She didn't dare turn around. "Thanks,
but you don't have to pretend. I haven't lived here long
enough to make any real difference in your life, or Jeff's.
You're a better cook than I am, and you've had people
to help you straighten up. I'm just a temporary conve-
nience. Nothing more."

He was conscious of a terrible wounding in her and
in himself. Had he made her feel so inadequate that she
thought he was better off without her than with her?

"The boy wants to see that new adventure movie that just came out. It's playing at the Longview. Want to come with us?"

"Oh, no, I don't think so," she forced herself to say. "I'm very tired. You two go ahead, and enjoy yourselves. I just want to go to bed and sleep the clock around."

He hesitated. "Fay, we can wait until you're rested."

"I don't like movies, honestly," she said quickly. "But thanks all the same."

He moved closer, his eyes narrow and concerned. "You've had a rough time lately, and I haven't been much help. Listen, Fay…"

"I don't need pity," she said, her voice steady despite the turmoil his nearness aroused. She dried her hands and sidestepped away from him. "I'm learning to stand on my own two feet. I won't pretend it's easy, but I think I'm finally getting the hang of it. After the custody hearing next week, I may see about moving back to my apartment house."

"You're assuming that I'll win it," he said formally. "There's a good chance that I won't. And if you tip out the front door hours later, Jeff's stepfather may appeal the court's decision even if I do win. Proof of an unstable home life would cost dearly."

Incredible that he sounded so determined to keep her with him, when she knew that wasn't what he wanted at all. Of course, it was for Jeff's sake. He loved the boy, if he loved no one else.

"All right," she said, sounding and feeling trapped. She sighed deeply. "I'll stay as long as you need me."

"If you stay that long, you'll never leave," he said curtly.

He turned and left the room, with Fay staring after

him in a daze, not quite sure that she'd really heard him right. Probably, she thought later, it was only wishful thinking on her part.

THEY FELL INTO a routine as the days passed. Fay went back to work, despite Donavan's comment that she was taking a job that someone else might really need, and Jeff went to school each day and began to look the very picture of a happy boy.

Fay worked harder than she ever had before, deliberately putting in late hours and paying more attention to detail than ever. Calhoun and Justin Ballenger were complimentary and appreciative of her efforts. Donavan was not.

"You do nothing but work!" he complained one evening when she wasn't working late—a rarity in recent days. "Don't Jeff and I count with you?"

"Uncle Don, Fay has to do her job right," Jeff pointed out. He grinned. "Besides, Mr. Ballenger says she's saved them plenty with all that hard work."

Donavan finished his dessert and reached for the carafe, to pour himself a second cup of coffee. "So I hear."

"You don't work any less hard yourself," Fay accused him. "And I don't complain."

His silver eyes met hers with cold impact. "Most brand-new wives would."

He was making an insinuation that, fortunately, went right over Jeff's head. But Fay knew what he was really saying, and she flushed.

"Yes, well, ours is hardly a normal situation."

"It could be," he said, startling her into looking up. There was no teasing, no mockery in his expression. He was deadly serious.

Fay flushed. "There's no time."

He lifted an eyebrow. "I beg your pardon?"

The flush grew worse. Jeff finished the last of his dessert and excused himself. "I want to get out of the line of fire," he said dryly, and closed the door into the living room. Seconds later, the TV blared out.

"Turn that damned thing down!" Donavan raged.

"You bet!" Jeff said irrepressibly and barely touched the knob.

Donavan, placated, was still glaring at Fay. "We're husband and wife," he reminded her. "There's no reason on earth that you can't share a bed with me."

"There's a very good one," she differed. She put down her napkin. "When Jeff's situation is resolved, I don't plan to stay here any longer than I have to. I won't risk getting pregnant."

His face drained of color. He looked…wounded. Cut to the bone. Fay felt sick at the careless comment when she saw its results. She hadn't even meant it. She loved him, but he only wanted her. She was fighting for her emotional survival, with the few weapons she had left.

"I didn't mean that," she said stiffly, averting her eyes. "Not like it sounded. But you must realize I'm right. A baby right now would…would complicate things."

"You don't think children can be prevented?" he asked with cutting sarcasm.

She lifted her eyes to his. "I won't be around that much longer," she said quietly. "I realize I must be stifling your sex life, and I'm sorry, but very soon I'll be gone and you can… Your life can get back to normal."

He grew colder in front of her eyes. He threw down his napkin and slowly got to his feet. "So that's what it's come down to in your mind. I'm hot for a woman and you're someone I can use in the meantime, until I'm free."

She went scarlet. "You can't pretend you feel anything other than desire for me," she said proudly. "After all, I'm rich."

His gaze averted to the table. He stared at it for a long moment. "Yes." He'd almost forgotten. Memories came back, of his father's greed, the censure after Rand Langley's second wife had committed suicide.

He left without another word. After a few minutes, Fay got up and cleared away the dishes. Well, what had she expected him to do, deny it? She laughed at her own folly and then had to bite back tears.

THE COURT HEARING was only two days away now, and both Jeff and Donavan were looking as if the pressure of it was giving them some problems.

Fay went by the video rental store and found three movies that would probably appeal to the two men in her life—both of whom were adventure fans—and presented them after supper.

"Wow!" Jeff enthused. "I've wanted to see these for ages! Thanks, Aunt Fay!"

"I didn't think you liked adventure films," Donavan remarked.

She shrugged. "I can take them or leave them. But I thought they might take Jeff's mind off court." She looked up at him curiously. "Have you heard anything from his stepfather, even through the lawyer?"

He shook his head. "It wouldn't surprise me to find that he's having us watched, though."

"Why?"

"Looking for anything to further his case." He laughed coldly. "It would be like him."

"Neither of us has been indiscreet," she reminded him primly, but with a nervous glance.

He glared at her. "I told you, I don't have women on the side. As long as we're married, you're it."

She averted her face. "Thank you."

"I hope that I can expect the same courtesy?"

Her eyes on his face were explosive and expressive. "You don't have to worry about that. I don't attract too many men now that I'm not rich anymore!"

The slip caught Donavan's attention. "You just inherited a fortune," he reminded her.

"Oh. Oh, yes," she faltered. She turned away quickly. "Nevertheless, I'm not going to break my wedding vows."

"I never thought you would, Fay," he said unexpectedly. He moved close behind her and caught her waist gently in his lean hands. "You needn't flinch like that." His voice was quiet, tender. "I may be a 14-karat heel, but I wouldn't hurt you physically."

"I know that," she said breathlessly. "And I don't think you're a heel. You love Jeff very much, don't you?"

He heard the jerky sound of her breathing and moved even closer, his powerful body all but wrapping around hers from behind. His face eased down so that his cheek was against hers, his warm breath sighing out at the corner of her mouth.

Her cold hands rested uneasily atop his, tremulous as the spell of his nearness made her pulse race wildly.

"It's easy to love a child," he said heavily. "Even a neglected, temperamental one. A child accepts love and returns it. Adults know better than to trust it."

"I see."

His hands tightened and his mouth dropped to her soft neck, pressing there hotly. "You see nothing," he said huskily. "Lift your mouth. I want it."

She started to protest, but the stark need of his mouth silenced her. His lips parted hers ruthlessly. He whipped her around against him, his body hardening as he held hers possessively to it. He groaned softly, and the sound made her even weaker.

With a tiny sigh, her mind let go and made her vulnerable in his arms. She reached up, opening her mouth to the rough, insistent probing of his tongue. The sensations he was causing made her knees tremble, and eventually it was only the crush of his arms that kept her on her feet at all.

The sudden silence in the living room was as blatant as a gunshot. Donavan reluctantly lifted his head just as Jeff's footsteps impinged on the silence.

Fay tried to pull back, but Donavan wouldn't let go. "He isn't blind," he said unsteadily. "Stay put."

She didn't quite grasp what he meant until he moved deliberately against her, making her realize at once that his hunger for her was blatant and easily seen.

She subsided and laid her cheek on his broad chest, relaxing against him as Jeff pushed open the kitchen door, and made an embarrassed sound.

"Sorry," he faltered. "I needed a soft drink."

"Help yourself," Donavan said, chuckling. "We are married, you know," he added, lightening the atmosphere.

"It's about time you started acting like you were," Jeff murmured with a grin. He got his soft drink and closed the door behind him with a faint wink at Fay.

"I'll remind you of the same thing," he told her when he stepped back and her face flamed before she was able to avert her eyes. "And you've seen me with a hell of a lot less on, in this condition."

"Will you stop?" she moaned.

"You're very easily embarrassed for an old married woman." His eyes narrowed as he paused long enough to light a cigar. He watched her closely. "I'll keep you from getting pregnant. I want you in my bed tonight. Hear me out," he added when she started to speak. "Sophistication is the one thing you can't fake. If even Jeff realizes we aren't living like married people, his stepfather might realize it as well. We could still lose Jeff."

She hesitated. "I realize that."

"You can pretend all you like," he added, "but you want what I can give you in bed. You're as excited right now as you were in the motel room the night after we married. The difference," he said sensually, "is that now we can experience each other totally, Fay. I can satisfy you totally."

Her lips parted. She could still feel him on them, taste him on them. He looked at her and knew, at once, that she was totally at his mercy.

Slowly he put out the cigar. He opened the door. "Jeff, we're going to have an early night. Bed by eleven, got that?"

"What? Oh, sure, Uncle Don," he said distractedly, his eyes on the TV screen. "Sleep well."

"You, too."

He closed the door and caught Fay's cold hand in his. He tugged her with him to the hall door, opened and closed it behind them and then led her into the darkness of his own bedroom.

He closed that door, and locked it. Seconds later, in the warm dark, Fay felt him lever down completely against her, pushing her back against the cool wood of the door as the heat of his muscular body overwhelmed her.

While he kissed her, his hands slid under the dress she was wearing and played havoc with her aroused body. Long before he began to take her clothes off, she was barely able to stand alone.

Later, she lay quietly, trembling, in his bed while he removed his own clothes. She could barely see him in the faint light from the window, but what she saw was devastating, and her breath caught.

"You know what to expect already," he whispered as he eased down beside her and began to arouse her all over again. "Except that this time," he whispered into her mouth, "I'm going to fill you…"

She cried out. His mouth hurt, his body was hard and heavy, but she didn't notice, didn't care. She welcomed the warm weight of him, the fierce passion of his mouth and hands. She even welcomed the faint flash of pain when he came into her, her body arching up to receive him, her eyes wide with shock and awe as he slowly completed his possession and then paused, hovering with her on the brink of some sensual precipice.

One lean hand had her hip in its steely grasp. He looked at her, breathing unsteadily, his silver eyes glistening with excitement, beads of sweat on his lean, swarthy face.

His hand contracted and he moved, sensually, just enough to make her feverishly aware of how intimate their embrace was.

She caught her breath and he laughed, deep in his throat.

"Yes," he whispered roughly. "You didn't realize just how intimate it was going to be, did you, little one?"

"N-no," she got out. She looked at him in astonishment, feeling him in every cell of her body. It was embarrassing, shocking, to talk to a man in the throes of such intimacy. And he was laughing. "It isn't funny," she choked.

"I'm not laughing because I'm amused," he whispered, and bent to nibble with barely contained hunger at her softly swollen lips. His hips curled down into hers and lifted, creating a sudden sensual vortex that coaxed a cry of shocked pleasure from her lips. "I'm laughing because you're the most sensual little virgin in the world, and because despite the newness and fear, you're giving yourself to me without a single inhibition. Lift your hips. Let me feel you as close as you can get."

She obeyed him, her body on fire. Her dreams had never been so explicit. Her nails bit into his broad shoulders as he began to move with exquisite delicacy.

"I may be a little rough with you now," he whispered into her mouth. "Don't be afraid of my passion. If you give yourself to it, to me, I'll give you a kind of pleasure you can't even imagine. Match me. Match my rhythm. Don't pull back. That's it." His teeth clenched and he groaned as his body stiffened. "Oh, God, I'm losing it…!"

He did. He lost it completely, before he could give her the time she needed to experience fulfillment. He arched above her, his face contorted and terrible in its unearthly pleasure, and he bit off something explicit and harsh as he gave in to the silky convulsions.

"I'm sorry," he whispered, lying drained and heavy over her. "My God, I'm so sorry!"

"Sorry that you made love to me?" she asked in a curious whisper.

"Sorry that I didn't satisfy you!"

"Oh." She stroked his dark hair gently. "You mean, the way you did the night we were married?" She smiled. "Now you can, can't you?"

He stared at her poleaxed. "You think that what just happened was only for my benefit?"

She frowned. "Wasn't it?"

He pulled her close and his arms tightened. "You're one in a million, do you know that? Lift this leg…yes!"

She gasped as his body suddenly became part of hers. She hadn't expected this again so soon. Weren't men supposed to be incapable for several minutes after intimacy?

He moved slowly, exquisitely, and her breath caught. She clung to him, as the most astounding sensations worked through her tightening body.

"Donavan," she began, and suddenly cried out at the unexpected spasm of staggering pleasure.

"Be quiet, sweetheart," he whispered at her mouth, his hips moving with more insistence now, more purpose. "Hold on tight. Yes, Fay, feel it, yes…yes!"

She wept brokenly as the pleasure burst inside her like an overfilled balloon. She had no control whatsoever over her body or the vicious contractions that convulsed her under his openly watchful eyes.

He whispered to her, words of encouragement, praise, flattery, while his mouth touched quickly over her flushed, taut face. It went on and on. She shuddered and clung, convulsed and clung, experiencing sensations beyond her wildest dreams of perfection.

At last, the world stopped rocking and whirling

around her. She trembled helplessly in the aftermath, drenched in sweat, weeping softly from the onrush of pleasure and its abrupt loss.

Donavan cradled her in his hard arms, smoothing back her damp hair as he comforted her.

"This," he said after a few minutes, "is what intimacy really is."

"I thought…before, at the motel…" She couldn't quite find the words.

"An alternate way of making love," he said quietly. "But nothing like the real thing. Was it, Fay?"

He wasn't mocking, or teasing. His voice was soft and deep and matter-of-fact.

"We…were like one person," she whispered into his cool, hair-roughened chest.

"Yes." His cheek moved against hers and he kissed her, very gently.

Her body felt pleasantly tired. She went boneless against him and slid even closer, her legs tangling with his. "Can I stay with you?" she asked drowsily.

His arms tightened. "Let me put it this way—just try to get away."

She smiled sleepily. "I don't think I want to."

He bit the lobe of her ear softly. "I want you again, right now," he said huskily, feeling her heart jump under his palm. "But we'll wait until the morning. It didn't hurt? Even the first time?"

"No," she lied, and snuggled closer. It hadn't hurt very much. And the second time had been heaven.

"Fay," he said hesitantly. His fingers threaded through her soft hair. "Fay, I forgot to use anything."

She didn't stir, or answer. He looked down and realized belatedly that she was asleep.

He bent and kissed her closed eyelids. "Maybe it's just as well that you didn't hear me," he whispered. His lean hand found her soft belly and rested there possessively. "You'd love a baby, Fay. So would I. Maybe it's already happened. If it has, perhaps I can convince you that it would be a bonus, not a complication."

Fay was wavering between consciousness and sleep. She heard Donavan say something about a bonus, but her mind was already headed for oblivion. She clung closer and gave in to it.

CHAPTER NINE

FAY WAS HUMMING softly to herself when Donavan came in from the barn. He'd gone out without waking her, and she was disappointed. She'd been hoping that the night before might have coaxed him to want her again, but obviously that hope had been doomed.

She stopped humming when he walked in, her eyes a little shy and nervous. "Good morning," she began, searching for the right words.

He paused in the doorway, and he could have been playing poker for all the expression in his face. Her stiff composure told him things he didn't want to know. He'd pleased her in the night. He'd hoped that things would change between them now that she knew what married life could be. But he wasn't reassured. She looked uncomfortable and poised to run. If she felt anything for him, it didn't show. And he needed some reassurance before he paraded his own feelings in front of her; his pride would take a mighty blow if she didn't care anymore.

"Good morning," he replied with equal formality. "Breakfast ready?"

"Almost."

He turned. "I'll call Jeff."

And not a word was said, either about the night before, or about what he felt. Fay watched him surrepti-

tiously, hoping to see some flicker of warmth in those
silver eyes. But they never met hers. He was polite,
nothing more. Fay left the table resolved not to expect
anything from that encounter in the darkness the night
before. It was just as well, because that night he didn't
come near her.

The next morning, they went to church, and then
spent a lazy afternoon in front of the television watching old movies. There had hardly been three words spoken in front of Jeff, who looked worried.

"Something bothering you?" Donavan asked curtly
after supper.

Jeff looked uncomfortable. "Yes, sir. Sort of."

"What is it?"

"It's you and Aunt Fay," he said miserably, wincing
at Fay's shock and Donavan's quick anger. "I'm sorry,
but if you two go into court tomorrow looking like you
do right now, I guess I'll be back in military school by
the next morning. Could you pretend to like each other,
just while we're in court?"

"No problem there," Donavan assured him. "Now
you'd better get your bath and go to sleep. We've got a
big day ahead tomorrow."

When he left the room, Donavan got up and turned
off the television. His eyes lingered on Fay's flushed
cheeks for a few seconds before he spoke.

"He's dead right," he told her. "If we don't present a
united front, he won't be able to stay here."

"I know." She folded her hands in her lap and clenched
them, staring at her nails. "I don't want him to have to
leave, Donavan, whatever you think."

His broad shoulders lifted and fell in an offhand
gesture. He lit a cigar and stared at its tip. "I shouldn't

have lost my head night before last," he said tersely. "It made things worse between us."

She didn't know how to answer that. She picked at one of her fingernails and didn't look up. "It was my fault, too."

"Was it? You didn't seduce me, honey," he drawled.

She sighed heavily. "I'm not on the pill," she said.

He hesitated. "Yes, I know."

"And you...well, you didn't do anything..."

"That's right," he replied. "Keep going."

She cleared her throat, glancing up at him. "You might have made me pregnant."

One corner of his mouth curved gently. "There's an old family christening gown around here somewhere. My great-grandmother made the lace it's edged in. There's a high chair and even a cradle that date back to the first settlers in Jacobsville."

Fay's green eyes softened as they met his. Her cheeks warmed as she looked at him. "I... I have a baptismal set, too. The furniture's all gone. But there's one antique that Great-Aunt Tessie kept—a silver baptismal bowl. I saved it from the auction."

The mention of her deceased relative made his expression become grim. He averted his face and smoked his cigar, still pacing slowly. "You inherited a lot of money," he said. "Can't you keep the furniture, or don't you want it?"

"I have no place for it in my apartment," she said simply.

He spun on his heel, glaring at her. "This is your home. There's no way on earth you're leaving here until I know if you're pregnant."

She started. "It's unlikely..."

"Why? Because it was the first time?" he asked with mocking amusement.

His sophisticated attitude angered her. "Can't we talk about something else?" she asked stiffly.

"Sure." He raised the cigar to his firm lips. He felt optimistic for the first time. She still reacted to him. She couldn't hide the way he affected her. It made him feel proud to realize that she was as helplessly attracted to him as he was to her.

Now, if only her heart was involved…

"Why don't you sleep with me tonight?" he asked sensuously. "After all, one more time isn't going to make much difference now."

"You don't want me to stay here," she said. "I don't want a child who has to grow up without his father."

"I didn't say I didn't want you to stay here," he returned.

"You did so!" she raged, standing. "You said that you didn't want me anymore because my great-aunt died and left me rich again! You let me go to Florida all by myself—"

"Not quite. Henry went with you," he pointed out.

She continued as if he hadn't interrupted "—and then you said I could find somewhere else to live!"

"I didn't say that," he murmured dryly. "Surely not?"

"Yes, you did!"

"That was before I slept with you, of course," he pointed out, letting his eyes punctuate the flat statement. "Now I'm hopelessly addicted."

"Any woman would do," she muttered.

"Not really, or I'd have had a few in the past year or so. I'd all but lost interest in sex until you came along and knocked my legs out from under me."

"A likely story, after the things you did to me night before last…!"

She stopped very suddenly, her hand going to her mouth as she realized what she'd said. She sat down again, hard.

"I had experience, Fay," he said softly.

She flushed. "I noticed!"

"You might consider that those early encounters made your life a little easier."

She stared at her feet, still smoldering. "You did things to me that I never even read in books."

"I'll tell you a secret, honey," he mused, putting out his cigar before he came to kneel between her legs where she sat rigidly on the sofa. He was almost on a level with her shocked eyes as he looked into them. "I've never done with anyone some of those things I did to you. And never could."

"C-couldn't you?" she whispered.

"No." His hands caught her waist and pulled gently, suddenly overbalancing so that she landed breathlessly on his chest. He rolled, pinning her under him on the big throw rug. As he held her eyes, one long leg inserted itself between both of hers and he moved slowly.

"I want you again. Now," he told her, his body screaming it in the intimate embrace. His lean hand smoothed blatantly over her soft breast and then began to slip buttons out of buttonholes.

"But the door…" she began.

"Isn't closed. I know." He slid his hand inside her bodice and under her soft bra, to find even softer flesh. His fingers gently caressed it, and she arched, gasping. "I'm going to carry you to bed now," he breathed.

"And I'm going to do all those things I did two nights ago. Right now."

He got to his feet and picked her up, shifting her gently as he carried her down the long hall and into his bedroom. He placed her on the bedspread and went to close and lock the door. Then he stood at the foot of the bed, his black hair half in his eyes, his face devoid of expression, his body blatantly aroused.

She eased up onto her elbows, feeling feminine and hotly desired, her green eyes lost in the glitter of his gray ones. He nodded slowly. And then he moved toward her.

But just as he reached her, bent over her, warmed her mouth with his breath in a deliciously tense bit of provocation—the telephone rang noisily on the bedside table.

Donavan stared at it blankly, as if for a moment he didn't even realize what was making the noise.

Impatiently he jerked up the receiver and spoke into it.

A familiar, sarcastic voice came over the line—Brad Danner, Jeff's stepfather.

"I'm looking forward to tomorrow, Donavan," he told the angry man on the other end of the line. "If you think that sham marriage is going to make any difference in a custody suit, you're very wrong."

"It isn't a sham marriage," Donavan said tersely, without looking at Fay, who was sitting shocked and disoriented beside him now, on the bed.

"I'll let you prove that tomorrow. Take good care of my stepson, won't you? I'm looking forward to having him home again."

"Yes, it would be something of a luxury, wouldn't

it?" Donavan asked icily. "When you stuck him in military school at his first show of spirit."

"One of you in a family is enough," the other man replied, obviously straining to keep his temper. "All my married life, Debbie threw you up to me. Nothing I did was ever right, ever the same thing *you* would have done in my place. My God, you don't know how I hated you!"

"Debbie always had a tendency to romanticize everything," Donavan said curtly. "After Dad died, I was all she had. As for her opinion of you," he added with mocking amusement, "I had nothing to do with it. You were a spineless complainer from day one. And don't tell me the dowry I gave her wasn't the real inducement to get you to the altar. You spent half of it the first week you were married to Debbie—on your mistress!"

The other receiver slammed down. Donavan slowly replaced his, chuckling with bitter amusement.

"Jeff's would-be guardian," he said, nodding toward the telephone. "He fancies himself a man. Imagine that?"

"He might have loved your sister," she began.

"Really? If he did, why was he involved with another woman before, during and after the marriage? The woman he's married to now, by the way. Debbie's insurance money set them up real well. He made sure that Jeff wasn't mentioned as a beneficiary."

"He sounds very mercenary," she said quietly.

"He thinks he can prove that our marriage is a fraud," he said. His eyes narrowed on her face. "It's imperative that we act like lovers. You understand that?"

She nodded. Her eyes fell to his broad chest, where his shirt was unbuttoned over a thick mat of curling black hair.

"I understand." Her lips parted with helpless hunger, but she lowered her eyes so that he wouldn't see how she felt. "That's why you brought me in here, isn't it, Donavan? So that it would show, in court tomorrow, that we'd been intimate."

He hesitated, but only for an instant. "Yes," he said curtly. "That's right. I wanted to make you look loved, so that I wouldn't risk losing Jeff."

"I see."

Her defeated expression made him wild. "He might run away if he gets sent back, don't you see? He's high-strung. I can't let that happen. He's all the family I have left in the world, Fay!"

She stood up with a long, gentle sigh. "Funny," she said as she turned. "Once upon a time, I thought I was part of your family. It just goes to show how money can warp you. Being rich must have made me stupid."

He rammed his hands into his pockets. He felt guilty, and he didn't like it. She was rich. She had the world. She didn't need a poor husband and a ready-made family, anyway. Even *if* he wanted her for keeps, which he didn't. He had one scandal to live down. He couldn't take another.

He only hoped he hadn't made her pregnant in that feverish coupling. It would make her life impossible, because he knew he'd never be able to turn his back on his own child. She'd be trapped then, and so would he.

"It's just as well that Brad interrupted us," he said tersely, thinking aloud. "I've been unforgivably careless about taking precautions. It's just as well if we don't take any more risks. I'll see you in the morning, Fay."

It was a dismissal. He looked as unapproachable as a porcupine. Fay couldn't understand why he'd bothered trying to seduce her in the first place. Now he seemed concerned about not making her pregnant. She left him there and went to bed, hurt and bitter and totally confused.

She dressed very carefully for court the next morning, in her off-white suit and leather high heels. She carried the one designer purse she had left, and wore a very becoming and very expensive spring hat. She looked what she was—a young woman with breeding who'd been raised to be a lady.

Donavan, in his pale gray suit, was openly appreciative of the way she looked. In fact, he could hardly keep his eyes off her.

"You look...lovely," he said.

She managed a cool smile. "Why thank you, darling," she said, playing her part to the hilt. Only her eyes gave the show away, because they were like two green pieces of ice. His hot-cold attitude had worn her out. She was giving up all hope of a happy marriage, but first she was going to help Jeff out of his predicament. It was a matter of honor. She'd given her word.

"Very nice," he replied curtly. "You'll convince anyone who doesn't look at your face too closely."

"I can handle that." She pulled the hat's matching veil down over her nose. "Now. One wife, properly accounted for, ready to go on stage."

He stiffened and turned away, his anger evident and blatant.

Jeff came out of his bedroom in a suit. He looked from Fay to Donavan and grimaced. "Well, I guess I'm as ready as I'll ever be, but I'm sure not looking forward to it."

"Neither are we," Donavan said. "All the more reason to get it over with as soon as possible. Try not to worry," he added gently, placing an affectionate hand on the boy's stooped shoulder. "And stand up straight. Don't let him think he's got you buffaloed."

"Yes, Uncle Don."

He herded Fay and Jeff out to the car and drove them to the county courthouse in a silence filled with worried looks and cigar smoke.

BRAD DANNER WASN'T at all what Fay had expected. He was short and redheaded and looked as if he had a massive ego.

"So you're the brand-new Mrs. J. D. Langley," Brad said mockingly, shaking off the firm hand of a suited man who was probably his attorney. "Well, it won't work. You might as well go back to whichever bar he found you at and throw in your chips. You'll never pull this off. I've got too much on you!"

"Have you indeed?" Fay asked, enjoying herself now. "Actually, Donavan did find me in a bar." She leaned closer. "But I didn't work there."

"Oh, of course not," he agreed amiably, and laughed as he turned back to the bleached blonde with the over-lipsticked mouth who was obviously pregnant and almost certainly his wife.

Donavan motioned for Fay to sit down at the table with him. Jeff had already been taken away by a juvenile officer for the course of the hearing.

Formalities had to be observed. Once those were out of the way, Donavan's attorney—an elderly man with keen eyes and alarming dignity—offered Brad's attorney the opportunity to present his case first.

Donavan looked nervous, but Mr. Flores only smiled and winked.

Brad's attorney got up and made a long speech about the things Brad had done for his stepson, most recently having enrolled him in a top-flight educational facility, which would lead him to an admirable career.

"We do concede that Mr. Danner has no blood relationship with the boy, as does Mr. Langley. However, despite his hasty marriage in an attempt to present a stable home environment, Mr. Langley overlooked one small detail. He neglected to keep his new wife close to home."

Fay and Donavan exchanged puzzled glances. The opposing attorney opened his briefcase and dragged out several photographs of Fay with her uncle on the way to Florida, and at Tessie's apartment, where they'd stayed until the funeral was over.

"This is the kind of monkey business the new Mrs. Langley gets up to when her husband's back is turned," the attorney said haughtily, glaring at Fay as if she were a fallen woman. "Hardly a moral example for a young boy!"

Donavan chuckled.

"You find these photographs amusing, Mr. Langley? You had been married for only a matter of days, I believe, when Mrs. Langley and her gentleman friend flew to Florida alone?"

"You aren't from here, are you?" Donavan asked the attorney. "And apparently neither is your private detective."

"He isn't a private detective, he's a friend of mine who used to be in intelligence work during the Korean

War," Brad said stiffly. "But you won't lie your way out of this. That man in the photographs is…!"

"…my uncle," Fay said. She glanced at Judge Ridley, who was an old friend of her family—and who was also trying not to break up.

"I'm afraid so," Judge Ridley agreed, wiping the unjudicial smile off his face. "I've known Henry for years."

"If he's her uncle, why doesn't he have the same surname she does?" the other attorney argued.

"Henry is Fay's mother's brother," Judge Ridley explained. "Surely your detective checked?"

"He said Donavan had probably found her at a bar," Brad began.

"Mrs. Langley and her uncle went to Florida to make the final arrangements for Mrs. Langley's great-aunt," Donavan's attorney clarified. "As for your friend's assertion that Mrs. Langley worked in a bar, let me assure you that nothing could be further from the truth. In point of fact, she was a debutante. And now, with the death of her great-aunt, she stands to inherit a large share of the estate."

Brad looked sick.

"I am also reliably told," Judge Ridley interrupted, "by the young boy whose custody is in question, that his uncle and Mrs. Langley have a warm, loving relationship, which gives him a much-needed feeling of security. Your accusation that the marriage is fraudulent hardly concurs with the home life the young man describes."

"He'd do anything to get Jeff, even pretending to be happily married. Ask him if he loves her," he challenged the judge. "Go ahead! He never lies. Make him tell her how he really feels about her!"

Fay stood up. "I know how my husband feels about me, Mr. Danner," she said stiffly. "I also know how you feel about him. Jeff is only a pawn to you. But he's a flesh-and-blood boy to Donavan. They're very happy together. Jeff will get a good education and caring company, and it won't be in a military school where he isn't even allowed weekend visits home more than twice a year! If you wanted him so badly, why send him away in the first place?"

"A good question," the judge agreed. He stared at Brad, who was slowly turning red. "Answer it, please."

"My wife is pregnant," Brad said shortly. "Jeff makes her nervous. Isn't that right, honey?"

"I fail to see why you sought custody, Mr. Danner," the judge persisted.

"Oh, tell him, Bradley," the blonde muttered. She sanded a nail to perfection. "He only wants the insurance money. He's afraid if he loses custody, he'll have to give Jeff his share of it, and he's already spent it."

"You idiot!" Brad raged at his wife.

"What's so terrible about the truth?" she asked with careless unconcern. "You were so scared of your brother-in-law finding out. Well, now he knows. Big deal. It's only a thousand dollars, anyway. If you hadn't bought that stupid boat, you could have afforded to pay it back."

The courtroom erupted. Before the fur stopped flying, Fay got a glimpse of the real Brad Danner, and she was very sorry for his second wife. By the time Fay and Donavan left the courtroom, with custody of Jeff and the promise of repayment of the insurance money Jeff should have had, Fay's head was whirling.

"Aunt Fay, I'm so relieved!" Jeff laughed, and hugged her impulsively. "I can stay, isn't it radical?"

"Just radical," she agreed happily.

"And you and Uncle Don fooled them all," he added. "Everybody thought you were the most devoted couple anywhere!"

"That was the joke of the century, all right," Fay said quietly, and met Donavan's angry eyes over Jeff's head. "Congratulations. You've got what you wanted."

"Yes," he said. "I've got everything I wanted."

She smiled coolly, grateful for the veil that hid her sadness, and put an affectionate arm around Jeff as they walked toward the car.

Donavan walked a little behind them. He didn't know how he felt exactly, but elated wouldn't have covered it. He was glad to have Jeff with him, of course, but in the process he was certain to lose Fay.

That shouldn't bother him. Fay was rich; he wasn't. Their lifestyles would never mix, and everyone would think that he'd married her for her money. Hell, they probably thought it already. He laughed at his own folly. Even if he divorced her, they'd say he was after a big cash settlement in return for her freedom. They'd say like father, like son.

Suddenly the public censure that had worried him so much before fell into place. If he knew what his motives were, did it really matter what a few small-minded people thought? It was usually the hypocrites who gossiped, anyway—the people who lived public lives of high morality and private lives of glaring impurity. The few friends he had wouldn't sit in judgment on him. So why was he agonizing over his plight?

He glanced at Fay hungrily. Hell, he wanted her.

He'd grown used to having her around the house. He enjoyed watching her stumbling attempts to cook edible meals. He liked the smell of her perfume when he stood close to her, and the way she fussed over him and Jeff, as if it really mattered to her that something might happen to one of them. He liked her, most especially, sliding under his body in bed, giving him her warmth and exquisite sensuality, giving him ecstasy that even in memory could make him weak in the knees. He wanted to stay with her. He wanted a child with her. Was it too late? Had he done too much damage?

"Suppose we stop off at the pizza place and get a supreme to go?" Jeff suggested. "After all, we are celebrating."

"Good idea. We'll give Aunt Fay the night off," Donavan agreed.

"He's just tired of bouncing biscuits and black steak," she told Jeff with a sigh. "I guess one well-cooked meal won't kill us all."

Jeff laughed, but Fay didn't. Now that Donavan had Jeff, she wondered how much time she had left until Donavan wanted her out of his life for good.

CHAPTER TEN

THE PIZZA WAS DELICIOUS. Fay enjoyed it as much as the rest of the family seemed to, but her heart wasn't in the celebration. She wanted to stand up and scream that life was unfair, that she'd been shortchanged all the way around. She'd always had money. But she'd never had love. Now it seemed that she didn't have either. Great-Aunt Tessie's legacy would be nice, but it would hardly allow her to give up her job. With some careful investing, it would grow, as long as she could live on what she made.

She worried about that for the rest of the day, trying to put on a happy face for Jeff. But Donavan saw through it. He joined her on the porch swing while Jeff played with one of three new snow-white puppies in the barn.

"We won," he reminded her as he smoked his cigar. Like her, he'd changed into casual clothes—jeans and a cotton shirt. He propped one booted foot on the swing and glanced down at her. "Aren't you glad?"

"Of course," she said absently. "I know how worried Jeff was."

He stared out over the horizon. "There really wasn't too much to worry about," he mused. "I had a contact of mine feed his Korean War veteran buddy a few scandalous facts about you and Uncle Henry. It's not my fault the man took it for gospel and didn't double check. His loss, my gain."

"Donavan!" she burst out. "That's devious!"

"That's how I am when people I love get threatened." He looked down at her. "I'll fight under the table, any way at all, to win when someone else's life depends on it. I couldn't let that strutting rooster get Jeff. It wasn't a tug of war with me—it was Jeff's whole life."

"I know he appreciates what you've done for him."

"I don't imagine you do. I'm sorry to have made you look, even temporarily, like a fallen angel. But I had no choice."

"I understood. Even the judge was having a hard time keeping a straight face."

"Where do we go from here, Fay?" he asked solemnly.

She listened to the creak as the wooden swing pulled against the chains rhythmically.

"I'll stay until your brother-in-law is safely back home and over his defeat," she said. "We've already discussed where I'll go."

"No we haven't," he disagreed. "You said you were going to move back to the apartment house and I said you weren't. My God, buy yourself a place, why don't you?"

Her hands clasped together painfully. Didn't he know he was tearing the heart out of her?

"I might, later on."

She wasn't giving an inch. He couldn't tell anything by her voice or her expression.

"You could stay on here," he remarked casually. "There's plenty of room. Jeff likes you. So does Bee."

"I've burned up enough good food already."

"We haven't complained."

She smiled to herself. Amazingly they hadn't. Only three days ago, Jeff had complimented her on one small side dish that was actually fit to eat.

"I might get the hang of it one day."

He studied his boot. "How about getting the hang of making formula and changing dirty diapers?" he asked, his eyes on the horizon.

She hesitated. He sounded…serious. "What do you mean?"

He shrugged. He lifted the cigar to his mouth and took a draw from it, blowing out a large cloud of pungent smoke. "I mean, suppose we stayed married. If you'd let me, I think I could make you pregnant eventually. We could raise a family, give Jeff a stable environment to finish growing up in."

She studied his profile. Nothing there. He looked as formidable as he had the first time she'd ever seen him. Just as handsome, too, she thought wistfully.

He glanced down and saw that wistfulness and one eyebrow went up. He looked at her openly now, from her forehead down to her mouth and back up to her eyes. "You're thinner. I've been cruel to you, Fay. Give me a chance to put things right."

"By making me pregnant?" she asked with pretended lightness.

"If it's what you want, yes. If not, we can put it off for a few years. You're still very young, little one. You might like to go to college or do some traveling before you get tied down with children."

"I've already done my traveling, and I don't want to go to college. I have a nice job already."

"You can resign from that," he said. "You don't need it."

She stared at him for a long moment, until he scowled. "Actually," she confessed, "I'm afraid I do."

"If you just want a way to get out of the house…"

She rested her cool fingers atop the lean hand that was propped on his jean-clad knee. "Donavan, I'm not exactly going to inherit a fortune."

"Yes, I know. Henry said you'll only get about a third, when it's all wrapped up. It doesn't matter," he said doggedly, averting his face. "I don't give a damn what people think anymore. I don't know now why I ever did. I'm not like my father. I married you for Jeff's sake, not because I stood to gain a fortune."

She felt the impact of that statement down to her toes. If only he'd married her for love of her. She sighed, audibly.

He tilted her face up to his. "What a wistful little sound," he said quietly. "You don't like thinking that I only married you for Jeff. You liked it even less when you thought it was for money."

"It doesn't bother me," she lied.

"Sure it does," he countered quietly. "I wanted you," he said softly. "You knew that already, I imagine."

"Yes."

"You wanted me back. I didn't have to coerce you into my bed. You came willingly."

She flushed and looked down at the lean fingers that slowly wrapped around hers in a close embrace. "It was new and...exciting."

"More than just exciting, I think, little one." His voice was soft, deep, sensual. "I lost you for a few seconds just as I fulfilled you. It made me feel pretty good to know I could give you that much pleasure."

"As you said," she swallowed, "you've had a lot of experience."

"I've had a lot of *bodies*," he said with faint cynicism. "Just that, Fay, a lot of bodies in the dark. I went through the motions and learned the right moves. But it was nothing like what I had with you, even on our wedding night, when my hands were all but tied. I knew then that it was more than physical attraction. But I knew it for certain when I put you on that plane to Florida and let you walk away from me. I didn't sleep all night, for thinking how cruel I'd been. You loved Tessie, and I'd given you no comfort, no support at all. I'm sorry for that. I owed you more than that."

"You owed me nothing," she told him dully. "We got married for Jeff, that's all."

His free hand spread against her soft cheek and lifted her face. "Haven't you been listening to me at all?" he asked softly.

"Yes," she said nervously. "You've got me on your conscience."

"Fay, listen with your heart, not your ears," he replied. He searched her face with eyes that adored it. "Can't you see it? Can't you feel it? Fay, can't you put your mouth on mine and taste it...?"

He pulled her lips under his and kissed her with such tenderness that she felt her body ripple with sheer pleasure.

His tongue probed inside her mouth, increasing the heat, making her moan. While he built the kiss, he lifted and turned her, so that she was lying completely in his arms, pressed close against the heat of his muscular chest.

Unseen, his lean hand eased inside her shirt and began to trace the warm, taut contours of her breast until he made the nipple go hard against his fingers.

He lifted his head minutes later, and looked down at her swollen mouth and dazed eyes before his gaze dropped to the taut nipple so evident under the thin fabric.

"You look as out of control as I feel," he said huskily, his gray eyes pure silver in the daylight. "If we were alone, I wouldn't even bother to strip you. I'd just get the necessary things out of the way and I'd take you like a tornado."

She shivered, pressing her hot face into his throat.

"Want it like that?" he whispered at her ear. "Rough and quick and blazing hot?" He glanced over her head at Jeff, who was sprawled in the aisle of the barn playing with the dogs while one of Donavan's older hands watched him.

Donavan stood up abruptly and put Fay on her feet. Catching the older hand's attention, he indicated that he wanted him to keep an eye on Jeff. The cowhand nodded, grinned and waved. Then Donavan turned back to Fay, his eyes glittery with intent.

"Oh…we can't," she faltered as he came toward her and she began backing toward the screen door. "Surely, you were kidding, with Jeff right outside…!"

"Like hell I was kidding," he whispered against her mouth.

He picked her up and carried her straight into his bedroom, pausing just long enough to lock the door before he backed her up against the waist-high vanity and opened the fastening of her jeans.

She gasped and started to protest, but he had her mouth under his, and she couldn't manage speech. She heard the rasp of another zipper, felt him move, and then her jeans slid off her legs. His tongue went roughly into her mouth, in quick, sharp thrusts that were unbelievably arousing.

He lifted her sharply and she felt him suddenly in an intimacy that took her breath. He half lifted her from the vanity, his body levering between her legs while he invaded her with urgent, exquisite mastery. She clung to his neck, feeling the force of his desire with faint awe as she experienced for the first time the unbridled violence of passion.

He wasn't tender, or particularly gentle, but the pleasure that convulsed her was beyond anything he'd given her before. She heard him cry out and felt him tense, then he was heavy in her arms, damp with sweat, trembling faintly from the strength he'd had to exert in the uncomfortable position.

"I like the noises that boil out of you when we make love," he said roughly. "You excite me."

"I can't stop shaking." She laughed shyly.

"Neither can I. We went high this time."

"Yes. Oh, yes!"

He drew back, finally, and looked at her. His face was solemn, his eyes quiet and gentle. He brushed back her damp hair and smiled. "That will have to last us until tonight," he whispered. "Think you can manage?"

"If you can," she teased. His eyes were telling her impossible things, too wonderful for reality. "Am I dreaming?" she asked.

"No, sweetheart. Not at all."

He lifted her, separating his body from hers, and grinned wickedly when she flushed.

"You needn't look so shocked," he chided as he rearranged his own clothing. "Five minutes ago you wouldn't have noticed if we were lying under a table in a restaurant."

"Neither would you!" she accused.

He drew her close and kissed her gently. "That's a fact," he whispered. "God, I love you, Fay."

She stiffened. She couldn't have heard that. She opened her eyes, very wide, and stared at him.

"I haven't given you much reason to believe it, but it's true just the same," he told her quietly. "You're all I want, you and Jeff and however many kids we can have together. If we can't have any, then you and Jeff will more than suffice."

"How long?" she asked gently, desperate now to believe him.

"Since the very first night we met," he replied. "I fought it. God, I did! But in the end, I couldn't do without you. After I made love to you, even light love, I was lost. I knew I'd never be able to let you go."

"Then I inherited Tessie's money," she began.

"I told you. It doesn't matter. I love you. Do whatever you like with your inheritance."

"In that case," she murmured, "I'll put it in the bank for Jeff's education. It should just about cover college."

"Where are we sending him to college—the Waldorf Astoria?"

She smiled warmly, convinced at last that she was awake and aware. "I only inherit part of the proceeds from the sale of her furniture," she told him, and proceeded to explain where the rest of the money was going.

He was surprised, and frankly pleased, that Fay's inheritance wouldn't amount to very much. "She must have been some kind of lady," he remarked.

"She was. A very special one. My share will just about pay for Jeff's college. Now you know why I wouldn't give up my job. I couldn't afford to."

"Just as well the Ballengers made one for you," he

murmured. He sighed heavily. "I guess this means that I'll have to start being, ugh, nice to Calhoun."

"That wouldn't hurt," she agreed.

"And your uncle," he added irritably.

"Also a nice touch."

He searched her eyes. "I won't reform completely. You know that. I'm exactly what you see. I won't change."

"Neither will I," she replied. "I might get a little rounder eventually, and have a few gray hairs."

"That's okay," he said pleasantly. "I might do that myself." He pulled her closer. "Fay, I'll never be a rich man. But I'll love you, and take care of you when you need it. If we have nothing else, we'll have each other."

She had to fight tears at the tenderness in his deep voice. She kissed him and then reached up and locked her arms gently around his neck. "I haven't said it," she whispered.

"You said it the night you gave yourself to me completely," he replied, surprised. "Don't you remember? You said it over and over again while you were trembling in my arms at the last."

"I must have been half out of my mind. Loving you does that to me," she whispered with her heart in her eyes.

"And to me," he replied. He bent, fusing her mouth with his in a slow, sweet expression of love.

"Uncle Don!" came a loud voice from below the window.

Donavan groaned. "What now?"

He opened the window and looked down. Jeff was waiting with two of Donavan's foreman's sons, both of whom were carrying fishing poles and tackle boxes.

"Please?" he pleaded with his uncle. "I haven't gotten to go fishing since the last time you took me. I'll bring home supper, honest, can I?"

"Go ahead." Donavan chuckled. "But you'd better bring home supper."

"We'll make sure he does, sir!" one of the older boys called. "Even if we have to swim under his line and hook the fish on it ourselves."

"Thanks!" Jeff laughed.

The boys were out of sight in no time. Donavan closed the window and took the phone off the hook. He moved toward her with a wicked smile.

"Sometimes," he told a breathlessly excited Fay as he began to caress her out of her clothing, "fate can be kind."

A sentiment that Fay would gladly have echoed, except that Donavan's mouth was hard over her own, and seconds later, she was in no condition to think at all...

THE NEXT MORNING, Fay was hard at work when Donavan showed up unexpectedly at the feedlot.

Calhoun, just coming out of his office, grimaced.

"No need to rush, finding excuses to get out of the office right away," Donavan drawled. "I'm reformed. I didn't come to complain. I actually dropped by to see about moving in some more cattle."

Calhoun's eyebrows went up. "You don't say!"

"I just did. While I'm about it, I might add a word of thanks about keeping my wife on," he added ruefully. "We figure her inheritance from her great-aunt will just about put one kid through college. Since we plan on more than our nephew taking up residence, every penny is going to count."

"We like the job Fay does. But it's tough luck," Calhoun ventured, "about the inheritance."

Donavan smiled lazily. "Not in my book. I like the idea of working toward something." He glanced at Fay with his heart in his eyes. "Struggling together brings two people close."

"Indeed it does," Fay agreed with a sigh.

"If you'd like to take your wife to lunch, we might be able to let her off a little early," Calhoun said.

"I was hoping you'd say that," Donavan said and grinned.

He took Fay to the local hamburger joint and they ate cheeseburgers and drank milkshakes until they were pretty well stuffed.

"You won't have an easy life with me," he said when they were outside again. He paused, catching her hand in his to stop and look down at her. "You'll probably always have to work. I can take some of the burden off you at home, because I can cook and do dishes and sweep. But when the kids come along, things could get pretty hectic."

"Am I worried?" she asked, smiling. "Am I complaining? I've got you. I don't need promises, assurances or anything else. I'm happier than I ever dreamed of being."

"Are you sure?" he asked, and looked worried. "You've always had everything you wanted."

"I still do."

"You know what I mean," he said irritably.

"Yes. Money was nice, but it wasn't particularly easy to cuddle up to. I don't mind living like ordinary working people. In fact," she said honestly, "I really like the challenge. It's nice to feel independent, and to know that you're earning what you have. I never had to earn anything before."

"You're giving me a lot to live up to, honey," he said quietly. "I hope I won't let you down. I'm not the easiest man to live with."

"Yes, you are," she replied. She put her arms around him and pressed close. "As long as I'm holding you, you're the easiest man in the world to get along with. So suppose I just never let go?"

He laughed and let out his breath in a long, contented sigh as he pulled her close and returned the gentle embrace. "I'll tell you something, sweetheart," he murmured contentedly. "That suits me just fine!"

And she never did.

* * * * *

JORDAN

CHAPTER ONE

LIBBY COLLINS COULDN'T figure out why her stepmother, Janet, had called a real estate agent out to the house. Her father had only been dead for a few weeks. The funeral was so fresh in her mind that she cried herself to sleep at night. Her brother, Curt, was equally devastated. Riddle Collins had been a strong, happy, intelligent man who'd never had a serious illness. He had no history of heart trouble. So his death of a massive heart attack had been a real shock. In fact, the Collinses' nearest neighbor, rancher Jordan Powell, said it was suspicious. But then, Jordan thought everything was suspicious. He thought the government was building cloned soldiers in some underground lab.

Libby ran a small hand through her wavy black hair, her light green eyes scanning the horizon for a sight of her brother. But Curt was probably up to his ears in watching over the births of early spring cattle, far in the northern pasture of the Powell ranch. It was almost April and the heifers, the two-year-old first-time mothers, were beginning to drop their calves right on schedule. There was little hope that Curt would show up before the real estate agent left.

Around the corner of the house, Libby heard the real estate agent speaking. She moved closer, careful to keep out of sight, to see what was going on. Her father had loved his small ranch, as his children did. It had been in their family almost as long as Jordan Powell's family had owned the Bar P.

"How long will it take to find a buyer?" Janet was asking.

"I can't really say, Mrs. Collins," the man replied. "But Jacobsville is growing by leaps and bounds. There are plenty of new families looking for reasonable housing. I think a subdivision here would be perfectly situated and I can guarantee you that any developer would pay top dollar for it."

Subdivision? Surely she must be hearing things!

But Janet's next statement put an end to any such suspicion. "I want to sell it as soon as possible," Janet continued firmly. "I have the insurance money in hand. As soon as this sale is made, I'm moving out of the country."

Another shattering revelation! Why was her stepmother in such a hurry? Her husband of barely nine months had just died, for heaven's sake!

"I'll do what I can, Mrs. Collins," the real estate agent assured her. "But you must understand that the housing market is depressed right now and I can't guarantee a sale—as much as I'd like to."

"Very well," Janet said curtly. "But keep me informed of your progress, please."

"Certainly."

Libby ran for it, careful not to let herself be seen. Her heart was beating her half to death. She'd wondered at Janet's lack of emotion when her father died. Now her mind was forming unpleasant associations.

She stood in the shadows of the front porch until she

heard the real estate agent drive away. Janet left immediately thereafter in her Mercedes.

Libby's mind was whirling. She needed help. Fortunately, she knew exactly where to go to get it.

She walked down the road toward Jordan Powell's big Spanish-style ranch house. The only transportation Libby had was a pickup truck, which was in the shop today having a water pump replaced. It was a long walk to the Powell ranch, but Libby needed fortifying to tackle her stepmother. Jordan was just the person to put steel in her backbone.

It took ten minutes to walk to the paved driveway that led through white fences to the ranch house. But it took another ten minutes to walk from the end of the driveway to the house. On either side of the fence were dark red-coated Santa Gertrudis cattle, purebred seed stock, which were the only cattle Jordan kept. One of his bulls was worth over a million dollars. He had a whole separate division that involved artificial insemination and the care of a special unit where sperm were kept. Libby had been fascinated to know that a single straw of bull semen could sell for a thousand dollars, or much more if it came from a prize bull who was dead. Jordan sold those straws to cattle ranchers all over the world. He frequently had visitors from other countries who came to tour his mammoth cattle operation. Like the Tremayne brothers, Cy Parks, and a number of other local ranchers, he was heavily into organic ranching. He used no hormones or dangerous pesticides or unnecessary antibiotics on his seed stock, even though they were never sold for beef. The herd sires he kept on the ranch lived in a huge breeding barn—as luxurious as a modern hotel—that was on property just adjacent to the Collinses' land. It was so close that they could hear the bulls bellowing from time to time.

Jordan was a local success story, the sort men liked to tell their young sons about. He started out as a cowboy long before he ever had cattle of his own. He'd grown up the only child of a former debutante and a hobby farmer. His father had married the only child of wealthy parents, who cut her off immediately when she announced her marriage. They left her only the property that Jordan now owned. His father's drinking cost him almost everything. When he wasn't drinking, he made a modest living with a few head of cattle, but after the sudden death of Jordan's mother, he withdrew from the world. Jordan was left with a hard decision to make. He took a job as a ranch hand on Duke Wright's palatial ranch and in his free time he went the rounds of the professional rodeo circuit. He was a champion bull rider, with the belt buckles and the cash to prove it.

But instead of spending that cash on good times, he'd paid off the mortgage that his father had taken on the ranch. Over the years he'd added a purebred Santa Gertrudis bull and a barn, followed by purebred heifers. He'd studied genetics with the help of a nearby retired rancher and he'd learned how to buy straws of bull semen and have his heifers artificially inseminated. His breeding program gave him the opportunity to enter his progeny in competition, which he did. Awards starting coming his way and so did stud fees for his bull. It had been a long road to prosperity, but he'd managed it, despite having to cope with an alcoholic father who eventually got behind the wheel of a truck and plowed it into a telephone pole. Jordan was left alone in the world.

Well, except for women. He sure seemed to have plenty of those, to hear her brother, Curt, talk.

Libby loved the big dusty-yellow adobe ranch house Jordan had built two years ago, with its graceful arches and black wrought-iron grillwork. There was a big fountain in the front courtyard, where Jordan kept goldfish and huge koi that came right up out of the water to look at visitors. It even had a pond heater, to keep the fish alive all winter. It was a dream of a place. It would have been just right for a family. But everybody said that Jordan Powell would never get married. He liked his freedom too much.

She went up to the front door and rang the doorbell. She knew how she must look in her mud-stained jeans and faded T-shirt, her boots caked in mud, like her denim jacket. She'd been helping the lone part-time worker on their small property pull a calf. It was a dirty business, something her pristine stepmother would never have done. Libby still missed her father. His unexpected death had been a horrible blow to Curt and Libby, who were only just getting used to Riddle Collins's new wife.

No sooner was Riddle buried than Janet fought to get her hands on the quarter-of-a-million-dollar insurance policy he'd left behind, of which she alone was listed as beneficiary. She'd started spending money the day the check had arrived, with no thought for unpaid bills and Riddle's children. They were healthy and able to work, she reasoned. Besides, they had a roof over their heads. Temporarily, at least. Janet's long talk with the real estate agent today was disquieting. Riddle's new will, which his children knew nothing about, had given Janet complete and sole ownership of the house as well as Riddle's comfortable but not excessive savings account. Or so Janet said. Curt was furious. Libby hadn't said anything. She missed her father so much. She felt as if she were still walking around in a daze and it was almost April. A windy, cold almost-April, at that, she thought, feeling the chill.

She was frowning when the door opened. She jumped involuntarily when instead of the maid, Jordan Powell himself opened it.

"What the hell do you want?" he asked coldly. "Your brother's not here. He's supervising some new fencing up on the north property.

"Well?" he asked impatiently when she didn't speak immediately. "I've got things to do and I'm late already!"

He was so dashing, she thought privately. He was thirty-two, very tall, lean and muscular, with liquid black eyes and dark, wavy hair. He had a strong, masculine face that was dark from exposure to the sun and big ears and big feet. But he was handsome. Too handsome.

"Are you mute?" he persisted, scowling.

She shook her head, sighing. "I'm just speechless. You really are a dish, Jordan," she drawled.

"Will you please tell me what you want?" he grumbled. "And if it's a date, you can go right back home. I don't like being chased by women. I know you can't keep your eyes off me, but that's no excuse to come sashaying up to my front door looking for attention."

"Fat chance," she drawled, her green eyes twinkling up at him. "If I want a man, I'll try someone accessible, like a movie star or a billionaire...."

"I said I'm in a hurry," he prompted.

"Okay. If you don't want to talk to me..." she began.

He let out an impatient sigh. "Come in, then," he

muttered, looking past her. "Hurry, before you get trampled by the other hopeful women chasing me."

"That would be a short list," she told him as she went in and waited until he closed the door behind him. "You're famous for your bad manners. You aren't even housebroken."

"I beg your pardon?" he said curtly.

She grinned at him. "Your boots are full of red mud and so's that fabulously expensive wool rug you brought back from Morocco," she pointed out. "Amie's going to kill you when she sees that."

"My aunt only lives here when she hasn't got someplace else to go," he pointed out.

"Translated, that means that she's in hiding. Why are you mad at her this time?" she asked.

He gave her a long-suffering stare and sighed. "Well, she wanted to redo my bedroom. Put yellow curtains at the windows. With ruffles." He spat out the word. "She thinks it's too depressing because I like dark wood and beige curtains."

She lifted both eyebrows over laughing eyes. "You could paint the room red…."

He glared down at her. "I said women chased me, not that I brought them home in buckets," he replied.

"My mistake. Who was it last week, Senator Merrill's daughter, and before her, the current Miss Jacobs County…?"

"That wasn't my fault," he said haughtily. "She stood in the middle of the parking lot at that new Japanese place and refused to move unless I let her come home with me." Then he grinned.

She shook her head. "You're impossible."

"Come on, come on, what do you want?" He looked

at his watch. "I've got to meet your brother at the old line cabin in thirty minutes to help look over those pregnant heifers." He lifted an eyebrow and his eyes began to shimmer. They ran up and down her slender figure. "Maybe I could do you justice in fifteen minutes...."

She struck a pose. "Nobody's sticking me in between roundup and supper," she informed him. "Besides, I'm abstaining indefinitely."

He put a hand over his heart. "As God is my witness, I never asked your brother to tell you that Bill Paine had a social disease..."

"I am not sweet on Bill Paine!" she retorted.

"You were going to Houston with him to a concert that wasn't being given that night and I knew that Bill had an apartment and a bad reputation with women," he replied with clenched lips. "So I just happened to mention to one of my cowhands, who was standing beside your brother, that Bill Paine had a social disease."

She was aghast, just standing there gaping at his insolence. Curt had been very angry about her accepting a date with rich, blond Bill, who was far above them in social rank. Bill had been a client of Blake Kemp's, where he noticed Libby and started flirting with her. After Curt had told her what he overheard about Bill, she'd cancelled the date. She was glad she did. Later she'd learned that Bill had made a bet with one of his pals that he could get Libby anytime he wanted her, despite her standoffish pose.

"Of course, I don't have any social diseases," Jordan said, his deep voice dropping an octave. He checked his watch again. "Now it's down to ten minutes, if we hurry."

She threw up her hands. "Listen, I can't possibly be

seduced today, I've got to go to the grocery store. What I came to tell you is that Janet's selling the property to a developer. He wants to put a subdivision on it," she added miserably.

"A what?" he exploded. "A subdivision? Next door to my breeding barn?" His eyes began to burn. "Like hell she will!"

"Great. You want to stop her, too. Do you have some strong rope?"

"This is serious," he replied gravely. "What the hell is she doing, selling your home out from under you? Surely Riddle didn't leave her the works! What about you and Curt?"

"She says we're young and can support ourselves," she said, fighting back frustration and fury.

He didn't say anything. His silence was as eloquent as shouting. "She's not evicting you. You go talk to Kemp."

"I work for Mr. Kemp," she reminded him.

He frowned. "Which begs the question, why aren't you at work?"

She sighed. "Mr. Kemp's gone to a bar association conference in Florida," she explained. "He said I could have two vacation days while he's gone, since Mabel and Violet were going to be there in case the attorney covering his practice needed anything." She glowered at him. "I don't get much time off."

"Indeed you don't," he agreed. "Blake Kemp is a busy attorney, for a town the size of Jacobsville. You do a lot of legwork for him, don't you?"

She nodded. "It's part of a paralegal's job. I've learned a lot."

"Enough to tempt you to go to law school?"

She laughed. "No. Not that much. A history degree is enough, not to mention the paralegal training. I've had all the education I want." She frowned thoughtfully. "You know, I did think about teaching adult education classes at night...."

"Your father was well-to-do," he pointed out. "He had coin collections worth half a million, didn't he?"

"We thought so, but we couldn't find them. I suppose he sold them to buy that Mercedes Janet is driving," she said somberly.

"He loved you and Curt."

She had to fight tears. "He wrote a new will just after he married her, leaving everything to her," she said simply. "She said she had it all in his safe-deposit box, along with the passbook to his big savings account, which her name was on as well as his. The way it was set up, that account belonged to her, so there was no legal problem with it," she had to admit. "Daddy didn't leave us a penny."

"There's something fishy going on here," he said, thinking out loud.

"It sounds like it, I guess. But Daddy gave everything to her. That was his decision to make, not ours. He was crazy about her."

Jordan looked murderous. "Has the will gone through probate yet?"

She shook her head. "She said she's given it to an attorney. It's pending."

"You know the law, even better than I do. This isn't right. You should get a lawyer," he repeated. "Get Kemp, in fact, and have him investigate her. There's something not right about this, Libby. Your father was the healthiest man I ever knew. He never had any symptoms of heart trouble."

"Well, I thought that, too, and so did Curt." She sighed, glancing down at the elegant blue-and-rose carpet, and her eyes grew misty. "He was really crazy about her, though. Maybe he just didn't think we'd need much. I know he loved us...." She choked back a sob. It was still fresh, the grief.

Jordan sighed and pulled her close against his tall, powerful body. His arms were warm and comforting as they enfolded her. "Why don't you just cry, Libby?" he asked gently. "It does help."

She sniffed into his shoulder. It smelled nice. His shirt had a pleasant detergent smell to it. "Do you ever cry?"

"Bite your tongue, woman," he said at her temple. "What would happen to the ranch if I sat down and bawled every time something went wrong? Tears won't come out of Persian carpet, you just ask my aunt!"

She laughed softly, even through the tears. He was a comforting sort of man and it was surprising, because he had a quick temper and an arrogance that put most people's backs up at first meeting.

"So that's why you yell at your cowboys? So you won't cry?"

"Works for me," he chuckled. He patted her shoulder. "Feel better?"

She nodded, smiling through tears. She wiped them away with a paper towel she'd tucked into her jeans. "Thanks."

"What are prospective lovers for?" he asked, smiling wickedly, and laughing out loud when she flushed.

"You stop corrupting me, you bad influence!"

"I said nothing corrupting, I just gave advance notice of bad intentions." He laughed at her expression. "At least it stopped the cascading waterfalls," he added, tongue in cheek, as he glanced at the tear tracks down her cheeks.

"Those weren't tears," she mumbled. "It was dew." She held up a hand. "I feel it falling again!"

"Talk to Kemp," he reiterated, not adding that he was going to do the same. "If she's got a new will and a codicil, signed, make her prove it. Don't let her shove you off your own land without a fight."

"I guess I could ask to see it," she agreed. Then she winced. "I hate arguments. I hate fights."

"I'll remember that the next time you come chasing after me," he promised.

She shook her head impotently, turning to go.

"Hey."

She glanced at him over her shoulder.

"Let me know what you find out," he said. "I'm in this, too. I can't manage a subdivision right near my barn. I can't have a lot of commotion around those beautiful Santa Gerts, it stresses them out too much. It would cost a fortune to tear down that barn and stick it closer to the house. A lawsuit would be cheaper."

"There's an idea," she said brightly. "Take her to court."

"For what, trying to sell property? That's rich."

"Just trying to help us both out," she said.

He glanced at his watch again. "Five minutes left and even I'm not that good," he added. "Pity. If you hadn't kept running your mouth, by now we could have…"

"You hush, Jordan Powell!" she shot at him. "Honestly, of all the blatant, arrogant, sex-crazed ranchers in Texas…!"

She was still mumbling as she went out the door. But when she was out of sight, she grinned. He was a tonic.

THAT NIGHT, Janet didn't say a word about any real estate deals. She ate a light supper that Libby had prepared, as usual without any compliments about it.

"When are you going back to work?" she asked Libby irritably, her dyed blond hair in an expensive hairdo, her trendy silk shell and embroidered jeans marking her new wealth. "It can't be good for you to lie around here all day."

Curt, who was almost the mirror image of his sister, except for his height and powerful frame, glared at the woman. "Excuse me, since when did you do any housework or cooking around here? Libby's done both since she turned thirteen!"

"Don't you speak to me that way," Janet said haughtily. "I can throw you out anytime I like. I own everything!"

"You don't own the property until that will goes through probate," Libby replied sweetly, shocked at her own boldness. She'd never talked that way to the woman before. "You can produce it, I hope, because you're going to have to. You don't get the property yet. Maybe not even later, if everything isn't in perfect order."

"You've been talking to that rancher again, haven't you?" Janet demanded. "That damned Powell man! He's so suspicious about everything! Your father had a heart attack. He's dead. He left everything to me. What else do you want?" she raged, standing.

Libby stood, too, her face flushed. "Proof. I want

proof. And you'd better have it before you start making any deals with developers about selling Daddy's land!"

Janet started. "De...developers?"

"I heard you this afternoon with that real estate agent," Libby said, with an apologetic glance at her brother, who looked shocked. She hadn't told him. "You're trying to sell our ranch and Daddy hasn't even been dead a month!"

Curt stood up. He looked even more formidable than Libby. "Before you make any attempt to sell this land, you're going to need a lawyer, Janet," he said in that slow, cold drawl that made cowhands move faster.

"How are you going to afford one, Curt, dear?" she asked sarcastically. "You just work for wages."

"Oh, Jordan will loan us the money," Libby said confidently.

Janet's haughty expression fluttered. She threw down her napkin. "You need cooking lessons," she said spitefully. "This food is terrible! I've got to make some phone calls."

She stormed out of the room.

Libby and Curt sat back down, both angry. Libby explained about the real estate agent's visit and what she'd overheard. Curt had only just come in when Libby had put the spaghetti and garlic bread on the table. It was Curt's favorite food and his sister made it very well, he thought, despite Janet's snippy comment.

"She's not selling this place while there's a breath left in my body," he told his sister. "Anyway, she can't do that until the will is probated. And she'd better have a legitimate will."

"Jordan said we needed to get Mr. Kemp to take a

look at it," she said. "And I think we're going to need a handwriting expert to take a look, too."

He nodded.

"But what are we going to do about money to file suit?" she asked. "I was bluffing about Jordan loaning us the money. I don't know if he would."

"He's not going to want a subdivision on his doorstep, I'll tell you that," Curt said. "I'll talk to him."

"I already did," she said, surprising him. "He thinks there's something fishy going on, too."

"You can't get much past Jordan," he agreed. "I've been working myself to death trying not to think about losing Dad. I should have paid more attention to what was going on here."

"I've been grieving, too." She sighed and folded her small hands on the tablecloth. "Isn't it amazing how snippy she is, now that Daddy's not here? She was all over us like poison ivy before he died."

"She married him for what he had, Libby," he said bitterly.

"She seemed to love him…."

"She came on to me the night they came back from that Cancún honeymoon," he said bitterly.

Libby whistled. Her brother was a very attractive man. Their father, a sweet and charming man, had been overweight and balding. She could understand why Janet might have preferred Curt to his father.

"I slapped her down hard and Dad never knew." He shook his head. "How could he marry something like that?"

"He was flattered by all the attention she gave him, I guess," Libby said miserably. "And now here we are. I'll bet she sweet-talked him into changing that will. He would have done anything for her, you know that—he was crazy in love with her. He might have actually written us out of it, Curt. We have to accept that."

"Not until they can prove to me that it wasn't forged," he said stubbornly. "I'm not giving up our inheritance without a fight. Neither are you," he asserted.

She sighed. "Okay, big brother. What do you want to do?"

"When do you go back to work?"

"Monday. Mr. Kemp's out of town."

"Okay. Monday, you make an appointment for both of us to sit down with him and hash this out."

She felt better already. "Okay," she said brightly. "I'll do that very thing. Maybe we do have a chance of keeping Daddy's ranch."

He nodded. "There's always hope." He leaned back in his chair. "So you went to see Jordan." He smiled indulgently. "I can remember a time not so long ago when you ran and hid from him."

"He always seemed to be yelling at somebody," she recalled. "I was intimidated by him. Especially when I graduated from high school. I had a sort of crush on him. I was scared to death he'd notice. Not that he was ever around here that much," she added, laughing. "He and Daddy had a fight a week over water rights."

"Dad usually lost, too," Curt recalled. He studied his sister with affection. "You know, I thought maybe Jordan was sweet on you himself—he's only eight years older than you."

"He's never been sweet on me!" she flashed at him, blushing furiously. "He's hardly even smiled at me, in all the years we've lived here, until the past few months! If anything, he usually treats me like a contagious virus!"

Curt only smiled. He looked very much like her, with the same dark wavy hair and the same green eyes. "He picks at you. Teases you. Makes you laugh. You do the same thing to him. People besides me have noticed. He bristles if anyone says anything unkind about you."

Her eyes widened. "Who's been saying unkind things about me?" she asked.

"That assistant store manager over at Lord's Department Store."

"Oh. Sherry King." She leaned back in her chair. "She can't help it, you know. She was crazy about Duke Wright and he wanted to take me to the Cattleman's Ball. I wouldn't go and he didn't ask anybody else. I feel sorry for her."

"Duke's not your sort of man," he replied. "He's a mixer. Nobody in Jacobsville has been in more brawls," he said, pausing. "Well, maybe Leo Hart has."

"Leo Hart got married, he won't be brawling out at Shea's Roadhouse and Bar anymore."

"Duke's not likely to get married again. His wife took their five-year-old son to New York City, where her new job is. He says she doesn't even look after the little boy. She's too busy trying to get a promotion. The child stays with her sister while she jets all over the world closing real estate deals."

"It's a new world," Libby pointed out. "Women are competing with men for the choice jobs now. They have to move around to get a promotion."

Curt's eyes narrowed. "Maybe they should get promotions before they get pregnant," he said impatiently.

She shrugged. "Accidents happen."

"No child of mine is ever going to be an accident," Curt said firmly.

"Nice to be so superior," she teased, eyes twinkling. "Never to make mistakes…"

He swiped at her with a napkin. "You don't even stick your toes in the water, so don't lecture me about drowning."

She chuckled. "I'm sensible, I am," she retorted. "None of this angst for me. I'll just do my routine job and keep my nose out of emotional entanglements."

He studied her curiously. "You go through life avoiding any sort of risk, don't you, honey?" he mused.

She moved one shoulder restlessly. "Daddy and Mama fought all the time, remember?" she said. "I swore I'd never get myself into a fix like that. She told me that she and Daddy were so happy when they first met, when they first married. Then, six months later, she was pregnant with you and they couldn't manage one pleasant meal together without shouting." She shook her head. "That means you can't trust emotions. It's better to use your brain when you think about marrying somebody. Love is…sticky," she concluded. "And it causes insanity, I'm sure of it."

"Why don't you ask Kemp if that's why he's stayed single so long? He's in his middle thirties, isn't he, and never even been engaged."

"Who'd put up with him?" she asked honestly. "Now there's a mixer for you," she said enthusiastically. "He actually threw another lawyer out the front door and onto the sidewalk last month. Good thing there was a welcome mat there, it sort of broke the guy's fall."

"What did he want?" Curt asked.

She shook her head. "I have no idea. But I don't expect him to be a repeat client."

Curt chuckled. "I see what you mean."

LIBBY WENT TO bed early that night, without another word to Janet. She knew that anything she said would be too much. But she did miss her father and she couldn't believe that he wouldn't have mentioned Libby and Curt in his will. He did love them. She knew he did.

She thought about Jordan Powell, too, and about Curt's remark that he thought Jordan was sweet on her. She tingled all over at the thought. But that wasn't going to happen, she assured herself. Jordan was gorgeous and he could have his pick of pretty women. Libby Collins would be his last resort. The world wasn't ending yet, so she was out of the running.

She rolled over, closed her eyes, and went to sleep.

CHAPTER TWO

JANET WASN'T AT breakfast the next morning. Her new gold Mercedes was gone and she hadn't left a note. Libby saw it as a bad omen.

The weekend passed with nothing remarkable except for Janet's continued absence. The truck was ready Saturday and Curt picked it up in town, catching a lift with one of Jordan's cowboys. It wasn't as luxurious as a Mercedes, but it had a good engine and it was handy for hauling things like salt blocks and bales of hay. Libby tried to picture hauling hay in Janet's Mercedes and almost went hysterical with laughter.

Libby went back to work at Blake Kemp's office early Monday morning, dropped off by Curt on his way to the feed store for Jordan. She felt as if she hadn't really had a vacation at all.

Violet Hardy, Mr. Kemp's secretary, who was dark-haired, blue-eyed, pretty and somewhat overweight, smiled at her as she came in the door. "Hi! Did you have a nice vacation?"

"I spent it working," Libby confessed. "How did things go here?"

Violet groaned. "Don't even ask."

"That bad, huh?" Libby remarked.

Mabel, the blonde grandmother who worked at reception, turned in her chair after transferring a call into Mr. Kemp's office. "Bad isn't the word, Libby," she said in a whisper, glancing down the hall to make sure the doors were all closed. "That lawyer Mr. Kemp got to fill in for him got two cases confused and sent the clients to the wrong courtrooms in different counties."

"Yes—" Violet nodded "—and one of them came in here and tried to punch Mr. Kemp."

Libby pursed her lips. "No. Did he have insurance?"

All three women chuckled.

"For an attorney who handles so many assault cases," Violet whispered, "he doesn't practice what he preaches. Mr. Kemp punched the guy back and they wound up out on the street. Our police chief, Cash Grier, broke it up and almost arrested Mr. Kemp."

"What about the other guy? Didn't he start it?" Libby exclaimed.

"The other guy was Duke Wright," Violet confessed, watching Libby color. "And Chief Grier said that instead of blaming Mr. Kemp for handling Mrs. Wright's divorce, he should thank him for not bankrupting Mr. Wright in the process!"

"Then what?" Libby asked.

All three women glanced quickly down the hall.

"Mr. Wright threw a punch at Chief Grier."

"Well, that was smart thinking. Duke's in the hospital, then?" Libby asked facetiously.

"Nope," Violet said, her blue eyes twinkling. "But he was in jail briefly until he made bail." She shook her head. "I don't expect he'll try that twice."

"Crime has fallen about fifty percent since we got Cash Grier as chief," Violet sighed, smiling.

"And Judd Dunn as assistant chief," Libby reminded her.

"Poor Mr. Wright," Mabel said. "He does have the worst luck. Remember that Jack Clark who worked for him, who was convicted of murdering that woman in Victoria? Mr. Wright sure hated the publicity. It came just when he was trying to get custody of his son."

"Mr. Wright would have a lot less trouble if he didn't spend so much time out looking for it," came a deep, gruff voice from behind them.

They all jumped. Blake Kemp was standing just at the entrance to the hallway with a brief in one hand and a coffee cup in the other. He was as much a dish as Jordan Powell. He had wavy dark hair and blue eyes and the most placid, friendly face—until he got in front of a jury. Nobody wanted to be across the courtroom from Kemp when a trial began. There was some yellow and purple discoloration on one high cheekbone, where a fist had apparently landed a blow. Duke Wright, Libby theorized silently.

"Libby, before you do anything else, would you make a pot of coffee, please?" he asked in a long-suffering tone. He impaled a wincing Violet with his pale blue eyes. "I don't give a damn what some study says is best for me, I want caffeine. C-A-F-F-E-I-N-E," he added, spelling it letter by letter for Violet's benefit.

Violet lifted her chin and her own blue eyes glared right back at him. "Mr. Kemp, if you drank less of it, you might not be so bad-tempered. I mean, really, that's the second person you've thrown out of our office in a month! Chief Grier said that was a new city record…."

Kemp's eyes were blazing now, narrow and intent. "Miss Hardy, do you want to still be employed here tomorrow?"

Violet looked as if she was giving that question a lot of deliberation. "But, sir…" she began.

"I like caffeine. I'm not giving it up," Kemp said

curtly. "You don't change my routine in this office. Is that clear?"

"But, Mr. Kemp—!" she argued.

"I don't remember suggesting anything so personal to you, Miss Hardy," he shot back, clearly angry. "I could, however," he added, and his cold blue eyes made insinuations about her figure, which was at least two dress sizes beyond what it should have been.

All three women gasped at the outrageous insinuation and then glared at their boss.

Violet flushed and stood up, as angry as he was, but not intimidated one bit by the stare. "My...my father always said that a woman should look like a woman and not a skeleton encased in skin. I may be a little overweight, Mr. Kemp, but at least I'm doing something about it!"

He glanced pointedly at a cake in a box on her desk.

She colored. "I live out near the Hart Ranch. I promised Tess Hart I'd pick that up at the bakery for her before I came to work and drop it by her house when I go home for lunch. It's for a charity tea party this afternoon." She was fuming. "I do not eat cake! Not anymore."

He stared at her until she went red and sat back down. She averted her eyes and went back to work. Her hands on the computer keyboard were trembling.

"You fire me if you want to, Mr. Kemp, but nothing I said to you was as mean as what you were insinuating to me with that look," Violet choked. "I know I weigh too much. You don't have to rub it in. I was only trying to help you."

Mabel and Libby were still glaring at him. He shifted uncomfortably and put the brief down on Violet's desk with a slap. "There are six spelling errors in that. You'll have to redo it. You can buzz me when the coffee's ready," he added shortly. He turned on his heel and took his coffee cup back into his office. As an afterthought, he slammed the door.

"Oh, and like anybody short of a druggist could read those chicken scratches on paper that you call handwriting!" Violet muttered, staring daggers after him.

Libby let out the breath she'd been holding and gaped at sweet, biddable Violet, who'd never talked back to Mr. Kemp in the eight months she'd worked for him. So did Mabel.

"Well, it's about time!" Mabel said, laughing delightedly. "Good for you, Violet. It's no good, letting a man walk all over you, no matter how crazy you are about him!"

"Hush!" Violet exclaimed, glancing quickly down the hall. "He'll hear you!"

"He doesn't know," Libby said comfortingly, putting an arm around Violet. "And we'll never tell. I'm proud of you, Violet."

"Me, too," Mabel grinned.

Violet sighed. "I guess he'll fire me. It might not be a bad thing. I spend too much time trying to take care of him and he hates it." Her blue eyes were wistful under their long, thick lashes. "You know, I've lost fifteen pounds," she murmured. "And I'm down a dress size."

"A new diet?" Libby asked absently as she checked her "in" tray.

"A new gym, just for women," Violet confessed with a grin. "I love it!"

Libby looked at the other woman with admiration. "You're really serious about this, aren't you?"

Violet's shoulder moved gently. She was wearing a purple dress with a high collar and lots of frills on the bodice and a very straight skirt that clung to her hips. It was the worst sort of dress for a woman who had a big bust and wide hips, but nobody had the heart to tell Violet. "I had to do something. I mean, look at me! I'm so big!"

"You're not that big. But I think it's great that you're trying so hard, Violet," Libby said gently. "And to keep you on track, Mabel and I are giving up dessert when you eat lunch with us."

"I have to go home and see about Mother most every day at lunchtime," Violet confessed. "She hates that. She said I was wasting my whole life worrying about her, when I should be out having fun. But she's already had two light strokes in the past year since Daddy died. I can't leave her alone."

"Honey, people like you are why there's a heaven," Mabel murmured softly. "You're one in a million."

Violet waved her away. "Everybody's got problems," she laughed. "For all we know, Mr. Kemp has much bigger ones than we do. He's such a good person. When Mother had that last stroke, the bad one, he even drove me to the hospital after I got the call."

"He is a good person," Libby agreed. "But so are you."

"You'd better make that coffee, I guess," Violet said wistfully. "I really thought I could make it half and half and he wouldn't be able to taste the difference. He's so uptight lately. He's always in a hurry, always under pressure. He drinks caffeine like water and it's so bad for his heart. I know about hearts. My dad died of a heart attack last year. I was just trying to help."

"It's hard to help a rattlesnake across the road, Violet," Mabel said, tongue in cheek.

Libby was curious about the coincidence of Violet's father dying of a heart attack, like her father, such a short time ago. "Violet could find one nice thing to say about a serial killer," Libby agreed affectionately. "Even worse, she could find one nice thing to say about my stepmother."

"Ouch," Mabel groaned. "Now there's a hard case if I ever saw one." She shook her head. "People in Branntville are still talking about her and old man Darby."

Libby, who'd just finished filling the coffeepot, started it brewing and turned jerkily. "Excuse me?"

"Didn't I ever tell you?" Mabel asked absently. "Just a sec. Good morning, Kemp Law Offices," she said. "Yes, sir, I'll connect you." She started to push the intercom button when she saw with shock that it was already depressed. The light was on the switch. She and Libby, who'd also seen it, exchanged agonized glances. Quickly, without telling Violet, she pushed it off and then on again. "Mr. Kemp, it's Mrs. Lawson for you on line two." She waited, hung up, and swung her chair around. She didn't dare tell poor Violet that Mr. Kemp had probably heard every single word she'd said about him.

"Your stepmother, Janet," Mabel told Libby, "was working at a nursing home over in Branntville. She sweet-talked an old man who was a patient there into leaving everything he had to her." She shook her head. "They said that Janet didn't even give him a proper funeral. She had him cremated and put in an urn and there was a graveside service. They said she bought a designer suit to wear to it."

Libby was getting cold chills. There were too many

similarities there to be a coincidence. Janet had wanted to have Riddle Collins cremated, too, but Curt and Libby had talked to the funeral director and threatened a lawsuit if he complied with Janet's request. They went home and told Janet the same thing and also insisted on a church funeral at the Presbyterian church where Riddle had been a member since childhood. Janet had been furious, but in the end, she reluctantly agreed.

Violet wasn't saying anything, but she had a funny look on her face and she seemed pale. She turned away before the others saw. But Libby's expression was thought-provoking.

"You're thinking something. What?" Mabel asked Libby.

Fortunately, the phone rang again while Libby was deciding if it was wise to share her thoughts.

Violet got up from her desk and went close to Libby. "She wanted to cremate your father, too, didn't she?"

Libby nodded.

"You should go talk to Mr. Kemp."

Libby smiled. "You know, Violet, I think you're right." She hugged the other girl and went back to Mabel. "When he gets off the phone, I need to talk to him."

Mabel grinned. "Now you're talking." She checked the board. "He's free. Just a sec." She pushed a button. "Mr. Kemp, Libby needs to speak to you, if it's convenient."

"Send her in, Mrs. Jones."

"Good luck," Mabel said, crossing her fingers.

Libby grinned back.

"COME IN," Kemp said, opening the door for Libby and closing it behind her. "Have a seat. I don't need ESP to know what's on your mind. I had a call from Jordan Powell at home last night."

Her eyebrows arched. "Well, he jumped the gun!"

"He's concerned. Probably with good reason," he added. "I went ahead on my own and had a private detective I know run a check on Janet's background. This isn't the first time she's become a widow."

"I know," Libby said. "Mabel says an elderly man in a nursing home left her everything he had. She had him sent off to be cremated immediately after they got him to the funeral home."

He nodded. "And I understand from Don Hedgely at our funeral home here that she tried to have the same thing done with your father, but you and your brother threatened a lawsuit."

"We did," Libby said. "Daddy didn't believe in cremation. He would have been horrified."

Kemp leaned back in his desk chair and crossed his long legs, with his hands behind his head. He pursed his lips and narrowed his blue eyes, deep in thought. "There's another thing," he said. "Janet was fired from that nursing home for being too friendly with their wealthiest patients. One of whom—the one you know about—was an elderly widower with no children. He died of suspicious causes and left her his estate."

Libby folded her arms. She felt chilled all over now. "Wasn't it enough for her?" she wondered out loud.

"Actually, it took the entire estate to settle his gambling debts," he murmured. "Apparently, he liked the horses a little too much."

"Then there was our father." She anticipated his next thought.

He shook his head. "That was after Mr. Hardy in San Antonio."

Libby actually gasped. It couldn't be!

Kemp leaned forward quickly. "Do you think Violet is happy having to live in a rented firetrap with her invalid mother? Her parents were wealthy. But a waitress at Mr. Hardy's favorite restaurant apparently began a hot affair with him and talked him into making her a loan of a quarter of a million dollars to save her parents from bankruptcy and her father from suicide. He gave her a check and had a heart attack before he could stop payment on it—which he planned to do. He told his wife and begged forgiveness of her and his daughter before he died." His eyes narrowed. "He died shortly after he was seen with a pretty blonde at a San Antonio motel downtown."

"You think it was Janet? That it wasn't a heart attack at all—that she killed him?"

"I think there are too many coincidences for comfort in her past," Kemp said flatly. "But the one eyewitness who saw her with Hardy at that motel was unable to pick her out of a lineup. She'd had her hair color changed just the day before the lineup. She remained a brunette for about a week and then changed back to blond."

Libby's face tightened. "She might have killed my father," she bit off.

"That is a possibility," Kemp agreed. "It's early days yet, Libby. I can't promise you anything. But if she's guilty and I can get her on a witness stand, in a court of law, I can break her," he said with frightening confidence. "She'll tell me everything she knows."

She swallowed. "I don't want her to get away with it," she began. "But Curt and I work for wages..."

He flapped his hand in her direction. "Every lawyer takes a pro bono case occasionally. I haven't done it in months. You and Curt can be my public service for the year," he added, and he actually smiled. It made him look younger, much less dangerous than he really was.

"I don't know what to say," she said, shaking her head in disbelief.

He leaned forward. "Say you'll be careful," he replied. "I can't find any suspicion that she ever helped a young person have a heart attack, but I don't doubt for a minute that she knows how. I'm working with Micah Steele on that aspect of it. There isn't much he doesn't know about the darker side of medicine, even if he is a doctor. And what he doesn't know about black ops and untimely death, Cash Grier does."

"I thought Daddy died of a heart condition nobody knew he had." She took a deep breath. "When I tell Curt, he'll go crazy."

"Let me tell him," Kemp said quietly. "It will be easier."

"Okay."

"Meanwhile, you have to go back home and pretend that nothing's wrong, that your stepmother is innocent of any foul play. That's imperative. If you give her a reason to think she's being suspected of anything, she'll bolt, and we may never find her."

"We'd get our place back without a fight," Libby commented wistfully.

"And a woman who may have murdered your father, among others, would go free," Kemp replied. "Is that really what you want?"

Libby shook her head. "Of course not. I'll do whatever you say."

"We'll be working in the background. The most important thing is to keep the pressure on, a little at a time, so that she doesn't get suspicious. Tell her you've spoken to an attorney about the will, but nothing more."

"Okay," she agreed.

He got up. "And don't tell Violet I said anything to you about her father," he added. His broad shoulders moved restlessly under his expensive beige suit, as if he were carrying some difficult burden. "She's...sensitive."

What a surprising comment from such an insensitive man, she thought, but she didn't dare say it. She only smiled. "Certainly."

She was reaching for the doorknob when he called her back. "Yes, sir?"

"When you make another pot of coffee," he said hesitantly, "I guess we could use some of that half and half."

Her dropped jaw told its own story.

"She means well," he said abruptly, and turned back to his desk. "But for now, I want it strong and black and straight up. Call me when it's made and I'll bring my cup."

"It should be ready right now," she faltered. Even in modern times, few bosses went to get their own coffee. But Mr. Kemp was something of a puzzle. Perhaps, Libby thought wickedly as she followed him down the hall, even to himself.

He glanced at Violet strangely, but he didn't make any more comments. Violet sat with her eyes glued to her computer screen until he poured his coffee and went back to his office.

Libby wanted so badly to say something to her, but she didn't know what. In the end, she just smiled and made a list of the legal precedents she would have to look up for Mr. Kemp at the law library in the county courthouse. Thank God, she thought, for computers.

SHE WAS ON her way home in the pickup truck after a long day when she saw Jordan on horseback, watching several men drive the pregnant heifers into pastures close to the barn. He had a lot of money invested in those purebred calves and he wasn't risking them to predators or difficult births. He looked so good on horseback, she thought dreamily. He was arrow-straight and his head, covered by that wide-brimmed creamy Stetson he favored, was tilted in a way that was particularly his. She could have picked him out of any crowd at a distance just by the way he carried himself.

He turned his head when he heard the truck coming down the long dirt road and he motioned Libby over to the side.

She parked the truck, cut off the engine, and stood on the running board to talk to him over the top of the old vehicle. "I wish I had a camera," she called. "Mama Powell, protecting his babies..."

"You watch it!" he retorted, shaking a finger at her.

She laughed. "What are you going to do, jump the fence and run me down?"

"Poor old George here couldn't jump a fence. He's twenty-four," he added, patting the old horse's withers. "He hates his corral. I thought I'd give him a change of scenery, since I wasn't going far."

"Everything gets old, I guess. Most everything, anyway," she added with a faraway, wistful look in her eyes. She had an elderly horse of her own, that she might yet have to give away because it was hard to feed and keep him on her salary.

He dismounted and left George's reins on the ground to jump the fence and talk to her. "Did you see Kemp?" he asked.

"Yes. He said you phoned him."

"I asked a few questions and got some uncomfortable answers," he said, coming around the truck to stand beside her. His big lean hands went to her waist and he lifted her down close to him. Too close. She could smell his shaving lotion and feel the heat off his body under the Western cut long-sleeved shirt. In her simple, jacketed suit, she felt overly dressed.

"You don't look too bad when you fix up," he commented, approving her light makeup and the gray suit that made her eyes look greener than they were.

"You don't look too bad when you don't," she replied. "What uncomfortable answers are you getting?"

His eyes were solemn. "I think you can guess. I don't like the idea of you and Curt alone in that house with her."

"We have a shotgun somewhere. I'll make a point of buying some shells for it."

He shook her by the waist gently. "I'm not teasing. Can you lock your bedroom door? Can Curt?"

"It's an old house, Jordan," she faltered. "None of the bedroom doors have locks."

"Tell Curt I said to get bolts and put them on. Do it when she's not home. In the meantime, put a chair under the doorknob."

"But why?" she asked uncertainly.

He drew a long breath. His eyes went to her soft bow of a mouth and he studied it for several seconds before he spoke. "There's one very simple way to cause a heart attack. You can do it with a hypodermic syringe filled with nothing but air."

She couldn't speak for a moment. "Could they...tell that if they did an autopsy on my father?"

"I'm not a forensic specialist, despite the fact that there are half a dozen shows on TV that can teach you how to think you are. I'll ask somebody who knows," he added.

She hated the thought of disinterring her father. But it would be terrible if he'd met with foul play and it never came out.

He tilted her face up to his narrow dark eyes. "You're worrying. Don't. I'm as close as your phone, night or day."

She smiled gently. "Thanks, Jordan."

His thumbs moved on her waist while he looked down at her. His face hardened. His eyes were suddenly on her soft mouth, with real hunger.

The world stopped. It seemed like that. She met his searching gaze and couldn't breathe. Her body felt achy. Hungry. Feverish. She swallowed, hoping it didn't show.

"If you play your cards right, I might let you kiss me," he murmured.

Her heart skipped. "Excuse me?"

One big shoulder lifted and fell. "Where else are you going to get any practical experience?" he asked. "Duke Wright is a candidate for the local nursing home, after all..."

"He's thirty-six!" she exclaimed. "That isn't old!"

"I'm thirty-two," he pointed out. "I have all my own teeth." He grinned to display them. "And I can still outrun at least two of my horses."

"That's an incentive to kiss you?" she asked blankly.

"Think of the advantages if you kiss me during a stampede," he pointed out.

She laughed. He was a case. Her eyes adored him. "I'll keep you in mind," she promised. "But you mustn't get your hopes up. This town is full of lonely bachelors who can't get women to kiss them. You'll have to take a number and wait."

"Wait until what?" he asked, tweaking her waist with his thumbs.

"I don't know. Christmas? I could kiss you as part of your present."

His eyebrows arched. "What's the other part?"

"It's not Christmas. Listen, I have to get home and make supper."

"I'll send Curt on down," he said.

She was seeing a new pattern. "To make sure I'm not left alone with Janet, is that right?"

"For my peace of mind," he corrected. "I've gotten... used to you," he added slowly. "As a neighbor," he added deliberately. "Think how hard it would be to break in another one, at my age."

"You just said you weren't old," she reminded him.

"Maybe I am, just a little," he confessed. He drew her up until she was standing completely against him, so close that she could feel the hard press of his muscular legs against her own. "Come on," he taunted, bending his head with a mischievous little smile. "You know you're dying to kiss me."

"I am?" she whispered dreamily as she studied the long, wide, firm curve of his lips.

"Desperately."

She felt his nose brushing against hers. Somewhere, a horse was neighing. A jet flew over. The wind ruffled leaves in a small tree nearby. She was deaf to any sound other than the throb of her own heartbeat. There was nothing in the world except Jordan's mouth, a scant inch from her own. He'd never kissed her. She wanted him to. She ached for him to.

His hands tightened on her waist, lifting her closer. "Come on, chicken. Give it all you've got."

Her hands were flat against his chest, feeling the warm muscles under his cotton shirt. She tasted his breath. Her arms slid up to his shoulders. He had her hypnotized. She wanted nothing more than to drown in him.

"That's it," he whispered.

She closed her eyes and lifted up on her tiptoes as she felt the slow, soft press of her own lips against his for the first time.

Her knees were weak. She didn't think they were going to support her. And still Jordan didn't move, didn't respond.

Frustrated, she tried to lift up higher, her arms circled his neck and pulled, trying to make his mouth firm and deepen above hers. But she couldn't budge him.

"Oh, you arro…!"

It was the opening he'd been waiting for. His mouth crushed down against her open lips and his arms contracted hungrily. Libby moaned sharply at the rush of sensation it caused in her body. It had never been like this in her life. She was burning alive. She ached. She longed. She couldn't get close enough….

"Hey, Jordan!"

The distant shout broke the spell. Jordan jerked his head around to see one of his men waving a wide-brimmed hat and gesturing toward a pickup truck that was driving right out into the pasture where Jordan was putting those pregnant heifers.

"It's the feed supplement I ordered," he murmured, letting her go slowly. "Damn his timing."

He didn't smile when he said that. She couldn't manage even a word.

He touched her softly swollen mouth with his fingertips. "Maybe you could take me on a date and we could get lost on some deserted country road," he suggested.

She took a breath and shook her head to clear it. "I do not seduce men in parked cars," she pointed out.

He snapped his fingers. "Damn!"

"He's waving at you again," she noted, looking over his shoulder.

"All right, I'll go to work. But I'll send Curt on home." He touched her cheek. "Be careful, okay?"

She managed a weak smile. "Okay."

He turned and vaulted the fence, mounting George with the ease of years of practice as a horseman. "See you."

She nodded and watched him ride away. Her life had just changed course, in the most unexpected way.

CHAPTER THREE

BUT ALL JORDAN'S WORRY—and Libby's unease—was for nothing. When she got home, Janet's Mercedes was gone. There was a terse little note on the hall table that read, Gone to Houston shopping, back tomorrow.

Even as she was reading it, Curt came in the back door, bareheaded and sweaty.

"She's gone?" he asked.

She nodded. "Left a note. She's gone to Houston and won't be back until tomorrow."

"Great. It'll give me time to put locks on the bedroom doors," he said.

She sighed. "Jordan's been talking to you, hasn't he?" she asked.

"Yes, and he's been kissing you, apparently," he murmured, grinning. "Old Harry had to yell himself hoarse to get Jordan's attention when they brought those feed supplements out."

She flushed. She couldn't think of a single defense. But she hadn't heard Harry yelling, except one time. No wonder people were talking.

"Interested in you, is he?" Curt asked softly.

"He wanted me to ask him out on a date and get him lost on a dirt road," she said.

"And you said...?"

She moved restively. "I said that I didn't seduce men

in parked cars on deserted roads, of course," she assured him.

He looked solemn. "Sis, we've never really talked about Jordan...."

"And we really don't need to, now," she interrupted. "I'm a big girl and I know all about Jordan. He's only teasing. I'm older and he's doing it in a different way, that's all."

Curt wasn't smiling. "He isn't."

She cleared her throat. "Well, it doesn't matter. He's not a marrying man and I'm not a frivolous woman. Besides, his tastes run to beauty queens and state senators' daughters."

He hesitated.

She smiled before he could say anything else. "Let it drop. We've got enough on our minds now without adding more to them. Let's rush to the hardware store and buy locks before she gets back."

He shrugged and let it go. There would be another time to discuss Jordan Powell.

WHEN LIBBY GOT home from work Tuesday evening she was still reeling from the shocking news that a fed-up Violet had quit her job and gone to work for Duke Wright. Blake Kemp had not taken the news well. Her mood lifted when she found Jordan's big burgundy double-cabbed pickup truck sitting in her front yard. He was sitting on the side of the truck bed, whittling a piece of wood with a pocket knife, his broad-brimmed hat pushed way back on his head. He looked up at her approach and jumped down to meet her.

"You're late," he complained.

She got out of her car, grabbing her purse on the

way. "I had to stay late and type up some notes for Mr. Kemp."

He scowled. "That's Violet's job."

"Violet's leaving," she said on a sigh. "She's going to work for Duke Wright."

"But she's crazy for Kemp, isn't she?" Jordan wondered.

She scowled at him. "You aren't supposed to know that," she pointed out.

"Everybody knows that." He looked around the yard. "Janet hasn't shown up. Curt said she'd gone to Houston."

"That's what the note said," she agreed, walking beside him to the front porch. "Curt put the locks on last night."

"I know. I asked him."

She unlocked the door and pushed it open. "Want some coffee?"

"I'd love some. Eggs? Bacon? Cinnamon toast?" he added.

"Oh, I see," she mused with a grin. "Amie's gone and you're starving, huh?"

He shrugged nonchalantly. "She didn't have to leave. I only yelled a little."

"You shouldn't scare her. She's old."

"Dirt's old. Amie's a spring chicken." He chuckled. "Anyway, she was shopping for antique furniture on the Internet and she found a side table she couldn't live without in San Antonio. She drove up to look at it. She said she'd see me in a couple of days."

"And you're starving."

"You make the nicest scrambled eggs, Libby," he coaxed. "Nice crisp bacon. Delicious cinnamon toast. Strong coffee."

"It isn't the time of day for breakfast."

"No law that you can't have breakfast for supper," he pointed out.

She sighed. "I was planning a beef casserole."

"It won't go with scrambled eggs."

She put her hands on her hips and gave him a considering look. "You really are a pain, Jordan."

He moved a step closer and caught her by the waist with two big lean hands. "If you want me to marry you, you have to prove that you're a good cook."

"Marry...?"

Before she could get another word out, his mouth crushed down over her parted lips. He kissed her slowly, tenderly, his big hands steely at her waist, as if he were keeping them there by sheer will when he wanted to pull her body much closer to his own.

Her hands rested on his clean shirt while she tried to decide if he was kidding. He had to be. Certainly he didn't want to marry anybody. He'd said so often enough.

He lifted his head scant inches. "Stop doing that."

She blinked. "Doing what?"

"Thinking. You can't kiss a man and do analytical formulae in your head at the same time."

"You said you'd never marry anybody...."

His eyes were oddly solemn. "Maybe I changed my mind."

Before she could answer him, he bent his head and kissed her again. This time it wasn't a soft, teasing sample of a kiss. It was bold, brash, invasive and possessive. He enveloped her in his hard arms and crushed her down the length of his powerful body. She felt a husky groan go into her mouth as he grew more insistent.

Against her hips, she felt the sudden hardness of his body. As if he realized that and didn't like having her feel it, he moved away a breath. Slowly, he lifted his hard mouth from her swollen lips and looked down at her quietly, curiously.

"This is getting to be a habit," she said breathlessly. Her body was throbbing, like her heart. She wondered if he could hear it.

His dark eyes fell to the soft, quick pulsing of her heart, visible where her loose blouse bounced in time with it. Beneath it, two hard little peaks were blatant. He saw them and his eyes began to glitter.

"Don't look at me like that," she whispered gruffly.

His eyes shot up to catch hers. "You want me," he said curtly. "I can see it. Feel it."

Her breath was audible. "You conceited…!"

His hands caught her hips and pushed them against his own. "It's mutual."

"I noticed!" she burst out, jerking away from him, red-faced.

"Don't be such a child," he chided, but gently. "You're old enough to know what desire feels like."

Her face grew redder. "I will not be seduced by you in my own kitchen over scrambled eggs!"

His eyebrows arched. "You're making them, then?" he asked brightly.

"Oh!" She pushed away from him. "You just won't take no for an answer!"

He smiled speculatively. "You can put butter on that," he agreed. His eyes went up and down her slender figure while she walked through to the kitchen, leaving her purse on the hall table as she went. "Not going to change before you start cooking?" he drawled, following her in. "I don't mind helping."

She shot him a dark glare.

He held up both hands. "Just offering to be helpful, that's all."

She laughed helplessly. "I can dress myself, thanks."

"I was offering to help you undress," he pointed out.

She had to fight down another blush. She was a modern, independent woman. It was just that the thought of Jordan's dark eyes on her naked body had an odd, pleasurable effect on her. Especially after that bone-shaking kiss.

"You shouldn't go around kissing women like that unless you mean business," she pointed out as she got out a big iron skillet to cook the bacon in.

"What makes you think I didn't mean it?" he probed, straddling a kitchen chair to watch her work.

"You? Mr. I'll-Never-Marry?"

"I didn't say that. I said I didn't want to get married."

"Well, what's the difference?" she asked, exasperated.

His dark eyes slid down to her breasts with a boldness that made her uncomfortable. "There's always the one woman you can't walk away from."

"There's no such woman in your life."

"Think so?" He frowned. "What are you doing with that?" he asked as she put the skillet on the burner.

"You're the one who wanted bacon!" she exclaimed.

"Bacon, yes, not liquid fat!" He got up from the chair, pulled a couple of paper towels from the roll and pulled a plate from the cabinet. "Don't you know how to cook bacon?"

He proceeded to show her, layering several strips of bacon on a paper-towel-coated plate and putting another paper towel on top of it.

She was watching with growing amusement. "And it's going to cook like that," she agreed. "Uh-huh."

"It goes in the microwave," he said with exaggerated patience. "You cook it for…"

"What's wrong?"

He was looking around, frowning, with the plate in one big hand. He opened cupboards and checked in the china cabinet. "All right, I'll bite. Where is it?"

"Where is what?"

"Your microwave oven!"

She sighed. "Jordan, we don't have a microwave oven."

"You're kidding." He scowled at her. "Everybody's got a microwave oven!"

"We haven't got one."

He studied her kitchen and slowly he put the plate back on the counter with a frown. The stove was at least ten years old. It was one of the old-fashioned ones that still had knobs instead of buttons. She didn't even have a dishwasher. Everything in the kitchen was old, like the cast-iron skillet she used for most every meal.

"I didn't realize how hard things were for you and Curt," he said after a minute. "I thought your father had all kinds of money."

"He did, until he married Janet," she replied. "She wanted to eat out all the time. The stove was worn-out and so was the dishwasher. He was going to re-place them, but she had him buy her a diamond ring she wanted, instead."

He scowled angrily. "I'm sorry. I'm really sorry."

His apology was unexpected and very touching. "It's all right," she said gently. "I'm used to doing things the hard way. Really I am."

He moved close, framing her oval face in his big warm hands. "You never complain."

She smiled. "Why should I? I'm healthy and strong and able to do anything that needs doing around here."

"You make me ashamed, Libby," he said softly. He bent and kissed her with aching tenderness.

"Why?" she whispered at his firm mouth.

"I'm not really sure. Do that again."

He nibbled her upper lip, coaxing her body to lean heavily against his. "This is even better than dessert," he murmured as he deepened the pressure of his mouth. "Come here!"

He lifted her against him and kissed her hungrily, until her mouth felt faintly bruised from the slow, insistent pressure. It was like flying. She loved kissing Jordan. She hoped he was never going to stop!

But all at once, he did, with a jerky breath. "This won't do," he murmured a little huskily. "Curt will be home any minute. I don't want him to find us on the kitchen table."

Her mouth flew open. "Jordan!"

He shrugged and looked sheepish. "It was heading that way. Here." He handed her the plate of bacon. "I guess you'd better fry it. I don't think it's going to cook by itself."

She smiled up at him. "I'll drain it on paper towels and get rid of some of the grease after it's cooked."

"Why are you throwing those away?" he asked when she put the bacon on to fry and threw away the paper towels it had laid on.

"Bacteria," she told him. "You never put meat back on a plate where it's been lying, raw."

"They teach you that in school these days, I guess?"

She nodded. "And lots of other stuff."

"Like how to use a prophylactic…?" he probed wickedly.

She flushed. "They did not! And I'll wash your mouth out with soap if you say that again!" she threatened.

"Never mind. I'll teach you how to use it, when the time comes," he added outrageously.

"I am not using a prophylactic!"

"You want kids right away, then?" he persisted.

"I am not having sex with you on my kitchen table!"

There was a sudden stunned silence. Jordan was staring over her shoulder and his expression was priceless. Grimacing, she turned to find her older brother standing there with his mouth open.

"Oh, shut your mouth, Curt," she grumbled. "It was a hypothetical discussion!"

"Except for the part about the prophylactic," Jordan said with a howling mad grin. "Did you know that they don't teach people how to use them in school?"

Curt lost it. He almost doubled over laughing.

Libby threw a dish towel at him. "Both of you, out of my kitchen! I'll call you when it's ready. Go on, out!"

They left the room obediently, still laughing.

Libby shook her head and started turning the bacon.

"HASN'T JANET EVEN phoned to say if she was coming back today?" Jordan asked the two siblings when they were seated at the kitchen table having supper.

"There wasn't anything on the answering machine," Libby said. "I checked it while the bacon was cooking. Maybe she thinks we're on to something and she's running for it."

"No, I don't think so," Curt replied at once. "She's

not about to leave this property to us. Not considering what it would be worth to a developer."

"I agree," Jordan said. "I've given Kemp the phone number of a private detective I know in San Antonio," he added. "He's going to look into the case for me."

"We'll pay you back," Curt promised, and Libby nodded.

"Let's cross our bridges one at a time," Jordan replied. "First order of business is to see if we can find any proof that she's committed a crime in the past."

"Mabel said she was suspected in a death at a nursing home in Branntville," she volunteered.

"So Kemp told me," Jordan said. "This is good bacon," he added.

"Thanks," she said with a smile.

"Violet's father was another one of her victims," Libby added.

Jordan nodded while Curt scowled curiously at both of them. "But they can't prove that. Not unless there's enough evidence to order an exhumation. And, considering the physical condition of Violet's mother," he added, "I'm afraid she'd never be able to agree to it. The shock would probably kill her mother."

Libby sighed. "Poor Violet. She's had such a hard life. And now to have to change jobs…"

"She works for Kemp, doesn't she?" Curt asked.

"She did. She quit today," Libby replied. "She's going to work for Duke Wright."

"Oh, Sherry King's going to love that," Curt chuckled.

"She doesn't own Duke," Libby said. "He doesn't even like her."

"She's very possessive about men she wants."

"More power to her if she can put a net over him and lock him in her closet."

Jordan chuckled. "He's not keen on the thought of a second wife."

"He's still trying to get custody of his son, isn't he?" Curt asked. "Poor guy."

"He won't be the first man who lost a woman to a career," Jordan reminded him. "Although it's usually the other way around." He glanced at Libby. "Just for the record, I think you're more important than a new bull, no matter what his ancestry is."

"Gee, thanks," she replied, tongue in cheek.

"It never hurts to clear up these little details before they become issues," he said wryly. "On the other hand, it would be nice if you'd tell me if you have plans to go to law school and move to a big city to practice law?"

"Not me, thanks," she replied. "I'm very happy where I am."

"You don't know any other life except this one," he persisted. "What if you regret not spreading your wings further on down the road?"

"We can't see into the future, Jordan," she replied thoughtfully. "But I don't like cities, although I'm sure they're exciting for some people. I don't like parties or business and I wouldn't trade jobs with Kemp for anything on earth. I'm happy looking up case precedents and researching options. I wouldn't like having to stand up in a courtroom and argue a case."

"You don't know that," he mused, and a shadow crossed his face. "What if you got a taste of it one day and couldn't live without it, but it was too late?"

"Too late?"

"What if you had kids and a husband?" he prompted.

"You're thinking about Duke Wright," she said slowly.

He drew in a hard breath, aware that Curt was watching him curiously. "Yes," he told her. "Duke's wife was a secretary. She took night courses to get her law degree and then got pregnant just before she started practice. While Duke was giving bottles and changing diapers, she was climbing the ladder at a prestigious San Antonio law firm, living there during the week and coming home on weekends. Then they offered her a job in New York City."

Libby couldn't quite figure out the look on his face. He was taking it all quite seriously and she'd thought he was teasing.

"So you see," he continued, "she didn't know she wanted a career until it was too late. Now she's making a six-figure annual income and their little boy's in her way. She doesn't want to give him up, but she doesn't have time to take care of him properly. And Duke's caught in the middle."

"I hadn't realized it was that bad," she confessed. "Poor Duke."

"He had a choice," he told her. "He married her thinking she wanted what he did, a nice home and a comfortable living, and kids." He drew a breath. "But she was very young," he added, his eyes studying her covertly. "Maybe she didn't really know what she wanted. Then."

"I suppose some women don't," she replied. "It's a new world. Maybe it took her a long time to realize the opportunities and then it was too late to go back."

He lowered his eyes to his boots. "That's very possible."

"But it's Duke's problem," she added, smiling. "Want

some pie? I've got a cherry one that I made yesterday in the refrigerator."

He shook his head. "Thanks. But I won't stay." He got to his feet. "I'll tell Kemp to let you know what the private detective finds out. Meanwhile," he added, glancing at Curt, "not a word to Janet. Okay?"

They both nodded.

"Thanks, Jordan," Curt added.

"What are neighbors for?" he replied, and he chuckled. But his eyes didn't quite meet Libby's.

"JORDAN WAS ACTING very oddly tonight, wasn't he?" Libby asked her brother after they'd washed the dishes and put them away.

"He's a man with a lot on his mind," he replied. "Calhoun Ballenger's making a very powerful bid for that senate seat that old man Merrill's had for so many years. They say old man Merrill's worried and so's his daughter, Julie. You remember, she's been pursuing Jordan lately."

"But he and Calhoun have been friendly for years," she said.

"So they have. There's more. Old man Merrill got pulled over for drunk driving by a couple of our local cops. Now Merrill's pulling strings at city hall to try and make the officers withdraw the charges. Merrill doesn't have a lot of capital. Jordan does."

"Surely you don't think Jordan would go against Cash Grier, even for Julie?" she wondered, concerned.

He started to speak and then thought better of it. "I'm not sure I really know," he said.

She rubbed at a clean plate thoughtfully. "Do you suppose he's serious about her? She and her father are very big socially and they have a house here that they stay in from time to time. She has a college degree. In fact, they say she may try her hand at politics. He was talking about marriage and children to us—like he was serious about it." She frowned. "Does that kind of woman settle down? Or was that what he meant, when he said some women don't know what they want until they find it?"

"I don't know that he's got marriage on his mind," Curt replied slowly. "But he's spent a good deal of time with Julie and the senator just lately."

That hurt. She bit her lower lip, hard, and forced her mind away from the heat and power of Jordan's kisses. "We've got a problem of our own. What are we going to do about Janet?"

"Kemp's working on that, isn't he? And Jordan's private detective will be working with him. They'll turn up something. She isn't going to put us out on the street, Libby," he said gently. "I promise you she isn't."

She smiled up at him. "You're sort of nice, for a brother."

He grinned. "Glad you noticed!"

She didn't sleep all night, though, wondering about Jordan's odd remarks and the way he'd looked at her when he asked if she had ambitions toward law practice. She really didn't, but he seemed to think she was too young to know her own mind.

Well, it wasn't really anything to worry about, she assured herself. Jordan had no idea of marrying her, regardless of her ambition or lack thereof. But Curt had said he was seeing a lot of Julie Merrill. For some unfathomable reason, the thought made her sad.

CHAPTER FOUR

IT WAS LATE afternoon before Janet came back, looking out of sorts. She threw herself onto the sofa in the living room and lit a cigarette.

"You'll stink up the place," Libby muttered, hunting for an ashtray. She put it on the table.

"Well, then, you'll have to invest in some more air freshener, won't you, darling?" the older woman asked coldly.

Libby stared at her angrily. "Where have you been for three days?"

Janet avoided looking at her. "I had some business to settle."

"It had better not have been any sales concerning this property," Libby told her firmly.

"And who's going to stop me?" the other woman demanded hotly.

"Mr. Kemp."

Janet crushed out the cigarette. "Let him try. You try, too! I own everything here and I'm not letting you take it away from me! No matter what I have to do," she added darkly. "I earned what I'm getting, putting up with your father handling me like a live doll. The repulsive old fool made my skin crawl!"

"My father loved you," Libby bit off, furious that the awful woman could make such a remark about her father, the kindest man she'd ever known.

"He loved showing me off, you mean," Janet muttered. "If he'd really loved me, he'd have given me the things I asked him for. But he was so cheap! Well, I'm not being cheated out of what's mine," she added, with a cold glare at Libby. "Not by you or your brother. I have a lawyer, too, now."

Libby felt sick. But she managed a calm smile. "We have locks on our bedroom doors, by the way," she said out of the blue. "And Mr. Kemp is having a private detective check you out."

Janet looked shocked. "W-what?"

"Violet who works in my office thinks you might have known her father— Mr. Hardy from San Antonio?" she added deliberately. "He had a heart attack, just like Daddy...?"

Janet actually went pale. She jumped to her feet as if she'd been stung.

"Where are you going?" Libby asked seconds later, when the older woman rushed from the room.

Janet went into her bedroom and slammed the door. The sound of objects bouncing off walls followed in a furious staccato.

Libby bit her lip. She'd been warned not to do anything to make Janet panic and make a run for it, but the woman had pricked her temper. She wished she hadn't opened her mouth.

With dark thoughts, she finished baking a ham and made potato salad to go with it, along with homemade rolls. It gave her something to do besides worry.

But when Curt came home to eat, he was met by Janet with a suitcase, going out the door.

"Where are you off to?" he asked her coolly.

She threw a furious glance at the kitchen. "Anywhere I don't have to put up with your sister!" she snarled. "I'll get a motel room in town. You'll be hearing from my attorney in a day or so."

Curt's eyebrows lifted. "Funny. I was just about to tell you the same thing. I had a phone call from Kemp while I was at work. His private investigator has turned up some very interesting information about your former employment at a nursing home in Branntville...?"

Janet brushed by him in a mad rush toward her Mercedes. She threw her case in and jumped in behind it, spraying dirt as she spun out of the driveway.

"Well, that's clinched it," Curt mused as he joined his troubled sister in the kitchen. "She won't be back, or I'll miss my bet."

"I don't think it was a good idea to run her off," she commented as she set the table. "I'd already opened my big mouth and mentioned the locks on our bedroom doors and Violet's father to her."

"It's okay," Curt said gently. "I'm doing what Kemp told me to. I put her on the run."

"Mr. Kemp said to do that?"

He nodded, tossing his hat onto a side table and pulling out a chair. "Any coffee going? We've been mucking out line cabins all day. I'm beat!"

"Mucking out line cabins, not stables?"

"The river ran out of its banks right into that cabin on the north border," he said heavily. "We've been shoveling mud all afternoon. Crazy, isn't it? We had drought for four years, now it's floods. God must really be mad at somebody!"

"Don't look at me, I haven't done a single thing out of line."

He smiled. "When have you ever?" He studied her

as she put food on the table. "Jordan says he's taking you out to a movie next week…watch it!"

Her hands almost let go of the potato salad bowl. She caught it and put it down carefully, gaping at her brother. "Jordan's taking me to a movie?"

"It's what usually happens when men start kissing women," he said philosophically, leaning back in his chair with a wicked grin. "They get addicted."

"How did you know he was kissing me last night?"

He grinned wickedly. "I didn't."

She cleared her throat and turned away, reddening as she remembered the passionate kiss she and Jordan had shared before the supper he'd coaxed her to cook for him. She hadn't slept well all night thinking about it. Or about what Curt had said, that Jordan was spending a lot of time with Julie Merrill. But he couldn't be interested in the woman, if he wanted to take Libby out!

"You never got addicted to any women," she pointed out.

He shrugged. "My day will come. It just hasn't yet."

"What were you telling Janet about a private investigator and the nursing home?"

"Oh, yes." He waited until she sat down and they said grace before he continued, while piling ham on his plate. "I'm not sure how much Kemp told you already but it seems that Janet has changed her legal identity since she worked in the nursing home. Also her hair color. She was under suspicion for the death of that elderly patient who liked to play the horses. She was making off with his bank account when it seems she was paid a visit by a gentleman representing a rather shadowy figure who was owed a great deal of money by the deceased. She left everything and ran for her life." He smiled complacently. "You see, there were more debts than money left in the elderly gentleman's entire estate!"

Libby was listening intently.

"There's more." He took a bite of ham. "This is nice!" he exclaimed when he tasted it.

"Isn't it?" She smiled. "I got it from Duke Wright. He's sidelining into a pork products shop and he's marketing on the Internet. He's doing organic bacon and ham."

"Smart guy."

She nodded. "There's more, you said?"

"Yes. They've just managed to convince Violet's mother that her husband might have been murdered. She's agreed to an exhumation."

"But they said the shock might be fatal!"

"Mrs. Hardy loved her husband. She never believed it was a heart attack. He'd had an echocardiogram that was misread, leading to a heart catheterization. They found nothing that would indicate grounds for a heart attack."

"Poor Violet," Libby said sadly. "It's going to be hard on her, too." She glanced up at her brother. "I still can't believe she quit and is going to work for Duke Wright."

"I know," he said. "She was crazy about Kemp!"

She nodded sadly. "Serves him right. He's been unpleasant to her lately. Violet's tired of eating her heart out for him. And who knows. It might prompt Mr. Kemp to do some soul-searching."

"More than likely he'll just hire somebody else and forget all about her. If he wanted to be married, he could be," he added.

"He doesn't date anybody, does he?" she asked curiously.

He shook his head. "But he's not gay."

"I never thought he was. I just wondered why he keeps so much to himself."

"Maybe he's like a lot of other bachelors in Jacobsville, he's got a secret past that he doesn't want to share!"

"We're running out of bachelors," she retorted. "The Hart boys were the last to go and nobody ever thought they'd end up with families."

"Biscuits were their downfall," he pointed out.

"Jordan doesn't like biscuits," she mused. "I did ask, you know."

He chuckled. "Jordan doesn't have a weakness and he's never lacked dates when he wanted them." He eyed her over his coffee cup. "But he may be at the end of his own rope."

"Don't look at me," she said, having spent too much time lately thinking about Jordan's intentions toward her. "I may be the flavor of the week, but Jordan isn't going to want to marry down, if you see what I mean."

His eyes narrowed. "We may not be high society, but our people go back a long way in Jacobs County."

"That doesn't put us in monied circles, either," she reminded him. Her eyes were dreamy and faraway. "He's got a big, fancy house and he likes to keep company with high society. Maybe that's why he's been taking Senator Merrill's daughter around. It gets him into places he was never invited to before. We'd never fit. Especially me," she added in a more wistful tone than she realized.

"That wouldn't matter."

She smiled sadly. "It would and you know it. He'll need a wife who can entertain and throw parties, arrange sales, things like that. Most of all, he'll want a woman who's beautiful and intelligent, someone he'll be proud to show off. He might take me to a movie. But believe me, he won't take me to a minister."

"You're sure of that?"

She looked up at him. "You said it yourself—Jordan has been spending a lot of time with the state senator's daughter. He's running for reelection and the latest polls say that Calhoun Ballenger is almost tied with him. He needs all the support he can get, financial and otherwise. I think Jordan's going to help him, because of Julie."

"Then why is he kissing you?"

"To make her jealous?" she pondered. "Maybe to convince himself that he's still attractive to women. But it's not serious. Not with him." She looked up. "And I don't have affairs, whether it's politically correct or not."

He sighed. "I suppose we all have our pipe dreams."

"What's yours, while we're on the subject?"

He smiled. "I'd like to start a ranch supply company. The last one left belonged to Ted Regan's father-in-law. When he died, the store went bust, and then his daughter Corrie married Ted Regan and didn't need to make her own living. The hardware store can order most supplies, but not cattle feed or horse feed. Stuff like that."

She hadn't realized her brother had such ambitions. "If we weren't in such a financial mess, I'd be more than willing to cosign a loan with the house as collateral."

He stared at her intently. "You'd do that for me?"

"Of course. You're my brother. I love you."

He reached out and caught her hand. "I love you, too, sis."

"Pipe dreams are nice. Don't you give yours up. Eventually we'll settle this inheritance question and we might have a little capital to work with." She studied him with pride. "I think you'd make a great success of it. You've kept us solvent, up until Janet's unexpected arrival."

"She'll be out for blood. I should probably call Kemp and update him on what's happened."

"That might not be a bad idea. Maybe we should get a dog," she added slowly.

"Bad idea. We can hardly afford to feed old Bailey, your horse. We'd have to buy food for a dog, too, and it would break us."

She saw his eyes twinkle and she burst out laughing, too.

JANET'S ATTORNEY NEVER showed up and two days later, Janet vanished, leaving a trail of charges to the Collinses for everything from clothes to the motel bill.

"You won't have to pay that," Kemp told Libby when he'd related the latest news to her. "I've already alerted the merchants that she had no authority to charge anything to you or Curt, or the estate."

"Thanks," she said with relief. "What do we do now?"

"I've got the state police out looking for her," he replied, his hands deep in his slacks' pockets. "On suspicion of murder. You won't like what's coming next."

"What?"

"I want to have your father exhumed."

She ground her teeth together. "I was afraid of that."

"We'll be discreet. But we need to have the crime lab check for trace evidence of poisoning. You see, we know what killed the old man at the nursing home where she worked. I believe she did kill him. Poisoners tend to stick to the same routine."

"Poor Daddy," she said, feeling sick. Now she won-

dered if they might have saved him, if they'd only realized sooner that Janet was dangerous.

"Don't play mind games with yourself, Libby," Kemp
said quietly. "It does no good."

"What a terrible way to go."

"The poison she used was quick," he replied. "Some
can cause symptoms for months and the victim dies a
painfully slow death. That wasn't the case here. It's the
only good news I have for you, I'm afraid. But after
they autopsy Mr. Hardy, there may be more forensic
evidence to make a case against her. We've found a
source for the poison."

"But the doctor said that Daddy died of a heart attack," she began.

"He might have," Kemp had to admit. "But he could
as easily have died of poison or an air embolism."

"Jordan mentioned that," she recalled.

He smiled secretively. "Jordan doesn't miss a trick."

"But Janet's gone. What if they discover that Daddy's
death was foul play and then they can't find her?" Libby
pointed out. "She's gotten away with it at least two times,
by being cagey."

"Every criminal eventually makes a mistake," he said
absently. "She'll make one. Mark my words."

She only nodded. She glanced at Violet's empty desk
and winced.

"I have an ad in the paper for a new secretary," he
said coldly. "Meanwhile, Mabel's going to do double
duty," he added, nodding toward Mabel, who was on
the phone taking notes.

"It's going to be lonely without her," she said without thinking.

Kemp actually ground his teeth, turned on his heel

and went back into his office. As an afterthought, he slammed the door.

Libby lost it. She laughed helplessly. Mabel, off the phone now and aware of Kemp's shocking attitude, laughed, too.

"It won't last long," Mabel whispered. "Violet was the only secretary he's ever had who could make and break appointments without hurting people's feelings. She was the fastest typist, too. He's not going to find somebody to replace her overnight."

Libby agreed silently. But it promised to be an interesting working environment for the foreseeable future.

Libby didn't even notice there was a message on the answering machine until after supper, when she'd had a lonely sandwich after Curt had phoned and said he was eating pizza with the other cowboys over at the Regan place for their weekly card game.

Curious, Libby punched the answer key and listened to the message. In a silken tone, the caller identified himself as an attorney named Smith and said that Mrs. Collins had hired him to do the probate on her late husband's will. He added that the children of Riddle Collins would have two weeks to vacate the premises.

Libby went through the roof. Her hands trembled as she tried to call Kemp and failing to reach him, she punched in Jordan's number.

It took a long time for him to answer the phone and when he finally did, there was conversation and music in the background.

"Yes?" he asked curtly.

Libby faltered. "Am I interrupting? I can call you another time..."

"Libby?" His voice softened. "Wait a minute." She

heard muffled conversation, an angry reply, and the sound of a door closing. "Okay," he said. "What's wrong?"

"I can't get Mr. Kemp," she began urgently, "and Janet's attorney just called and said we had two weeks to get out of the house before they did the probate!"

"Libby," he said softly, "just sit down and use your mind. Think. When has anybody ever been asked to vacate a house just so that probate papers could be filed?"

She took a deep breath and then another. Her hands were still cold and trembling but she was beginning to remember bits and pieces of court documents. She was a paralegal. For God's sake, she knew about probate!

She sighed heavily. "Thanks. I just lost it. I was so shocked and so scared!"

"Is Curt there?"

"No, he went to his weekly card game with the cowboys over at Ted Regan's ranch," she said.

"I'm sorry I can't come over and talk to you. I'm having a fundraising party for Senator Merrill tonight."

Merrill. His daughter Julie was the socialite. She was beautiful and rich and…socially acceptable. Certainly, she'd be at the party, too.

"Libby?" he prompted, when she didn't answer him.

"That's…that's okay, Jordan, I don't need company, honest," she said at once. "I just lost my mind for a minute. I'm sorry I bothered you. Really!"

"You don't have to apologize," he said, as if her statement unsettled him.

"I'll hang up now. Thanks, Jordan!"

He was still talking when she put the receiver down, very quickly, and put the answering machine back on. If he called back, she wasn't answering him. Janet's vicious tactics had unsettled her. She knew Janet had gotten someone to make that phone call deliberately, to upset Riddle's children.

It was her way of getting even, no doubt, for what Libby and Curt had said to her. She wondered if there was any way they could trace a call off an answering machine? A flash of inspiration hit her. Before Jordan would have time to call and foul the connection, she jerked up the phone and pressed the *69 keys. It gave her the number of the party who'd just phoned and she wrote it down at once, delighted to see that it was not a local number. She'd give it to Kemp the next morning and let his private investigator look into it.

Feeling more confident, she went back to the kitchen and finished washing up the few dishes. She couldn't forget Jordan's deep voice on the phone and the sound of a woman's voice arguing angrily when he went into another room to talk to Libby. It must be that senator's daughter. Obviously she felt possessive of Jordan and was wary of any potential rival. But Libby was no rival, she told herself. Jordan had just kissed her. That was all.

If only she could forget how it had felt. Then she remembered something else: Jordan's odd statements about Duke Wright's wife, and how young she was, and how she didn't quite know she wanted a career until she was already married and pregnant. He'd given Libby an odd, searching look when he said that.

The senator's daughter, Julie Merrill, was twenty-six, she recalled, with a degree in political science. Obviously she already knew what she wanted. She wanted Jordan. She was at his house tonight, probably hostessing the party there. Libby looked down at her worn jeans and faded blouse and then around her at the shabby but useful furniture in the old house. She laughed mirthlessly. What in the world would Jordan want with her, anyway? She'd been daydreaming. She'd better wake up, before she had her heart torn out.

SHE DIDN'T PHONE Jordan again and he didn't call her back. She did give the telephone number of the so-called attorney to Mr. Kemp, who passed it along to his investigator.

Several days later, he paused by Libby's desk while she was writing up a precedent for a libel case, and he looked smug.

"That was quick thinking on your part," he remarked with a smile. "We traced the number to San Antonio. The man isn't an attorney, though. He's a waiter in a high-class restaurant who thinks Janet is his meal ticket to the easy life. We, uh, disabused him of the idea and told him one of her possible futures. We understand that he quit his job and left town on the next bus to make sure he wasn't involved in anything she did."

She laughed softly. "Thank goodness! Then Curt and I don't have to move!"

Kemp glared at her. "As if I'd stand by and let any so-called attorney toss you out of your home!"

"Thanks, boss," she said with genuine gratitude.

He shrugged. "Paralegals are thin on the ground," he said with twinkling blue eyes.

"Callie Kirby and I are the only ones that I know of in town right now," she agreed.

"And Callie's got a child," he said, nodding. "I don't think Micah's going to want her to come back to work until their kids are in school."

"I expect not. She's got Micah's father to help take care of, too," she added, "after his latest stroke."

"People die," he said, and his eyes seemed distant and troubled.

"Mabel called in sick," she said reluctantly. "She's got some sort of stomach virus."

"They go around every spring," he agreed with a sigh. "Can you handle everything, or do you want to get a temp? If you do, call the agency. Ask if they've got somebody who can type."

She gave him her most innocent look. "Of course I can do the work of three women, sir, and even make coffee…"

He laughed. "Call the agency."

"Yes, sir."

He glowered. "It's Violet's fault," he muttered, turning. "I'll bet she's cursed us. We'll have sick help from now on."

"I'm sure she'd never do that, Mr. Kemp," she assured him. "She's a nice person."

"Imagine taking offense at a look and throwing in the towel. Hell, I look at people all the time and they don't quit!"

She cleared her throat and nodded toward the door, which was just opening.

A lovely young woman with a briefcase and long blond hair came in. "I'm Julie Merrill," she said with a haughty smile. "Senator Merrill's daughter? You advertised for a secretary, I believe."

Libby could not believe her eyes. Jordan's latest love and she turned up here looking for work! Of all the horrible bad luck…

Kemp stared at the young woman without speaking.

"Oh, not me!" Julie laughed, clearing her throat. "Heavens, I don't need a job! No, it's my friend Lydia.

She's just out of secretarial school and she can't find anything suitable."

"Can she type?"

"Yes! Sixty words a minute. And she can take shorthand, if you don't dictate too fast."

"Can she speak?"

Julie blinked. "I beg your pardon?"

Kemp gave her a scrutiny that would have stopped traffic. His eyes became a wintry blue, which Libby knew from experience meant that his temper was just beginning to kindle.

"I don't give jobs through third persons, Miss Merrill, and I don't give a damn who your father is," he said with a cool smile.

She colored hotly and gaped at him. "I... I...just thought... I mean, I could ask...!"

"Tell your friend she can come in and fill out an application, but not to expect much," he added shortly. "I have no respect for a woman who has to be helped into a job through favoritism. And in case it's escaped your attention," he added, moving a step closer to her, "nobody works for me unless they're qualified."

Julie shot a cold glare at Libby, who was watching intently. "I guess you think she's qualified," she said angrily.

"I have a diploma as a trained paralegal," Libby replied coolly. "It's on the wall behind you, at my desk."

Kemp only smiled. It wasn't a nice smile.

Julie set her teeth together so hard that they almost clicked. "I don't think Lydia would like this job, anyway!"

Kemp's right eyebrow arched. "Was there anything else, Miss Merrill?"

She turned, jerking open the door. "My father will not be happy when I tell him how you've spoken to me."

"By all means, tell him, with my blessing," Kemp said. "One of his faults is a shameful lack of discipline with his children. I understand you've recently expressed interest in running for public office in Jacobs County, Miss Merrill. Let me give you a piece of advice. Don't."

Her mouth fell open. "How dare you…!"

"It's your father's money, of course. If he wants to throw it away, that's his concern."

"I could win an election!"

Kemp smiled. "Perhaps you could. But not in Jacobs County," he said pleasantly. His eyes narrowed and became cold and his voice grew deceptively soft. "Closet skeletons become visible baggage in an election. And no one here has forgotten your high-school party. Especially not the Culbertsons."

Julie's face went pale. Her fingers on the briefcase tightened until the knuckles showed. She actually looked frightened.

"That was…a terrible accident."

"Shannon Culbertson is still dead."

Julie's lower lip trembled. She turned and went out the door so quickly that she forgot to close it.

Kemp did it for her, his face cold and hard, full of repressed fury.

Libby wondered what was going on, but she didn't dare ask.

Later, of course, when Curt got home from work, she couldn't resist asking the question.

He scowled. "What the hell did Julie want in Kemp's office? Lydia doesn't need a job, she already has a job—a good one—at the courthouse over in Bexar County!"

"She said Lydia wanted to work for Mr. Kemp, but she was giving me the evil eye for all she was worth."

"She wants Jordan. You're in the way."

"Sure I am," she laughed coldly. "What about that girl, Shannon Culbertson?"

Curt hesitated. "That was eight years ago."

"What happened?"

"Somebody put something in her drink—which she wasn't supposed to have had in the first place. It was a forerunner of the date-rape drug. She had a hidden heart condition. It killed her."

"Who did it?"

"Nobody knows, but Julie tried to cover it up, to save her father's senate seat. Kemp dug out the truth and gave it to the newspapers." He shook his head. "A vindictive man, Kemp."

"Why?" she asked.

"They say Kemp was in love with the girl. He never got over it."

"But Julie's father won the election," she pointed out.

"Only because the leading lights of the town supported him and contributed to his reelection campaign. Most of those old-timers are dead or in nursing homes and the gossip around town is that Senator Merrill is already over his ears in debt from his campaign. Besides which, he's up against formidable opposition for the first time in recent years."

CHAPTER FIVE

So that was Kemp's secret, Libby thought. A lost love. "Yes, I know," she said. "Calhoun Ballenger has really shaken up the district politically. A lot of people think he's going to win the nomination right out from under Merrill."

"I'm almost sure he will," Curt replied. "The powers that be in the county have changed over the past few years. The Harts have come up in the world. So have the Tremaynes, the Ballengers, Ted Regan, and a few other families. The power structure now isn't in the hands of the old elite. If you don't believe that, notice what's going on at city hall. Chief Grier is making a record number of drug busts and I don't need to remind you that Senator Merrill was arrested for drunk driving."

"That never was in the paper, you know," she said with a wry smile.

"The publisher is one of his cronies—he refused to run the story. But Merrill's up to his ears in legal trouble. So he's trying to get the mayor and two councilmen who owe him favors to fire the two police officers who made the arrest and discredit them. The primary election is the first week of May, you know."

"Poor police," she murmured.

"Mark my words, they'll never lose their jobs. Grier has contacts everywhere and despite his personal problems, he's not going to let his officers go down without a fight. I'd bet everything I have on him."

She grinned. "I like him."

Curt chuckled. "I like him, too."

"Mr. Kemp said they traced the lawyer's call to San Antonio," she added, and told him what was said. "Why would she want us out of the house?"

"Maybe she thinks there's something in it that she hasn't gotten yet," he mused. "Dad's coin collection, for instance."

"I haven't seen that in months," she said.

"Neither have I. She probably sold it already," he said with cold disgust. "But Janet's going to hang herself before she quits." He gave his sister a sad look. "I'm sorry about the exhumation. But we really need to know the truth about how Dad died."

"I know," she replied. The pain was still fresh and she had to fight tears. She managed a smile for him. "Daddy wouldn't mind."

"No. I don't think he would."

"I wish we'd paid more attention to what was going on."

"He thought he loved her, Libby," he said. "Maybe he did. He wouldn't have listened to us, no matter what we said, if it was something bad about her. You know how he was."

"Loving her blindly may have cost him his life."

"Try to remember that he died happy. He didn't know what Janet was. He didn't know that she was cheating him."

"It doesn't help much."

He nodded. "Nothing will bring him back. But maybe

we can save somebody else's father. That would make it all worthwhile."

"Yes," she agreed. "It would."

THAT EVENING WHILE they were watching television, a truck drove up. A minute later, there was a hard knock on the door.

"I've got it," Curt said, leaving Libby with her embroidery.

There were muffled voices and then heavy footsteps coming into the room.

Jordan stared at Libby curiously. "Julie came to your office today," he said.

"She was looking for a job for her friend Lydia," Libby said in a matter-of-fact tone.

"That's not what she said," Jordan replied tersely. "She told me that you treated her so rudely that Kemp made her leave the office."

Libby lifted both eyebrows. "Wow. Imagine that."

"I'm not joking with you, Libby," Jordan said, and his tone chilled. "That was a petty thing to do."

"It would have been," she agreed, growing angry herself, "if I'd done it. She came into the office in a temper, glared at me, made some rude remarks to Mr. Kemp and got herself thrown out."

"That's not what she told me," he repeated.

Libby got to her feet, motioning to Curt, who was about to protest on her behalf. "I don't need help, Curt. Stay out of it, that's a nice brother." She moved closer to Jordan. "Miss Merrill insinuated that Mr. Kemp had better offer Lydia a job because of her father's position in the community. And he reminded her about her high-school graduation party where a girl died."

"He what?" he exploded.

"Mr. Kemp doesn't take threats lying down," she said, uneasy because of Jordan's overt hostility. "Miss Merrill was very haughty and very rude. And neither of us can understand why she'd try to get Lydia a job at Kemp's office, because she's already got one in San Antonio!"

Jordan didn't say anything. He just stood there, silent.

"She was with you when I phoned your house, I guess, and she got the idea that I was chasing you," she said, gratified by the sudden blinking of his eyelids. "You can tell her, for me," she added with saccharine sweetness, "that I would not have you on a hot dog bun with uptown relish. If she thinks I'm the competition, all she has to do is look where I live." Her face tautened. "Go ahead, Jordan, look around you. I'm not even in your league, whatever your high-class girlfriend thinks. You're a kind neighbor whom I asked for advice and that's all you ever were. Period," she lied, trying to save face.

He still wasn't moving or speaking. But his eyes were taking on a nasty glitter. Beside his lean hips, one of his hands was clenched until the knuckles went white. "Ever?" he prodded, his tone insinuating things.

She knew what he meant. She swallowed hard, trying not to remember the heat and power of the kisses they'd shared. Obviously, they'd meant nothing to him!

"Ever," she repeated. "I certainly wasn't trying to tie you down, Jordan. I'm not at all sure that I want to spend the rest of my life in Jacobsville working for a lawyer, anyway," she added deliberately, but without looking at him. "I've thought about that a lot, about what you said. Maybe I do have ambitions."

He didn't speak for several seconds. His eyes became narrow and cold.

"If you'd like to show your Julie that I'm no competition, you can bring her down here and show her how we live," she offered with a smile. "That would really open her eyes, wouldn't it?"

"Libby," Curt warned. "Don't talk like that."

"How should I talk?" she demanded, her throat tightening. "Our father is dead and it looks like our stepmother killed him right under our noses! She's trying to take away everything we have, getting her friends to call and threaten and harass us, and now here's Jordan's Goody-two-shoes girlfriend making me out to be a man-stealer, or somebody. How the hell should I talk?"

Jordan let out a long breath. "I thought you knew what you wanted," he said after a minute.

"I'm young. Like you said," she said cynically. "Sorry I ever asked you for help, Jordan, and made your girlfriend mad. You can bet I'll never make that mistake twice."

She turned and went into the kitchen and slammed the door behind her. She was learning really bad habits from Mr. Kemp, she decided, as she wiped tears away with a paper towel.

She heard the door open behind her and close again, firmly. It was Curt, she supposed, coming to check on her.

"I guess I handled that badly," she said, choking on tears. "Has he gone?"

Big, warm hands caught her shoulders and turned her around. Jordan's eyes glittered down into hers. "No, he hasn't gone," he bit off.

He looked ferocious like that. She should have been

intimidated, but she wasn't. He was handsome, even bristling with temper.

"I've said all I have to say," she began.

"Well, I haven't," he shot back, goaded. "I've never looked down on you for what you've got and you know it."

"Julie Merrill does," she muttered.

His hands tightened and relaxed. He looked vaguely embarrassed. His dark eyes slid past her to the worn calendar on the wall. "You know how I grew up," he said heavily. "We had nothing. I was never invited to parties. My parents were glorified servants in the eyes of the town's social set."

She drew in a short breath. "And now Julie's opening the doors and inviting you in and you like it."

He seemed shocked by the statement. His eyes dropped to meet hers. "Maybe."

"Can't you see why?" she asked quietly. "You're rich now. You made something out of nothing. You have confidence, and power, and you know how to behave in company. But there's more to it than that, where the Merrills are concerned."

"That's not your business," he said shortly.

She smiled sadly. "They need financial backing. Their old friends aren't as wealthy as they used to be. Calhoun Ballenger has the support of the newer wealthy people in Jacobsville and they don't deal in 'good old boy' politics."

"In other words, Julie only wants me for money to run her father's reelection campaign."

"You know better than that," she replied, searching his hard face hungrily. "You're handsome and sexy. Women adore you."

One eyebrow lifted. "Even you?"

She wanted to deny it, but she couldn't. "Even me," she confessed. "But I'm no more in your class, really, than you're in Julie's. They're old money. It doesn't really matter to them how rich you get, you'll never be one of them."

His eyes narrowed angrily. "I am one of them," he retorted. "I'm hobnobbing with New York society, with Kentucky Thoroughbred breeders, with presidential staff members—even with Hollywood producers and actors!"

"You could do that on your own," she said. "You don't need the Merrills to make you socially acceptable. And in case you've forgotten, Christabel and Judd Dunn have been hobnobbing with Hollywood people for a year. They're not rich. Not really."

He was losing the argument and he didn't like it. He glared down at her with more riotous feelings than he'd entertained in years. "Julie wants to marry me," he said, producing the flat statement like a weapon.

She managed not to react to the retort, barely. Her heart was sinking like lead in her chest as she pictured Julie in a designer wedding gown flashing diamonds like pennies on her way to the altar.

"She doesn't want a career," he added, smiling coldly.

Neither did Libby, really. She liked having a job, but she also liked living in Jacobsville and working around the ranch. She'd have liked being Jordan's wife more than anything else she could think of. But that wasn't going to happen. He didn't want her.

She tried to pull away from Jordan's strong hands, but he wasn't budging.

"Let me go," she muttered. "I'm sure Julie wouldn't like this!"

"Wouldn't like what?" he drawled. "Being in my arms, or having you in them?"

"Are you having fun?" she challenged.

"Not yet," he murmured, dropping his gaze to her full lips. "But I expect to be pretty soon…"

"You can't…!"

But he could. And he was. She felt the warm, soft, coaxing pressure of his hard mouth before she could finish the protest. Her eyes closed. She was aware of his size and strength, of the warmth of his powerful body against hers. She could feel his heartbeat, feel the rough sigh of his breath as he deepened the kiss.

He hadn't really meant to do this. But when he had her so close that he could feel her heart beating like a wild thing against him, nothing else seemed to matter except pleasing her, as she was pleasing him.

He drew her up closer, so that he could feel the soft, warm imprint of her body on the length of his. He traced her soft mouth with his lips, with the tip of his tongue. He felt her stiffen and then lift up to him. He gathered her completely against him and forgot Julie, forgot the argument, forgot everything.

She felt the sudden ardor of his embrace grow unmanageable in a space of seconds. His mouth was insistent on hers, demanding. His hands had gone to her hips. They were pressing her against the sudden rigidity of his powerful body. Even as she registered his urgent hunger for her, she felt one of his big, lean hands seeking between them for the soft, rounded curve of her breast…

She pulled away from him abruptly, her mouth swollen, her eyes wild. "N-no," she choked.

He tried to pull her back into his arms. "Why not?" he murmured, his eyes on her mouth.

"Curt," she whispered.

"Curt." He spoke the name as if he didn't recognize it. He blinked. He took a deep breath and suddenly realized where they were and what he'd been doing.

He drew in a harsh, deep breath.

"You have to go home," she said huskily.

He stood up straight and stared down his nose at her. "If you keep throwing yourself into my arms, what do you expect?" he asked outrageously.

She gaped at him.

"It's no use trying to look innocent," he added as he moved back another step. "And don't start taking off your blouse, it won't work."

"I am not...!" she choked, crossing her arms quickly.

He made a rough sound in his throat. "A likely story. Don't follow me home, either, because I lock my doors at night."

She wanted to react to that teasing banter that she'd enjoyed so much before, but she couldn't forget that he'd taken Julie's side against her.

She stared at him coldly. "I won't follow you home. Not while you're spending all your free time defending Julie Merrill, when I'm the one who was insulted."

He froze over. "The way Julie tells it, you started on her first."

"And you believe her, of course. She's beautiful and rich and sophisticated."

"Something no man in his right mind could accuse

you of," he shot back. With a cold glare, he turned and went out the door.

He didn't pause to speak to Curt, who was just coming in the front door. He shot him a look bare of courtesy and stormed outside. He was boiling over with emotion, the strongest of which was frustrated desire.

LIBBY DIDN'T EXPLAIN anything to her brother, but she knew he wasn't blind or stupid. He didn't ask questions, either. He just hugged her and smiled.

She went to bed feeling totally at sea. How could an argument lead to something so tempestuous that she'd almost passed out at Jordan's feet? And if he really wanted Julie, then how could he kiss Libby with such frustrated desire? And why had he started another fight before he left?

She was still trying to figure out why she hadn't slapped his arrogant face when she fell asleep.

THE TENSION BETWEEN Jordan and his neighbors was suddenly visible even to onlookers. He never set foot on their place. When he had a barbecue for his ranch hands in April, to celebrate the impressive calf sale he'd held, Curt wasn't invited. When Libby had a small birthday party to mark her twenty-fourth birthday, Jordan wasn't on the guest list. Jacobsville being the small town it was, people noticed.

"Have you and Jordan had some sort of falling out?" Mr. Kemp asked while his new secretary, a sweet little brunette fresh out of high school named Jessie, was out to lunch.

Libby looked up at him with wide-eyed innocence. "Falling out?"

"Julie Merrill has been telling people that she and Jordan have marriage plans," he said. "I don't believe it. Her father's in financial hot water and Jordan's rich. Old man Merrill is going to need a lot of support in today's political climate. He made some bad calls on the budget and education and the voters are out to get him."

"So I've heard. They say Calhoun Ballenger's just pulled ahead in the polls."

"He'll win," Kemp replied. "It's no contest. Regardless of Jordan's backing."

"Mr. Kemp, would they really use what happened at Julie's party as a weapon against her father?" she asked carefully.

"Of course they would!" he said shortly. "Even in Jacobs County, dirty laundry has a value. There are other skeletons in that closet, too. Plenty of them. Merrill has already lost the election. His way of doing business, under the table, is obsolete. He's trying to make Cash Grier fire those arresting officers and swear they lied. It won't happen. He and his daughter just don't know it and she refuses to face defeat."

"She's at Jordan's house every day now," she said on a sigh that was more wistful than she knew. "She's very beautiful."

"She's a tarantula," Kemp said coldly. "She's got her finger in a pie I can't tell you about, but it's about to hit the tabloids. When it does, her father can kiss his career goodbye."

"Sir?"

He lifted both eyebrows. "Can you keep a secret?"

"If I can't, why am I working for you?" she asked pertly.

"Those two officers Grier's backing, who caught the

senator driving drunk—" he said. "They've also been investigating a house out on the Victoria road where drugs are bought and sold. That's the real reason they're facing dismissal. Merrill's nephew is our mayor."

"And he's in it up to his neck, I guess?" she fished.

He nodded. "The nephew and Miss Merrill herself. That's where her new Porsche came from."

Libby whistled. "But if Jordan's connected with her…" she said worriedly.

"That's right," he replied. "He'll be right in hot water with her, even though he's not doing anything illegal. Mud not only sticks, it rubs off."

She chewed her lower lip. "You couldn't warn him, I guess?"

He shook his head. "We aren't speaking."

She stared at him. "But you're friends."

"Not anymore. You see, he thinks I took your side unjustly against Miss Merrill."

She frowned. "I'm sorry."

He chuckled. "It will all blow over in a few weeks. You'll see."

She wasn't so confident. She didn't think it would and she hated the thought of seeing Jordan connected with such an unsavory business.

SHE WALKED DOWN to Barbara's Café for lunch and ran right into Julie Merrill and Jordan Powell, who were waiting in line together.

"Oh, look, it's the little secretary," Julie drawled when she saw Libby in line behind them. "Still telling lies about me, Miss Collins?" she asked with a laugh.

Jordan was looking at Libby with an expression that was hard to classify.

Libby ignored her, turning instead to speak to one of the girls from the county clerk's office, who was in line behind her.

"Don't you turn your back on me, you little creep!" Julie raged, attracting attention as she walked right up to Libby. Her eyes were glazed, furious. "You told Jordan that I tried to throw my weight around in Kemp's office and it was a lie! You were just trying to make yourself look good, weren't you?"

Libby felt sick at her stomach. She was no good at dealing with angry people, despite the fact that she had to watch Kemp's secretaries do it every day. She wasn't really afraid of the other girl, but she was keenly aware of their differences on the social ladder. Julie was rich and well-known and sophisticated. Libby was little more than a rancher's daughter turned legal apprentice.

"Jordan can't stand you, in case you wondered, so it's no use calling him up all the time for help, and standing at his door trying to make him notice you!" Julie continued haughtily. "He wouldn't demean himself by going out with a dirty little nobody like you!"

Libby pulled herself up and stared at the older girl, keenly aware of curious eyes watching and people listening in the crowded lunch traffic. "Jordan is our neighbor, Miss Merrill," she said in a strained tone. Her legs were shaking, but she didn't let it show. "Nothing more. I don't want Jordan."

"Good. I'm glad you realize that Jordan's nothing more than a neighbor, because you're a nuisance! No man in his right mind would look at you twice!"

"Oh, I don't know about that," Harley Fowler said suddenly, moving up the line to look down at Julie Merrill with cold eyes. "I'd say her manners are a damned

sight better than yours and your mouth wouldn't get you
into any decent man's house in Jacobsville!"

Julie's mouth fell open.

"I wouldn't have her on toast!" one of the Tremaynes'
cowboys ventured from his table.

"Hey, Julie, how about a dime bag?" some anony-
mous voice called. "I need a fix!"

Julie went pale. "Who said that?" she demanded shakily.

"Julie, let's go," Jordan said curtly, taking her by the
arm.

"I'm hungry!" she protested, fighting his hold.

Libby didn't look up as he passed her with Julie
firmly at his side. He didn't look at her, either, and his
face was white with rage.

As she went out the door, there was a skirl of bellig-
erent applause from the patrons of the café. Julie made
a rude gesture toward them, which was followed by
equally rude laughter.

"Isn't she a pain?" The girl from the clerk's office
laughed. "Honestly, Libby, you were such a lady! I'd
have laid a chair across her thick skull!"

"Me, too," said another girl. "Nobody can stand her.
She thinks she's such a debutante."

Libby listened to the talk with a raging heartbeat.
She was sick to her stomach from the unexpected confrontation and glad that Jordan had gotten the girl out
of the room before things got ugly. But it ruined her
lunch. It ruined her whole day.

It DIDN'T OCCUR to Libby that Jordan would be upset
about the things that Julie had said in the café, especially since he hadn't said a word to Libby at the time.

But he actually came by Kemp's office the next day, hat in hand, to apologize for Julie's behavior.

He looked disappointed when Kemp was sitting perched on the edge of Libby's desk, as if he'd hoped to find her alone. But he recovered quickly.

He gave Kemp a quick glare, his gaze returning at once to Libby. "I wanted to apologize for Julie," he said curtly. "She's sorry she caused a scene yesterday. She's been upset about her father facing drunk-driving charges."

"I don't receive absentee apologies," Libby said coldly. "And you'll never convince me that she would apologize."

Kemp's eyebrows collided. "What's that?"

"Julie made some harsh remarks about me in Barbara's Café yesterday," Libby told him, "in front of half the town."

"Why didn't you come and get me?" Kemp asked. "I'd have settled her hash for her," he added, with a dangerous look at Jordan.

"Harley Fowler defended me," Libby said with a quiet smile. "So did several other gentlemen in the crowd," she added deliberately.

"She's not as bad as you think she is," Jordan said grimly.

"The hell she's not," Kemp replied softly. He got up. "I know things about her that you're going to wish you did and very soon. Libby, don't be long. We've got a case first thing tomorrow. I'll need those notes," he added, nodding toward the computer screen. He went to his office and closed the door.

"What was Kemp talking about?" Jordan asked Libby curiously.

"I could tell you, but you wouldn't believe me," she said sadly, remembering how warm their relationship had been before Julie Merrill clouded the horizon.

He drew in a long breath and moved a little closer, pushing his hat back over his dark hair. He looked down at her with barely contained hunger. Mabel was busy in the back with the photocopier and the girl who was filling in for Violet had gone to a dental appointment. Mr. Kemp was shut up in his office. Libby kept hoping the phone would ring, or someone would come in the front door and save her from Jordan. It was all she could do not to throw herself into his arms, even after the fights they'd had. She couldn't stop being attracted to him.

"Look," he said quietly, "I'm not trying to make an enemy of you. I like Julie. Her father is a good man and he's had some hard knocks lately. They really need my help, Libby. They haven't got anybody else."

She could just imagine Julie crying prettily, lavishing praise on Jordan for being so useful, dressing up in her best—which was considerably better than Libby's best—and making a play for him. She might be snippy and aggressive toward other women, but Julie Merrill was a practiced seducer. She knew how to wind men around her finger. She was young and beautiful and cultured and rich. She knew tricks that most men—even Jordan—wouldn't be able to resist.

"Why are you so attracted to her?" Libby wondered aloud.

Jordan gave her an enigmatic look. "She's mature," he said without thinking. "She knows exactly what she wants and she goes after it wholeheartedly. Besides that, she's a woman who could have anybody."

"And she wants you," she said for him.

He shrugged. "Yes. She does."

She studied his lean, hard face, surprising a curious rigidity there before he concealed it. "I suppose you're flattered," she murmured.

"She draws every man's eye when she walks into a room," he said slowly. "She can play the piano like a professional. She speaks three languages. She's been around the world several times. She's dated some of the most famous actors in Hollywood. She's even been presented to the queen in England." He sighed. "Most men would have a hard time turning up their noses at a woman like that."

"In other words, she's like a trophy."

He studied her arrogantly. "You could say that. But there's something more, too. She needs me. She said everyone in town had turned their backs on her father. Calhoun Ballenger is drawing financial support from some of the richest families in town, the same people who promised Senator Merrill their support and then withdrew it. Julie was in tears when she told me how he'd been sold out by his best friends. Until I came along, he actually considered dropping out of the race."

And pigs fly, Libby thought privately, but she didn't say it. The Merrills were dangling their celebrity in front of Jordan, a man who'd been shut out of high society even though he was now filthy rich. They were offering him entry into a closed community. All that and beautiful Julie, as well.

"Did you hear what she said to me in Barbara's Café?" she wondered aloud.

"What do you mean?" he asked curiously.

"You stood there and let her attack me, without saying a word."

He scowled. "I was talking to Brad Henry while we stood in line, about a bull he wanted to sell. I didn't realize what was going on until Julie raised her voice. By then, Harley Fowler and several other men were making catcalls at her. I thought the best thing to do would be to get her outside before things escalated."

"Did you hear her accuse me of chasing you? Did you hear her warn me off you?"

He cocked his head. "I heard that part," he admitted. "She's very possessive and more jealous of me than I realized. But I didn't like having her insult you, if that's what you mean," he said quietly. "I told her so later. She said she'd apologize, but I thought it might come easier from me. She's insecure, Libby. You wouldn't think so, but she really takes things to heart."

A revelation a minute, Libby was thinking. Jordan actually believed what he was saying. Julie had really done a job on him.

"She said that you wouldn't waste your time on a nobody like me," she persisted.

"Women say things they don't mean all the time." He shrugged it off. "You take things to heart, too, Libby," he added gently. "You're still very young."

"You keep saying that," she replied, exasperated. "How old do I have to be for you to think of me as an adult?"

He moved closer, one lean hand going to her slender throat, slowly caressing it. "I've thought of you like that for a long time," he said deeply. "But you're an addiction I can't afford. You said it yourself—you're ambitious. You won't be satisfied in a small town. Like the old-timers used to say, you want to go and see the elephant."

She was caught in his dark eyes, spellbound. She'd

said that, yes, because of the way he'd behaved about Julie's insults. She'd wanted to sting him. But she didn't mean it. She wasn't ambitious. All she wanted was Jordan. Her eyes were lost in his.

"The elephant?" she parroted, her gaze on his hard mouth.

"You want to see the world," he translated. But he was moving closer as he said it and his head was bending, even against his will. This was stupid. He couldn't afford to let himself be drawn into this sweet trap. Libby wanted a career. She was young and ambitious. He'd go in headfirst and she'd take off and leave him, just as Duke Wright's young wife had left him in search of fame and fortune. He'd deliberately drawn back from Libby and let himself be vamped by Julie Merrill, to show this little firecracker that he hadn't been serious about those kisses they'd exchanged. He wasn't going to risk his heart on a gamble this big. Libby was in love with love. She was attracted to him. But that wasn't love. She was too young to know the difference. He wasn't. He'd grabbed at Julie the way a drowning man reaches for a life jacket. Libby didn't know that. He couldn't admit it.

While he was thinking, he was parting her lips with his. He forgot where they were, who they were. He forgot the arguments and all the reasons he shouldn't do this.

"Libby," he growled against her soft lips.

She barely heard him. Her blood was singing in her veins like a throbbing chorus. Her arms went around his neck in a stranglehold. She pushed up against him, forcing into his mouth in urgency.

His arms swallowed her up whole. The kiss was slow,

deep, hungry. It was invasive. Her whole body began to throb with delight. It began to swell. Their earlier kisses had been almost chaste. These were erotic. They were…narcotic.

A soft little cry of pleasure went from her mouth into his and managed to penetrate the fog of desire she was drowning him in.

He jerked back from her as if he'd been stung. He fought to keep his inner turmoil from showing, his weakness from being visible to her. His big hands caught her waist and pushed her firmly away.

"I know," she said breathlessly. "You think I've had snakebite on my lip and you were only trying to draw out the poison."

He burst out laughing in spite of himself.

She swallowed hard and backed away another step. "Just think how Julie Merrill would react if she saw you kissing me."

That wiped the smile off his face. "That wasn't a kiss," he said.

"No kidding?" She touched her swollen mouth ironically. "I'll bet Julie could even give you lessons."

"Don't talk about her like that," he warned.

"You think she's honest and forthright, because you are," she said, a little breathless. "You're forgetting that her father is a career politician. They both know how to bend the truth without breaking it, how to influence public opinion."

"Politics is a science," he retorted.

"It can be a horrible corruption, as well," she reminded him. "Calhoun Ballenger has taken a lot of heat from them, even a sexual harassment charge that had no basis in fact. Fortunately, people around here know better, and it backfired. It only made Senator Merrill look bad."

His eyes began to glitter. "That wasn't fiction. The woman swore it happened."

"She was one of Julie's cousins," she said with disgust.

He looked as if he hadn't known that. He scowled, but he didn't answer her.

"Julie thinks my brother and I are so far beneath her that we aren't even worth mentioning," she continued, folding her arms over her chest. "She chooses her friends by their social status and bank accounts. Curt and I are losers in her book and she doesn't think we're fit to associate with you. She'll find a way to push you right out of our lives."

"I don't have social status, but I'm welcome in their home," he said flatly.

"There's an election coming up, they don't have enough money to win it, but you do. They'll take your money and make you feel like an equal until you're not needed anymore. Then you'll be out on your ear. You don't come from old money, Jordan, even if you're rich now…"

"You don't know a damned thing about what I come from," he snapped.

The furious statement caught her off guard. She knew Jordan had made his own fortune, but he never spoke about his childhood. His mother worked as a housekeeper. Everybody knew it. He sounded as if he couldn't bear to admit his people were only laborers.

"I didn't mean to be insulting," she began slowly.

"Hell! You're doing your best to turn me against Julie.

She said you would," he added. "She said something else, too—that you're involved with Harley Fowler."

She refused to react to that. "Harley's sweet. He defended me when Julie was insulting me."

That was a sore spot, because Jordan hadn't really heard what Julie was saying until it was too late. He didn't like Harley, anyway.

"Harley's a nobody."

"Just like me," she retorted. "I'd much rather have Harley than you, Jordan," she added. "He may be just a working stiff, but he's got more class than you'll ever have, even if you hang out with the Merrills for the next fifty years!"

That did it. He gave her a furious glare, spit out a word that would have insulted Satan himself and marched right out the door.

"And stay out!" she called after it slammed.

Kemp stuck his head out of his office door and stared at her. "Are you that same shy, introverted girl who came to work here last year?"

She grinned at him through her heartbreak. "You're rubbing off on me, Mr. Kemp," she remarked.

He laughed curtly and went back into his office.

LATER, LIBBY WAS MISERABLE. They'd exhumed her father's body and taken it up to the state crime lab in Austin for tests.

Curt was furious when she told him that Jordan had been to her office to apologize for the Merrill girl.

"As if she'd ever apologize to the likes of us," he said angrily. "And Jordan just stood by and let her insult you in the café without saying a word!"

She gaped at him. "How did you know that?"

"Harley Fowler came by where I was working this morning to tell me about it. He figured, rightly, that you'd try to keep it to yourself." He sank down into a chair. "I gave Jordan notice this afternoon. In two weeks, I'm out of there."

She grimaced. "But, Curt, where will you go?"

"Right over to Duke Wright's place," he replied with a smile. "I already lined up a job and I'll get a raise, to boot."

"That's great," she said, and meant it.

"We'll be fine. Don't worry about it." He sighed. "It's so much lately, isn't it, sis? But we'll survive. We will!"

"I know that, Curt. I'm not worried."

BUT SHE WAS. She hated being enemies with Jordan, who was basically a kind and generous man. She was furious with the Merrills for coming between them for such a selfish reason. They only wanted Jordan's money for the old man's reelection campaign. They didn't care about Jordan. But perhaps he was flattered to be included in such high society, to be asked to hang out with their friends and acquaintances.

But Libby knew something about the people the Merrills associated with that, perhaps, Jordan didn't. Many of them were addicts, either to liquor or drugs. They did nothing for the community; only for themselves. They wanted to know the right people, be seen in the right places, have money that showed when people looked. But to Libby, who loved her little house and little ranch, it seemed terribly artificial.

She didn't have much but she was happy with her life. She enjoyed planting things and watching them grow. She liked teaching Vacation Bible School in the summer and working in the church nursery with little children. She liked cooking food to carry to bereaved families when relatives died. She liked helping out with church bazaars, donating time to the local soup kitchen. She didn't put on airs, but people seemed to like her just the way she was.

Certainly Harley Fowler did. He'd come over to see her the day after Julie's attack in the café, to make sure she was all right. He'd asked her out to eat the following Saturday night.

"Only to Shea's," he chuckled. "I just paid off a new transmission for my truck and I'm broke."

She'd grinned at him. "That's okay. I'm broke, too!"

He shook his head, his eyes sparkling as he looked down at her with appreciation. "Libby, you're my kind of people."

"Thanks, Harley."

"Say, can you dance?"

She blinked. "Well, I can do a two-step."

"That's good enough." He chuckled. "I've been taking these dance courses on the side."

"I know. I heard about the famous waltz with Janie Brewster at the Cattleman's Ball last year."

He smiled sheepishly. "Well, now I'm working on the jitterbug and I hear that Shea's live band can play that sort of thing."

"You can teach me to jitterbug, Harley," she agreed at once. "I'd love to go dancing with you."

He looked odd. "Really?"

She nodded and smiled. "Really."

"Then I'll see you Saturday about six. We can eat there, too."

"Suits me. I'll leave supper for Curt in the refrigerator. That was really nice of you to go to bat for him with your boss, Harley," she added seriously. "Thanks."

He shrugged. "Mr. Parks wasn't too pleased with the way Powell's sucking up to the Merrills, either," he said. "He knows things about them."

"So do I," she replied. "But Jordan doesn't take well-meant advice."

"His problem," Harley said sharply.

She nodded. "Yes, Harley. It's his problem. I'll see you Saturday!" she added, laughing.

When she told Curt about the upcoming date, he seemed pleased. "It's about time you went out and had some fun for a change."

"I like Harley a lot," she told her brother.

He searched her eyes knowingly. "But he's not Jordan."

She turned away. "Jordan made his choice. I'm making mine." She smiled philosophically. "I dare say we'll both be happy!"

CHAPTER SIX

LIBBY AND HARLEY raised eyebrows at Shea's Roadhouse and Bar with their impromptu rendition of the jitterbug. It was a full house, too, on a Saturday night. At least two of the Tremayne brothers were there with their wives, and Calhoun Ballenger and his wife, Abby, were sitting at a table nearby with Leo Hart and his wife, Janie.

"I'm absolutely sure that Calhoun's going to win the state senate seat," Harley said in Libby's ear when they were seated again, drinking iced tea and eating hamburgers. "It looks like he's going to get some support from the Harts."

"Is Mr. Parks in his corner, too?" she asked.

He nodded. "All the way. The political landscape has been changing steadily for the past few years, but old man Merrill just keeps going with his old agenda. He hasn't got a clue what the voters want anymore. And, more important, he doesn't control them through his powerful friends."

"You'd think his daughter would be forward thinking," she pointed out.

He didn't say anything. But his face was eloquent.

"Somebody said she was thinking of running for public office in Jacobsville," she began.

"No name identification," Harley said at once. "You

have to have it to win an office. Without it, all the money in the world won't get you elected."

"You seem to know something about politics," she commented.

He averted his eyes. "Do I?" he mused.

Harley never talked about his family, or his past. He'd shown up at Cy Parks's place one day and proved himself to be an exceptional cowboy, but nobody knew much about him. He'd gone on a gigantic drug bust with Jacobsville's ex-mercenaries and he had a reputation for being a tough customer. But he was as mysterious in his way as the town's police chief, Cash Grier.

"Wouldn't you just know they'd show up and spoil everything?" Harley said suddenly, glaring toward the door.

Sure enough, there was Jordan Powell in an expensive Western-cut sports coat and Stetson and boots, escorting pretty Julie Merrill in a blue silk dress that looked simple and probably cost the earth.

"Doesn't she look expensive?" Harley mused.

"She probably is," Libby said, trying not to look and sound as hurt as she really was. It killed her to see Jordan there with that terrible woman.

"She's going to find out, pretty soon, that she's the equivalent of three-day-old fish with this crowd," Harley predicted coolly, watching her stick her nose up at the Ballengers as she passed them.

"I just hope she doesn't drag Jordan down with her," Libby said softly. "He started out like us, Harley," she added. "He was just a working cowboy with ambition."

Jordan seated Julie and shot a cool glance in Harley and Libby's direction, without even acknowledging them. He sat down, placing his Stetson on a vacant chair and motioned a waiter.

"Did you want something stronger to drink?" Harley asked her.

She grinned at him. "I don't have a head for liquor, Harley. I'd rather stick to iced tea, if you don't mind."

"So would I," he confided, motioning for a waiter.

The waiter, with a fine sense of irony, walked right past Jordan to take Harley's order. Julie Merrill was sputtering like a stepped-on garden hose.

"Two more iced teas, Charlie," Harley told the waiter. "And thanks for giving us preference."

"Oh, I know who the best people are, Harley," the boy said with a wicked grin. And he walked right past Jordan and Julie again, without even looking at them. A minute later, Jordan got up and stalked over to the counter to order their drinks.

"He'll smolder for the rest of the night over that," Harley mused. "So will she, unless I miss my guess. Isn't it amazing," he added thoughtfully, "that a man with as much sense as Jordan Powell can't see right through that debutante?"

"How is it that you can?" Libby asked him curiously.

He shrugged. "I know politicians all too well," he said, and for a moment, his expression was distant. "Old man Merrill has been hitting the bottle pretty hard lately," he said. "It isn't going to sit well with his constituents that he got pulled over and charged with drunk driving by Jacobsville's finest."

"Do you think they'll convict him?" she wondered aloud.

"You can bet money on it," Harley replied. "The world has shifted ten degrees. Local politicians don't meet in parked cars and make policy anymore. The sunshine laws mean that the media get wind of anything crooked and they report it. Senator Merrill has been living in the past. He's going to get a hell of a wake-up call at the primary election, when Calhoun Ballenger knocks him off the Democratic ballot as a contender."

"Mr. Ballenger looks like a gentleman," Libby commented, noticing the closeness of Calhoun and his brunette wife, Abby. "He and his wife have been married a long time, haven't they?"

"Years," Harley said. "He and Justin are honest and hardworking men. They came up from nothing, too, although Justin's wife, Shelby, was a Jacobs before she married him," he reminded her. "A direct descendant of Big John Jacobs. But don't you think either of the Ballenger brothers would have been taken in by Julie Merrill, even when they were still single."

She paused to thank the waiter, who brought their two glasses of tall, cold iced tea. Jordan was still waiting for his order at the counter, while Julie glared at Libby and Harley.

"She's not quite normal, is she?" Libby said quietly. "I mean, that outburst in Barbara's Café was so… violent."

"People on drugs usually are violent," Harley replied. "And irrational." He looked right into Libby's eyes. "She's involved in some pretty nasty stuff, Libby. I can't tell you what I know, but Jordan is damaging himself just by being seen in public with her. The campaigns will get hot and heavy later this month and some dirty linen is about to be exposed to God and the general public."

Libby was concerned. "Jordan's a good man," she

said quietly, her eyes going like homing pigeons to his lean, handsome face.

He caught her looking at him and glared. Julie, seeing his attention diverted, looked, too.

Once he returned to the table Julie leaned over and whispered something to Jordan that made him give Libby a killing glare before he started ignoring her completely.

"Watch your back," Harley told Libby as he sipped his iced tea. "She considers you a danger to her plans with Jordan. She'll sell you down the river if she can."

She sighed miserably. "First my stepmother, now Julie," she murmured. "I feel like I've got a target painted on my forehead."

"We all have bad times," Harley told her gently, and slid a big hand over one of hers where it lay on the table. "We get through them."

"You, too?" she wondered aloud.

"Yeah. Me, too," he replied, and he smiled at her.

Neither of them saw the furious look on Jordan Powell's face, or the calculating look on Julie's.

THE FOLLOWING WEEK, when Libby went to Barbara's Café for lunch, she walked right into Jordan Powell on the sidewalk. He was alone, as she was, and his expression made her feel cold all over.

"What's this about you going up to San Antonio for the night with Harley last Wednesday?" he asked bluntly.

Libby couldn't even formulate a reply for the shock. She'd driven Curt over to Duke Wright's place early Wednesday afternoon and from there she'd driven up to San Antonio to obtain some legal documents from the county clerk's office for Mr. Kemp. She hadn't even seen Harley there.

"I thought you were pure as the driven snow," Jordan continued icily. His dark eyes narrowed on her shocked face. "You put on a good act, don't you, Libby? I don't need to be a mind reader to know why, either. I'm rich and you and your brother are about to lose your ranch."

"Janet hasn't started probate yet," she faltered.

"That's not what I hear."

"I don't care what you hear," she told him flatly. "Neither Curt nor I care very much what you think, either, Jordan. But you're going to run into serious problems if you hang out with Julie Merrill until her father loses the election."

He glared down at her. "He isn't going to lose," he assured her.

She hated seeing him be so stubborn, especially when she had at least some idea of what Julie was going to drag him down into. She moved a step closer, her green eyes soft and beseeching. "Jordan, you're an intelligent man," she began slowly. "Surely you can see what Julie wants you for..."

A worldly look narrowed his eyes as they searched over her figure without any reaction at all. "Julie wants me, all right," he replied, coolly. "That's what's driving you to make these wild comments, isn't it? You're jealous because I'm spending so much time with her."

She didn't dare let on what she was feeling. She forced a careless smile. "Am I? You think I don't know when a man is teasing me?"

"You know more than I ever gave you credit for and that's the truth," he said flatly. "You and Harley Fowler." He made it sound like an insult.

"Harley is a fine man," she said, defending him.

"Obviously you think so, or you wouldn't be shacking up with him," he accused. "Does your brother know?"

"I'm a big girl now," she said, furious at the insinuation.

"Both of you had better remember that I make a bad enemy," he told her. "Whatever happens with your ranch, I don't want to have a subdivision full of people on my border."

He didn't know that Libby and Curt had already discussed how they were going to manage without their father's life insurance policy to pay the mortgage payments that were still owed. Riddle had taken out a mortgage on the ranch to buy Janet's Mercedes. Janet had waltzed off with the money and the private detective Jordan had recommended to Mr. Kemp had drawn a blank when he tried to dig into Janet's past. The will hadn't been probated, either, so there was no way Riddle Collins's children could claim any of their inheritance with which to pay bills or make that huge mortgage payment. They'd had to let their only helper—their part-time cowboy—go, for lack of funds to pay him. They only had one horse left and they'd had to sell off most of their cattle. The only money coming in right now was what Curt and Libby earned in their respective jobs, and it wasn't much.

Of course, Libby wasn't going to share that information with a hostile Jordan Powell. Things were so bad that she and Curt might have to move off the ranch anyway because they couldn't make that mortgage payment at the end of the month. It was over eight hundred dollars. Their collective take-home pay wouldn't amount to that much and there were still other bills owing. Janet had run up huge bills while Riddle was still alive.

Jordan felt sick at what he was saying to Libby. He was jealous of Harley Fowler, furiously jealous. He couldn't bear the thought of Libby in bed with the other man. She wasn't even denying what Julie had assured him had happened between them. Libby, in Harley's arms, kissing him with such hunger that his toes tingled. Libby, loving Harley…

Jordan ached to have her for himself. He dreamed of her every night. But Libby was with Harley now. He'd lost his chance. He couldn't bear it!

"Is Harley going to loan you enough money to keep the ranch going until Janet's found?" he wondered aloud. He smiled coldly. "He hasn't got two dimes to rub together, from what I hear."

Libby remembered the mortgage payments she couldn't make. Once, she might have bent her pride enough to ask Jordan to loan it to her. Not anymore. Not after what he'd said to her.

She lifted her chin. "That's not your business, Jordan," she said proudly.

"Don't expect me to lend it to you," he said for spite.

"Jordan, I wouldn't ask you for a loan if the house burned down," she assured him, unflinching. "Now, if you'll excuse me, I'm using up my lunch hour."

She started to go around him, but he caught her arm and marched her down the little alley between her office and the town square. It was an alcove, away from traffic, with no prying eyes.

While she was wondering what was on his mind, he backed her up against the cold brick and brought his mouth down on her lips.

He lifted his head a bare inch and looked into her wide green eyes with possession and desire. It never stopped. He couldn't get within arm's length of her without giving in to temptation. Did she realize? No. She had no idea. She thought it was a punishment for her harsh words. It was more. It was anguish.

"You still want me," he ground out. "Do you think I don't know?"

"What?" she murmured, her eyes on his mouth. She could barely think at all. She felt his body so close that when he breathed, her chest deflated. Her breasts ached at the warm pressure of his broad chest. It was heaven to be so close to him. And she didn't dare let it show.

"Are you trying to prove something?" she murmured, forcing her hands to push instead of pull at his shoulders.

"Only that Harley isn't in my league," he said in a husky, arrogant tone, as he bent again and forced her mouth open under the slow, exquisite skill of his kisses. "In fact," he bit off against her lips, "neither are you, cupcake."

She wanted to come back with some snappy reply. She really did. But the sensations he was arousing were hypnotic, drugging. She felt him move one long, powerful jean-clad leg in between both of hers. It was broad daylight, in the middle of town. He was making love to her against a wall. And she didn't care.

She moved against him, her lips welcoming, her hands spreading, caressing, against his rib cage, his chest. There was no tomorrow. There was only Jordan, wanting her.

Her body throbbed in time with her frantic heartbeat.

She was hot all over, swelling, aching. She wanted relief. Anything…!

Voices coming close pushed them apart when she would have said that nothing could. Jordan stepped back, his face a rigid mask. She looked up at him, her crushed mouth red from the ardent pressure, her eyes soft and misty and dazed.

Her pocketbook was on the ground. He reached down and handed it back to her, watching as she put the strap over her shoulder and stared up at him, still bemused.

She wanted to tell him that Harley was a better lover, to make some flip remark that would sting him. But she couldn't.

He was in pretty much the same shape. He hated the very thought of Harley. But even through the jealousy, he realized that Libby's responses weren't those of any experienced woman. When Julie kissed him, it was with her whole body. She was more than willing to do anything he liked. But he couldn't take Julie to bed because he didn't want her that way. It was a source of irritation and amazement to him. And to Julie, who made sarcastic remarks about his prowess.

It wasn't a lack of ability. It was just a lack of desire. But he raged with it when he looked at Libby. He'd never wanted a woman to the point of madness until now and she was the one woman he couldn't have.

"Women and their damned ambitions," he said under his breath. "Damn Harley. And damn you, Libby!"

"Damn you, too, Jordan," she said breathlessly. "And don't expect me to drag you into any more alleys and make love to you, if that's going to be your attitude!"

She turned and walked away before he had time to realize what she'd said. He had to bite back a laugh. This was no laughing matter. He had to get a grip on himself before Libby realized what was wrong with him.

AFTER THEIR DISTURBING ENCOUNTER, she wondered if she and Curt wouldn't do better to just move off their property and live somewhere else. In fact, she told herself, that might not be a bad idea.

Mr. Kemp didn't agree.

"You have to maintain a presence on the property," he told Libby firmly. "If you move out, Janet might use that against you in court."

"You don't understand," she groaned. "Jordan is driving me crazy. And every time I look out the window, Julie's speeding down the road to Jordan's house."

"Jordan's being conned," he ventured.

"I know that, but he won't listen," Libby said, sitting down heavily behind her desk. "Julie's got him convinced that I'm running wild with Harley Fowler."

"That woman is big trouble," he said. "I'd give a lot to see her forced to admit what she did to the Culbertson girl at that party."

"You think it was her?" she asked, shocked.

He shrugged. "Nobody else had a motive," he said, his eyes narrow and cold. "Shannon Culbertson was running against her for class president and Julie wanted to win. I don't think she planned to kill her. She was going to set her up with one of the boys she was dating and ruin Shannon's reputation. But it backfired. At least, that's my theory. If this gets out it's going to disgrace her father even further."

"Isn't he already disgraced enough because of the drunk-driving charges?" she asked.

"He and his cronies at city hall are trying desperately to get those charges dropped, before they get into some newspaper whose publisher doesn't owe him a favor," Kemp replied, perching on the edge of her desk. "There's a disciplinary hearing at city hall next month for the officers involved. Grier says the council is going to try to have the police officers fired."

She smiled. "I can just see Chief Grier letting that happen."

Kemp chuckled. "I think the city council is going to be in for a big surprise. Our former police chief, Chet Blake, never would buck the council, or stand up for any officer who did something politically incorrect with the city fathers. Grier isn't like his cousin."

"What if they fire him, too?" she asked.

He stood up. "If they even try, there will be a recall of the city council and the mayor," Kemp said simply. "I can almost guarantee it. A lot of people locally are fed up with city management. Solid waste is backing up, there's no provision for water conservation, the fire department hasn't got one piece of modern equipment, and we're losing revenue hand over fist because nobody wants to mention raising taxes."

"I didn't realize that."

"Grier did." He smiled to himself. "He's going to shake up this town. It won't be a bad thing, either."

"Do you think he'll stay?"

Kemp nodded. "He's put down deep roots already, although I don't think he realizes how deep they go just yet."

Like everyone else in Jacobsville, Libby knew what was going on in Cash Grier's private life. After all, it had been in most of the tabloids. Exactly what the situation was between him and his houseguest, Tippy

Moore, was anybody's guess. The couple were equally tight-lipped in public.

"Could I ask you to do something for me, sir?" she asked suddenly.

"Of course."

"Could you find out if they've learned anything about…Daddy at the state crime lab and how much longer it's going to be before they have a report?" she asked.

He frowned. "Good Lord, I didn't realize how long it had been since the exhumation," he said. "Certainly. I'll get right on it, in fact."

"Thanks," she said.

He shrugged. "No problem." He got to his feet and hesitated. "Have you talked to Violet lately?" he asked reluctantly.

"She's lost weight and she's having her hair frosted," she began.

His lips made a thin line. "I don't want to know about her appearance. I only wondered how she likes her new job."

"A lot," she replied. She pursed her lips. "In fact, she and my brother are going out on a date Saturday night."

"Your brother knows her?" he asked.

She nodded. "He's working for Duke Wright, too…"

"Since when?" he exclaimed. "He was Jordan's right-hand man!"

She averted her eyes. "Not anymore. Jordan said some pretty bad things about me and Curt quit."

Kemp cursed. "I don't understand how a man who was so concerned for both of you has suddenly become an enemy. However," he added, "I imagine Julie Merrill has something to do with his change of heart."

"He's crazy about her, from what we hear."

"He's crazy, all right," he said, turning back toward his office. "He'll go right down the tubes with her and her father if he isn't careful."

"I tried to tell him. He accused me of being jealous."

He glanced back at her. "And you aren't?" he probed softly.

Her face closed up. "What good would it do, Mr. Kemp? Either people like you or they don't."

Kemp had thought, privately, that it was more than liking on Jordan's part. But apparently, he'd been wrong right down the line.

"Bring your pad, if you don't mind, Libby," he said. "I want you to look up a case for me at the courthouse law library."

"Yes, sir," she said, picking up her pad. It was always better to stay busy. That way she didn't have so much time to think.

She was walking into the courthouse when she met Calhoun Ballenger coming out of it. He stopped and grinned at her.

"Just the woman I was looking for," he said. "On the assumption that I win this primary election for the Democratic candidate, how would you like to join my campaign staff in your spare time?"

She caught her breath. "Mr. Ballenger, I'm very flattered!"

"Duke Wright tells me that you have some formidable language skills," he continued. "Not that my secretaries don't, but they've got their hands full right now trying to get people to go to the polls and vote for me in May. I need someone to write publicity for me. Are you interested?"

"You bet!" she said at once.

"Great! Come by the ranch Saturday about one. I've invited a few other people, as well."

"Not…the Merrills or Jordan Powell?" she asked worriedly.

He glowered at her. "I do not invite the political competition to staff meetings," he said with mock hauteur. He grinned. "Besides, Jordan and I aren't speaking."

"That's a relief," she said honestly.

"You're on the wrong side of him, too, I gather?"

She nodded. "Me and half the town."

"More than half, if I read the situation right," he said with a sigh. "A handful of very prominent Democrats have changed sides and they're now promoting me." He smiled. "More for our side."

She smiled back. "Exactly! Well, then, I'll see you Saturday."

"I've already invited your boss and Duke Wright, but Duke won't come," he added heavily. "I invited Grier, and Duke's still browned off about the altercation he had with our police chief."

"He shouldn't have swung on him," she pointed out.

"I'm sure he knows that now," he agreed, his eyes twinkling. "See you."

She gave him a wave and walked into the courthouse lobby. Jordan Powell was standing there with a receipt for his automobile tag and glaring daggers at Libby.

"You're on a friendly basis with Calhoun Ballenger, I gather?" he asked.

"I'm going to work on his campaign staff," she replied with a haughty smile.

"He's going to lose," he told her firmly. "He doesn't have name identification."

She smiled at him. "He hasn't been arrested for drunk driving, to my knowledge," she pointed out.

His eyes flashed fire. "That's a frame," he returned. "Grier's officers planted evidence against him."

She glared back. "Chief Grier is honest and open-handed," she told him. "And his officers would never be asked to do any such thing!"

"They'll be out of work after that hearing," he predicted.

"You swallow everything Julie tells you, don't you, Jordan?" she asked quietly. "Maybe you should take a look at the makeup of our city council. Those were people who once owned big businesses in Jacobsville and had tons of money. But their companies are all going downhill and they're short of ready cash. They aren't the people who have the power today. And if you think Chief Grier is going to stand by and let them railroad his employees, you're way off base."

Jordan didn't reply at once. He stared at Libby until her face colored.

"I never thought you'd go against me, after all I've done for you and Curt," he said.

She was thinking the same thing. It made her ashamed to recall how he'd tried to help them both when Janet was first under suspicion of murder and fraud. But he'd behaved differently since he'd gotten mixed up with Senator Merrill's daughter. He'd changed, drastically.

"You have done a lot for us," she had to agree. "We'll always be grateful for it. But you took sides against us first, Jordan. You stood by with your mouth closed in Barbara's Café and let Julie humiliate me."

Jordan's eyes flashed. It almost looked like guilt. "You had enough support."

"Yes, from Harley Fowler. At least someone spoke up for me."

He looked ice-cold. "You were rude to Julie first, in your own office."

"Why don't you ask Mr. Kemp who started it?" she replied.

"Kemp hates her," he said bluntly. "He'd back your story. I'm working for Senator Merrill and I'm going to get him reelected. You just side with the troublemakers and do what you please. But don't expect me to come around with my hat in my hand."

"I never did, Jordan," she said calmly. "I'm just a nobody around Jacobsville and I'm very aware of it. I'm not sophisticated or polished or rich, and I have no manners. On the other hand, I have no aspirations to high society, in case you wondered."

"Good thing. You'd never fit in," he bit off.

She smiled sadly. "And you think you will?" she challenged softly. "You may have better table manners than I do—and more money—but your father was poor. None of your new high-class friends is ever going to forget that. Even if you do."

He said something nasty. She colored a little, but she didn't back down.

"Don't worry, I know my place, Mr. Powell," she replied, just to irritate him. "I'm a minor problem that you've put out beside the road. I won't forget."

She was making him feel small. He didn't like it.

"Thank you for being there when we needed you most," she added quietly. "We aren't going to sell our land to developers."

"If you ever get title to it," he said coldly.

She shrugged. "That's out of our hands."

"Kemp will do what he can for you," he said, feeling guilty, because he knew that she and Curt had no money for attorneys. He'd heard that Janet was still missing and that Kemp's private detective had drawn a blank when he looked into her past. Libby and Curt must be worried sick about money.

"Yes, Mr. Kemp will do what he can for us." She studied his face, so hard and uncompromising, and wondered what had happened to make them so distant after the heated promises of those kisses they'd exchanged only weeks before.

"Curt likes working for Wright, I suppose?" he asked reluctantly.

She nodded. "He's very happy there."

"Julie had a cousin who trains horses. He's won trophies in steeplechase competition. He's working in Curt's place now, with my two new Thoroughbreds."

"I suppose Julie wants to keep it all in the family," she replied.

He glared down at her. "Keep all what in the family?"

"Your money, Jordan," she said sweetly.

"You wouldn't have turned it down, if I'd given you the chance," he accused sarcastically. "You were laying it on thick."

"Who was kissing whom in the alley?" she returned huskily.

He didn't like remembering that. He jerked his wide-brimmed hat down over his eyes. "A moment of weakness. Shouldn't have happened. I'm not free anymore."

Insinuating that he and Julie were much more than friends, Libby thought correctly. She looked past Jordan to Julie, who was just coming out of the courthouse looking elegant and cold as ice. She saw Libby standing with Jordan and her lips collided furiously.

"Jordan! Let's go!" she called to him angrily.

"I was only passing the time of day with him, Julie," Libby told the older woman with a vacant smile.

"You keep your sticky hands to yourself, you little liar," Julie told her as she passed on the steps. "Jordan is mine!"

"No doubt you mean his money is yours, right?" Libby ventured.

Julie drew back her hand and slapped Libby across the cheek as hard as she could. "Damn you!" she raged.

Libby was shocked at the unexpected physical reply, but she didn't retaliate. She just stood there, straight and dignified, with as much pride as she could muster. Around the two women, several citizens stopped and looked on with keen disapproval.

One of them was Officer Dana Hall, one of the two police officers who had arrested Senator Merrill for drunk driving.

She walked right up to Libby. "That was assault, Miss Collins," she told Libby. "If you want to press charges, I can arrest Miss Merrill on the spot."

"Arrest!" Julie exploded. "You can't arrest me!"

"I most certainly can," Officer Hall replied. "Miss Collins, do you want to press charges?"

Libby stared at Julie Merrill with cold pleasure, wondering how it would look on the front page of Jacobsville's newspaper.

"Wouldn't that put another kink in your father's re-election campaign?" Libby ventured softly.

Julie looked past Libby and suddenly burst into tears.

She threw herself into Jordan Powell's arms. "Oh, Jordan, she's going to have me arrested!"

"No, she's not," Jordan said curtly. He glanced at Libby. "She wouldn't dare."

Libby cocked her head. "I wouldn't?" She glared at him. "Look at my cheek, Jordan."

It was red. There was a very obvious handprint on it.

"She insulted me," Julie wailed. "I had every right to hit her back!"

"She never struck you, Miss Merrill," Officer Hall replied coldly. "Striking another person is against the law, regardless of the provocation."

"I never meant to do it!" Julie wailed. She was sobbing, but there wasn't a speck of moisture under her eyes. "Please, Jordan, don't let them put me in jail!"

Libby and Officer Hall exchanged disgusted looks.

"Men are so damned gullible," Libby remarked with a glare at Jordan, who looked outraged. "All right, Julie, have it your way. But you'd better learn to produce tears as well as broken sobs if you want to convince another woman that you're crying."

"Jordan, could we go now?" Julie sobbed. "I'm just sick...!"

"Not half as sick as you'll be when your father loses the election, Julie," Libby drawled sweetly, and walked up the steps with Officer Hall at her side. She didn't even look at Jordan as she went into the courthouse.

CHAPTER SEVEN

CALHOUN BALLENGER'S MEETING with his volunteer staff was a cheerful riot of surprises. Libby found herself working with women she'd known only by name a few months earlier. Now she was suddenly in the cream of society, but with women who didn't snub her or look down their noses at her social position.

Libby was delighted to find herself working with Violet, who'd come straight from her job at Duke Wright's ranch for the meeting.

"This is great!" Violet exclaimed, hugging Libby. "I've missed working with you!"

"I've missed you, too, Violet," Libby assured her. She shook her head as she looked at the other woman. "You look great!"

Violet grinned. She'd dropped at least two dress sizes. She was well-rounded, but no longer obese even to the most critical eye. She'd had her brown hair frosted and it was waving around her face and shoulders. She was wearing a low-cut dress that emphasized the size of her pretty breasts, and her small waist and voluptuous hips, along with high heels that arched her small feet nicely.

"I've worked hard at the gym," Violet confessed. She was still laughing when her eyes collided with Blake Kemp's across the room. The expression left her face. She averted her eyes quickly. "Excuse me, won't you,

Libby? I came with Curt. You, uh, don't mind, do you?" she added worriedly.

"Don't be silly," Libby said with a genuine smile. "Curt's nice. So are you. I think you'd make a lovely couple…"

"Still happy with Duke Wright, Miss Hardy?" came a cold, biting comment from Libby's back.

Blake Kemp moved into view, his pale eyes expressive on Violet's pretty figure and the changes in the way she dressed.

"I'm…very happy with him, Mr. Kemp," Violet said, clasping her hands together tightly. "If you'll excuse me…"

"You've lost weight," Kemp said gruffly.

Violet's eyes widened. "And you actually noticed?"

The muscles in his face tautened. "You look…nice."

Violet's jaw dropped. She was literally at a loss for words. Her eyes lifted to Kemp's and they stood staring at each other for longer than was polite, neither speaking or moving.

Kemp shifted restlessly on his long legs. "How's your mother?"

Violet swallowed hard. "She's not doing very well, I'm afraid. You know…about the exhumation?"

Kemp nodded. "They're still in the process of evaluating Curt and Libby's father's remains, as well, at the crime lab. So far, they have nothing to report."

Violet looked beside him at Libby and winced. "I didn't know, Libby. I'm so sorry."

"So am I, for you," Libby replied. "We didn't want to do it, but we had to know for sure."

"Will they really be able to tell anything, after all

this time?" Violet asked Kemp, and she actually moved a step closer to him.

He seemed to catch his breath. He was looking at her oddly. "I assume so." His voice was deeper, too. Involuntarily, his lean fingers reached out and touched Violet's long hair. "I like the frosting," he said reluctantly. "It makes your eyes look...bluer."

"Does it?" Violet asked, but her eyes were staring into his as if she'd found treasure there.

With an amused smile, Libby excused herself and joined her brother, who was talking to the police chief.

Cash Grier noticed her approach and smiled. He looked older somehow and there were new lines around his dark eyes.

"Hi, Chief," she greeted him. "How's it going?"

"Don't ask," Curt chuckled. "He's in the middle of a controversy."

"So are we," Libby replied. "We're on the wrong side of the election and Jordan Powell is furious at us."

"We're on the right side," Cash said carelessly. "The city fathers are in for a rude awakening." He leaned down. "I have friends in high places." He paused. "I also have friends in low places." He grinned.

Libby and Curt burst out laughing, because they recognized the lines from a country song they'd all loved.

Calhoun Ballenger joined them, clapping Cash on the back affectionately. "Thanks for coming," he said. "Even if it is putting another nail in your coffin with the mayor."

"The mayor can kiss my..." Cash glanced at Libby and grinned. "Never mind."

They all laughed.

"She's lived with me all her life," Curt remarked. "She's practically unshockable."

"How's Tippy?" Calhoun asked.

Cash smiled. "Doing better, thanks. She'd have come, too, but she's still having a bad time."

"No wonder," Calhoun replied, recalling the ordeal Tippy had been through in the hands of kidnappers. It had been in all the tabloids. "Good thing they caught the culprits who kidnapped her."

"Isn't it?" Cash said, not giving away that he'd caught them, with the help of an old colleague. "Nice turnout, Calhoun," he added, looking around them. "I thought you invited Judd."

"I did," Calhoun said at once, "but the twins have a cold."

"Damn!" Cash grimaced. "I told Judd that he and Crissy needed to stop running that air conditioner all night!"

"It wasn't that," Calhoun confided. "They went to the Coltrains' birthday party for their son—his second birthday—and that's where they got the colds."

Cash sighed. "Poor babies."

"He's their godfather," Calhoun told Libby and Curt. "But he thinks Jessamina belongs to him."

"She does," Cash replied haughtily.

Nobody mentioned what the tabloids had said—that Tippy had been pregnant with Cash's child a few weeks earlier and lost it just before her ordeal with the kidnapping.

Libby diplomatically changed the subject. "Mr. Kemp said that you can put up campaign posters in our office windows," she told Calhoun, "and Barbara's willing to let you put up as many as you like in her café," she added with a grin. "She said she's never going to forgive Julie Merrill for making a scene there."

Calhoun chuckled. "I've had that sort of offer all week," he replied. "Nobody wants Senator Merrill back in office, but the city fathers have thrown their support behind him and he thinks he's unbeatable. What we really need is a change in city government, as well. We're on our second mayor in eight months and this one is afraid of his own shadow."

"He's also Senator Merrill's nephew," Curt added.

"Which is why he's trying to make my officers back down on those DWI charges," Cash Grier interposed.

"I'd like to see it. Carlos Garcia wouldn't back down from anybody," Calhoun mused. "Or Officer Dana Hall, either."

"Ms. Hall came to my assistance at the courthouse this week," Libby volunteered. "Julie Merrill slapped me. Officer Hall was more than willing to arrest her, if I'd agreed to press charges."

"Good for Dana," Cash returned. "You be careful, Ms. Collins," he added firmly. "That woman has poor impulse control. I wouldn't put it past her to try and run somebody down."

"Neither would I," Curt added worriedly. "She's already told Jordan some furious lies about us and he believes her."

"She can be very convincing," Libby said, not wanting to verbally attack Jordan even now.

"It may get worse now, with all of you backing me," Calhoun told the small group. "I won't have any hard feelings if you want to withdraw your support."

"Do I look like the sort of man who backs away from trouble?" Cash asked lazily, with a grin.

"Speaking of Duke Wright," Libby murmured dryly, "he's throwing his support to Mr. Ballenger, too. But he had, uh, reservations about coming to the meeting."

Cash chuckled. "I don't hold grudges."

"Yes, but he does," Calhoun said on a chuckle. "He'll get over it. He's got some personal problems right now."

"Don't we all?" Cash replied wistfully, and his dark eyes were troubled.

Libby and Curt didn't add their two cents' worth, but they exchanged quiet looks.

THE CAMPAIGN WAS winding down for the primary, but all the polls gave Calhoun a huge lead over Merrill. Printed materials were ordered, along with buttons, pencils, bumper stickers and key chains. There was enough promotional matter to blanket the town and in the days that followed, Calhoun's supporters did exactly that in Jacobs County and the surrounding area in the state senatorial district that Merrill represented.

Julie Merrill was acting as her father's campaign manager and she was coordinating efforts for promotion with a group of teenagers she'd hired. Some of them were delinquents and there was a rash of vandalisms pertaining to the destruction of Calhoun's campaign posters.

Cash Grier, predictably, went after the culprits and rounded them up. He got one to talk and the newspapers revealed that Miss Merrill had paid the young man to destroy Calhoun's campaign literature. Julie denied it. But the vandalism stopped.

Meanwhile, acting mayor Ben Brady was mounting a fervent defense for Senator Merrill on the drunk-driving charges and trying to make things hot for the two officers. He ordered them suspended and tried to get the city council to back him up.

Cash got wind of it and phoned Simon Hart, the state's attorney general. Simon phoned the city attorney and they had a long talk. Soon afterward, the officers were notified that they could stay on the job until the hearing the following month.

Meanwhile, the state crime lab revealed the results of its report to Blake Kemp. He walked up to Libby's desk while she was on the phone and waited impatiently for her to hang up.

"They can't find any evidence of foul play, Libby," he said at once.

"And if there was any, they would?" she asked quickly.

He nodded. "I'm almost certain of it. The crime lab verified our medical examiner's diagnosis of myocardial infarction. So Janet's off the hook for that one, at least."

Libby sat back with a long sigh and closed her eyes. "Thank God. I couldn't have lived with it if she'd poisoned Daddy and we never knew."

He nodded. "On the other hand, they hit pay dirt with Violet's father," he added.

She sat up straight. "Poison?"

"Yes," he said heavily. "I'm not going to phone her. I'm going over to Duke Wright's place to tell her in person. Then I'll take her home to talk to her mother. She'll need someone with her."

Yes, she would, and Libby was secretly relieved that Kemp was going to be the person. Violet would need a shoulder to cry on.

"I'll phone Curt and tell him," she said.

"Libby, give me half an hour first," he asked quietly. "I don't want him to tell Violet."

She wondered why, but she wasn't going to pry. "Okay."

He managed a brief smile. "Thanks."

"What about Janet?" she wondered miserably. "They still haven't found her."

"They will. Now all we need is a witness who can place her with Mr. Hardy the night of his death, and we can have her arrested and charged with murder," he replied.

"Chance would be a fine thing, Mr. Kemp," she said heavily.

"Don't give up hope," he instructed. "She's not going to get away with your inheritance. I promise."

She managed a smile. "Thanks."

But she wasn't really convinced. She went home that afternoon feeling lost and alone. She'd told Curt the good news after Violet had gone home with Kemp. Curt had been as relieved as she had, but there was still the problem of probate. Everything was in Janet's name, as their father had instructed. Janet had the insurance money. Nobody could do anything with the estate until the will was probated and Janet had to sign the papers for that. It was a financial nightmare.

There was a message on the answering machine when Libby got home. She pushed the Play button and her heart sank right to her ankles.

"This is the loan officer at Jacobsville Savings and Loan," came the pleasant voice. "We just wanted to remind you that your loan payment was due three days ago. Please call us if there's a problem." The caller gave her name and position and her telephone number. The line went dead.

Libby sat down beside the phone and just stared at it. Curt had told her already that they weren't going to be able to make the payment. Jordan had assured her that he wasn't going to loan her the money to pay it. There was nobody else they would feel comfortable asking. She put her face in her hands and let the tears fall. The financial establishment would repossess the ranch. It wouldn't matter where Janet was or what state the probate action was in. They were going to lose their home.

SHE WENT OUT to the barn and ran the currycomb over Bailey, her father's horse. He was the last horse they had.

The barn leaked. It was starting to rain and Libby felt raindrops falling on her shoulder through a rip in the tin roof from a small tornado that had torn through a month earlier. The straw on the floor of the barn needed changing, but the hay crop had drowned in the flooding. They'd have to buy some. Libby looked down at her worn jeans, at the small hand resting on them. The tiger's-eye ring her father had given her looked ominous in the darkened barn. She sighed and turned back to the horse.

"Bailey, I don't know what we're going to do," she told the old horse, who neighed as if he were answering her.

The sound of a vehicle pulling up in the yard diverted her. She looked down the long aisle of the barn to see Jordan's pickup truck sitting at the entrance. Her heart skipped as he got out and came striding through the dirty straw, his cotton shirt speckled with raindrops that had escaped the wide brim of his white straw hat.

"What do you want?" she asked, trying to ignore him to finish her grooming job on the horse.

"My two new Thoroughbreds are missing."

She turned, the currycomb suspended in her small hand. "And you think we took them?" she asked incredulously. "You honestly think we'd steal from you, even if we were starving?"

He averted his face, as if the question had wounded him.

"Please leave," she said through her teeth.

He rammed his hands into his pockets and moved a step closer, looking past her to Bailey. "That horse is useless for ranch work. He's all of twenty."

"He's my horse," she replied. "I'm not getting rid of him, whatever happens."

She felt his lean, powerful body at her back. "Libby," he began. "About that bank loan…"

"Curt and I are managing just fine, thanks," she said without turning.

His big, strong hands came down heavily on her shoulders, making her jump. "The bank president is a good friend of the Merrills."

She pulled away from him and looked up, her unspoken fears in her green eyes. "They can't do anything to us without Janet," she told him. "She has legal power of attorney."

"Damn it, I know that!" he muttered. "But it's not going to stop the bank from foreclosing, don't you see? You can't make the loan payment!"

"What business is that of yours?" she asked bitterly.

He drew in a slow breath. "I can talk to the president of the Jacobsville Merchant Bank for you," he said. "He might be willing to work out something for the land. You and Curt can't work it, anyway, and you don't have the capital to invest in it. The best you could do is sell off your remaining cattle and give it up."

She couldn't even manage words. She had no options at all and he had to know it. She could almost hate him.

"We can't sell anything," she said harshly. "I told you, Janet has power of attorney. And she was named in Daddy's will as the sole holder of the property. We can't even sell a stick of furniture. We're going to have to watch the bank foreclose, Jordan, because Janet has our hands tied. We're going to lose everything Daddy worked for, all his life..."

Her lower lip trembled. She couldn't even finish the sentence.

Jordan stepped forward and wrapped her up tight in his arms, holding her while she cried. "Damn, what a mess!"

She beat a small fist against his massive chest. "Why?" she moaned. "Why?"

His arms tightened. "I don't know, baby," he whispered at her ear, his voice deep and soothing. "I wish I did."

She nuzzled closer, drowning in the pleasure of being close to him. It had been so long since he'd held her.

His chest rose and fell heavily. "Kemp's detective hasn't tracked her down yet?"

"Not yet. But she didn't...kill Daddy. The autopsy showed that he died of a heart attack."

"That's something, I guess," he murmured.

"But Violet's daddy was poisoned," she added quietly, her eyes open as they stared past Jordan's broad chest toward his truck parked at the front of the barn. "So they'll still get her for murder, if they can ever find her."

"Poor Violet," he said.

"Yes."

His hand smoothed her hair. It tangled in the wavy soft strands. "You smell of roses, Libby," he murmured deeply, and the pressure of his arms changed in some subtle way.

She could feel the sudden tautness of his lean body against her, the increasing warmth of his embrace. But he'd taken Julie's side against her and she wasn't comfortable being in his arms anymore.

He lifted his head and looked down into her misty and wet green eyes. His voice was deep with feeling. "You haven't stopped wanting me."

"I want hot chocolate, too, Jordan, but it still gives me migraines, so I don't drink it," she said emphatically.

His dark eyebrows lifted. "That's cute. You think you convinced me?"

"Sure," she lied.

He laughed mirthlessly, letting his dark eyes fall to her lips. "Let's see."

He bent, drawing his lips slowly, tenderly, across her mouth in a teasing impression of a kiss. He was lazy and gentle and after a few seconds of imitating a plank of wood, her traitorous body betrayed her.

She relaxed into the heat of his body with a shaky little sigh and found herself enveloped in his arms. He kissed her again, hungrily this time, without the tenderness of that first brief exchange.

"Yes," he groaned. His long leg slid lazily against hers, and between them, while his big, warm hands smoothed blatantly over her rib cage, his thumbs sliding boldly right over her breasts. "Don't think," he whispered against her parted lips. "Just give in. I won't hurt you."

"I know that," she whispered. "But..."

He nibbled on her lower lip. His thumbs edged out gently and found her nipples. They moved lazily, back and forth, coaxing the tips into hard little nubs. She shivered with unexpected pleasure.

He lifted his head and looked into her eyes while he did it again. If she was used to this sort of love play, it certainly didn't show. She was pliable, yielded, absolutely fascinated with what he was doing to her body. She liked it.

That was all he needed to know. His leg became insistent between hers, coaxing them to move apart, to admit the slow, exquisite imprint of his hips between her long legs. It was like that day in the alley beyond her office, when she hadn't cared if all of Jacobsville walked by while he was pressing her aching body against the brick wall. She was drowning in pleasure.

Surely, she thought blindly, it couldn't be wrong to give in to something so sweet! His hands on her body were producing undreamed of sensations. He was giving her pleasure in hot, sweeping waves. He touched her and she ached for more. He kissed her and she lifted against him to find his mouth and coax it into ardor. One of her legs curled helplessly around his powerful thigh and she moaned when he accepted the silent invitation and moved into near intimacy with her.

He was aroused. He was powerful. She felt the hard thrust of him against her body and she wanted to rip off her clothes and invite his hands, his eyes, his body, into complete surrender with her. She wanted to feel the ecstasy she knew he could give her. He was skilled, masterful. He knew what she needed, what she wanted. He could give her pleasure beyond bearing, she knew it.

His lean hands moved under her blouse, searching for closeness, unfastening buttons, invading lace. She felt his fingers brush tenderly, lovingly, over her bare breasts in an intimacy she'd never shared with anyone.

Her dreams of him had been this explicit, but she'd never thought she would live them in such urgent passion. As he touched her, she arched to help him, moved to encourage him. Her mouth opened wide under his. She felt his tongue suddenly thrust into it with violent need.

She moaned loudly, her fingertips gripping the hard muscle of his upper arms as he thrust her blouse and bra up to her throat and bent at once to put his mouth on her breasts.

The warm, moist contact was shattering. She stiffened with the shock of pleasure it produced. He tasted her in a hot, feverish silence, broken only by his urgent breathing and the rough sigh of her own voice in his ear.

"Yes," he groaned, opening his mouth. "Yes, Libby. Here. Right here. You and me. I can give you more pleasure than damned Harley ever dreamed of giving you!"

Harley. Harley. She felt her body growing cold. "Harley?" she whispered.

He lifted his head and looked down at her breasts with grinding urgency. "He's had you."

"He has not!" she exclaimed, shocked.

He scowled, in limbo, caught between his insane need to possess her and his jealousy of the other man.

She took advantage of his indecision by jerking out of his arms and pulling her blouse down as she dragged herself out of the stall. She groped for fastenings while she flushed with embarrassment at what she'd just let him do to her.

She looked devastated. Her hair was full of straw, like her clothes. Her green eyes were wild, her face flushed, her mouth swollen.

He got to his feet, still in the grip of passion, and started toward her. His hat was off. His hair was wild, from her searching fingers, and his shirt was half-open over hair-matted muscle.

"Come back here," he said huskily, moving forward.

"No!" she said firmly, shivering. "I'm not standing in for Julie Merrill!"

The words stopped him in his tracks. He hesitated, his brows meeting over turbulent dark eyes.

"Remember Julie? Your girlfriend?" she persisted shakily. Throwing his lover in his face was a way to cover her hurt for the insinuation he'd made about her and Harley. "What in the world would she think if she could see you now?"

He straightened, but with an effort. His body was raging. He wanted Libby. He'd never wanted anyone, anything, as much as he wanted her.

"Julie has nothing to do with this," he ground out. "I want you!"

"For how long, Jordan?" she asked bitingly. "Ten minutes? Thirty?"

He blinked. His mind wasn't working.

"I am nobody's one-night stand," she flashed at him. "Not even yours!"

He took a deep breath, then another one. He stared at her blankly while he tried to stop thinking about how sweet it was to feel her body under his hands.

"I want you to leave, now," she repeated, folding her arms over her loose bra. She could feel the swollen contours of her breasts and remembered with pure shame how it felt to have him touching and kissing them.

"That isn't what you wanted five minutes ago," he reminded her flatly.

She closed her eyes. "I'm grass-green and stupid," she said curtly. "It wouldn't be the first time an experienced man seduced an innocent girl."

"Don't make stupid jokes," he said icily. "You're no innocent."

"You believe what you like about me, Jordan, it doesn't matter anymore," she interrupted him. "I've got work to do. Why don't you go home?"

He glared at her, frustrated desire riding him hard. He cursed himself for ruining everything by bringing up Harley Fowler. "You're a hard woman, Libby," he said. "Harder than I ever realized."

"Goodbye, Jordan," she said, and she turned away to pick up the curry comb she'd dropped.

He gave her a furious glare and stormed out of the barn to his truck. Bailey jumped as Jordan slammed the door and left skid marks getting out of the driveway. She relaxed then, grateful that she'd managed to save herself from that masterful seduction. She'd had a close call. She had to make sure that Jordan never got so close to her again. She couldn't trust him. Not now.

CHAPTER EIGHT

JANET WAS STILL in hiding before the primary election
and probate hadn't begun. But plenty had changed in
Jacobsville. Libby and Curt had been forced to move
out of the farmhouse where they'd grown up, because
the bank had foreclosed.

They hadn't said a word to Jordan about it. Curt
moved into the bunkhouse at the Wright ranch where
he worked. Libby moved into a boardinghouse where
two other Jacobsville career women lived.

Bailey would have had to be boarded and Libby didn't
have the money. But she worked out a deal with a dude
ranch nearby. Bailey would be used for trail rides for
people who were nervous of horses and Libby would
help on the weekends. It wasn't the ideal solution, but
it was the only one she had. It was a wrench to give up
Bailey, even though it wasn't going to be forever.

Jordan and Julie Merrill were apparently engaged.
Or so Julie was saying, and she was wearing a huge
diamond on her ring finger. Her father was using every
dirty trick in the book to gain his party's candidacy.

Julie Merrill was vehemently outspoken about some
unnamed dirty tactics being used against her father in
the primary election campaign, and she went on television to make accusations against Calhoun Ballenger.

The next morning, Blake Kemp had her served as the defendant in a defamation lawsuit.

"THEY'RE NOT GOING to win this case," Julie raged at Jordan. "I want you to get me the best attorney in Austin! We're going to put Calhoun Ballenger right in the gutter where he belongs, along with all these jump-up nouveau riche that think they own our county!"

Jordan, who was one of those jump-ups, gave her a curious look. "Excuse me?" he asked coolly.

"Well, I'm not standing by while Ballenger talks my father's constituents into deserting him!"

"You're the one who's been making allegations, Julie," Jordan said quietly. "To anyone who was willing to listen."

She waved that away. "You have to do that to win elections."

"I'm not going to be party to anything dishonest," Jordan said through his teeth.

Julie backed down. She curled against him and sighed. "Okay. I'll tone it down, for your sake. But you aren't going to let Calhoun Ballenger sue me, are you?"

Jordan didn't know what he was going to do. He felt uneasy at Julie's temperament and her tactics. He'd taken her side against Kemp when she told him that one of the boys at her graduation party had put something in the Culbertson girl's drink and she couldn't turn him in. She'd cried about Libby Collins making horrible statements against her. But Libby had never done such a thing before.

He'd liked being Julie's escort, being accepted by the social crowd she ran around with. But it was getting old and he was beginning to believe that Julie was only playing up to him for money to put into her father's campaign. Libby had tried to warn him and he'd jumped down her throat. He felt guilty about that, too. He felt guilty about a lot of things lately.

"Listen," he said. "I think you need to step back and take a good look at what you're doing. Calhoun Ballenger isn't some minor citizen. He and his brother own a feedlot that's nationally known. Besides that, he has the support of most of the people in Jacobsville with money."

"My father has the support of the social set," she began.

"Yes, but Julie, they're the old elite. The demographics have changed in Jacobs County in the past ten years. Look around you. The Harts are a political family from the roots up. Their brother is the state attorney general and he's already casting a serious eye on what's going on in the Jacobsville city council, about those police officers the mayor's trying to suspend."

"They can't do anything about that," she argued.

"Julie, the Harts are related to Chief Grier," he said shortly.

She hesitated. For the first time, she looked uncertain.

"Not only that, they're related to the governor and the vice president. And while it isn't well-known locally, Grier's people are very wealthy."

She sat down. She ran a hand through her blond hair. "Why didn't you say this before?"

"I tried to," he pointed out. "You refused to listen."

"But Daddy can't possibly lose the election," she said with a child's understanding of things. "He's been state senator from this district for years and years."

"And now the voters are looking for some new blood," he told her. "Not only in local government, but in state and national government. You and your father don't really move with the times, Julie."

"Surely, you don't think Calhoun can beat Daddy?" she asked huskily.

"I think he's going to," he replied honestly, ramming his hands into his pockets. "He's way ahead of your father in the polls. You know that. You and your father have made some bad enemies trying to have those police officers fired. You've gotten on the wrong side of not only Cash Grier, but the Harts, as well. There will be repercussions. I've already heard talk of a complete recall of the mayor and the city council."

"But the mayor is Daddy's nephew. How could they…?"

"Don't you know anything about small towns?" he ground out. "Julie, you've spent too much time in Austin with your father and not enough around here where the elections are decided."

"This is just a hick town," she said, surprised. "Why should I care what goes on here?"

Jordan's face hardened. "Because Jacobs County is the biggest county in your father's district. He can't get reelected without it. You've damaged his campaign by the way you've behaved to Libby Collins."

"That nobody?" she scoffed.

"Her father is a direct descendant of old John Jacobs," he pointed out. "They may not have money and they may not be socially acceptable to you and your father, but the Collinses are highly respected here. The reason Calhoun's got such support is because you've tried to hurt Libby."

"But that's absurd!"

"She's a good person," he said, averting his eyes as he recalled his unworthy treatment of her—and of Curt—on Julie's behalf. "She's had some hard knocks recently."

"So have I," Julie said hotly. "Most notably, having a lawsuit filed against me for defamation of character by that lawyer Kemp!" She turned to him. "Are you going to get me a lawyer, or do I have to find my own?"

Jordan was cutting his losses while there was still time. He felt like ten kinds of fool for the way he'd behaved in the past few weeks. "I think you'd better do that yourself," he replied. "I'm not going against Calhoun Ballenger."

She scoffed. "You'll never get that Collins woman to like you again, no matter what you do," she said haughtily. "Or didn't you know that she and her brother have forfeited the ranch to the bank?"

He was speechless. "They've what?"

"Nobody would loan them the money they needed to save it," she said with a cold smile. "So the bank president foreclosed. Daddy had a long talk with him."

He looked furious. His big fists clenched at his hips. "That was low, Julie."

"When you want to win, sometimes you have to fight dirty," she said simply. "You belong to me. I'm not letting some nobody of a little dirt rancher take you away from me. We need you."

"I don't belong to you," he returned, scooping up his hat. "In fact, I've never felt dirtier than I do right now."

She gaped at him. "I beg your pardon! You can't talk to me like that!"

"I just did." He started toward the door.

"You're no loss, Jordan," she yelled after him. "We

needed your money, but I never wanted you! You're one of those jump-ups with no decent background. I'm sorry I ever invited you here the first time. I'm ashamed that I told my friends I liked you!"

"That makes two of us," he murmured icily, and he went out the door without a backward glance.

KEMP WAS GOING over some notes with Libby when Jordan Powell walked into the office without bothering to knock.

"I'd like to talk to Libby for a minute," he said solemnly, hat in hand.

Libby stared at him blankly. "I can't think what you have to say," she replied. "I'm very busy."

"She is," Kemp replied. "I'm due in court in thirty minutes."

"Then I'll come back in thirty minutes," Jordan replied.

"Feel free, but I won't be here. I have nothing to say to you, Jordan," she told him bluntly. "You turned your back on me when I needed you the most. I don't need you now. I never will again."

"Listen," he began impatiently.

"No." She turned back to Kemp. "What were you saying, boss?"

Kemp hesitated. He could see the pain in Jordan's face and he had some idea that Jordan had just found out the truth about Julie Merrill. He checked his watch. "Listen, I can read your writing. Just give me the pad and I'll get to the courthouse. It's okay," he added when she looked as if he were deserting her to the enemy. "Really."

She bit her lower lip hard. "Okay."

"Thanks," Jordan said stiffly, as Kemp got up from the desk.

"You owe me one," he replied, as he passed the taciturn rancher on the way out the door.

MINUTES LATER, Mabel went into Kemp's office to put some notes on his desk, leaving Jordan and Libby alone.

"I've made some bad mistakes," he began stiffly. He hated apologies. Usually, he found ways not to make them. But he'd hurt Libby too badly not to try.

She was staring at her keyboard, trying not to listen.

"You have to understand what it's been like for me," he said hesitantly. He sat down in a chair next to her desk, with his wide-brimmed hat in his hands. "My people were like yours, poor. My mother had money, but her people disinherited her when she married my dad. I never had two nickels to rub together. I was that Powell kid, whose father worked for wages, whose mother was reduced to working as a housekeeper." He stared at the floor with his pride aching. "I wanted to be somebody, Libby. That's all I ever wanted. Just to have respect from the people who mattered in this town." He shrugged. "I thought going around with Julie would give me that."

"I don't suppose you noticed that her father belongs to a group of respectable people who no longer have any power around here," she said stiffly.

He sighed. "No, I didn't. I had my head turned. She was beautiful and rich and cultured, and she came at me like a hurricane. I was in over my head before I knew it."

Libby, who wasn't beautiful or rich or cultured, felt her heart breaking. She knew all this, but it hurt to hear him admit it. Because it meant that those hungry, sweet kisses she'd shared with him meant nothing at all. He wanted Julie.

"I've broken it off with her," he said bluntly.

Libby didn't say anything.

"Did you hear me?" he asked impatiently.

She looked up at him with disillusioned eyes. "You believed her. She said I was shacking up with Harley Fowler. She said I attacked her in this office and hurt her feelings. You believed all that, even though you knew me. And when she attacked me in Barbara's Café and on the courthouse steps, you didn't say a thing."

He winced.

"Words don't mean anything, Powell," she said bitterly. "You can sit there and apologize and try to smooth over what you did for the rest of your life, but I won't listen. When I needed you, you turned your back on me."

He drew in a long breath. "I guess I did."

"I can understand that you were flattered by her attention," she said. "But Curt and I have lost everything we had. Our father is dead and we don't even have a home anymore."

He moved his hat in his hands. "You could move in with me."

She laughed bitterly. "Thanks."

"No, listen," he said earnestly, leaning forward.

She held up a hand. "Don't. I've had all the hard knocks I can handle. I don't want anything from you, Jordan. Not anything at all."

He wanted to bite something. He felt furious at his own stupidity, at his blind allegiance to Julie Merrill and her father, at his naivete in letting them use him. He felt even worse about the way he'd turned on Libby.

But he was afraid of what he'd felt for her, afraid of her youth, her changeability. Now he only felt like a fool.

"Thanks for the offer and the apology," she added heavily. "Now, if you'll excuse me, I have to get back to work."

She turned on the computer, brought up her work screen and shut Jordan out of her sight and mind.

He got up slowly and moved toward the door. He hesitated at it, glancing back at her. "What about the autopsy?" he asked suddenly.

She swallowed hard. "Daddy died of a heart attack, just like the doctors said," she replied.

He sighed. "And Violet's father?"

"Was poisoned," she replied.

"Riddle had a lucky escape," he commented. "So did you and Curt."

She didn't look at him. "I just hope they can find her, before she kills some other poor old man."

He nodded. After a minute, he gave her one last soulful glance and went out the door.

LIFE WENT ON as usual. Calhoun's campaign staff cranked up the heat. Libby spent her free time helping to make up flyers and make telephone calls, offering to drive voters to the polls during the primary election if they didn't have a way to get to the polls.

"You know, I really think Calhoun's going to win," Curt told Libby while they were having a quick lunch together on Saturday, after she got off from work.

She smiled. "So do I. He's got all kinds of support."

He picked at his potato chips. "Heard from Jordan?"

She stiffened. "He came by the office to apologize a few days ago."

He drew in a long breath. "Rumor is that Julie Merrill's courting Duke Wright now."

"Good luck to her. He's still in love with his wife. And he's not quite as gullible as Jordan."

"Jordan wasn't so gullible," he defended his former boss. "When a woman that pretty turns up the heat, most normal men will follow her anywhere."

She lifted both eyebrows. "Even you?"

He grinned. "I'm not normal. I'm a cowboy."

She chuckled and sipped her iced tea. "They're still looking for Janet. I've had an idea," she said.

"Shoot."

"What if we advertise our property for sale in all the regional newspapers?"

"Whoa," he said. "We can't sell it. We don't have power of attorney and the will's not even in probate yet."

"She's a suspected murderess," she reminded him. "Felons can't inherit, did you know? If she's tried and convicted, we might be able to get her to return everything she got from Daddy's estate."

He frowned, thinking hard. "Do you remember Dad telling us about a new will he'd made?"

She blinked. "No."

"Maybe you weren't there. It was when he was in the hospital, just before he died. He could hardly talk for the pain and he was gasping for breath. But he said there was a will. He said he put it in his safest place." He frowned heavily. "I never thought about that until just now, but what if he meant a new will, Libby?"

"It wouldn't have been legal if it wasn't witnessed," she said sadly. "He might have written something down and she found it and threw it out. I doubt it would stand up in court."

"No. He went to San Antonio without Janet, about two days before he had the heart attack," he persisted.

"Who did he know in San Antonio?" she wondered aloud.

"Why don't you ask Mr. Kemp to see if his private detective could snoop around?" he queried softly.

She pursed her lips. "It would be a long shot. And we couldn't afford to pay him...."

"Dad had a coin collection that was worth half a million dollars, Libby," Curt said. "It's never turned up. I can't find any record that he ever sold it, either."

Her lips fell open. In the agony of the past few months, that had never occurred to her. "I assumed Janet cashed it in...."

"She had the insurance money," he reminded her, "and the property—or so she assumed. But when we were sorting out Dad's personal belongings, that case he kept the coins in was missing. What if—" he added eagerly "—he took it to San Antonio and left it with someone, along with an altered will?"

She was trying to think. It wasn't easy. If they had those coins, if nothing else, they could make the loan payment.

"I can ask Mr. Kemp if he'll look into it," she said. "He can take the money out of my salary."

"I can contribute some of mine," Curt added.

She felt lighter than she had in weeks. "I'll go ask him right now!"

"Finish your sandwich first," he coaxed. "You've lost weight, baby sister."

She grimaced. "I've been depressed since we had to leave home."

"Yeah. Me, too."

She smiled at him. "But things are looking up!"

SHE FOUND KEMP just about to leave for the day. She stopped him at the door and told him what she and Curt had been discussing.

He closed the door behind them, picked up the phone, and dialed a number. Libby listened while he outlined the case to someone, most likely the private detective he'd hired to look for Janet.

"That's right," he told the man. "One more thing, there's a substantial coin collection missing, as well. I'll ask." He put his hand over the receiver and asked Libby for a description of it, which he gave to the man. He added a few more comments and hung up, smiling.

"Considering the age of those coins and their value, it wouldn't be hard to trace them if they'd been sold. Good work, Libby!"

"Thank my brother," she replied, smiling. "He remembered it."

"You would have, too, I expect, in time," he said in a kindly tone. "Want me to have a talk with the bank president?" he added. "I think he might be more amenable to letting you and Curt back on the property with this new angle in mind. It might be to his advantage," he added in a satisfied tone.

"You mean, if we turn out to have that much money of our own, free and clear, it would make him very uncomfortable if we put it in the Jacobsville Municipal Bank and not his?"

"Exactly."

Her eyes blazed. "Which is exactly where we will put it, if we get it," she added.

He chuckled. "No need to tell him that just yet."

Her eyebrows lifted. "Mr. Kemp, you have a devious mind."

He smiled. "What else is new?"

LIBBY WAS FURIOUS at herself for not thinking of her father's impressive coin collection until now. She'd watched those coins come in the mail for years without really noticing them. But now they were important. They meant the difference between losing their home and getting it back again.

She sat on pins and needles over the weekend, until Kemp heard from the private detective the following Monday afternoon.

He buzzed Libby and told her to come into the office.

He was smiling when she got there. "We found them," he said, chuckling when she made a whoop loud enough to bring Mabel down the hall.

"It's okay," Libby told her coworker, "I've just had some good news for a change!"

Mabel grinned and went back to work.

Libby sat down in the chair in front of Kemp's big desk, smiling and leaning forward.

"Your father left the coins with a dealer who locked them in his safe. He was told not to let Janet have them under any circumstances," he added gently. "Besides that, there was a will. He's got that, too. It's not a self-made will, either. It was done by a lawyer in the dealer's office and witnessed by two people who work for him."

Libby's eyes filled with tears. "Daddy knew! He knew she was trying to cut us out of the will!"

"He must have," he conceded. "Apparently she'd made some comments about what she was going to do when he died. And she'd been harassing him about his health, making remarks about his heart being weak, as well." His jaw clenched. "Whatever the cause, he changed the will in your favor—yours and Curt's. This will is going to stand up in a court of law and it changes the entire financial situation. You and Curt can go home and I'll get the will into probate immediately."

"But the insurance…"

He nodded. "She was the beneficiary for one of his insurance policies." He smiled at her surprise. "There's another one, a half-a-million-dollar policy, that he left with the same dealer who has the will. You and Curt are co-beneficiaries."

"He didn't contact us!" she exclaimed suddenly.

"Yes, and that's the interesting part," he said. "He tried to contact you and Janet told him that you and Curt were out of the country on an extended vacation. She planned to go and talk to him the very day you made the remarks about Violet's father and having locks put on your bedroom doors. She ran for her life before she had time to try to get to the rest of your inheritance." He chuckled. "Maybe she had some idea of what the seller was guarding and decided that the insurance policy would hold her for a while without risking arrest."

"Oh, thank God," she whispered, shivering with delight. "Thank God! We can go home!"

"Apparently," he agreed, smiling. "I'm going to drive up to San Antonio today and get those documents and the coin collection."

She was suddenly concerned. "But what if Janet hears about it? She had that friend in San Antonio who called and tried to get us off the property…" She stopped abruptly. "That's why they were trying to get us out of the house! They knew about the coin collection!" She sat back heavily. "But they could be dangerous…."

"Cash Grier is going with me."

She pursed her lips amusedly. "Okay."

He chuckled. "Nobody is going to try to attack me with Grier in the car. Even if he isn't armed."

"Good point," she agreed.

"So call your brother and tell him the news," he said. "And stop worrying. You're going to land on your feet, Libby."

"How's Violet?" she asked without thinking.

He stood up, his hands deep in his pockets. "She and her mother are distraught, as you might imagine. They never realized that Mr. Hardy had been the victim of foul play. I've tried to keep it out of the papers, but when Janet's caught, it's going to be difficult."

"Is there anything I can do?"

He smiled. "Take them a pizza and let Violet talk to you about it," he suggested. "She misses working here."

"I miss her, too."

He shifted, averting his gaze. "I offered to let her come back to work here."

"You did?" she asked, enthused.

"She's going to think about it," he added. "You might, uh, tell her how shorthanded we are here, and that the temporary woman we got had to quit. Maybe she'll feel sorry for us and come back."

She smiled. "I'll do my best."

He looked odd. "Thanks," he said stiffly.

CHAPTER NINE

THE VERY NEXT DAY, Kemp came into the office grinning like a lottery winner. He was carrying a cardboard box, in which was a mahogany box full of rare gold coins, an insurance policy, a few personal items that had belonged to Riddle Collins and a fully executed new will.

Libby had to sit down when Kemp presented her with the hard evidence of her father's love for herself and Curt.

"The will is legal," he told her. "I'm going to take it right to the courthouse and file it. It will supersede the will that Janet probably still has in her possession. You should take the coins to the bank and put them in a safe-deposit box until you're ready to dispose of them. The dealer said he'll buy them from you at market value anytime you're ready to sell them."

"But I'll have to use them as collateral for a loan to make the loan payment..."

"Actually, no, you won't," Kemp said with a smile, drawing two green-covered passbooks out of the box and handing them to her.

"What are these?" she asked blankly.

"Your father had two other bank accounts, both in San Antonio." He smiled warmly. "There's more than enough there to pay off the mortgage completely so that the ranch is free and clear. You'll still have a small fortune left over. You and your brother are going to be rich, Libby. Congratulations."

She cried a little, both for her father's loving care of them even after death and for having come so close to losing everything.

She pulled a tissue out of the pocket of her slacks and wiped her red eyes. "I'll take these to the Jacobsville Municipal Bank right now," she said firmly, "and have the money transferred here from San Antonio. Then I'll have them issue a cashier's check to pay off the other bank," she added with glee.

"Good girl. You can phone the insurance company about the death benefit, too. How does it feel, not to have to worry about money?"

She chuckled. "Very good." She eyed him curiously. "Does this mean you're firing me?"

"Well, Libby, you won't really need to work for a living anymore," he began slowly.

"But I love my job!" she exclaimed, and had the pleasure of watching his high cheekbones go ruddy. "Can't I stay?"

He drew in a long breath. "I'd be delighted if you would," he confessed. "I can't seem to keep a paralegal these days."

She smiled, remembering that Callie Kirby had been one, until she'd married Micah Steele. There had been two others after her, but neither had stayed long.

"Then it's settled. I have to go and call Curt!"

"Go to the bank first, Libby," he instructed with a grin. "And I'll get to the courthouse. Mabel, we're going to be out of the office for thirty minutes!"

"Okay, boss!"

They went down the hall together and they stopped dead.

Violet was back at her desk, across from a grinning Mabel, looking radiant. "You said I could come back," she told Kemp at once, looking pretty and uncertain at the same time.

He drew in a sharp breath and his eyes lingered on her. "I certainly did," he agreed. "Are you staying?"

She nodded.

"How about making a fresh pot of coffee?" he asked.

"Regular?" she asked.

He averted his gaze to the door. "Half and half," he murmured. "Caffeine isn't good for me."

He went out the door, leaving Violet's jaw dropped.

"I told you he missed you," Libby whispered as she followed Kemp out the door and onto the sidewalk.

LIBBY AND CURT were able to go home the next morning. But their arrival was bittersweet. The house had been ransacked in their absence.

"We'd better call the sheriff's office," Curt said angrily, when they'd ascertained that the disorder was thorough. "We'll need to have a report filed on this for insurance purposes."

"Do we even have insurance?"

He nodded. "Dad had a homeowner's policy. I've been keeping up the payments, remember?"

She righted a chair that had been turned over next to the desk her father had used in his study. The filing cabinet had been emptied onto the floor, along with a lot of other documents pertaining to the ranch's business.

"They were looking for that coin collection," Curt

guessed as he picked up the phone. "I'll bet anything Janet knew about it. She must be running short of cash already!"

"Thank God Mr. Kemp was able to track it down," she said.

"Sheriff's department?" Curt said into the telephone receiver. "I need you to send someone out to the Collins ranch. That's right, it's just past Jordan Powell's place. We've had a burglary. Yes. Okay. Thanks!" He hung up. "I talked to Hayes. He's going to come himself, along with his investigator."

"I thought he was overseas with his army unit in Iraq," she commented.

"He's back." He glanced at her amusedly. "You used to have a case on him, just before you went nuts over Jordan Powell."

She hated hearing Jordan's name mentioned. "Hayes is nice."

"So he is." He toyed with the telephone cord. "Libby, Jordan's having some bad times lately. His association with the Merrills has made him enemies."

"That was his choice," she reminded her brother.

"He was good to us, when Dad died."

She knew that. It didn't help. Her memories of Jordan's betrayal were too fresh. "Think I should do anything before they get here?"

"Make coffee," he suggested dryly. "Hayes's investigator is Mack Hughes, and he lives on caffeine."

"I'll do that."

SHERIFF HAYES CARSON pulled up at the front steps in his car, a brightly polished black vehicle with all sorts of antennae sticking out of it. The investigator, Mack

Hughes, pulled up beside it in his black SUV with a deck of lights on the roof.

"Thanks for coming so quickly," Curt said, shaking hands with both men. "You remember my sister, Libby."

"Hello, Elizabeth," Hayes said with a grin, having always used her real first name instead of the nickname most people called her by. He was dashing, with blond hair and dark eyes, tall and muscular and big. He was in his mid-thirties; one tough customer, too. He and Cash Grier often went head-to-head in disputes, although they were good colleagues when there was an emergency.

"Hi, Hayes," she replied with a smile. "Hello, Mack."

Mack, tall and dark, nodded politely. "Let's see what you've got."

They ushered the law-enforcement officers inside and stood back while they went about searching for clues.

"Any idea who the perpetrators were?" Hayes murmured while Mack looked around.

"Someone connected to our stepmother, most likely," Libby commented. "Dad had a very expensive coin collection and some secret bank accounts that even we didn't know about. If that's what they were looking for, they're out of luck. Mr. Kemp tracked them to San Antonio. Everything's in the bank now and a new will we recovered is in the proper hands."

Hayes whistled softly. "Lucky for you."

There was a sudden commotion in the front yard, made by a truck skidding to a stop between the two law-enforcement vehicles. A dusty, tired Jordan Powell came up the steps, taking them two at a time, and stopped abruptly in the living room.

"What's happened?" he asked at once, his eyes homing to Libby with dark concern.

"The house was ransacked," Hayes told him. "Have you seen anything suspicious?"

"No. But I'll ask my men," Jordan assured them. He looked at Libby for a long time. "You okay?"

"Curt and I are fine, thanks," she said in a polite but reserved tone.

Jordan looked around at the jumble of furniture and paper on the floor, along with lamps and broken pieces of ceramic items that had been on the mantel over the fireplace.

"This wasn't necessary," Jordan said grimly. "Even if they were looking for something, they didn't have to break everything in the house."

"It was malicious, all right," Hayes agreed. He moved just in front of Libby. "I heard from Grier that you've had two confrontations with Julie Merrill, one of them physically violent. She's also been implicated in acts of vandalism. I want to know if you think she might have had any part in this."

Libby glanced at Jordan apprehensively.

"It could be a possibility," Jordan said, to her dismay. "She was jealous of Libby and I've just broken with Julie and her father. She didn't take it well."

"I'll add her to the list of suspects," Hayes said quietly. "But I have to tell you, she isn't going to like being accused."

"I don't care," Curt replied, answering for himself as well as Libby. "Nobody has a right to do something like this."

"Boss!" Mack called from the back porch. "Could you ask the Collinses to come out here, please?"

Curt stood aside to let Libby go first. On the small back stoop, Mack was squatting down, looking at a big red gas can. "This yours?" he asked Curt.

Curt frowned. "We don't have one that big," he replied. "Ours is locked up in the outbuilding next to the barn."

Mack and Hayes exchanged curious looks.

"There's an insurance policy on the house," Libby remarked worriedly. "It's got Janet, our stepmother, listed as beneficiary."

"That narrows down the suspects," Hayes remarked.

"Surely she wouldn't..." Libby began.

"You've made a lot of trouble for her," Jordan said grimly. "And now she's missed out on two savings accounts and a will that she didn't even know existed."

"How did you know that?" Libby asked belligerently.

"My cousin owns the Municipal Bank," Jordan said nonchalantly.

"He had no business telling you anything!" Libby protested.

"He didn't, exactly," Jordan confessed. "I heard him talking to one of his clerks about opening the new account for you and setting up a safe-deposit box."

"Eavesdropping should be against the law," she muttered.

"I'll make a note of it," Hayes said with a grin.

She grinned back. "Thanks, Hayes."

He told Mack to start marking evidence to be collected. "We'll see if we can lift any latent prints," he told the small group. "If it was Janet, or someone she hired, they'll probably have been wearing gloves. If it was Julie Merrill, we might get lucky."

"I hope we can connect somebody to it," Libby said

wearily, looking around. "If for no other reason than to make them pay to help have this mess cleaned up!"

"I'll take care of that," Jordan said at once, and reached for his cell phone.

"We don't need—!" Libby began hotly.

But Jordan wasn't listening. He was talking to Amie at his ranch, instructing her to phone two housekeepers she knew who helped her with heavy tasks and send them over to the Collins place.

"You might as well give up," Hayes remarked dryly. "Once Jordan gets the bit between his teeth, it would take a shotgun to stop him. You know that."

She sighed angrily. "Yes. I know."

Hayes pushed his wide-brimmed hat back off his forehead and smiled down at Libby. "Are you doing anything Saturday night?" he asked. "They're having a campaign rally for Calhoun's supporters at Shea's."

"I know, I'm one of them," she replied, smiling. "Are you going to be there?"

He shrugged. "I might as well. Somebody'll have a beer too many and pick a fight, I don't doubt. Tiny the bouncer will have his hands full."

"Great!" she said enthusiastically.

Jordan was eavesdropping and not liking what he heard. He wanted to tell Hayes to back off. He wanted to tell Libby what he felt. But he couldn't get the words out.

"If you two are moving back in," Hayes added, "I think we'd better have somebody around overnight. I've got two volunteer deputies in the Sheriff's Posse who would be willing, I expect, if you'll keep them in coffee."

She smiled. "I'd be delighted. Thanks, Hayes. It would

make me feel secure. We've got a shotgun, but I don't even know where it is."

"You could both stay with me until Hayes gets a handle on who did this," Jordan volunteered.

"No, thanks," Libby said quietly, trying not to remember that Jordan had already asked her to do that. No matter how she felt about the big idiot, she wasn't going to step into Julie Merrill's place.

"This is our home," Curt added.

Jordan drew in a long, sad breath. "Okay. But if you need help…"

"We'll call Hayes, thanks," Libby said, turning back to the sheriff. "I need to tidy up the kitchen. Is it all right?"

Hayes went with her into the small room and looked around. There wasn't much damage in there and nothing was broken. "It looks okay. Go ahead, Libby. I'll see you Saturday, then?"

She grinned up at him. "Of course."

He grinned back and then rejoined the men in the living room. "I'm going to talk to my volunteers," he told Curt. "I'll be in touch."

"Thanks a lot, Hayes," Curt replied.

"Just doing my job. See you, Jordan."

"Yeah." Jordan didn't offer to shake hands. He glared after the other man as he went out the front door.

"I can clean my own house," Libby began impatiently.

Jordan met her eyes evenly. "I've made a lot of mistakes. I've done a lot of damage. I know I can't make it up to you in one fell swoop, but let me do what I can to make amends. Will you?"

Libby looked at her brother, who shrugged and walked away, leaving her to deal with Jordan alone.

"Some help you are," Libby muttered at his retreating back.

"I don't like the idea of that gas can," Jordan said, ignoring her statement. "You can't stay awake twenty-four hours a day. If Janet is really desperate enough to set fire to the house trying to get her hands on the insurance money, neither you nor Curt is going to be safe here."

"Hayes is getting us some protection," she replied coolly.

"I know that. But even deputies have to use the bathroom occasionally," he said flatly. "Why won't you come home with me?"

She lifted her chin. "This is my place, mine and Curt's. We're not running anymore."

He sighed. "I admire your courage, Libby. But it's misplaced this time."

She turned away. "I've got a lot to do, Jordan. Thanks anyway."

He caught her small waist from behind and held her just in front of him. His warm breath stirred the hair at the back of her head. "I was afraid."

"Of…what?" she asked, startled.

His big hands contracted. "You're very young, even for a woman your age," he said stiffly. "Young women are constantly changing."

She turned in his hold, curious. She looked up at him without understanding. "What has that got to do with anything?"

He reached out and traced her mouth with his thumb. He looked unusually solemn. "You really don't know, do you?" he asked quietly. "That's part of the problem."

"You aren't making any sense."

"I am. You're just not hearing what I'm saying." He bent and kissed her softly beside her ear, drawing away almost at once. "Never mind. You'll figure it out one day. Meanwhile, I'm going to do a better job of looking after you."

"I can—"

He interrupted at once. "If you say 'look after myself,' so help me, I'll…!"

She glared at him.

He glared back.

"You're up against someone formidable, whoever it is," he continued. "I'm not letting anything happen to you, Libby."

"Fat lot you cared before," she muttered.

He sighed heavily. "Yes, I know. I'll eat crow without catsup if it will help you trust me again."

"Julie's very pretty," she said reluctantly.

"She isn't a patch on you, butterfly," he said quietly.

She hesitated. But she wasn't giving in easily. He'd hurt her. No way was she going to run headfirst into his arms the first time he opened them.

She watched him suspiciously.

His broad chest rose and fell. "Okay. We'll do it your way. I'll see you at Shea's."

"You're the enemy," she pointed out. "You're not on Calhoun's team."

He shrugged. "A man can change sides, can't he?" he mused. "Meanwhile, if you need me, I'll be at the house. If you call, I'll come running."

She nodded slowly. "All right."

He smiled at her.

Curt came back in. He was as cool to Jordan as his

sister. The older man shrugged and left without another word.

"Now he's changed sides again," Libby told Curt when Jordan was gone.

"Jordan's feeling his age, Libby," Curt told her. "And some comments were made by his cowboys about that kiss they saw."

Her eyebrows arched. "What?"

He sighed. "I never had the heart to tell you. But one of the older hands said Jordan was trying to rob the cradle. It enraged Jordan. But it made him think, too. He knows how sheltered you've been. I think he was trying to protect you."

"From what?"

"Maybe from a relationship he didn't think you were ready for," he replied. "Julie was handy, he'd dated her a time or two, and she swarmed all over him just about the time he was drawing back from you. I expect he was flattered by her attention and being invited into that highbrow social set that shut out his mother after she was disinherited because she married his father. The local society women just turned their backs on her. She was never invited anywhere ever again. Jordan felt it keenly, that some of his playmates weren't allowed to invite him to their houses."

"I didn't know it was so hard on him. He's only told me bits and pieces about his upbringing."

"He doesn't advertise it," he added. "She gave up everything to marry his father. She worked as a housekeeper in one of the motels owned by her father's best friend. It was a rough upbringing for Jordan."

"I can imagine." She sighed, unable to prevent her heart from thawing.

SHEA'S WAS FILLED to capacity on Saturday evening. Cash Grier got a lot of attention because he brought Tippy with him. She looked good despite her ordeals, except for the small indications of healing cuts on her lovely face. She was weak and still not totally recovered and it showed. Nevertheless, she was still the most beautiful woman in the room. But she had eyes only for Cash and that showed, too.

When they got on the dance floor together, Libby was embarrassed to find herself staring wistfully at them. Tippy melted into Cash's tall body as if she'd found heaven. He looked that way, as well. They clung together to the sound of an old love song. And when she looked up at him, he actually stopped dancing and just stared at her.

"They make a nice couple," Jordan said from behind her.

She glanced up at him. He looked odd. His dark eyes were quiet, intent on her uplifted face.

"Yes, they do," she replied. "They seem to fit together very well."

He nodded. "Dance with me," he said in a deep voice, and drew her into his arms.

She hesitated, but only for a few seconds. She'd built dreams on those kisses they'd shared and she thought it was all over. But the way he was holding her made her knees weak. His big hand covered hers against his chest and pressed it hard into the warm muscle.

"I've been an idiot," he said at her ear.

"What do you mean?" she wondered aloud, drugged by his closeness.

"I shouldn't have backed off," he replied quietly. "I got cold feet at the very worst time."

"Jordan…"

"…mind if I cut in?" Hayes Carson asked with a grin.

Jordan stopped, his mind still in limbo. "We were talking," he began.

"Plenty of time for that later. Shall we, Libby?" he asked, and moved right in front of Jordan. He danced Libby away before she had a chance to stop him.

"Now that's what I call a jealous man," Hayes murmured dryly, glancing over her shoulder at Jordan. "No need to ask about the lay of the land."

"Jordan doesn't feel that way about me," Libby protested.

"He doesn't?"

She averted her eyes to the crowded dance floor. "He isn't a marrying man."

"Uh-huh."

She glanced up at Hayes, who was still grinning.

She flushed at the look in his eyes.

Across the room, Jordan Powell saw that flush and had to restrain himself from going over there and tearing Libby out of Hayes's embrace.

"What the devil are you doing here?" Calhoun Ballenger asked abruptly.

Jordan glanced at him wryly. "Not much," he murmured. "But I came to ask if you needed another willing ally. I've, uh, changed camps."

Calhoun's eyebrows went up almost to his blond hairline.

"I do like to be on the winning side," Jordan drawled.

Calhoun burst out laughing. "Well, you're not a bad diplomat, I guess," he confessed, holding out his hand. "Welcome aboard."

"My pleasure."

JORDAN CONTRIVED TO drive Libby and Curt home, but he was careful to let Curt go into the ranch house before he cut off the engine and turned to Libby.

"There's been some news," he said carefully.

"About Janet?" she exclaimed.

"About Julie," he corrected. He toyed with a strand of her hair in the dim light of the car interior. "One of Grier's men saw her with a known drug dealer earlier today. She's put her neck in a noose and she doesn't even know it."

"She uses, doesn't she?" she asked.

He shrugged. "Her behavior is erratic. She must."

"I'm sorry. You liked her..."

He bent and kissed her hungrily, pulling her across his lap to wrap her up in his warm, strong arms. "I like you," he whispered against her mouth. "More than I ever dreamed I could!"

She wanted to ask questions, but she couldn't kiss him and breathe at the same time. She gave up and ran her arms up around his neck. She relaxed into his close embrace and kissed him back until her mouth grew sore and swollen.

He sighed into her throat as he held her and rocked her in his arms in the warm darkness.

"Libby, I think we should start going out together."

She blinked. "You and me?"

He nodded. "You and me." He drew back and looked down at her possessively. "I could give up liver and onions, if I had to. But I can't give you up."

"Listen, I don't have affairs..."

He kissed her into silence. "Neither do I. So I guess maybe we won't sleep together after all."

"But if we go out together..." she said worriedly.

He grinned. "You have enough self-restraint for both of us, I'm sure," he drawled. "You can keep me honest."

She drew back a little and noted the position of his big lean hands under her blouse. She looked at him intently.

He cleared his throat and drew his hands out from under the blouse. "Every man is entitled to one little slip. Right?" His eyes were twinkling.

She laughed. "Okay."

He touched her mouth with his one last time. "In that case, you'd better rush inside before I forget to be honest."

"Thanks for bringing us home."

"My pleasure. Lock the doors," he added seriously. "And I'm only a phone call away if you need me. You call me," he emphasized. "Not Hayes Carson. Got that?"

"And since when did I become your personal property?" she asked haughtily.

"Since the minute you let me put my hands under your blouse," he shot right back, laughing. "Think about it."

She got out of the vehicle, dizzy and with her head swimming. In one night, everything had changed.

"Don't worry," he added gently, leaning out the window. "I have enough restraint for both of us!"

Before she could answer him, he gunned the engine and took off down the road.

CHAPTER TEN

FOR THE NEXT FEW DAYS, Jordan was at Libby's house more than at his own. He smoothed over hard feelings with her brother and became a household fixture. Libby and Curt filed the insurance claim, paid off the mortgage, and started repurchasing cattle for the small ranch.

Janet was found a couple of days later at a motel just outside San Antonio, with a man. He turned out to be the so-called attorney who'd phoned and tried to get Libby and Curt out of their home. She was arrested and charged with murder in the death of Violet's father. There was DNA evidence taken from the dead man's clothing and the motel room that was directly linked to Janet. It placed her at the motel the night Mr. Hardy died. When she realized the trouble she was in, she tried to make a deal for a reduced sentence. She agreed to confess to the murder in return for a life sentence without hope of parole. But she denied having a gas can. She swore that she never had plans to burn down Riddle Collins's house with his children in it. Nobody paid her much attention. She'd told so many lies.

It was a different story for Julie Merrill. She continued to make trouble, and not only for Calhoun Ballenger. She was determined that Jordan wasn't going to desert her for little Libby Collins. She had a plan. Two days before the hearing to decide the fate of the police officers who'd arrested her father—Saturday—she put it into practice.

She phoned Libby at work and apologized profusely for all the trouble she'd caused.

"I never meant to be such a pain in the neck," she assured Libby. "I want to make it up to you. You get off at one on Saturdays, don't you? Suppose you come over here for lunch?"

"To your house?" Libby replied warily.

"Yes. I've had our cook make something special," she purred. "And I can tell you my side of the story. Will you?"

Dubious, Libby hesitated.

"Surely you aren't afraid of me?" Julie drawled. "I mean, what could I do to you, even if I had something terrible in mind?"

"You don't need to feed me," Libby replied cautiously. "I don't hold grudges."

"You'll come, then," Julie persisted. "Today at one. Will you?"

It was against her better judgment. But it was a bad idea to keep a feud going, especially now that Jordan seemed really interested in her.

"Okay," Libby said finally. "I'll be there at one."

"Thanks!" Julie said huskily. "You don't know how much I appreciate it! Uh, I don't guess you'd like to bring your brother, too?" she added suddenly.

Libby frowned. "Curt's driving a cattle truck for Duke Wright up to San Antonio today."

"Well, then, another time, perhaps! I'll see you at one." Julie hung up, with a bright and happy note in her voice.

Libby frowned. Was she stupid to go to the woman's

home? But why would Julie risk harming her now, with the primary election so close? It was the following Tuesday.

She phoned Jordan. "Guess what just happened?" she asked.

"You've realized how irresistible I am and you're rushing over to seduce me?" he teased. "Shall I turn down the covers on my bed?"

"Stop that," she muttered. "I'm serious."

"So am I!"

"Jordan," she laughed. "Julie just called to apologize. She invited me to lunch."

"Did she?" he asked. "Are you going?"

"I thought I might." She hesitated. "Don't you think it's a good idea, to mend fences, I mean?"

"I don't know, Libby," he replied seriously. "She's been erratic and out of control lately. I don't think it's a good idea. I'd rather you didn't."

"Are you afraid she might tell me something about you that I don't know?" she returned, suspicious.

He sighed. "No. It's not that. She wasn't happy when I broke off with her. I don't trust her."

"What can she do to me in broad daylight?" she laughed. "Shoot me?"

"Of course not," he scoffed.

"Then stop worrying. She only wants to apologize."

"You be careful," he returned. "And phone me when you get home. Okay?"

"Okay."

"How about a movie tonight?" he added. "There's a new mystery at the theater. You can even have popcorn."

"That sounds nice," she said, feeling warm and secure.

"I'll pick you up about six."

"I'll be ready. See you then."

She hung up and pondered over his misgivings. Surely he was overreacting. He was probably afraid Julie might make up a convincing lie about how intimate they'd been. Or perhaps she might be telling the truth. She only knew that she had to find out why Julie wanted to see her in person. She was going.

BUT SOMETHING NIGGLED at the back of her mind when she drove toward Julie's palatial home on the Jacobs River. Julie might have wanted to invite Libby over to apologize, but why would she want Curt to come, too? She didn't even know Curt.

Libby's foot lifted off the accelerator. Her home was next door to Jordan's. Julie was furious that Jordan had broken off with her. If the house was gone, Libby and Curt would have to move away again, as they had before…!

Libby turned the truck around in the middle of the road and sped toward her house. She wished she had a cell phone. There was no way to call for help. But she was absolutely certain what was about to happen. And she knew immediately that her stepmother hadn't been responsible for that gas can on the porch.

The question was, who had Julie convinced to set that fire for her? Or would she be crazy enough to try and do it herself?

Libby sped faster down the road. If only there had been state police, a sheriff's deputy, a policeman watching. She was speeding. It was the only time in her life she'd ever wanted to be caught!

But there were no flashing lights, no sirens. She was going to have to try and stop the perpetrator all by herself. She wasn't a big woman. She had no illusions about being able to tackle a grown man. She didn't even have a weapon. Wait. There was a tire tool in the boot! At least, she could threaten with it.

She turned into the road that led to the house. There was no smoke visible anywhere and no sign of any traffic. For the first time, she realized that she could be chasing make-believe villains. Why would she think that Julie Merrill would try to burn her house down? Maybe the strain of the past weeks was making her hysterical after all.

She pulled up in front of the house and got out, grabbing the tire tool out of the back. It wouldn't hurt to look around, now that she was here.

She moved around the side of the house, her heart beating wildly. Her palms were so sweaty that she had to get a better grip on the tire tool. She walked past the chimney, to the corner, and peered around. Her heart stopped.

There was a man there. A young man. He had a can of gasoline. He was muttering to himself as he sloshed it on the back porch and the steps.

Libby closed her eyes and prayed for strength. There was nobody to help her. She had to do this alone.

She walked around the corner with the tire tool raised. "That's enough, you varmint! You're trespassing on private property and you're going to jail. The police are right behind me!"

Startled, the man dropped the gas can and stared wild-eyed at Libby.

Sensing an advantage, she started to run toward him, yelling at the top of her lungs.

To her amazement, he started running down a path

behind the house, with Libby right on his heels, still yelling.

Then something happened that was utterly in the realm of fantasy. She heard an engine behind her. An accomplice, she wondered, almost panicking.

Jordan Powell pulled up right beside her in his truck and threw open the passenger door. "Get in!" he called.

She didn't need prompting. She jumped right in beside him, tire tool and all, and slammed the door. "He was dousing the back porch with gas!" she panted. "Don't let him get away!"

"I don't intend to." His face was grim as he stood down on the accelerator and the truck shot forward on the pasture road, which was no more than tracks through tall grass.

The attempted arsonist was tiring. He was pretty thick in the middle and had short legs. He was almost to a beat-up old car sitting out of sight of the house near the barn when Jordan came alongside him on the driver's side.

"Hold it in the ruts!" he called to Libby.

Just as she grabbed the wheel, he threw open the door and leaped out on the startled, breathless young man, pinning him to the ground.

By the time Libby had the truck stopped, Jordan had the man by his shirt collar and was holding him there.

"Pick up the phone and call Hayes," he called to Libby.

Her hands were shaking, but she managed to dial 911 and give the dispatcher an abbreviated account of what had just happened. She was told that they contacted a deputy who was barely a mile away and he was starting toward the Collins place at that moment.

Libby thanked her nicely and cut off the phone.

"Who put you up to this?" Jordan demanded of the man. "Tell me, or so help me, I'll make sure you don't get out of prison until you're an old man!"

"It was Miss Julie," the young man sobbed. "I never done nothing like this in my life. My daddy works for her and he took some things out of her house. She said she'd turn him over to the police if I didn't do this for her."

"She'd have turned him over anyway, you fool," Jordan said coldly. "She was using you. Do you have any idea what the penalty is for arson?"

He was still sobbing. "I was scared, Mr. Powell."

Jordan relented, but only a little. He looked up as the sound of a siren was heard coming closer.

Libby opened the door of the truck and got out, just as a sheriff's car came flying down the track and stopped just behind the truck.

The deputy was Sammy Tibbs. They both knew him. He'd been in Libby's class in high school.

"What have you got, Jordan?" Sammy asked.

"A would-be arsonist," Jordan told him. "He'll confess if you ask him."

"I caught him pouring gas on my back porch and I chased him with my tire tool. I almost had him when Jordan came along," Libby said with a shy grin.

"Whew," Sammy whistled. "I hope I don't ever run afoul of you," he told her.

"That makes two of us," Jordan said, with a gentle smile for her.

"I assume you'll be pressing charges?" Sammy asked Libby as he handcuffed the young man, who was still out of breath.

"You can bet real money on it," Libby agreed. "And you'll need to pick up Julie Merrill as well, because this man said she told him to do it."

Sammy's hands froze on the handcuffs. "Julie Merrill? The state senator's daughter?"

"That's exactly who I mean," Libby replied. "She called and invited me over to lunch. Since she doesn't like me, I got suspicious and came home instead, just in time to catch this weasel in the act."

"Is this true?" the deputy asked the man.

"Mirandize him first," Jordan suggested. "Just so there won't be any loopholes."

"Good idea," Sammy agreed, and read the suspect his rights.

"Now, tell him," Libby prodded, glaring at the man who'd been within a hair of burning her house down.

The young man sighed as if the weight of the world was sitting on his shoulders. "Miss Merrill had something on my daddy, who works for her. She said if I'd set a fire on Miss Collins's back steps, she'd forget all about it. She just wanted to scare Miss Collins is all. She didn't tell me to burn the whole place down."

"Arson is arson," Sammy replied. "Don't touch anything," he told Libby. "I'll send our investigator back out there and call the state fire marshal. Arson is hard to prove, but this one's going to be a walk in the park."

"Thanks, Sammy," Libby said.

He grinned. "What for? You caught him!"

He put the scared suspect in the back of his car and sped off with a wave of his hand.

"That was too damned close," Jordan said, looking down at Libby with tormented eyes. "I couldn't believe it when I saw you chasing him through the field with a tire iron! What if he'd been armed?"

"He wasn't," she said. "Besides, he ran the minute I chased him, just like a black snake."

He pulled her into his arms and wrapped her up tight. There was a faint tremor in those strong arms.

"You brave idiot," he murmured into her neck. "Thank God he didn't get the fire started first. I can see you running inside to grab all the sentimental items and save them. You'd have been burned alive."

She grimaced, because he was absolutely right. She'd have tried to save her mementos of her father and mother, at any cost.

"Libby, I think we'd better get engaged," he said suddenly.

She was hallucinating. She said so.

He pulled back from her, his eyes solemn. "You're not hallucinating. If Julie realizes how serious this is between us, she'll back off."

"She's going to be in jail shortly, she'll have to," she pointed out.

"They can afford bail until her hearing, even so," he replied. "She'll be out for blood. But if she hears about the engagement, it might be enough to make her think twice."

"I'm not afraid of her," she said, although she really was.

"Humor me," he coaxed, bending to kiss her gently.

She smiled under the warm, comforting feel of his hard mouth on her lips. "Well…"

He nibbled her upper lip. "I'll get you a ring," he whispered.

"What sort?"

"What do you want?"

"I like emeralds," she whispered, standing on tiptoe to coax his mouth down again.

"An emerald, then."

"Nobody would know?"

He chuckled as he kissed her. "We might have to tell a few hundred people, just to make it believable. And we might actually have to get married, but that's okay, isn't it?"

She blinked. "Get...married?"

"That's what the ring's for, Libby," he said against her warm mouth. "Advance notice."

"But...you've always said you never wanted to get married."

"I always said there's the one woman a man can't walk away from," he added. He lifted his head and looked down at her, all the teasing gone. "I can't walk away from you. The past few weeks have been pure hell."

Her eyes widened with unexpected delight.

He traced her eyebrows with his forefinger. "I missed you," he whispered. "It was like being cut apart."

"You wanted Julie," she accused.

He grimaced. "I wanted you to think about what was happening. You've been sheltered your whole life. Duke Wright's wife was just like you. Then she married and had a child and got career-minded. That poor devil lives in hell because she didn't know what she wanted until it was too late!"

She searched his face quietly. "You think I'd want a career."

"I don't know, Libby," he bit off. He looked anguished. "I'm an all-or-nothing kind of man. I can't just stick my toe in to test the water. I jump in headfirst."

He…loved her. She was stunned. She couldn't believe she hadn't noticed, in all this time. Curt had seen it long before this. He'd tried to tell her. But she hadn't believed that a man like Jordan could be serious about someone like her.

Her lips fell apart with a husky sigh. She was on fire. She'd never dreamed that life could be so sweet. "I don't want a career," she said slowly.

"What if you do, someday?" he persisted.

She reached up and traced his firm, jutting chin with her fingertips. "I'm twenty-four years old, Jordan," she said. "If I don't know my own mind by now, I never will."

He still looked undecided.

She put both hands flat on his shirt. Under it, she could feel the muted thunder of his heartbeat. "Why don't we go to a movie?" she asked.

He seemed to relax. He smiled. "We could grab a hamburger for lunch and talk about it," he prompted.

"Okay."

"Then we'll go by the sheriff's department and you can write out a statement," he added.

She grimaced. "I guess I'll have to."

He nodded. "So will I." His eyes narrowed. "I wish I could see the look on Julie's face when the deputy sheriff pulls up in her driveway."

"I imagine she'll be surprised," Libby replied.

SURPRISED WAS AN UNDERSTATEMENT. Julie Merrill gaped at the young man in the deputy sheriff's uniform.

"You're joking," she said haughtily. "I… I had nothing to do with any attempted arson!"

"We have a man in custody who'll swear to it," he

replied. "You can come peacefully or you can go out the door in handcuffs," he added, still pleasant and respectful. "Your choice, Miss Merrill."

She let out a harsh breath. "This is outrageous!"

"What's going on out here?" Her father, the state senator, came into the hall, weaving a little, and blinked when he saw the deputy. "What's he doing here?" he murmured.

"Your daughter is under arrest, senator," he was told as the deputy suddenly turned Julie around and cuffed her with professional dexterity. "For conspiracy to commit arson."

"Arson?" The senator blinked. "Julie?"

"She sent a man to burn down the Collins place," he was told. "We have two eyewitnesses, as well."

The senator gaped at his daughter. "I told you to leave that woman alone," he said, shaking his finger at her. "I told you Jordan would get involved if you didn't! You've cost me the election! Everybody around here will go to the polls Tuesday and vote for Calhoun Ballenger! You've ruined me!"

"Oh, no, sir, she hasn't," the deputy assured him with a grin. "Your nephew, the mayor, did that, by persecuting two police officers who were just doing their jobs." The smile faded. "You're going to see Monday night just how much hot water you've jumped into. That disciplinary hearing is going to be remembered for the next century in Jacobsville."

"Where are you taking my daughter?" the senator snorted.

"To jail, to be booked. You can call your attorney and arrange for a bail hearing whenever you like," the deputy added, with a speaking glance at the older man's condition. "If you're able."

"I'll call my own attorney," Julie said hotly. "Then I'll sue you for false arrest!"

"You're welcome to try," the deputy said. "Come along, Miss Merrill."

"Daddy, do try to sober up!" Julie said scathingly.

"What would be the point?" the senator replied. "Life was so good when I didn't know all about you, Julie. When I thought you were a sweet, kind, innocent woman like your mother…" He closed his eyes. "You killed that girl!"

"I did not! Think what you're saying!" Julie yelled at him.

Tears poured down his cheeks. "She died in my arms…"

"Let's go," the deputy said, tugging Julie Merrill out the door. He closed it on the sobbing politician.

Julie Merrill was lodged in the county jail until her bail hearing the following Monday morning. Meanwhile, Jordan and Libby had given their statements and the would-be arsonist was singing like a canary bird.

The disciplinary hearing for Chief Grier's two police officers was Monday night at the city council meeting.

It didn't take long. Within thirty minutes, the council had finished its usual business, Grier's officers were cleared of any misconduct, and the surprise guests at the hearing had Jacobsville buzzing for weeks afterward.

CHAPTER ELEVEN

JORDAN DROVE LIBBY to his house in a warm silence. He led her into the big, elegant living room and closed the door behind them.

"Want something to drink?" he asked, moving to a pitcher of iced tea that Amie had apparently left for them, along with a plate of homemade cake, covered with foil. "And a piece of pound cake?"

"I'd love that," she agreed.

He poured tea into two glasses and handed them to her, along with doilies to protect the coffee table from spots. He put cake onto two plates, with forks, and brought them along. But as he bent over the coffee table, he obscured Libby's plate. When he sat down beside her, there was a beautiful emerald solitaire, set in gold, lying on her piece of cake.

"Look at that," he exclaimed with twinkling dark eyes. "Why, it's an engagement ring! I wonder who could have put it there?" he drawled.

She picked it up, breathless. "It's beautiful."

"Isn't it?" he mused. "Why don't you try it on? If it fits," he added slyly, "you might turn into a fairy princess and get your own true prince as a prize!"

She smiled through her breathless delight. "Think so?"

"Darlin', I can almost guarantee it," he replied tenderly. "Want to give it a shot?"

He seemed to hold his breath while he waited for her reply. She had to fight tears. It was the most poignant moment of her entire life.

"Why don't you put it on for me?" she asked finally, watching him lift the ring and slide it onto her ring finger with something like relief.

"How about that?" he murmured dryly. "It's a perfect fit. Almost as if it were made just for you," he added.

She looked up at him and all the humor went out of his face. He held her small hand in his big one and searched her eyes.

"You love emeralds. I bought this months ago and stuck it in a drawer while I tried to decide whether or not it would be suicide to propose to you. Duke Wright's situation made me uncertain. I was afraid you hadn't seen enough of the world, or life, to be able to settle down here in Jacobsville. I was afraid to take a chance."

She moved a step closer. "But you finally did."

He cupped her face in his big, warm hands. "Yes. When I realized that I was spending time with Julie just to keep you at bay. If she'd been a better sort of person, it would have been a low thing to do. I was flattered at her interest and the company I got to keep. But I felt like a traitor when she started insulting you in public. I was too wrapped up in my own uncertainties to do what I should have done."

"Which was what?" she asked softly.

He bent to her soft mouth. "I should have realized that if you really love someone, everything works out." He kissed her tenderly. "I should have told you how I felt and given you a chance to spread your wings if you wanted to. I could have waited while you decided what sort of future you wanted."

She still couldn't believe that he didn't know how she felt. "I was crazy about you," she whispered huskily. "Everybody knew it except you." She reached up and linked her arms around his neck. "Duke's wife wasn't like me, Jordan," she added, searching his dark eyes. "She lived with a domineering father and a deeply religious mother. They taught her that a woman's role in life was to marry and obey her husband. She'd always done what they told her to do. But after she married Duke, she ran wild, probably giving vent to all those feelings of suffocated restriction she'd endured all her life. Getting pregnant on her wedding night was a big mistake for both of them, because then she really felt trapped." She took a deep breath. "If Duke hadn't rushed her into it, she'd have gone off and found her career and come back to him when she knew what she really wanted. It was a tragedy in the making from the very beginning."

"She didn't love him enough," he murmured.

"He didn't love her enough," she countered. "He got her pregnant, thinking it would hold her."

He sighed. "I want children," he said softly. "But not right away. We need time to get to know each other before we start a family, don't we?"

She smiled. "See? You ask me about things. You don't order me around. Duke was exactly the opposite." She traced his mouth with her fingertips. "That's why I stopped going out with him. He never asked me what I wanted to do, even what I wanted to eat when we went out together. He actually ordered meals for me before I could say what I liked." She glowered. "He ordered me liver and onions and I never went out with him again."

He lifted an eyebrow and grinned. "Darlin', I swear

on my horse that I will never order you liver and onions." He crossed his heart.

He was so handsome when he grinned like that. Her heart expanded like a balloon with pure happiness. "Actually," she whispered, lifting up to him, "I'd even eat liver and onions for you."

"The real test of love," he agreed, gathering her up hungrily. "And I'd eat squash for you," he offered.

She smiled under the slow, sweet pressure of his mouth. Amie said he'd actually dumped a squash casserole in the middle of the living room carpet to make the point that he never wanted it again.

"This is nice," he murmured, lifting her completely off the floor. "But I can do better."

"Can you really?" she whispered, biting softly at his full lower lip. "Show me!"

He laughed, even though his body was making emphatic statements about how little time there was left for teasing. He was burning.

He put her down on the sofa and crushed her into it with the warm, hard length of his body.

"Jordan," she whispered breathlessly when he eased between her long legs.

"Don't panic," he said against her lips. "Amie's a scream away. Lift up."

She did, and he unfastened the bra and pushed it out of the way under her blouse. He deepened the kiss slowly, seductively, while his lean hands discovered the soft warmth of her bare breasts in a heated silence.

Her head began to spin. He was going to be her husband. She could lie in his arms all night long. They could have children together. After the tragedy of the past few months, it was like a trip to paradise.

She moaned and wrapped her long legs around his hips, urging him even closer. She felt the power and heat of him intimately. Her mouth opened, inviting the quick, hard thrust of his tongue.

"Oh, yes," she groaned into his hard mouth. Her hips lifted into his rhythmically, her breath gasping out at his ear as she clung to him. "Yes. That feels…good!"

A tortured sound worked out of his throat as he pressed her down hard into the soft cushions of the sofa, his hands already reaching for the zipper in the front of her slacks, so far gone that he was mindless.

The sound of footsteps outside the door finally penetrated the fog of passion that lay between them. Jordan lifted his head. Libby looked up at him, dazed and only half-aware of the sound.

"Amie," Jordan groaned, taking a steadying breath. "We have to stop."

"Tell her to go away," she whispered, laughing breathlessly.

"You tell her," he teased as he got to his feet. "She gets even in the kitchen. She can make squash look just like a corn casserole."

"Amie's Revenge?"

He nodded. "Amie's Revenge." Jordan paused. "I want to marry you," he said quietly. "I want it with all my heart."

She had to fight down tears to answer him. "I want it, too."

He drew her close, over his lap, and when he kissed her, it was with such breathless tenderness that she felt tears threatening again.

She slid her arms around his neck and kissed him back with fervent ardor. But he put her gently away.

"You don't want to ravish me?" she exclaimed. "You said once that you could do me justice in thirty minutes!"

"I lied," he said, chuckling. "I'd need two hours. And Amie's skulking out in the hall, waiting for an opportunity to congratulate us," he added in a whisper. "We can't possibly shock her so soon before the wedding."

She hesitated. "So soon…?"

"I want to get married as quickly as possible," he informed her. "All we need is the blood tests, a license, and I've already got us a minister. Unless you want a formal wedding in a big church with hundreds of guests," he added worriedly.

"No need, since you've already got us a minister," she teased.

He relaxed. "Thank God! The idea of a morning coat and hundreds of people…"

She was kissing him, so he stopped talking.

Just as things were getting interesting, there was an impatient knock at the door. "Well?" Amie called through it.

"She said yes!" Jordan called back.

The door opened and Amie rushed in, grinning from ear to ear.

"She hates squash," he said in a mock whisper.

"I won't ever make it again," Amie promised.

He hugged her. After a minute, Libby joined them. She hugged the housekeeper, too.

"Welcome to the family!" Amie laughed.

And that was the end of any heated interludes for the rest of the evening.

THE NEXT FEW days went by in a blur of activity. When the votes were counted on Tuesday at the primary election, Senator Merrill lost the Democratic candidacy by a ten-to-one margin. A recall of the city fathers was announced, along with news of a special election to follow. Councilman Culver and the mayor were both implicated in drug trafficking, along with Julie Merrill. Julie had managed to get bail the day before the primary, but she hadn't been seen since. She was also still in trouble for the arson conspiracy. Her father had given an impressive concession speech, in front of the news media, and congratulated Calhoun Ballenger with sincerity. It began to be noticed that he improved when his daughter's sins came to light. Apparently he'd been duty-bound to try and protect her, and it had almost killed his conscience. He'd started drinking heavily, and then realized that he was likely to lose his state senate seat for it. He'd panicked, gone to the mayor, and tried to get the charges dropped.

One irresponsible act had cost Senator Merrill everything. But, he told Calhoun, he still had his house and his health. He'd stand by his daughter, of course, and do what he could for her. Perhaps retirement wouldn't be such a bad thing. His daughter could not be reached for comment. She was now being hunted by every law-enforcement officer in Texas and government agents on the drug charges, which were formidable. Other unsavory facts were still coming to light about her doings.

Jordan finally understood why Libby had tried so hard to keep him out of Julie's company and he apologized profusely for refusing to listen to her. Duke Wright's plight had made him somber and afraid, especially when he realized how much he loved Libby. He was afraid to take a chance on her. He had plenty of regrets.

Libby accepted his apology and threw herself into

politics as one of Calhoun's speechwriters, a job she loved. But, she told Jordan, she had no desire to do it for a profession. She was quite happy to work for Mr. Kemp and raise a family in Jacobsville.

On the morning of Libby's marriage to Jordan, she was almost floating with delight. "I can't believe the things that have happened in two weeks," Libby told her brother at the church door as they waited for the music to go down the aisle together. "It's just amazing!"

"For a small town, it certainly is," he agreed. He grinned. "Happy?"

"Too happy," she confessed, blushing. "I never dreamed I'd be marrying Jordan."

"I did. He's been crazy about you for years, but Duke Wright's bad luck really got to him. Fortunately, he did see the light in time."

She took a deep breath as the first strains of the wedding march were heard. "I'm glad it's just us and not a crowd," she murmured.

He didn't speak. His eyes twinkled as he opened the door.

Inside, all the prominent citizens of Jacobsville were sitting in their pews, waiting for the bride to be given away by her brother. Cash Grier was there with Tippy. So were Calhoun Ballenger and Abby, Justin Ballenger and Shelby Jacobs Ballenger. And the Hart brothers, all five of them including the attorney general, with their wives. The Tremaynes. Mr. Kemp, with Violet! The Drs. Coltrain and Dr. Morris and Dr. Steele and their wives. Eb Scott and his wife. Cy Parks and his wife. It was a veritable who's who of the city.

"Surprise," Curt whispered in her ear, and tugged her along down the aisle. She was adorned in a simple white satin gown with colorful embroidery on the bodice and puffy sleeves, a delicate veil covering her face and shoulders. She carried a bouquet of lily of the valley and pink roses.

Jordan Powell, in a soft gray morning coat and all the trappings, was waiting for her at the altar with the minister. He looked handsome and welcoming and he was smiling from ear to ear.

Libby thought back over the past few agonizing weeks and realized all the hardships and heartache she'd endured made her truly appreciate all the sweet blessings that had come into her life. She smiled through her tears and stopped at Jordan's side, her small hand searching blindly for his as she waited to speak her vows. She'd never felt more loved or happier than she was at that moment. She only wished her parents had lived to see her married.

JUST AFTER THE WEDDING, there was a reception at the church fellowship hall, catered by Barbara's Café. The wedding cake was beautiful, with a colorful motif that exactly matched the embroidery on Libby's wedding gown.

She and Jordan were photographed together cutting the cake and then interacting with all their unexpected guests. The only sticky moment was when handsome Hayes Carson bent to kiss Libby.

"Careful, Hayes," Jordan said from right beside him. "I'm watching you!"

"Great idea," Hayes replied imperturbably and grinned. "You could use a few lessons."

And he kissed Libby enthusiastically while Jordan fumed.

WHEN THEY WERE finally alone, hours later in Galveston, Jordan was still fuming about that kiss.

"You know Hayes was teasing," she said, coaxing him into her arms. "But I'm not. I've waited twenty-four years for this," she added with a wry smile. "I have great expectations."

He drew her close with a worldly look. "And I expect to satisfy them fully!"

"I'm not going to be very good at this, at first," she said breathlessly, when he began to undress her. "Is it all right?"

He smiled tenderly. "You're going to be great at it," he countered. "The only real requirement is love. We're rich in that."

She relaxed a little, watching his dark eyes glow as he uncovered the soft, petal-pink smoothness of her bare skin. She was a little nervous. Nobody had seen her undressed since she was a little girl.

Jordan realized that and it made him even more gentle. He'd never been with an innocent, but he knew enough about women that it wasn't going to be a problem. She loved him. He wanted nothing more than to please her.

When she was standing in just her briefs, he bent and smoothed his warm mouth over the curve of her breasts. She smelled of roses. There was a faint moisture under his lips, which he rightly attributed to fear.

He lifted his head and looked down into her wide, uncertain eyes. "Women have been doing this since the dawn of time," he whispered. "If it wasn't fun, nobody would want to do it. Right?"

She laughed nervously. "Right."

He smiled tenderly. "So just relax and let me drive. It's going to be a journey you'll never forget."

Her hands went to his tie. "Okay. But I get to make suggestions," she told him impishly, and worked to unfasten the tie and then his white shirt. She opened it over a bronzed chest thick with dark, soft hair. He felt furry. But under the hair was hard, warm muscle. She liked the way he felt.

He kissed her softly while he coaxed her hands to his belt. She hesitated.

"Don't agonize over it," he teased, moving her hands aside to unfasten it himself. "We'll go slow."

"I'm not really a coward," she whispered unsteadily. "It's just uncharted territory. I've never even looked at pictures…"

He could imagine what sort of pictures she was talking about. He only smiled. "Next time, you'll be a veteran and it won't intimidate you."

"Are you sure?" she asked.

He bent to her mouth again. "I'm sure."

His warm lips moved down her throat to her breasts, but this time they weren't gently teasing. They were invasive and insistent as they opened on the hard little nubs his caresses had already produced. When his hands moved her hips lazily against the hard thrust of his powerful body, she began to feel drugged.

She'd thought it would be embarrassing and uncomfortable to make love in the light. But Jordan was slow and thorough, easing her into an intimacy beyond anything she'd ever dreamed. He cradled her against him on the big bed, arousing her to such a fever pitch that when he removed the last bit of her clothing, it was a relief to feel the coolness of the room against her hot skin. And by the time he removed his own clothes, she was too hungry to be embarrassed. In fact, she was as aggressive as he was, starving for him in the tempestuous minutes that followed.

She remembered the first kiss they'd shared, beside her pickup truck at his fence. She'd known then that she'd do anything he wanted her to do. But this was far from the vague dreams of fulfillment she'd had when she was alone. She hadn't known that passion was like a fever that nothing could quench, that desire brought intense desperation. She hadn't known that lovemaking was blind, deaf, mute slavery to a man's touch.

"I would die for you," Jordan whispered huskily at her ear as he moved slowly into total possession with her trembling body.

"Will it...hurt?" she managed in a stranger's voice as she hesitated just momentarily at the enormity of what was happening to her.

He laughed sensuously as he began to move lazily against her. "Are you kidding?" he murmured. And with a sharp, deft movement, he produced a sensation that lifted her clear of the bed and against him with an unearthly little cry of pleasure.

From there, it was a descent into total madness. She shivered with every powerful thrust of his body. She clung to him with her arms, her legs, her soul. She moaned helplessly as sensation built on sensation, until she was almost screaming from the urgent need for satisfaction.

She heard her own voice pleading with him, but she couldn't understand her own words. She drove for fulfillment, her body demanding, feverishly moving with his as they climbed the spiral of passion together.

She felt suddenly as if she'd been dropped from a great height into a hot, throbbing wave of pleasure that began and never seemed to end. She clung to him, terrified that he might stop, that he might draw back, that he might pull away.

"Shh," he whispered tenderly. "I won't stop. It's all right. It's all right, honey. I love you...so much!"

"I love you, too!" she gasped.

Then he began to shudder, even as she felt herself move from one plane of ecstasy to another, and another, and another, each one deeper and more satisfying than the one before. At one point she thought she might actually die from the force of it. Her eyes closed and she let the waves wash over her in succession, glorying in the unbelievably sweet aftermath.

Above her, Jordan was just reaching his own culmination. He groaned harshly at her ear and shuddered one last time before he collapsed in her arms, dead weight on her damp, shivering body.

"And you were afraid," he chided in a tender whisper, kissing her eyes, her cheeks, her throat.

She laughed. "So that's how it feels," she said drowsily. "And now I'm sleepy."

He laughed with her. "So am I."

"Will you be here when I wake up?" she teased.

He kissed her swollen mouth gently. "For the rest of my life, honey. Until the very end."

Her arms curved around him and she curled into his powerful body, feeling closer to him than she'd ever felt to another human being. It was poignant. She was a whole woman. She was loved.

"Until the very end, my darling," she repeated, her voice trailing away in the silence of the room.

She slept in his arms. It was the best night of her life. But it was only the beginning for both of them.

* * * * *